THE ET

The Eternity Fund

By

Liz Monument

Fahrenheit Press

Dedicated to Sarah Corbett, without whose patience and support this novel may never have come to fruition.

Prologue

Lindiwi says that Sister Enuncia is stealing the children after dark. She ties them up in the cellar, drains their blood, then takes the bodies into the desert for the nightbeetles to snip to pieces. I want Lindiwi to be wrong, but why are the dorm beds stripped, as though they aren't coming back? And why do I dream of the schaduw stalking the empty corridors after curfew, making Sister Enuncia do the things she's doing?

I

Two sections of the perimeter were down. Wind hissed through the Kevlar mesh either side of the gap. Beyond, the Cinderlands slid away into infinity, the dunes scarred by struts sticking out of the sand like stripped bones. Anything could've been staring back at us from underneath the bombed-out metal.

'Why would somebody remove the boundary?' I said to Mo, who stood to my right, one foot on a lump of blackglass.

He shrugged. In silhouette, his features were sharply cut, like a beautiful Old World sculpture, the kind that spends its entire life in a vault somewhere while the public get to gawp at a reproduction.

'This job came in as code amber. That's low alert, in case you've forgotten your basic training, Miss Green.'

Mo and me hadn't got off to a good start, but if there's one thing you don't do, its piss your handler off any more than is absolutely necessary.

'Look, Mo, I know you've got more field experience than me, but-'

'You have no field experience at all, Miss Green.'

He turned to face me, the setting sun glancing off one dark cheekbone. Mo wouldn't admit it, not straight out at least, but since the day Oxton pulled him from the senior guardians and gave him to me, he'd found various ways to let me know he had a problem with the status quo.

I turned my back on him and ran my fingers along the broken edge of Kevlar.

'The cuts are neat,' I said. 'This was no accident. Plus they've taken the fence, just to be sure we can't do a quick patch-up job.'

I scanned the earth around my feet, the black stuff they say is some kind of ash that blows off the Disaster Zone and gives the Cinderlands its name.

'See these vehicle marks?' I squatted down. A breeze scattered the dust, and the marks began to disappear. 'They're recent, made by an old fashioned hop - the sort that hovers rather than flies.'

Mo snorted.

'What?' I stood up. 'I recognise the pattern. The nuns had an old hop that left tracks just the same.'

'It isn't the hop. I'm wondering why the Unit brought in an empath to tell me what I can see with my own two eyes.'

Before the Unit, I'd had some pretty tricky customers, but I'd been a fool to think I could handle anything in trousers. Mo glared at me, his eyebrows taut over his shades. I wished he'd take them off, just once, so that I could see his eyes, but he never did. They were always there, melded to his face. He probably even slept in them. And he thought I was weird.

'I need a little longer.'

I faced the Cinderlands and closed my eyes. The vehicle had passed through the perimeter several times, carrying some kind of cargo. Whoever drove it slipped away fast into the dunes, carrying me along on his thought-stream. The driver was older than me, but not much, unkempt, and unfit. He resonated desperation, the kind that usually signifies somebody in over their head, somebody who's on the edge of losing it. Don't ask me how I know things like this - I just do. You could be scientific and say that something inside me responds to the displacement kinetic energy, or you might prefer the spiritual angle, whatever that might be. It doesn't make much difference to me. All I know is, this is what I am, and this is what I do. The sense of black earth and spent metal told me the vehicle was deep in the dunes, until, like a light that'd been turned out, it vanished.

I swore softly, and opened my eyes. Our driver was using the Cinderlands as a cover. Even the shifters wouldn't set foot over the boundary. But if I told Mo, he'd laugh in my face. He'd tell me he could've worked that much out for himself. I tried to focus in on the cargo, but all I saw was blackness, the kind of blackness that signifies something with no life signature.

As the last trace of the sun vanished, the temperature plummeted. Mo slid his foot off the blackglass and turned towards the hop, which was parked on the edge of the bone-yard behind us. Its landing pads stood leg-deep in a sea of half-submerged Old World headstones that pushed like broken teeth through the detritus.

'We should go,' he said, pulling his jacket tight around his body. 'We'll report back to Oxton and request a repair team.'

Mo stalked off between the stones. Beyond, throughout North Side, night lights were flicking on, fragmenting the expanse of darkness with chains of colour. It was almost curfew.

'Just give me another minute,' I said.

I switched my awareness, scanning the broken fence for life-lights. The faintest glimmer of the last living person to touch the metal hung over it in a streak, so faint that in another few days, it would vanish completely. The life-light belonged to a single male, most likely the hop driver. He'd laser-clipped the fence open three and a half weeks ago, four at most, and hadn't touched it again since. The kind of laser needed to cut through Kevlar wasn't something you could get hold of on the street; it was strictly Unit issue.

None of it made sense.

The wind tore my hair from its band and whipped it around my face in dark whorls. I held it back off my forehead and took a deep breath. Three months at the Unit, and the most I'd achieved was basic training, which was virtually pointless, considering my one-and-only hop piloting lesson had almost ended in a crash, and that I still couldn't aim a laser weapon at a double-door and be sure I'd hit it. I stared out towards the horizon. The wind shrieked through the mesh, and wrapped itself around me like a shroud. At least at Torches I'd known the score. Sure, the guys got fresh from time to time, but security made sure everything stayed friendly. And now, after five years in a world I'd known, here I was staring into the dark and listening to the wind sift sand and roar off a landscape made of mutilated scrap. I pulled my jacket tight around my waist, and turned away.

Mo was already in the vehicle. The thrusters hissed softly, sending puffs of blacksand up around the landing pads. He put his headset on as I climbed into the passenger seat.

'How can you wear that thing over your shades?' I said.

He ignored me. I fastened my harness and we rose up.

'Did you get anything else?' Mo's voice was light, but the sarcasm bled through.

'Yes,' I said. 'The fence was cut down a month ago. The hop driver is a single male, and the cargo has no life signature. Our driver is using the Cinderlands as a cover for his operation. He also has access to a Unit issue Kevlar-cutter.'

Just for a beat Mo's block fell away and a sharp flash of shock burned through the space between us. A moment later, he'd stamped on it. It was an effort not to let the corners of my mouth twitch up. The guy wasn't as impervious as he wanted to think.

As the hop turned, we faced a fiesta of light garlands in every colour imaginable. They hung in chains, sporadic here, but further into North Side more dense, crawling up the tall houses and coiling around the courtyards. So pretty, it was difficult to believe that there were more unexplained disappearances in this part of the city than any other. Unless you understood shifters.

Across the boundary bridge into South Side, the buildings were bigger, and the street lights hung in regular rows like little white pearls. The squares teemed with people, some at flash-food stands, others seated underneath heat lamps in pavement café bars or dawdling between the shopping arcades. Virtual childmoms shepherded groups of kids in neon jackets, and android enforcers clustered under the fake-trees, watching. After the solitude of the bone-yard, we might've been flying into a carnival.

'I suggest we see Oxton immediately to report on the perimeter. If she doesn't want anything else, I'll take you home, Miss Green.'

We touched down on HQ roof top. Mo slipped the headset off and put it on the dash.

'Can't you cut the Miss Green thing and just call me Jess?'

'No.'

'Why not?'

'Protocol.'

'That's such bull, Mo. At least let's soften the boundaries a little so we don't have to pretend that I give the orders.'

Mo ignored me, and opened his side visor.

I laid my hand on his elbow. 'Can we at least try to-'

He pulled away and twisted round to face me in one quick move.

'I'd prefer it if you didn't touch me, Miss Green.'

'What?'

'The last empath I knew read by touch.'

'But I don't.'

'Even so.'

Mo slid out the door. I flicked down my side-visor, and followed him out onto the roof. An Eye shot past the landing lights, its lenses glittering. It saw us, then darted over the edge of the building and plummeted down into the square below.

We checked through security and took the lift in silence facing our reflections, Mo's dark face high above my own pale one. My shirt collar had fallen open to reveal the Old World button on a chain that I never took off, the only thing I had of my brother's. Instinctively, I reached up and tucked it away. The sight of my hair still shocked me - the hair I'd worn long at Torches, the hair that'd brought me extra tips, now cut to my shoulders and tied back, reduced to a dark smudge. Then, they'd called me beautiful; now, stripped of the artifice the Torches clientele seemed to love, I wasn't so sure. I closed my eyes and waited for the stomach-surge to tell me that we'd stopped moving.

The lift opened on floor Eighty Nine. Oxton was waiting for us in her office, her lips anus-tight and her eyes bloodshot. She shut the door.

'What have you got for me Miss Green, Mr Okoli?'

'The shifters' report was correct, Oxton,' I said.

'I suspected so.' Oxton sank into a plush swivel behind the desk, and slid her com into a rack. 'North Side might not be the Unit's favourite location, but the shifters would never lie about a perimeter breach. Please, continue.'

I opened my mouth to speak. Mo cut me off.

'Miss Green detected a possible single male driving some kind of cargo to and from North Side into the Cinderlands.'

A possible single male? What the hell was one of those, when it was at home?

'Whatever he's doing, it can't be any more than small-time,' Mo continued. 'It wouldn't be the first time a petty racketeer has made the mistake of using North Side as a cover. Let's plant the seed with the shifters, let them take him out, and then repair the breach. It should take forty eight hours tops.'

Oxton sat back and laced her fingers. Her nails were long and sharp, painted the same scarlet as her lips. She regarded us both in silence.

'I don't necessarily agree,' I said.

Mo twitched.

'With respect, Mo, you only saw what your eyes told you, and that wasn't an awful lot.'

He stiffened and looked down at me.

'I have an alternative recommendation,' I said to Oxton. 'If we operate a minimum-surveillance operation, we can find out exactly what this guy is up to.'

'Minimum surveillance is perhaps a term Miss Green remembers from her basic training.'

'No, I-'

'Which hardly makes up for almost crashing a hop, and discharging a laser weapon in a dangerous environment.'

'When a lone ranger rips open the perimeter in shiftersville, and drives out into the Cinderlands carrying an unspecified cargo, then it isn't a code amber situation, Mo. There's more to it.'

Mo smiled. 'Thank you for your expert opinion.'

'Can I have exactly what you picked up in your words, Miss Green?' said Oxton.

She wasn't sitting any more. She stood, and leaned across her desk, her eyes so pale blue they were ghostly, the circles underneath cavernous.

'He travels alone when he crosses the border. This guy's stress levels are off the scale. Everything about him carries the hallmark of somebody who's in over his head. To me, that only means one thing: that somebody bigger is running him. And if somebody bigger is running him, then sooner or later, something bigger is going to happen.'

Nobody spoke. The water cooler in the corner hummed. Oxton's com bleeped, once, then kicked into messages. Mo bristled and didn't bother to block.

'And for the record, my assessment has nothing to do with my basic training,' I said. 'It's based on five years of watching the same thing happen over again.'

Torches might've been a sexclub, but thanks to its dodgy reputation, it was also a racketeers' hothouse. Subversives used the place as a front, and conducted their business behind closed doors. I guess the girls and the drink were just a light diversion. When you've worked a place like that for a while, you get a feel for the kind of guys who operate below the radar.

Oxton watched us closely, her eyes rolling in their sockets.

'You are no longer a senior guardian, Mr Okoli. You are Miss Green's handler. Your role is to support her work and not to question her judgement.' Oxton turned to me. 'How would you like to see this matter handled, Miss Green?'

'Put a motion-sensor on the broken fence, and have all film footage forwarded straight to me,' I said. 'Once we've located this man, I only have to look into his eyes. He never need know I'm onto him. That's better than taking him off the street and alerting his boss in the process.'

Oxton nodded. 'I accept your recommendation. Keep me informed.'

She flicked through some holo-files, sending them out into the air around her head where they fluttered like little mirages. Seconds later, they vanished.

'The arrangements are made. I have a team from Forty Three attending the perimeter before dawn. Footage will be sent to you both immediately the motion sensors are deployed. You are dismissed.'

My stomach turned itself over, that horrible, taut feeling you get when you find yourself praying you've made the right call.

Mo nodded stiffly and turned towards the door.

'Oh, and Mr Okoli?'

He stopped with his hand stretched towards the handle.

'Do you have a personal issue with Miss Green?'

Mo spun around on his heels. 'No, ma'am.'

'Good. Do you have a professional issue with Miss Green?'

He hesitated. 'No, ma'am.'

Like hell he didn't.

'Good. You may no longer be a senior guardian, but I expect you to employ the same level of professionalism. Dismissed.'

We stepped into the corridor. The door closed behind us with a soft sucking sound. When Mo's footsteps began to disappear in the opposite direction, I realised I'd turned the wrong way to the lift. I spun around. Light from the strips slid over the surface of his jacket as he loped away. I wanted to ask him if the leather was real, because if it was, he earned more than double what I was on, but I kept my mouth shut and caught up.

Mo palm-scanned and we stepped into the lift. I pretended to watch the digi-display, staring at him out the corner of my eye. A pale scar cut the underside of his jaw.

'What's with the old wound on your chin?'

He ran a finger along the skin. 'Laser burn.'

'You're kidding. I didn't think a human could survive a beam.'

The corner of Mo's mouth twitched up. He continued to stare at the door.

'In the line of duty?'

'Uhuh.'

'Was that the only time?'

He hesitated, then pulled back his jacket to reveal a laser arm that nestled in a body holster. Mo lifted his top. There wasn't an ounce of fat on the guy. A faint sheen of damaged tissue paled the muscular ribs above his waistband.

'Nasty. Is that the worst you ever had?'

Mo dropped his top and his jacket swung back into place. 'I have others. But not in places I can show.'

'Why didn't you have corrective treatment?'

'Because I can't stand holo-nurses.'

I laughed, despite the fact it wasn't funny.

The lift stopped, and the door flew back.

'If there's nothing else you need, I'll take you home, Miss Green.'

'Thanks, but I'll make my own way back.'

I headed for security check-out, took an exit palm-print and walked through the double doors into the square.

Outside, the stones glistened with rain. A fragrant furze of steam hung between the food cabins. At the cab point, an electro sat waiting. I got in. The passenger door opened and Mo slid in next to me.

'If you want to take a cab, we'll take a cab. But I have to see you home.'

Exasperated, I fastened my harness and settled back into the seat. The cab pulled away with a whine, sending a slosh of rainwater onto the kerb.

'What if I don't want to go home?'

Mo didn't respond, but I felt the frustration coming off him in waves. He turned his head away, and stared outside.

'For three months, the only journey I've made is between HQ and my apartment,' I said. 'What if I want to meet up with a friend?'

The cab slowed down to let a crowd of young women cross the walkway. They were my age, laden with sparkly bags, chased by holo-promotions that fluttered to their feet and fizzled out. Laughing, they disappeared into a restaurant. Something tugged me inside, a longing for something I'd never had, something normal – like carrying a sparkly bag, and walking through a shoal of disintegrating holo-ads.

'I didn't think you had any friends,' Mo said.

'Of course I have friends,' I snapped. 'I have Saskia.'

'And would this Saskia be the prostitute you shopped when your sexclub burned down?'

'I did not shop Saskia. And don't use the word prostitute - she's a professional consort. Anyway, what the hell do you know about the club?'

'I did my background on you, Green.'

'I have no background,' I said. 'Not one that went on the records.'

'Don't you believe it.'

He was bluffing – he had to be. We crossed town in silence, the stone and concrete eventually giving way to the softer suburbs of Riverbank. Fake-grass lined the walkways, and the tops of real trees were visible over the smaller buildings. Security was discreet here, Kevlar mesh wound with real creepers. The cab pulled up at the entrance.

'Thanks for the company, Mo. I'll see you tomorrow morning.'

I released the visor but Mo flicked the interior lock. My knees butted into the side.

'Why did you do that?'

'Because you and I have to get something clear. When Oxton recruited you, she told you security was paramount.'

'Which is how I ended up here,' I said, gesturing to the apartment blocks that sat inside the boundary. 'I'm not complaining about the view, but the additional security seems a little excessive.'

'Thirteen may be a new department, but you need protection. Take it seriously.'

'I get it. I knew the score when they brought me in. Either assimilate and enjoy the benefits, or disappear into a street compressor with the rest of the human detritus they drag out of the sewers once in a while. But please don't tell me I'm not allowed to walk a few paces without you shadowing my every step.'

I flicked the visor release again. It didn't move.

'That's the point. You're not allowed to, Miss Green. When you were told you go nowhere without me, Oxton meant it.'

I didn't respond. Mo exhaled slowly, his eyebrows unknitting as his face relaxed. It might've been weariness, or it could've been desperation. I couldn't tell.

'If Oxton thinks you'll be a target once Thirteen takes off, believe her. This perimeter job, on North Side? It's small fry. Oxton's just giving you your head. You've got far worse to come, believe me.'

'What, exactly?' I shrugged. 'Kidnap? Imprisonment? Murder?'

The last word came out as a laugh, but an unexpected tension wound its way around my throat, twisting my voice into a whine.

'Don't be facetious. This isn't a game. If you do your job properly, you'll get a price on your head.'

'What?'

Mo nodded, once, the way he does when he's letting me know he doesn't expect to be challenged.

'Why do you think I carry this?' He patted the laser arm that nestled underneath his jacket. 'It's not for my own good, it's for your protection. Remember that.'

Mo stared out the front of the electro-cab, the night-lights glancing off his lenses. I looked at him, properly, the set of his jaw and the way his eyebrows knitted together over his shades. There was a hardness about Mo, but it wasn't directed at me – it was utterly impersonal.

'OK,' I said. 'I understand.'

For the second time that day, a shimmer of shock danced in the air between us.

'You shouldn't do that,' I said.

'Do what?'

'Forget yourself and let your block go.'

'I didn't.'

'Yes you did. You lose it just for a second every time I take you by surprise.'

Mo's head snapped towards me. He scowled.

'Can I get out, now, please?'

The visor release bleeped and it sprung open. Outside, the air was heavy with the scent of rain on real leaves, and damp earth - heady, exotic, something I was still getting used to.

'We have to work together,' I said, climbing out. 'The least we can be is pleasant to each other.'

Mo stared at me from the back of the cab, his expression unfathomable.

'Come see my new apartment,' I said. 'I have an old cat, a real one. His name is Claws - he belonged to my aunt, but she died. Oxton pushed me an animal license through when I was recruited, although I doubt the cat is grateful. He hates people. I have vodka, mineral water, just-like-juice, or whatever it is you drink. I also have an excellent music collection.'

The mizzle suddenly thickened to rain, dripping off my nose in freezing globs.

'We can't be friends, Miss Green.'

The Kevlar mesh cracked open and the laser wire flicked off. I stepped through to the other side.

'Why not?'

'Because I'm your handler.'

The perimeter sealed itself and the cab visor shut. Mo pulled away. I watched the empty road after him, as the rain ran in drivels down my neck. I'd never bloody well fitted in anywhere, but if Torches hadn't finished me off, then the Unit certainly wouldn't. I set off in the direction of my apartment block, my footsteps drowned out by the white noise of rain on naked leaves.

II

The following morning, when I checked in at reception, HQ computer told me I had an appointment with Rosie, the secretary. I found her chatting to a vending machine in the rest area. She spun around when she heard me coming.

'Good morning. I'm to take you to your secure pod. You have a delivery.'

The vending machine pushed a protein shake out. Rosie snatched it and stuffed it in her handbag.

'After the pod, you're to meet our Chief Archivist, and then the senior staff from Fifty Nine,' she said. 'The former is eccentric but harmless. The latter pull limbs off stress toys and lay bets on who'll get the biggest scream and the most blood. Neither is to be regarded as friendship material. Come on.'

Rosie set off down the corridor, her heels stabbing the tiles and her blonde curls unravelling around her shoulders like a multitude of golden yo-yos. I jogged to catch up.

'How come you know everything about everybody?' I hissed.

Rosie shrugged. 'My memory is enhanced so I never forget a face or a voice. Plus, I'm programmed not to reveal anything inappropriate. I guess that makes me a safe confidante.'

'Programmed? You mean... you're not real?'

'Oh, Miss Green,' Rosie smiled indulgently, 'you are funny. Half the people here think you aren't real.'

We headed to the rear of ground floor, where the tiles gave out and the Kevlar doors became double-thickness. Rosie pulled up sharp at a corridor junction. Strip lighting, grey walls, and an expanse of identical doors disappeared into infinity in both directions.

'Behold the reason I get the job of showing you to appointments for the first two years,' she said, dodging in front of me. 'After that, you're on your own.'

We arrived at a bank of doors. Rosie palm-scanned the pad, and half the wall slid back on a vault lined with cubicles. I whistled.

'Don't waste your breath, Miss Green – this is only a fraction of HQ. Floors one through nineteen are admin and accommodation. The twenties and thirties are biological sciences. Forty through Sixty Nine is investigative, and the seventies are brute force, but don't quote me on that. Anything upwards of Eighty is top brass, no first names. Above Ninety, they don't have faces. Oh, and beware of getting involved with departments thirty through forty. They have a long-running feud. They'll do anything to shop each other. '

'You're kidding me, right?'

Rosie smirked. 'Welcome to the podbay. It's alphabetic. You're this way.'

We carried on walking until my name appeared above a door. I slid open the hatch. A light flicked on. Something gelatinous sat on the middle shelf, pulsating from a puddle of black goo.

'What the hell is that?'

'What's the matter?' Rosie peered over my shoulder and retreated, wrinkling her nose. 'Looks like something that should've been euthanized by Twenty One. Wildlife is banned from the pods.'

I swung around to face her. 'Who would've left me this?'

Rosie shrugged. 'How should I know?'

'Because you know everything about everybody here.'

She held up her hands. 'Don't shoot the messenger.'

I turned back to the mess on the shelf. A trail of slime ran across its length, pocked with bubbles. Somewhere deep within the translucent body, three things that looked like eyes were staring up at me, unblinking. The creature moved, setting off a wave of flatulence among its folds.

Rosie smirked.

'It isn't funny,' I snapped.

'Of course it isn't, Miss Green.'

'For goodness' sake, call me Jess. And please don't tell me you can't.'

'Why shouldn't I be able to?'

Rosie and I stared at each other in awkward silence.

'I didn't mean to snap. I'm sorry,' I said at last. 'It's just that this place pisses me off sometimes. This is probably some sad idiot's idea of a joke.'

Rosie smiled, which dimpled her cheeks winsomely. She looked too young and sweet to know everybody on all ninety nine floors. Or maybe the winsome sweetness was engineered in the same way her memory was.

'Any idea who might be behind it?' she said.

I leaned against a cubicle and scrubbed my face with my hands. 'You're a safe confident, right?'

'Always.'

'I'm having problems with my handler. Mo might not have done the dirty work on this one, but I suspect he got one of his chums to.'

Rosie's dimples straightened out and she tilted her head on one side. She knew something, I could tell, but she clearly wasn't about to spill.

'I'll sort it out, Jess.'

She stepped away from the cubicle door, pressed two fingers into one temple, then turned away and began to pace, slowly, the same as you do when you're talking on a com. After a few seconds she dropped her hand.

'Twenty One have acknowledged that one of their lab-rat colony went missing earlier this morning,' she said. 'It's sticky and smelly but it's basically harmless. Just don't touch it – the slime stains. And the odour takes forever to remove, especially if it splits open. If it does, we're in trouble, because dividing is how they reproduce. We could end up knee-deep in the things in no time.'

The twist in her lips told me she found the prospect amusing.

'Did you just communicate with Twenty One through your head?' I said.

'I have a direct link to HQ computer. It's so I can keep tabs on everybody, and make contact fast.'

I turned back to the pod. The thing had spread itself out on the shelf so that the eyes were more prominent. They swivelled towards me, sending up a pouf of unpleasant odour. I reached out to close the pod door, and caught sight of a small envelope on the top shelf. The printed label read Miss Jess Green, Secure Pod, HQ. I turned it over in my hand. The back was blank.

'Come on, let's get out,' said Rosie. 'A clean-up guy from Twenty One will be here soon.' She closed the cabinet on the black jelly, which whimpered as the lock engaged. 'And don't let it bother you, Jess. It's just a new recruit joke, like sending you for a long weight, or a left-handed com.'

We headed for the exit, the clap of our heels ricocheting off the cubicle doors. When we got back to reception, Rosie gestured to the rest area.

'Take a minute to check your delivery. I'm going to intercept the lab tech. He might know who set this up.'

Rosie vanished into a lift nearby. I reached into my pocket and pulled out the envelope, slitting it open with one nail. A card fell into the palm of my hand. A pale pink rose was sketched in one corner. In the middle, were the words:

Abigail Tempest Green.

My mother's name: a name I hadn't spoken in years; a name I'd never read, anywhere, not once - until now.

At the bottom, in smaller print, was River City Crematorium, followed by a plot number.

The writing on the card wavered as though the words were sliding over the surface. I sagged back onto the settee, the tip of the card trembling in my fingers. My flesh was white where I gripped it.

I didn't hear footsteps until it was too late. When I looked up, Mo stood in front of me, peering down into my face, furious.

'Where the hell have you been?'

'With Rosie.'

'You didn't answer your com.'

'It didn't tell me to.'

'Rubbish,' snapped Mo. 'I've tried to com you continually. The motion sensors picked up movement near the bone-yard.'

Hell - the footage.

I'd forgotten all about it.

An alert should've gone straight to my com.

I checked my pockets. No com. I shucked off my backpack, and rifled through it, spilling stuff out the sides onto the floor. The com fell into my hand, its signal panel blank. Mo tutted.

'You turned it off, when we're on an operation?'

'No, I didn't, I promise. I never turn it off. It must be malfunctioning.'

I shook the com. Mo snatched it out of my hand. The screen sprang to life with a dozen alerts and holo messages that shot out and hung in the air around our heads, chattering. Most of them were from him. Mo thrust the com back under my nose.

'You either turned it off, or deliberately ignored it, but we don't have time to argue. I've a hop out front. Come on - we have to go.'

'I need to tell Rosie. She's coming back for me.'

'Rosie already knows,' said Mo, turning away.

I pushed myself up off the sofa. The pattern on the floor tiles swam. One little card with a few words and a number on it, that's all it took for me to fall to pieces all over again. I swore I'd done with this.

Mo was already half way to the scan point when I stooped to pile my stuff back into my pack. I tapped the com screen. A little icon in one corner told that that somebody had blocked my alerts remotely. I shoved the com into one pocket and the envelope in the other, and ran.

As I followed Mo through exit security, a lab tech with a white hold-all marked 'livestock' crossed my path in the direction of the secure pods. He averted his eyes when he saw me.

*

While Mo piloted, I ran the security film. Only an hour previously, an old hop with a single male driver had crossed from the bone-yard into the Cinderlands, activating the sensor. The hop was dark and battered, virtually limping, its trim hanging off and trailing the dirt. A random sandstorm thrashed waves of black grit around, making the film look like a retro-movie that some celluloid geek had discovered in an abandoned warehouse. The driver wore a wide-brim cap pulled down low over his face, but the size of his jowls agreed with my first impression. As the hop pulled past and vanished, the film cut out.

'Old hop, single guy, unfit. Told you so,' I said, tucking the com into my pocket.

Mo grunted. Below us, the river was grey, its waters choppy. Brewing storm clouds tainted the crooked buildings and cobbled alleyways of North Side with a darkness that rendered everything flat. As we flew on, the houses reduced in height, then disappeared altogether. Mo took the hop down in one corner of the bone-yard. The sandstorm had blown itself out, leaving drifts of blacksand sifted around the stones. I didn't wait for the thrusters to cut before I jumped out and ran to the fence. The dunes had shifted slightly, revealing melted girders and twisted beams that hadn't seen daylight for decades. The faintest impression of the driver still hung there, his thought-stream disappearing into the Cinderlands like the tail-end of a comet.

Mo's footsteps came up behind me.

'I need to go through,' I said, without turning around.

'No way, Green, it's forbidden. Why do you think there's a perimeter? Even the shifters won't go in there.'

'I think that's exactly what our moonlighter is relying on.'

'He's a fool. I'm not losing you to stupidity.'

I shut my eyes, and caught up with the driver's decaying thought-stream as he sailed on into the blackness. Sand hissed into the front screen of the hop, and the old engine puttered. Our moonlighter favoured this time of day; something to do with the shifter nightclubs. They closed after dawn, so it didn't take a genius to work out this was the best time to cross North Side unseen. The essence of him weakened, and fizzled out.

I opened my eyes.

'Graham,' I said. 'His name is Graham.'

Behind me, Mo exhaled a long, disappointed breath.

'Great. So we have an overweight guy in an unidentified hop, called Graham. Well, that narrows it down a bit.'

Beyond the edge of the city, a distant peal of thunder cracked open and rolled itself out.

I shrugged. 'Let's take the hop, then.'

'It's illegal to fly over the Cinderlands.'

'Nobody need know.'

'You will know, Miss Green.'

'And you don't want to give me anything to hold over you, right?'

Mo sighed a great, racking sigh and shook his head. 'You just don't get it, do you?'

I wedged my hands in my jacket pockets and stared up into his face. 'You want me to fail.'

'What?'

'If Thirteen doesn't work out, you can go back to being a senior guardian.'

The wind changed direction and lashed sand against our legs, heavy with the threat of rain.

'I can never go back to being a senior guardian.'

Somewhere over the Cinderlands, forked lightening slit the cloudbank open.

'Why not?'

'Because… I was demoted.' Mo's voice disappeared in the tail-end of a gust of wind.

So. My handler, the model of Unit perfection, the artificially enhanced goliath who wouldn't have looked out of place on a plinth in an art gallery, was flawed. I looked at my feet so he couldn't see me smile.

'What do you think will happen to you, if Thirteen fails?'

I shrugged. 'I'll end up filing in archives, or temping on floor one.'

'You don't understand. You won't get moved sideways, not in the Unit. I'm lucky. I was given this job because I have a blemish-free service record spanning more than one hundred and eighty two years.'

I stared at his face, the un-lined skin the colour of latte, the short-cropped black hair that didn't show a single grey. I laughed.

'That's such bull.'

He didn't even crack a smile. 'There's no such thing as an ex-Unit employee. Think brain-drain, then think street compressor for any bits that might be left. You'll be cube-crushed for bio-fuel. That's what they do with people who don't make it work.'

The wind vanished and the air stilled to the thick, brooding silence that screams imminent storm. Mo stepped away and stood between two of the closest bone-yard stones, laying a hand on each. The stones glowed in the eerie way they do when there isn't much light, like pieces of bleached bone. Between them, he seemed to vanish into a backdrop of blacksand. He glanced towards the Cinderlands.

'Providing we don't go far, I will accompany you on foot. But this is off the record. Understood?'

'I understand.'

I slipped through the gap and set off, fast, my feet kicking up chunks of blackglass. In the distance, banks of raincloud melded with the earth in dark columns. Mo drew his laser. If he'd asked me, I could've told him that I'd already scanned for life signs and found none in close proximity. But Mo preferred to do things his way. We carried on until I felt weak with the effort of dragging my legs. I cast around, but Graham and his hop were too long gone. I pulled up by a shell of metal that looked like it might once have been part of a building. The sand shifted and swallowed my feet.

'I can't find him, Mo.'

'Then we have to go back.'

I was breathing hard, but Mo hadn't even broken a sweat. Behind him, the perimeter caterpillared along the edge of the Cinderlands. The gap we'd come through looked tiny. Over our heads, the clouds weighed heavy. The endless space reminded me of things I hadn't confronted in years: freedom. Lack of boundaries; possibilities. When I looked down, Mo was watching me.

'So what's the problem with big horizons?' He flicked the safety on his laser.

'What?'

'I saw your face, just then, when you looked up. You flinched. And you're ducking. Just a little bit.'

I'm not often lost for words.

'You don't have to tell me if you don't want to.'

'I hadn't thought about it,' I lied. 'I guess... I haven't seen open spaces for too many years. Not as big as this. At the club, the doors were locked. The windows had shutters.'

Mo took a barrel off the laser, checked it and re-attached it. His fingers moved deftly. He looked through the sights, over the dunes.

'So what was with the shutters?'

I shrugged. 'Management said windows and doors weren't safe. We had Kevlar security screens everywhere. They locked them.'

Mo readjusted the sights and stared down the barrel some more.

'They locked you in?'

I nodded. 'Yeah. Luca said it was best.'

'Luca?'

'The club manager. Said we'd be safer that way.'

Mo gave a bitter little laugh, and moved the laser slowly as though he was tracking something across the horizon.

'Did this Luca ever let you out?'

'Course not. It was for our own protection.'

Mo lowered the laser and looked straight at me, his features impassive.

'How long were you there?'

I shrugged. 'I went there at seventeen, after my aunt died. If I hadn't run, they would've put me in temporary care and taken everything off me anyway. I made my own choices. But at least I saw the city first. Saskia worked the club since she was eleven. She never saw the outside again till Torches burned down. She'll be twenty nine this year.'

Saskia.

Even the feel of her name on my tongue reinforced the hole she'd left when I'd run.

I had to contact her, and soon, but my instincts screamed at me to wait at least a full year – long enough for Luca to suppose he'd never see me again.

Mo began to rub the laser handle vigorously with the edge of his shirt. The damn thing hardly needed polishing.

'Look, I can't go back without something more to take to Oxton,' I said.

'Then we'll wait it out in the bone-yard with the hop cloaked. This Graham. He has to come out some time. But the Unit is better than the club, right?'

I shrugged. 'It's not better, it's just different.'

Something glimmered at my feet. I scuffed it with one toe. A disk slid up out of the sand, and sat on the surface. I picked it up. It was metal, some obsolete compound which had tarnished over time, cut in a circle. One side was blank. I flipped it over. On the other, a fancy letter N stood out in black. I held it up and whistled.

'Some collectors pay a fortune for old rubbish from the Cinderlands.' I flicked the disk into the air and watched it spin.

Mo's hand shot out and caught it. His eyebrows knotted together.

'What's the matter?'

He turned it over, and exhaled sharply. 'This is from your old hop.'

I scanned around my feet for tracks, but the wind had erased them.

'It's an early New World thing. Vehicles used to have the maker's sigil on them. Nothing like now, where it's done in holographs.'

'Oh,' I tried to sound interested. 'Is it worth much?'

'Irrelevant. I recognise the sigil. It belongs to the Nemesis Corporation.'

'Never heard of them.'

'You wouldn't have. You'll never see their name written down or publicised anywhere. They're only ever represented by this.' Mo opened his palm. 'Nobody knows what goes on inside except the people who work there. The board isn't public, and their meeting house is floating. Although I believe they do have premises, I couldn't say where.'

'But that's impossible,' I said.

'Nothing is impossible if it's connected to the Unit. I wouldn't know about them either if I hadn't been asked to guard a high-level meeting, just the once.'

A violent gust of wind sent sand past us in horizontal slats. I pulled my jacket collar up.

'You need sand-glasses,' said Mo. 'I'll inform Seventeen.'

That meant he was intending on coming back out here. I pulled my lapels up around my face so he couldn't see me smile.

'Let's get back to the hop, Miss Green.'

'Can I have the sigil back?'

'No, you can't.'

Mo slid it into his pocket, and pushed the laser back into its holster. We began to walk, the wind buffeting our backs.

'I don't get a good feeling about this,' said Mo. 'You told Oxton that you picked up that somebody bigger was running Graham? Maybe that includes letting a minion take an old vehicle from the Nemesis Corporation de-conscript stock.'

So, he had listened to what I'd said.

We reached the perimeter as darkness closed in over our heads. The rain began to scythe down in silver sheets. Inside the hop, the noise was deafening. Mo and me sat in silence until the storm blew itself out and the sun slipped away below the horizon.

Graham never came back.

III

A high-pitched com alert forced its way into my dream. I heaved myself up on one elbow, disorientated. The image in my mind, of an empty cot with its covers stripped and the mattress leaned on one side, hung stubbornly behind my lids. I felt for the button around my neck and squeezed it, like I always did after one of the dreams, as though it was an amulet that might somehow bring him back. The digi-display on my living room wall read two thirty AM. I'd fallen asleep on the sofa. Outside, a peppering of stars showed through patchy cloud; I'd forgotten to throw the blackout.

The alert cut out, and Oxton's face appeared over a half-empty glass of just-like-juice on the coffee table. The cat shot off the settee and puttered into the bedroom, his black belly hugging the floor, the white patch on his back glowing faintly in the gloom. I struggled upright.

'This announcement may be untimely, but I'm afraid it can't wait until morning.'

'What is it, Oxton?'

'We have a crime scene. I need you to take a look at it right away. Mr Okoli is on his way to pick you up.' Oxton squinted and peered through the com at me, her eyes wide. 'Are you alright, Miss Green?'

'I'm fine. Bad dream,' I said, wiping my forehead.

Oxton stared right through me in that intense way she has, the circles under her eyes so deep she looked more like a poorly-sculpted puppet than a real person. Her face broke up in a shower of pixels and the com flicked itself off. I pulled on my boots, grabbed my jacket, and drained the juice. When the door alarm sounded, a holograph of Mo appeared on the security panel inside. I swung the door open.

'Never throw your door wide without scanning first. I could've been anybody.'

'I saw you on the screen, Mo.'

'Technology isn't infallible, Miss Green. The holo could've been faked.'

'OK,' I said. 'Next time.'

Mo led the way down the stairs. Outside, a black hop was waiting on the forecourt.

'A night hop?'

'We can't afford to attract attention. The less people who see us, the better.'

'Where are we going?'

'West Side.'

The night hop's thrusters were virtually silent. We cleared the banks of the little tributary that cut the apartment block grounds, the mist on its surface like latte foam. After curfew, traffic management disappeared, leaving the skies open and the lack of holographic lane markers and warnings starkly absent. We rose up, the stars a reverse imprint of the street lights below. We travelled in silence, seeing only the android enforcers that waited and watched from the deserted streets.

In West Side, light sliced the tower blocks on the floors occupied by night workers. The rest of the district was in darkness. We lost height, and drifted towards the back alleys and service areas. Mo took the hop down in the shadow of a vacant building.

'Follow me,' he said, sliding out. 'And stay out of the security beams.'

I fell in behind him, inhaling the scent of damp and mould. The wall we were tracing suddenly doubled in height, plunging us into blackness. The sound of Mo's breathing and the squeak of his leather jacket doubled in volume as my hearing took over.

'You've had night vision enhancement?' I whispered.

'Yep.'

I switched my awareness. A multitude of colours sprang up on the solid surfaces ahead, not bright enough to light the way, but intense where people had walked and leaned and touched, illuminating the route of human traffic. Mo was blinding neon blue. I squinted and looked past him.

We stopped at a hangar doorway. The surround was frosted with human contact, such a heavy pastiche that the colours bled together in a mess. The life lights were old, as though the place had been well used until three weeks ago, before being emptied out. Only a few recent prints stood out.

'In here,' Mo whispered.

'Am I allowed light?'

Mo held his com up, and shot a torch beam into the darkness. The floor was empty except for the odd piece of junk. I scanned for life signatures but there were none except mine and his. Mo stepped through the entrance and I followed, close enough to feel the heat from his body. He swept the torch beam left until it hit a bundle of rags on the floor. The scent of death was overpowering.

Blood spread around the rags in an arc, viscous and shiny in the torchlight. From above, something dripped into the pool with a rhythmic splat. Mo moved the light upwards. For a moment it disappeared into the depths of the hangar, the back wall too far away for the beam to touch, until, way above our heads, it settled on two naked feet. Ochre bloodstains streaked the white skin. I stepped away instinctively. As the beam crawled upwards, it picked out legs and a torso slit open by a single cut.

The victim was male, youngish, maybe my age. The edges of several cleanly sliced ribs winked white from between layers of darker muscle. His blood-matted head lolled forwards at an angle that told me he was suspended from a broken neck. Thankfully, I couldn't see his face. I shut my eyes and turned away.

At Torches, a regular had once smuggled in a knife and slashed one of the girls. Luca got to her just in time. The bit I remember most was the spray, arcs of it like little red jewels strewn on the mirrors. They found me standing in a corner, not speaking, just staring. Apparently he'd run right past me with the knife, and I'd just watched him go. But all I remember is the mirrors.

'Are you alright, Miss Green?'

My head swam. I felt sick.

'I'll be fine,' I whispered, and stepped away.

'Unfortunately, there is another body.'

Mo put on hand on my shoulder, lightly, and steered me around to face the bundle of rags.

'You've already seen the worst, I promise you,' he said.

We stepped towards the pile on the floor, avoiding the blood. Mo squatted down and moved the cloth back. Underneath, a girl with short brown hair was curled into a foetal position, her skin grey with death-pallor.

She was frozen solid.

The torch beam picked out her eyelashes, crisped with a silver coat, and the eyes which were still half open, glazed and opaque. At my feet, the pool of blood had two parts. That closest to the girl's body was frozen, but the blood which ran from the victim above was liquid.

'What can you see?' said Mo.

Images crowded my mind: men running; surgical tools; drained blood; fear. They slid over each other like quick-fire holo-movie stills, and vanished.

Mo pulled the cloth back over the body and suddenly she was just a heap of rags again. I turned away.

'I guess this must be difficult for you.' Mo averted the torch so the light fell in a full moon on the floor between us. The refractions hit him under the cheekbones, hollowing them.

'I'm fine. It's just... overwhelming.'

I checked the floor for life lights. The couple had come in here, together, only hours before. They'd stopped along the way, leaning on a wall here, kicking aside a piece of rubbish there. Their imprints were the most widely strewn. The other recent footsteps had come later, and were ordered and formal. They'd belong to whoever Oxton sent out from HQ to look at the mess. But who the hell were the running men I'd picked up, and why didn't they show a life signature?

Mo flicked the torch to our right. A film tripod stood close to the bodies.

'Looks like they decided to film their own little home movie.'

The torch-light rolled along the floor to a low platform of crates that'd been pushed together to form a makeshift bed. The tripod was angled directly towards it.

'And if you check out the ceiling,' Mo swung the beam up, missing the hanging body, 'you'll see why they chose this place.'

An assortment of lifting gear, including chains, straps, and cages, lined the ceiling nearby. I whistled through my teeth. Some people were crazily inventive. Torches had taught me that much.

'Where's the com that they filmed with?' I said.

'Fifty Nine picked it up and took it away earlier. The male victim had time to use a coded alert to call the Unit.'

'The victims were Unit employees?'

'No. The guy had just paid out for a new and very expensive personal alarm system with a direct link to HQ. It won't look good that Seventy One didn't arrive in time.'

I turned to the hanging body. I couldn't bear to look any higher than the feet. Mo obliged by pointing the torch beam low, which picked out the mauve lunula of his nails, and the hair around his ankles encrusted with dried blood. At least the dripping had stopped.

'His organs have been removed,' I said.

'I pretty much guessed that from the incision,' said Mo, but there was no sarcasm in his voice. 'I know this is difficult for you, but you have to toughen up. This is what you've been recruited for – you need to find a way to switch off and cope.'

Cope. That's what I'd been doing for years. Until now, I'd thought that coping related to the convent, to my brother's disappearance, to my mother vanishing... not to freshly-butchered bodies.

'Whoever did this took the victim's organs away for a reason, Mo. It wasn't a happy accident, and it wasn't just for the thrill of it. There's something messy about it, though. Something botched.'

Mo didn't respond. I turned to the girl on the floor.

'She was the second victim,' I said. 'Her boyfriend managed to throw her the com before he died. The girl was the one who activated the alert. She went down very quickly, faster than he did.' Something about the speed of the girl's demise made my mind reel, as though I was spinning, out of control. 'And they got it right with this one.'

'What do you mean?'

'Her vital organs are gone and her blood has been drained. Plus, she's frozen. That was in the game plan. The guy was a test-run. They botched him.'

Mo shifted the beam, plunging us into darkness. He ran it up to the hanging body and back down to the floor.

The ghost of an impression fleeted through my mind, a woman in long pale dress, the fabric of her skirts wrapping itself into a candy-twist around her legs as she turned towards me. I didn't get to see her face before she vanished.

Had I seen the victim, not long before she died?

Or had I caught a glimpse of somebody else, somebody who might hold a fundamental clue to what had happened here?

Right at that moment, I had no way of knowing.

'I'm calling Twenty One to retrieve the bodies for further tests,' said Mo. 'Let me get you out of here, Miss Green.'

Mo held his torch in one hand, and took my elbow with the other. We headed for the exit, where rain slapped the tarmac and bounced back up to knee height, silvered into little bullets by the security light. Mo didn't let go of my arm until we were at the hop. I leaned against the side, and retched on the tarmac. He passed me a compressed-water canister. I activated the spray and drank, gratefully, tilting back my head so that the rain could sluice my face. Mo's hand rested on my shoulder.

'You told me you preferred it if we don't touch.'

'Don't take this the wrong way, Green, but newbies aren't particularly careful in choosing where they pass out after their first big scene. I'd rather catch you, if you decide to nose-dive the tarmac. Are you going to be sick again?'

I shook my head. Mo flicked the visor down and helped me into the hop.

This wasn't the first time he'd seen butchered bodies, but for me, I'd crossed a line. How the hell was I supposed to think this was better than Torches?

We made the journey in silence. Back at HQ, night-lights waterfalled down the front, transforming its drab façade with spectral glitter, but inside, the web of grey corridors was the same. The security staff, the scurrying lab techs, even the junior secretaries in suits, carried on as though it was ten AM on a busy morning. In reality, the digi told me it was three fifteen AM. Nobody second-glanced our soaking clothes. Rosie was already waiting for us in reception rest area. As usual, she looked bizarrely immaculate.

'I have to take you straight to meet our Chief Archivist,' she said. 'Oxton thinks that talking to Reginald immediately is the best way forwards. He wants to know exactly what you picked up, so he can cross reference any detail with his records.' Rosie's eyes flickered over Mo. 'I've heard things were pretty grim out there.'

'Yeah.'

I caught my reflection in the scanner screen. My eyes were set in dark hollows, my skin unnaturally pale. Next to me Rosie's face was illuminated by a halo of curls. She was staring up at Mo with that weird kind of intensity that says something more is going on underneath the surface. As I caught her eye, she looked away.

'I intend to accompany Miss Green,' said Mo. 'She's had a shock, and she's exhausted.'

Rosie raised her eyebrows. 'As you wish. Follow me.'

'It's OK - I appreciate the gesture, but you don't have to. Go grab a coffee. Get dried off. I'll com you when I finish up in Archives.'

'But you look terrible.'

'I'll be better when I get out of these wet clothes.'

'I'll fetch something right away,' said Rosie.

We stopped by a lift, and she palm-scanned the pad. Mo remained in the corridor, staring at us, impassive, until the doors shut him out.

'I don't think he likes me,' I said, as we descended.

Rosie smirked.

'Seriously.'

'Mo has his reasons. Don't be too hard on him.' She glanced at me out of the corner of her eye.

'I know about his demotion,' I said.

Rosie twitched. 'It has nothing to do with his demotion.'

'Then what has it to do with?'

Rosie shrugged. 'It's nothing.' A flicker of something passed over her face, gone before I'd registered what.

'I'm supposed to work with the guy. I need to know.'

Rosie stared at her reflection in silence.

'Look, I know you can't say anything you're not supposed to, but surely you can tell me something?'

She sighed. 'I'm surprised nobody has mentioned it already.'

'Nobody in HQ speaks to me except you. And Mo, and Oxton. They don't like empaths.'

Rosie smirked. 'You haven't heard this from me, OK? Mo will never be comfortable around you, because you remind him of somebody.'

'Who?'

'His fiancée.'

'Why should that be a problem?'

'Because she died.'

The lift pulled up and my head cart-wheeled. The door flashed back, and Rosie was out in the corridor before I'd regained my balance, stabbing the floor with her sharp heels, her buttocks two juggling balls underneath the tight skirt. I caught up.

'When did she die?'

'Before you were born. Mo's been on his own for at least sixty years. It's too long ago for him not to have moved on, in my opinion, but I've been told it's none of my business.'

We turned left at an intersection. Rosie was walking too fast. Hanks of wet hair slapped my face as I broke into a jog to keep up.

'What was her name?'

'Zaphira. There's never been anybody since. Mo's had the odd fling, met girls out in town, but nothing that meant anything. Apparently.' Rosie rolled her eyes.

She stopped outside a door that looked identical to every other door, her irises sparking vivid blue under the strip lights, brighter than I'd noticed them before. Above her head, an Eye spotted us, its lights glittering like tiny darts.

'Reginald is in here,' she said, reaching for the handle.

'Wait.' I slid my hand onto Rosie's. 'Just one more question. How did Zaphira die?'

'I'm not authorised to discuss that with you,' Rosie said, and opened the door.

Inside, the lighting was low. I glanced at the ceiling. Most of the strips were out.

'Jess,' said Rosie, 'meet Reginald.' She motioned towards a small, wiry man slumped on a chair, playing with a retro digi-pad. His head was bald except for a ruff of hair that sat over his ears like an ermine crown. 'Reginald, this is Jess Green from Thirteen.'

Reg looked up without smiling. His eyes were blackened slits. Something about them drew me in and freaked me out at the same time.

'Hi,' I said. 'Nice to meet you, Reg.'

He twitched. 'Inald.'

'I'm sorry?'

'It's Reg. Inald. Reginald. I do not do unnecessary abbreviations, Miss Green.'

A single tear fell from the corner of one eye and rolled down his cheek. Reg pulled an old-fashioned handkerchief from an inside pocket, and dabbed his face.

'I'll leave you to it,' said Rosie, retreating.

The door clicked closed.

'Please, Miss Green, sit.'

Reg motioned to a chair next to him. As I slid into it, he flicked his com, and a holo-screen flared to life on the wall opposite. He flinched and turned the light down.

'Murder,' he snapped. 'Organ excision. Blood draining. Freezing. All against the wonderful backdrop of an abandoned warehouse filled with lifting gear, while a home porn movie was being filmed.'

'Except it wasn't a home porn movie,' I said.

Reg's head snapped towards me, his expanded pupils glittering like beads in the half-light.

'The film was intended for public consumption. They're made to be sold. My old manager used to buy them. He'd screen them in a private booth for the best customers. The actors make their living at it. Some of the films are horrible.'

Reg's eyes widened as he took in my face and my body all in one. I shifted back in my seat.

'In this instance, I'll bow to your greater experience, Miss Green. I'm aware you've come from a sexclub background.'

I didn't respond. Reg twitched, a tiny tremor than ran right through him, and smiled, all lips and teeth and nothing behind the eyes. He turned back to the screen, and sent a holo-photo shooting out. A dismembered boy a little younger than me lay in a gutter. His torso was raked with claw marks. I turned my head away.

'We've had similar incidences over the years,' Reg said cheerfully, changing the picture. 'Decapitations, dismemberings, Hen and Stag nights to the North Side that've gone horribly wrong…' the picture changed again. 'Please look at the screen, Miss Green. You might learn something.'

I lifted my head. A single, bloodied holographic eyeball shimmered in front of my nose, the rest of the decapitated head a blur in the background. Instinctively I put my hands to my mouth.

'Usually the shifters are involved, but not always,' said Reg, tapping his com again. 'Ah. This was one of my personal favourites. Twelve years ago, a coach-hop carrying a cheerleading team took a wrong turn down an alley in North Side and vanished. Fifty Two only ever found a couple of pom-poms, and the bits of the girls that'd been ripped off as souvenirs. Shifters were responsible. A renegade strain with a too-powerful hunting instinct. But I've never, in all my time in archives, known anybody to be frozen solid.'

In the half-light, the sensations came flooding back: the air heavy with the taste of iron; the splat of blood falling from somewhere high up; the girl's eyelashes cocooned in ice, her short hair frozen into solid spikes; and Mo, his hand on my shoulder, the scent of his leather jacket, his voice. Scythes of rain, hitting my face and drenching my clothes…

We sat in silence. The scrolling holo-files chattered softly. Somebody walked along the corridor outside, sending the fragile slat blinds trembling. Reg switched off the screen. The light around the rim vanished, and the strip above us failed, plunging the room into darkness. He was on his feet before I'd heard him move. He stopped at the door, and slid on an ocular shield that covered most of his face.

'It's time for you to meet my archives, Miss Green. Please, follow.'

On our way past reception, Rosie slipped me a neatly folded pile of black fabric.

'Dry clothes. Archives is big enough for you to find a corner to change in,' she whispered, continuing down the corridor without stopping.

In front of the lift, a man in restraints wearing Unit uniform lay on the floor screaming obscenities, strands of foam flecking his lips. One guard was standing over him with a taser, while three more struggled to hold him down as his body convulsed violently.

'Faulty implant,' Reg said too cheerfully over one shoulder. 'Try not to stare, Green. If he's lucky, they'll put him out of his misery.'

Reg stepped around him. I followed. As we got into the lift, the screaming stopped.

'He's gone. Bag him up,' said the man with the taser. 'I'll inform the widow.'

The lift door closed and the voices cut out. Trembling, I leaned back against the wall, clutching the clothes. Reg programmed the lights to 'very dim', and pulled his mask off.

'You're entering my world now, Green,' he said. 'We're going down.'

The floors flew by in a blur of neon. Seconds later, the lift stopped, and the door zipped back. I squinted into the gloom. Boxes and files were stacked in floor-to-ceiling racks, separated by narrow aisles that stretched as far as I could see in all directions. The dusty smell of long-term storage was punctuated by a sour, feral under-note, as though something was living alongside the records.

Reg whipped off his gloves and pushed past, his hand brushing mine lightly. 'Please, do step inside, Miss Green.'

'Call me Jess,' I said, but Reg had already set off down the aisle ahead of me.

'You'll notice that I favour Old World-style records,' he gestured to each side. 'This entire system owes everything to my diligence. Nothing, in my opinion, beats the feel of real paperwork, the smell of it... of course I have a digital version, but it fits the whole of Archives onto one tiny shelf. Such a disappointment. Now. I have a particularly magnificent collection of Old World murders,' Reg pointed left. 'Tell me, Green, have you heard of Jack the Ripper?'

'No,' I said, as I surveyed the endless racks with a sinking heart. 'Ancient history really isn't my thing.'

'This aisle here,' Reg gestured with both hands, 'deals with illegal cybernetic implants in mercantile armies. If we move to the left at this intersection, then we're in espionage and counter-espionage. Fertile ground for murder,' he chuckled. 'Over there we've got Alien Technology and the Dissection Records. Didn't make us very popular during the New World Peace Treaty, but then again, that won't really concern you... and here we have my favourite, the terrorism-through-the-ages section.' Reg stopped so suddenly I toppled into him. The strange smell seemed to be emanating from his clothes. 'The upper shelves are dedicated to Old World terrorist crimes - vulgar devices like nail bombs. The mid-section deals with the Transition Period and the Early New World. And here's my favourite bit: the New World itself.' Reg folded his hands and flashed a smile. The faintest trace of a tattoo, like pale snakeskin, flared up his neck where his collar fell a little low. 'Am I going too fast, Green?' he snapped, adjusting it.

'No,' I lied.

The truth was, I felt sick. The stacks of old records reminded me of the junk in the nuns' personal studies, the stuff you ended up facing when you got called in for punishment. I had a photographic recall of every single item on Sister Enuncia's shelf. I peeled off my jacket and hooked it over one arm.

'You'll get used to the temperature,' Reg said. 'It helps preserve the records. I hate going upstairs. It's like a morgue. Here,' he gestured at the lower boxes, 'are the New World terrorists: the Daughters of Bethelnau; Sirtees and Ali; even the most right-wing of the Tax Payers' Alliance... but we didn't come here to discuss old crimes. I intend to record a thorough first person account of your impressions of the scene. Then I can sift through your experience at my leisure, and see what can be teased out. Follow me, Green. My station is at the far end.'

Eventually, we arrived at a beaten-up desk butted against a wall. There was no overhead light.

'This is where I spend most of my time,' said Reg, proudly.

Piles of battered boxes sat on an Old World desk that looked as though several generations of tamewulf pups had teethed on its legs. I put the fresh clothes down on one corner, and draped my sodden jacket over a chair.

Reg's smirked. 'The desk is real wood. You can touch it, if you like. Where would you like to change, Miss Green?'

'I'm sorry?'

Reg's eyes roved my wet top and down my legs, one eyebrow shooting up. 'Your clothes. You need to remove them.'

'I – I'm fine. Let's get finished first.'

'As you wish,' Reg said primly.

He shoved in his hand into a box on the top of the desk, and rummaged around, muttering.

'Ah! Here!' he pulled a small chip from a wallet.

As he slid it into place, a snakeskin tattoo disappeared underneath his raised cuff. Reg twitched the sleeve down and hit 'open'. Underneath the electronic chatter of the files loading, came a faint scratching sound from a briefcase on its side on the desk.

'Reginald, I think there's something moving inside your briefcase.'

Reg snatched the briefcase and stowed it underneath the table, his eyes narrowed and his lips pursed.

'What is it?' I asked.

'Your imagination.' I swear his eyelids closed from side to side. 'Keep your nose out of my private things and your eyes and ears on the job in hand, Miss Green.'

I turned back to the screen.

'I need you to be as explicit as possible as to what you saw, thought and felt at the crime scene earlier,' said Reg.

'Your record will form the basis for a completely new file. These are exciting times, Miss Green.'

Reg regarded me for a moment, in silence. The expression on his face changed subtly. His mouth softened, his eyes rounded, and he sidled to the desk, then sat on it, leaving only the smallest space between his knee and my arm. I inched away, and plaited my fingers in my lap. Reg cleared his throat. Something about his manner reminded me of a customer at Torches, a man I hadn't trusted. Instinctively, my right hand crawled to my neck, the fingers twisting my wet shirt collar.

'Before I depart, Miss Green, there's something I feel moved to let you know.'

'I'm sorry?'

'I'll keep it simple. It's an offer. I'll scratch your back if you scratch mine. Mutual favours. Benefits. Call it what you will.'

I stared at him.

'The gist is, I can get hold of whatever information you want, off the record. For a small price, of course.' His eyes glowed greedily and his mouth went a little slack.

I slid back into the chair as far as I could, which had the effect of pushing my breasts out, so I hunched my shoulders and caved my chest in, sodden strips of hair falling around my face. At Torches we'd had minders; even Luca waded in from time to time if things got out of hand. But here, deep in the bowels of HQ, I was too far away from security for them to be of any use at all.

Reg watched me for a while, then pressed his lips together and slid off the table, hands clasped.

'As you wish,' he said curtly, then turned his back and vanished into the shadows.

In front of me, the com screen glowed like a wraith in the darkness.

What was it with Unit staff?

Mo never let me see his eyes and was way too old to look so good.

Rosie looked about twelve; she'd refused to enlighten me as to whether she was mainly cyborg with human bits or mainly human with cyborg bits.

Oxton was more cadaver than human, with her hollow eyes and perpetually pursed lips.

And now, Reg snakeskin-cuffs wanted to play friends-with-benefits.

I switched on the camera-mike and cleared my throat. A corner of Reg's briefcase peeked out from underneath the desk. Whatever was in there was still moving. Tap, tap, shhhhhh. Reg's footsteps tapped a diminuendo, then stopped. I adjusted the camera until my face filled the screen. The faintest sound of movement came from the direction of the desk. Then, silence, and eventually footsteps that started half way down an aisle, and grew fainter.

When I looked again, the briefcase had gone.

*

Oxton put me on work-from-home the following day. The plus was, I got to catch up on some sleep. The minus was, I had both Oxton and Reg springing onto my coffee table at regular intervals, asking awkward questions about Luca and the sex films. I couldn't believe that I was their best source of information on the industry. By late afternoon, none of us had got any further, so I clocked off and found myself staring at the crematorium card that sat on the side in the kitchen.

I flicked on the broadcast system and it picked up where it'd left off two days before: Mozart, a rare Old World recording of a piece of music called The Magic Flute. Sourcing the file was one of my proudest achievements. It was down to a favourite client from Torches who'd owned a reclamation facility. You'd think the remnants of an obliterated culture would be preserved, not discarded like trash, but whatever, the guy did me a favour. Thanks to him and a couple of other lucky breaks, I was well on my way to having the biggest Old World Mozart collection I knew of anywhere except a museum. As the melody soared high and clear, I asked the broadcast for full volume. It responded by swelling to a crescendo that made the beakers on my wall shelf tremble, the recycle unit flash with alarm, and Claws shoot off the settee and scuttle into my bedroom.

I stared into the crematorium card with its little pink flower, and felt my throat tighten. Mozart at full volume didn't ease my feelings about my mother, or the fractured memories. The image of her heading for the arch door without looking back replayed itself repeatedly: my little brother screaming, his arms flailing until Sister Enuncia picked him up and held him tight, not lovingly but spitefully; the cloth bunny falling to the floor, its black button eyes gleaming as the old nun kicked it under a nearby chair out of sight. I reached for the button around my neck, and squeezed.

I had to see my mother's grave for myself. It wouldn't give me the answers I craved, but it might bring me partial closure, which was at least something after all these years.

I cut the music, picked up my com and pressed speed-call for Mo. It rang and rang. Through the window, the faint glimmer of armed laser wire at the perimeter created an army of cat's eyes in the twilight. The birds were already flocking on the river bank, preparing to roost. Some of them had tucked their heads under their wings, making them look decapitated. The com cut itself off.

Just for a beat, the window seemed to stretch and change, and the river and birds were swallowed by sand. The hem of a white cotton night dress flapped around my ankles in a wind that rolled off the dunes. I was a child again, looking for nightbeetle tracks from the safety of the open doorway, knowing that I mustn't go outside…

My com hit the floor with a crack. As the casing slid over the floor and lodged itself underneath the entertainment unit, I was back in my living room staring down onto the river.

'Is everything OK?' computer asked.

'Voice off,' I snapped, irritated.

The dreams I could deal with, but the increasing severity of flashbacks was distressing. I retrieved the com parts and slotted them together, my fingers shaking.

Mo had told me I couldn't go anywhere without him, but he was supposed to be on call. I tried again, twice, but still nothing.

I had no choice but to go alone.

I snatched my jacket and bleep-code, and headed for the door.

IV

The flowers were carnations, the cloned sort that don't have any scent, with petals like bloodless flesh. I hurried to the nearest cab point with them tucked under my arm inside a flare of cellophane. I didn't know what else to do. It wasn't a mission borne of the desire to mourn the mother I hadn't heard from in years, it was more the necessity to see her memorial for myself, to accept that it was finally too late for me to find out why.

The driver took me out through Cheapside, past my old apartment. The takeaway underneath was boarded up. Somebody had stapled a Unit 'illegal meat' order to the door. A graffiti artist had sketched a rat over the top.

Why now?

Why, after all these years, when the sleepless nights and the bad dreams had at last been replaced by a life, a job, a purpose, why should a name on a card shake me up all over again?

We pulled away from Cheapside in a slick of rainwater, and within minutes, we'd arrived at the gates to River City Crematorium.

'You wanna be careful,' said the cabbie as I pushed my bleep code at him. 'Notice says it's only open another twenty minutes. You don't wanna be locked in that place all night. No sayin' what walks round in there after dark. Shall I wait?'

'Thank you, I'd appreciate that,' I said, sliding the door closed behind me.

In the half-light, with its big gates, Kevlar locks, and Old World perimeter wall, the place looked more abandoned prison than memorial facility.

I had to see Connie first. It seemed only right, somehow - she was the one who'd brought me up, after all. I turned west, and kept walking.

The damp air transformed the glow lamps into balls of white floss. Foggy mizzle oozed along the paths, turning the edges of the monuments into nebulous smears. Rows of plot markers gaped through the fake-grass like little open mouths. When I reached Connie's, it was dulled by a layer of grime. Was it really so long since I'd last been? I took out a cloth and wiped it clean.

Look after yourself, Jess. Keep yourself to yourself and never stay in one place too long. Promise me?

It was only now, years later, that I found myself wondering what the hell she'd meant.

I split the wrapping and laid half the flowers down, then changed my mind and pulled the rest from the cellophane. It didn't seem right to split them equally between Aunt Connie and my mother. My mother didn't deserve them. They spilled over onto the neighbouring plots in a tangle of stems. I said a prayer, then set off for the opposite side of the cemetery.

An android janitor was on duty on the main walkway. It wore a white suit with the word 'maintenance' printed on the back, and walked down the edge of the fake-grass flicking gravel back onto the path with a paddle. It turned and looked at me with its big, blank sensor eyes. Unnerved, I turned down the next path on the right. When I looked back, the carnations on Connie's grave stood out like the bleached bones of a small animal. The janitor had disappeared. A claxon rang from the chapel.

'Eight minutes until lock-down,' said the clock.

The markers at the end of the row were obfuscated by years of muck. I knelt down and started to rub them clean. If my mother was here, then she'd died while Aunt Connie was still alive. Why hadn't Connie told me?

I'd cleaned half a dozen before I realised there was no Abigail Tempest Green. I checked the plot number again. The number on the card, that should've been the end of the row, simply didn't exist. Confused, I stared up and down the endless rows, which vanished into the mizzle in both directions. If the memorial card had the wrong plot number, I'd never find my mother. She could be anywhere.

Or she might not be anywhere at all.

I felt sick. The one thing I'd been certain of when I'd set out for the cemetery, was that I'd get the chance to lay something to rest today. Now, I couldn't even do that.

A private hop hung overhead, its lights glowing in the twilight like the eyes of a huge hunting insect. They passed over me, briefly, slicing my jacket with a stray beam, at the same time as the janitor crossed my line of vision in a flash of white. A second later I was alone again, the mizzle thickening to rain and hitting me in stinging splats. I headed back towards the main path.

At the exit, I remembered the Book of Souls.

'Four minutes until...' said the clock.

Four minutes was enough time to check a name in a holo-book. I ran past the fake-roses, ignoring my splintered reflection as it ran alongside, jiggering over the leaded lights.

The chapel door was open. Inside, statuettes of the Virgin glowed softly from alcoves, their robes scored with shadow. Simulated candle light gave the impression of warmth, but it was so cold that my breath hung in a fog. The Book of Souls sat on a holographic lectern at the far end. I ran to it and rifled through the index. Outside, the lamps began to flick off in zones, killing the stained glass panel by panel. Abigail Tempest Green was missing from the book, and so was her plot number. The clock gave a one minute warning and began a count-down. The auto-bar activated in the inner doors, ready to engage. If Abigail Tempest Green wasn't remembered here, then somebody had sent me a fake memorial card.

Who would do that, and why?

I jumped off the podium and ran to the doors. They were already closing as I slipped outside. With twenty seconds to go, I slid between the gates and headed for the cab point, chased by darkness as the final lights went out behind me.

The driver opened the door, and I jumped inside.

'You OK?' he said, his face pale under the ceiling light.

'Yes. Thanks for waiting.' My voice came out as a whisper.

I leaned back and strapped myself in. As the cab pulled away, the locks clunked into place behind us, and a smudge of white appeared behind the grille. For a moment, I thought I was looking straight into the face of the janitor, its blank sensors trained on the cab, but the only thing staring back at me was the security Eye, which winked as we drove away, and the lights of the private hop, which rose and vanished into the darkness.

*

The memorial card and its package had no identifying features, and no traces of DNA or prints. Oxton had equipped me with enough personal kit to do the forensics myself, which was just as well, because Twenty One had re-programmed their main entrance to exclude my authorisation. Rosie said they did it from time to time if anybody pissed them off, which I found odd because the closest I'd ever got to Twenty One was walking past the entrance and catching a glimpse of a room full of skinny geeks in white lab coats and safety goggles. They'd stared at me as though I was a specimen in a jar which was funny considering they were the ones stuck behind the glass.

I'd just disposed of the spent forensics down a chute near reception, when Reg sprang out from behind a vending machine.

'Miss Green,' he hissed, glancing both ways along the corridor.

Wary, I hung back. Reg dodged into the alcove. His ocular shield was lop-sided, and the ruff of hair above his ears stuck out at random angles.

'Come closer,' he said. 'See the Eye, up there, behind you?'

I glanced over my shoulder. It was trained right on me, its sensors glittering. I stepped into the alcove.

'Protein shake, please,' Reg said to the vending machine, rather loudly, and then, lowering his voice, 'I have to go Upstairs, to Eighty Nine to see Oxton. I'm not looking forward to it. Please, order something from the vender, or the Eye will get suspicious.'

'Can I tempt you with a low-cal protein biscuit and some just-like-juice?' said the machine. 'This is my most popular breakfast for the demographic to which you belong, Miss Green.'

Reg moved so close I could feel the heat of his body through his shirt. I stepped away. He grabbed my wrist and yanked me back. He was surprisingly strong, for a little man.

'Please,' he hissed. 'I need your help.'

'If you don't require food I can always serve you beverage only,' said the machine.

'Earl Grey tea,' I said, my voice unnaturally high-pitched.

I snatched my hand away and rubbed my wrist. Reg mimed an apology and pushed a steri-pack at me. It was small, plain white and unlabelled, with a sealed top.

'I need you to take this into Archives and put it in my briefcase. It's on the table at my work station,' he hissed.

The sides of the pack bulged and retracted. I recoiled.

'It's perfectly safe,' Reg whispered. 'And it's properly sealed. Nothing will... escape, if that's what you're worried about.'

'Reginald, I can't get into the basement without your access.'

'Never mind the access code. I'll send you down in the chute with my authorisation.'

'What the hell is the chute?'

'My special high-speed link to Archives,' Reg's voice was smug. 'Makes the rank-and-file too queasy. The truth is, I need this pack putting somewhere safe before I go Upstairs. I can't take it with me. Don't ask why, I just can't.'

Reg snatched at my jacket pocket and dropped the pack inside. The sides heaved and then lay still.

'Please take your tea, and have a lovely morning. Is there anything else I can get for you?' said the machine.

'There's nothing to worry about, Green,' said Reg.

'There is no need to worry about anything on my menu,' said the machine huffily.

'I'll pay for the tea,' hissed Reg. 'Walk with me, to the chute, now.'

He pushed me out into the corridor, setting whatever was inside the sac wriggling like a foetus inside my pocket.

The chute was a slim door next to the main lift, the kind you wouldn't notice unless it was pointed out. Reg pushed me in, tapped in a command and retreated to the corridor. The door shushed closed and the descent began so fast that I pitched forwards and banged my head on the wall. Crap - no wonder only Reg used it. My pocket swelled and wriggled. Seconds later, the door pulled back, and I found myself facing the hinterland of Archives.

Gingerly, I drew the pack out. A flutter of movement set off inside. I held it at arm-length until I reached Reg's station, where his briefcase lay open on the desk. I dropped the package in and closed the lid. Sounds were amplified inside, tap-tap-shhhhhh, as though a scrum of tiny tentacles were writhing over each other. I threw the laser locks and stowed the case underneath the desk, sliding it as far back as I could with my foot. Reg's desk com sensed me and flared to life. I glanced at the screen. He'd been searching the memory vaults before he was called upstairs. He was still signed in. I pulled up a chair.

I took a steriwipe from a dispenser on the side, and slid it over the voice-reader on the top of the com.

'Information request,' I whispered.

For a moment, I thought the computer was going to refuse, but the search tool flickered.

'Go ahead, Mr Le Blanc.'

'Abigail Tempest Green.'

The com responded with a visual message that read searching memory vaults now. My palms began to prickle.

'I'm sorry, I'm afraid this file is restricted access, Mr Le Blanc.'

I fell back into Reg's chair, stunned. I'd expected a date of birth, an employment record, perhaps a Book of Souls entry from somewhere – but not HQ computer announcing that my mother's file was restricted access.

'More information needed,' I said.

'Abigail Tempest Green's file has been suspended from regular use. It is currently Upstairs.'

Upstairs?

What had I heard about Upstairs?

That it was never a good thing if your file found its way up there: that past floor Eighty there were no first names; past floor Ninety there were no faces. Right at the top were Perseus, Quimper and the other invisible suits of Ninety Nine, the ones who ran the city, and, if Rosie's stories were true, ate sushi together on a rooftop garden every Friday night. Upstairs had made Oxton sleepless and grey, and had put her on pills that she dissolved underneath her tongue. Why would my mother have a file Upstairs?

'Why has the file been suspended?' I said, my voice weak.

'Because Abigail Tempest Green's activities were monitored closely by Ninety One.'

Activities?

It didn't make sense – my mother was a laundrette assistant. She'd done shifts and hired a virtual-childmom to look after me and my brother... until it all got too much and she'd bottled out and dumped us.

'Is Abigail Tempest Green... is she... deceased?'

'The last post I am permitted to reveal is that Abigail Tempest Green was monitored for two years before her alleged disappearance.'

'Disappearance?' I said, my voice rising. 'Can you confirm where and when?'

'Alleged disappearance,' corrected the computer. 'I cannot confirm or deny. I have a holograph recorded twelve years ago. It's the most up-to-date image on public file for Abigail Tempest Green. Would you like to see it?'

'Yes,' I whispered.

It spun over the desk, unfurling itself and hanging in the void between me and the com. The face could've been my own, wraithlike, the eyes dark and severe with an expression I couldn't read. The only photograph Aunt Connie had ever shown me of my mother was identical. She'd put it in a retro frame on the kitchen wall of our little flat.

'Your mother may be a difficult person to think of fondly,' Aunt Connie's voice whispered in my memory, 'but she deserves to be remembered.'

I'd never quite worked out why. I'd thrown the photo down the recycle chute not long after Connie had gone into hospital. But I hadn't expected to see it again, rotating in front of me, translucent as a ghost, years later...

'Vanish photo,' I snapped. 'Grave marker card for Abigail Tempest Green.'

'No such card exists,' computer replied.

'Last known sighting of Abigail Tempest Green,' I said.

'Fort Burnout, Southern Disaster Zone, twelve years ago,' said the com.

Fort Burnout.

The words blazed through my memory and for a moment I was a child again in the unforgiving heat, stepping through ribbons of incense smoke in the long corridor. Why would my mother have last been seen twelve years ago, at Fort Burnout? That was where I last saw her.

'Mr Le Blanc,' the computer said, 'your voice-reader appears to be faulty. I will report the problem to maintenance.'

'Thank you,' I said. 'Delete this footprint from the memory vault search.'

'Request understood,' replied the com. 'Your search won't show on the general log, but if anybody asks specifically, I can't deny-'

'I understand. Disconnect vault access.'

'Preparing to comply.'

Reg's screen went blank. I peeled the steri-wipe off the voice reader, and threw it into the recycler. A thick silence hung over Archives, the scuff of my feet and the creak of the chair swallowed by the detritus crowding in around the table. Even the packet inside Reg's briefcase had stopped moving, as though whatever was inside was listening, waiting.

I left Reg's chair in the same position he'd vacated it, and headed for the lift.

V

When Mo appeared at my apartment door the following morning, his lips were pinched and his eyebrows were one long furrow over his shades.

'What?' I said.

I toed the old cat back inside the kitchen. Claws heaved himself onto the work surface and sat, eyeing us both with thinly disguised disgust, his ample black belly spilling over the edge. I shut the door and threw the laser lock.

Mo turned away and set off down the stairs in silence. We hit the exit as a blaze of sunlight splurged between the clouds. Above us, jigsaw bits of blue sky showed between them. The hop visors shot down automatically. We climbed inside.

'I know you aren't pleased,' I said as I fastened my harness. 'Can we cut to the chase, the bit where you tell me why, instead of sulking?'

'I don't sulk, Miss Green,' said Mo calmly. 'As a matter of professionalism, I felt that our conversation should take place behind closed doors in the hop.'

'You've got my attention.'

If Mo had found out that I'd used Reg's secure access in Archives, then Reg must know too. And if Reg knew, and Mo knew, that meant Oxton knew.

Mo slid the headset on and his face morphed into a deadpan of reflected cloud. He revved the thrusters, but we didn't rise up.

'You disobeyed direct orders, Miss Green. You left these premises just before dark yesterday, without any security protection.'

I opened my mouth to speak, then closed it again.

Left these premises?

This wasn't about Reg and the memory vaults at all – it was about my little excursion to the cemetery.

I stared out the window. From the river bank, the birds watched us suspiciously, their eyes like little beads. The first time they'd seen a hop so close they'd freaked, but they were slowly getting used to it.

'You and I need to build trust if our relationship is to work.' The tone of Mo's voice was mild, but he was fuming. It leaked through his block in hot flashes. 'Why did you leave your apartment at dusk, without protection, to visit a crematorium?'

'I... I took some flowers to my aunt's grave.'

'Why didn't you com me?'

I plaited my fingers in my lap. 'I did. You didn't answer.'

'I'm your handler. It's my job to answer. I am on call to you anytime, all the time. You know this.' Mo pulled his com from an inside pocket and held it up. 'You didn't even message me.'

'Your message-taker wasn't on.'

Mo shook his head. Needles of frustration pricked my skin. He slipped the com away, and leaned back in his seat.

'I tapped into the network and caught you on every Eye out through South Side, then watched you leave the crematorium.'

I flopped back in my seat and stared through the front screen, up into the clouds. 'Does anybody else know?'

'Rosie,' said Mo. 'She was checking footage with HQ computer when she spotted you.'

Rosie, with her sweet pink cheeks and her cute dimples and her tousled blonde curls. Rosie who was programmed not to give away anything she shouldn't... which clearly didn't cover what I got up to on the sly.

'Are you going to Oxton?'

Mo sighed. 'No. Contrary to what you think, I can't afford for you to fail, Miss Green. But I can't protect you if you won't let me.'

Mo reached for the headset on the dash, slowly, as though the weight of his thoughts was crushing him.

'I'm sorry.'

He paused. I waited, but he didn't speak. He slid the headset on and took the hop up.

I focussed on the clouds, and the random jets of sunshine that slit them open and then vanished again as they moved.

We'd just reached HQ when Oxton's voice came through.

'We have a crime scene,' she said, her voice steely. 'Don't land. I need you at Business Block Two on West Side, immediately.'

My stomach churned as the hop spun round. We joined a formation of other vehicles that'd peeled off HQ roof and were heading in the same direction.

'This morning, I received an emergency communication about a large number of vanished office workers,' Oxton continued. 'Prepare to receive the co-ordinates. Thirteen is to spearhead the investigation.'

The digi-display told me Oxton was speaking on fleet-line, so everybody in the formation could hear. I glanced at Mo out the corner of my eye. His face remained impassive, but he radiated tension.

'If the report is accurate, we have to prepare for a code red. Keep me informed.'

The connection died and the digi flicked to flat-line. I breathed, slowly, and felt for the bottle of calmers I kept in my jacket pocket.

They weren't there.

We passed over the Klone Zone, and the rows of windowless warehouses that force-grew veg. They slid away beneath us, grey anonymous blocks identical to every other in the district save for the neon leaves that identified their roof apexes. I'd heard tell the lights inside were so intensive that the vegetables grew six times faster than in real daylight. The catch was their adverse effect on human tissue. The non-robotic staff had bleached hands, white-filmed eyes and untreatable skin rashes. And that was only on the outside.

In silence, we closed on Business Block Two, which sat at the Western edge of the city, squatting between rows of identical buildings. The only outstanding feature was the Unit cordon that enclosed the front. A small crowd had gathered, whispering and watching the vehicles landing on the plaza, their lights rotating. I felt sick to the pit of my stomach.

We landed, and Mo led the way in. The bodies parted to let us pass, some watching from under lowered lids, others looking away. Mo lifted the security tape and stood back for me to duck underneath. Seconds later we were inside the building in an empty lobby, where sunlight slanted through a swathe of real jungle plants worth a fortune in bio-license.

The shock hit me in the chest. It hung in the spaces between the furniture like a shroud. I could almost hear the last breaths of the vanished staff.

'They've gone all right,' I said. 'Every last one of them. I'm not picking up any life signs at all.'

Reception front desk was huge, more hyper-spa than office block, with Old World alloy toe rails and faux-leather padding. Smears of life light frosted the surface. I crouched down and moved in closer.

'The marks aren't fresh.'

'How old?' said Mo.

'At least three hours.' I traced them with an outstretched finger. 'Hand prints, elbow marks... nothing you wouldn't expect in a busy reception. Somebody leaned here, and here... but no struggle. No fight.'

I stood up and turned towards the lift. Mo followed.

'Here,' I said, pointing to the closed doors. 'More marks. Normal lift usage. There's nothing except regular employees and a normal day.'

I pinged the controls and seconds later, the doors whooshed clear on an open-plan office.

'Death,' I said, stepping into the walkway. 'I can feel it. This is where a significant number of the staff died. Quickly, too.'

Work screens were open on the desks, most of them still active. Some were alive with screensaver holo-photos of spouses and children. I tapped the closest. A document leapt out. The text was overlaid by photo ID of a woman in her fifties called Margaret Cooke.

'She was half way through an inventory,' I said. 'The document auto-saved five minutes after it was last added to. Look.' I turned the screen towards Mo. 'Time of auto-save: three hours ago. Just like I said.'

Mo didn't reply. I slid the screen back and set off again, scanning the floor.

'Not even marks to suggest that anybody fell,' I said. 'What the hell happened here?'

A gust of air hit us both in the face. Mo drew his laser, his hand a blur. The eddy swirled between us and blew itself out. He lowered his weapon but didn't re-sheathe it. He walked to the window and passed a hand through where the glazing should have been. The frame was empty.

'Hang on, there's something on the floor.' I squatted and ran my fingers along a streak of shiny liquid. 'It's wet.'

I took a reading and flipped the analysis straight to Twenty Two, then showed the screen to Mo. He ignored it and began to shake his head slowly, radiating frustration.

'What?' I said.

'You just broke a golden rule.'

I took a steri-wipe from my pack and wiped my fingers.

'You touched a sample, Miss Green.'

'It was water. Look at the com reading.'

'But you didn't know that when you touched it. This is a crime scene. Over a hundred people have disappeared. The liquid could've been poison, acid, DNA-targeted blood coagulant. Never. Touch. Anything.'

Mo stalked away towards the lift. I cursed softly.

'We should take the stairs,' I called, turning towards the door.

In the stairwell, smears of life light glimmered where staff had touched the walls and hand rail. None of the marks were recent. On floor two, the manager's door was open, a swivel seat abandoned as though its owner had taken a short walk. Except this time, she'd never come back.

We stood for a moment in silence, the kind of silence you get when you're surrounded by the spaces left by vanished people, with no clue except empty rooms and the scent of sudden death.

Mo headed for the closest window. The frame was intact, but, just as with floor two, the glazing had gone. A slight residue of fractured material sat around the inside of the frame like cake frosting. I drew a sample kit from my pack and scraped up some crystals, careful not to touch them. I sealed the pouch and dropped it into my jacket pocket. Mo stared through the empty frame down onto the plaza, where the neighbouring blocks reached into the sky. Behind the tinted windows, faces were peering at Block Two, wondering what the hell the Unit cordon was for. It wouldn't take long for the rumours to start. An Eye appeared outside, and extended its lens into my face. I stepped back. The lens shrunk back and the Eye sped off over the square.

'Let's take the lift,' I said. 'But not up, Mo. Something's telling me we've got to go down.'

We travelled in silence. All around us, fading life-lights hung like spectral bunting from the walls. The lift announced that we'd arrived at basement level, a staff vehicle park. I stepped back instinctively as the door opened, and clamped my hand over my mouth. The scent of death was overpowering.

Mo's laser arm was tense again, the weapon already drawn.

'This way,' I said, stepping out of the lift.

'Slowly,' he whispered. 'You can't just blunder in-'

'The only life signatures here are yours and mine.'

Mo hung back as though he didn't believe me.

The basement bulkheads sensed our presence, and lit up in sequence, each with a metallic clang that threw a giant lily-pad of light onto the blackened tarmac. We stepped from one to the other, me in front, Mo following stealthily, scanning up and down the rows of vehicles. Most were tiny economy models, until, in the Director's Bay, a row of blacked-out multi-carriers sat waiting for owners who were never coming back. Behind us, the bulkheads flicked off, swallowing the perimeter in darkness.

I'd almost reached the bodies by the time I saw them.

They were stacked by the far wall in neat layers, their symmetry broken by the occasional bunch of fingers that lolled from the pile. Threads of blood-stained cloth hung from the melee, the edges showing clean cuts. Eyes were still open on the few visible faces. I walked towards them, slowly, freaked and fascinated at the same time. Behind me, Mo whistled softly.

'Too many for a head count but I'd bet they're all present and correct,' I said, making the figure eight of the Virgin against my chest (convent habits die hard).

'I'll make the call,' said Mo, reaching for his com.

'No,' I wheeled around touched his arm. Mo flinched, ever so slightly. 'Sorry.' I snatched my hand back. 'Not yet. Just give me a few more minutes. The longer I have here alone with the vics, the more I can tell Oxton.'

I turned back to the bodies. The closer I got, the colder the air became, and the thicker the smell of death. When I blocked, and nothing happened, I realised I wasn't dealing with sixth sense, but physical reality.

The bodies were frozen solid.

Close up, tiny crystals of ice formed intricate patterns on the torn fabric of jackets and trousers and skirts. Individual shafts of hair were solid inside silver sheaths; eyelashes were crisped. My breath bloomed white when I exhaled. A stray bleep-code hung off one of the bodies, a splash of frozen blood jewelling its surface.

'Whatever did this was powerful, organised, and fast... so why waste time and effort stacking the dead in a basement? It doesn't make sense.'

Mo didn't move, but the tautness in his body told me he was having just as much of an issue as I was. I closed my eyes and spread my hands.

'Organs,' I said, my voice cracking. 'Vital organs are missing.' I felt Mo wince. 'Blood. Drained in large quantities from all of them, just like the girl in the warehouse. Death was instantaneous in every case. None of them saw it coming. By the time they realised they were in trouble, the party was over.'

'Who did it?'

I opened my eyes. 'I don't have a clear picture. It's more of an impression. I can tell you that there were many assailants - lots of men, like a swarm. Figures, everywhere, moving fast; black shadows... like insects...' I dropped my hands to my sides, already exhausted. 'But it isn't enough. Not for Oxton. She expects more.'

I began to pace up and down in front of the bodies. Mo gave up trying to shadow me. He stood motionless, eyes front, the laser resting on one thigh. His shades reflected the scree of corpses in miniature, broken by a tiny me as I passed like a snake pupil from left to right in front of him. All the while I walked, I cast my mind out in increasing circles, concentrating, feeling...

My vision went dark, obfuscating the basement. Dizzy, I fell sideways into a wall. In my mind, a scrambled mess of black lines solidified into what looked like an Old World ink drawing. Two dark eyes stood out from a curly mass of hair: an animal's head. The eyes were framed by a pair of horns that coiled either side.

'I'm getting the sigil of a ram.'

The image forced itself out of its two dimensional background, the muzzle springing forwards, the horns pushing out. I got the sense of infinite size and incomprehensible power. My knees gave way. One cheek grazed the wall as I slid down.

'It's changing,' I said, blindly. 'Something's happening...'

The ram's head turned golden. It rotated, glinting, like an Old World statue on a spinning plinth. The eyes, which were facetted like jewels, began to glow red. Before I could make sense of it, the head vanished, leaving the sudden shock of a black hole in its place, and the familiar headache of my own poorly prepared mind.

I came to in the recovery position. Mo was crouched close by. His eyebrows were taut above his shades. I pushed myself up and sat with my back against the wall. My head throbbed. My cheek hurt. When I touched it, my fingers came away covered with blood and grit. A half-remembered image stirred in my memory, of something buried, its eyes flicking to life like miniature glow-balls when my fingers closed around it and pulled it free. The memory dissipated like sand in the wind, leaving me frustrated and confused.

'I'm fine,' I said. 'Just give me a minute.'

A trickle of dark liquid wound its way across the concrete from underneath the bodies.

'They're defrosting,' I said.

'I already called it in,' said Mo.

I pushed myself off the floor and slid up the wall. If Oxton was on her way down, she'd want more than some indiscernible rubbish about an arcane sketch that turned into a metallic ram's head. I pulled a wipe from my backpack and ran it over my injured cheek. The wound tightened instantly as the hormones got to work. I stuffed the wipe into my pack, scrubbed my palms on my trousers, and took a couple of deep breaths.

I set off past Mo, and past the bodies, averting my eyes. He fell in behind me. The banging in my head dulled to a throb.

'So they stack the bodies in the basement,' I said, 'and they leave with the blood and the organs. But I didn't pick anything up in the lift. The life lights were too old, just like the warehouse. Maybe they took another route. Let's check the walkway.'

I headed towards a sign marked Exit, searching the gangways. The faintest gleam told me the last living being had been here that morning, and no later.

'There's nothing here,' I said, touching the wall. My own life light, vivid violet, drowned out the others. 'It's as though whoever was here didn't leave any residue at all.'

'Chemically removed?'

'Impossible. You can't apply the rules of physics to the laws of psychic energy. It's as though whatever was here, whatever did this, wasn't really alive at all...'

We reached the exit and stared out into the void. A faint breeze teased through the tunnel, carrying city scents: fast food, hot tarmac and fuel. Beyond, the hum of thousands of inhabitants ran like a resonant beat through the basement. I shut them out, and turned around.

Suddenly, I wasn't looking at Mo and the vehicle park any more. I was in a sunlit hall amid a crowd of people. In front of me stood a woman with brown hair coiled into a chignon, dressed in a long pale gown that wrapped itself in a candy-twist around her legs. Stunned, I stepped back, and the scene blanched out into whitewash. I blinked, and I was back in the basement. Mo was right in front of me.

'Green, what is it?'

'I've seen a woman. She's connected, somehow, to the freezings. She vanished before I saw her face, just like she did at the first crime scene. Only this time, I saw a little more detail.'

Mo cursed softly. 'Would this woman be the one you missed out of your first report?'

'I'm sorry. I don't always understand what I'm seeing.'

'Have you any idea what the connection is?'

I shrugged. 'I don't know. But I'll work it out. All I'm sure of is that the frozen girl and the mass freezing here are linked. The warehouse couple were a trial run.'

He shook his head slowly. 'The senior guardians have a saying. When a crime rears its head more than once and gets bigger, there are only two possibilities.'

'Tell me.'

'The first is a psychopath.'

'And the other?'

'Terrorists.'

Mo slid his laser into its holster, and led the way back to the lift, casting anger and helplessness around us both.

VI

Back at HQ, the corridors were empty except for security. There was no sign of Rosie. We took the lift down to Archives in silence. When we reached Reg's station, he was at his desk. Mo stood back against a rack of files and disappeared into the shadows, hands clasped in front.

'Multiple murder,' snapped Reg. 'Organ theft. Frozen bodies. Our latest insights add up to precisely nothing that makes any sense, Miss Green. I hope for your sake that you can deliver more than this. If not, Department Thirteen will find itself condemned before it's even fully staffed.'

I slid into a seat. Reg tapped his com, and a holophoto sprung onto the table top. I recognised the vehicle park, except the bodies had been bagged and tagged. One zipper wasn't done up properly. Bare toes poked out, right under my nose.

'The victims were inventoried by Twenty One only minutes ago,' Reg said. 'Every member of staff is accounted for. The bodies are coming back to HQ for more tests as I speak, but unfortunately, we are little the wiser about exactly what happened inside Block Two.'

Reg changed the photo to a close-up of a naked cadaver with a neat incision from neck to stomach. The wound was stitched clumsily with dark thread. I looked away.

'Scans showed vital organs missing, and blood drained, just as you described, Miss Green. Tests at the scene revealed no chemical traces. The cuts to the cadavers are surgically clean. Cause of death appears to be flash freezing. Twenty One sewed them back up again. It's a nasty new form of terrorism, I'm afraid, and one we've got to crack quickly.'

I glanced at Mo. His eyebrows twitched up.

'They get more cunning and inventive every decade,' said Reg.

'But why would anybody do this?'

Reg waved a hand. 'We don't deal in whys, Miss Green. We deal in whos, and then we deal in punishment. We've enough on our plates without making martyrs of them. I mean, what would we be trying to do next, for heaven's sake – understand their cause, perhaps?' he gave a mirthless guffaw. 'But these are exciting times. We don't get to start a file on a new terrorist group every day of the week. What do you think to the Brotherhood of the Golden Ram? It does have a certain ring about it, wouldn't you agree?'

The holo-photo of the cadaver vanished, to be replaced by an ID portrait of a young woman with dark skin and a shaved head.

'This is – or was – Aminah Amali. She was a sleeper for Forty Two, temporarily placed in Business Block Two to give weight to her forthcoming legend. Amali had her organs bleep-coded for reasons of religious belief. That helped us trace her kidneys to Body Bay. They were advertised for sale one hour ago.'

'Body Bay are supposed to check that the death was legitimate,' I said. 'Did the relatives agree to the sale?'

'Amali's relatives are squabbling over her kidneys as we speak. Her mother wants them back to cremate, but her father's family say it'd be a waste not to go ahead and sell them now she's gone.' Reg slid into the seat next to mine and plaited his fingers. 'Now, it's your turn. Tell me everything you can, Miss Green.'

I told Reg about the ram's head. His nostrils flared almost imperceptibly as he listened. He began to tap into his com.

'Would you describe it as a vision?'

'Yes,' I said, my gaze flickering towards Mo, who remained motionless in the shadows.

'Can you elaborate?'

It's difficult to explain to non-empaths that sometimes, I'm able to connect with things without understanding how. It's even more difficult to explain that it isn't an exact science, and that I simply can't pull all the information I need out of the aether immediately, or in the right order. Sometimes, it can take a while to distil. I did my best with Reg, but he was motionless while I spoke, leaking the vaguest whiff of suspicion, eventually pursing his lips.

'Am I to understand that your non-exact science of… seeing things… is one of the reasons Oxton has recruited you for her new department?'

I nodded.

Reg put up a new image. 'Look familiar?'

The hologram showed an Old World painting of a herd of sheep.

'Should it?'

'Then the sheep are wrong,' said Reg.

'The horns aren't big enough. What's the white stuff?'

'Snow. Painted by a famous artist. In days of old they were obsessed by vague approximations of livestock. Poor relation of holo-photography, if you ask me,' Reg sniffed, and sent another image to replace it.

'No, that's not right either. The horns were curly. Like this.' I used my hands to illustrate.

Reg frowned. 'How about this?'

'Getting closer.'

Reg lined up a series of holograms in the centre of the room.

'That's it!' I stood up and knocked my com onto the floor.

Reg enlarged the image. His face paled. He slumped back in his chair, arms folded.

'What aren't you telling me?'

Reg rubbed his eyes, which began to water. He pulled the handkerchief out of his pocket, and dabbed at his cheeks. When he sighed, he seemed to shrink in on himself, as though he was deflating.

'Look closely at the ram's head, Miss Green. This specimen dates from the Old World, perhaps even Pre-Old World. The original is buried somewhere in Unit HQ's vaults.'

'And?'

Reg shifted in his seat. 'You obviously have no idea that the golden ram is the personal sigil of Perseus.'

I shrugged.

A miniature animal head in the sand, its eyes red jewels...

The vaguest sensation of unease crept over my skin, accompanied by a half-formed memory. In a beat, it vanished.

'How long have you been in River City, Miss Green?'

'A few months.'

'Irrespective, there are only four major conurbations in the developed world. You have to be from one of them, and therefore you should know about Perseus, considering he has a hand in running them all.'

Reg was staring at me intensely, without blinking.

I fidgeted. 'Like I said. I've lived in every city at some point.'

Reg rolled his eyes, exasperated. 'The notion that a new terrorist group has appropriated Perseus's personal sigil will be taken very badly. And you, unfortunately, are the bearer of these tidings.'

Great. Something else to endear me to my colleagues.

Reg vanished the ram, and replaced it with a schematic diagram of Business Block Two.

'Herein lies our biggest mystery. Security in the building was top notch: bleep-codes; retina scans; full monitoring of staff in and out. Yet, at some point this morning, the entire staff was flash frozen and had their organs excised. We not only have the puzzle of how the terrorists gained access unnoticed, but how the organs of one hundred and twenty nine people were successfully got off site without so much as a blood smear.'

It's never easy to get the co-operation of a non-empath when you hinge everything on a flash of precognition, but I told Reg about the woman I'd 'seen', the one I'd omitted from my original report. While I spoke, he picked up a retro pen and began to weave it between his fingers, faster and faster.

'I've learned to trust my foresight, Reginald. All I know is, this woman is connected to the crimes and my instincts are telling me I'm going to meet her here, in River City, within a month at most. You may not like precognition, and I might not always understand it, but it's going to happen.'

Reg put the pen on the desk. 'Then there's only one thing for it. Mr Okoli?'

Mo straightened.

'I'll request central computer undertake a seek-and-find of every afternoon cocktail function in River City taking place within the next four weeks. Miss Green has a party to attend.'

Stunned, I slumped back in my chair.

'What is it? You almost look as though you thought I wouldn't believe you.'

'I – I expected to have to persuade you a little harder.'

Reg smirked and scooted his chair towards the desktop com.

Mo stepped out of the shadows into the aisle. 'Miss Green can't go alone.'

Reg spoke a series of commands, then broke off to face us both. 'As soon as we get our short list of venues, I'll have Twenty Seven get you both in as guests.'

Oh, great.

People falling left, right and centre, missing organs, drained blood, sex films, and now a party invite with Mr Odd as my date.

'Take a look at these,' said Reg.

Holograms shot out of the com with each flick of his fingers. Every one advertised a charity event or a function, none of which resonated until a black letter N in fancy script appeared. It rotated, its calligraphic flourishes writhing like little clasping hands on a plain white background. I ordered the image to freeze.

'This means something to you?' Reg's eyes flickered between me and Mo, his excitement palpable.

Mo pushed his hand into his pocket and drew out the disk I'd found in the sand. The trim glinted dully.

'A perfect match,' said Reg.

I swear his eyelids closed from side to side.

'May I?'

Mo stepped out of the shadows towards the table. He held out his hand. Reg snatched the disk so fast his fingers were a blur. He turned it over and over, crooning to himself, as though he'd forgotten we were there. After several seconds he stopped, coughed, and glanced up.

'I know this sigil. It belongs to the Nemesis Corporation. I have a file on them which has too many gaps in it.' Reg's eyes flickered from Mo to the disk and back again.

Above the table, the calligraphy on the holo-invite unravelled, and it opened. Inside, a date and time appeared underneath the words 'The Eternity Fund - Barbervil Towers.'

I saw her again, the pale dress twisting around her legs as she turned to face me. She slid away into darkness. Goosebumps ran along my arms.

'So what's The Eternity Fund?'

'A branch of the Nemesis Corporation,' said Mo, studying the hologram. 'Barbervil Towers is Shem Barber's place.'

'Barber is the entrepreneur,' said Reg. 'They say he's the only non-Unit employee to have eaten sushi with the faceless suits on their rooftop garden.'

Reg handed the disk back to Mo reluctantly.

'And Miss Green? You'll need something appropriate to wear to the party. A cocktail dress, perhaps.'

Oh, crap.

The first and last time I'd worn a cocktail dress was for a private party at Torches. The client had a fetish for straps, raw fish and ripped fabric, which wasn't a combination I'd ever encountered before. Just let's say the memories weren't particularly fond, even though the tips made it worth it.

Mo and me left Reg fussing with his files, and took the chute from Archives to ground floor in silence. Mo walked me to a rest area.

'I'm with Oxton for an hour at most,' he said. 'I'll be back to pick you up.'

'And what do you want me to do?' I called to his disappearing back.

Mo shrugged. 'Check out the Eternity Fund. Watch your messages. Have a coffee.'

I pulled an Earl Grey out of the vendor and watched him lope away, then took out my com. According to HQ computer, the Eternity Fund was a new incentive bankrolled by Shem Barber. It researched non-surgical 'cures' for ageing, sponsored by wealthy donors.

I'd only taken one sip of my tea when Rosie's head appeared around the corner.

'Hey.'

'Hey, Rosie.'

'Got time for lunch?'

I shrugged. 'I guess so. Mo's in a meeting. He's coming to get me in an hour.'

'Great. Let's go to Harry's. My treat.'

'I'm not supposed to leave HQ without protection.'

Rosie rolled her eyes. 'Harry's is only across the square. I can mind you for short distances.'

I hesitated, then shrugged my jacket on. 'If you say so, Rosie.'

We checked out. In the square, sunlight shot darts off the puddles on the flagstones. An android enforcer squatted underneath the trees, relaying instructions to a flying Eye hovering in front of its face. Either side of us, the bistros sent food scents drifting across the square, the hiss of steam and the shouts of kitchen staff pushing through the open windows.

'You'll love Harry's,' said Rosie. 'They do real cake. Not that I can eat it myself, of course.'

'Why can't you eat cake?'

'I only take liquids and supplement. I've had major internal systems reconstructed. It's all I can cope with.'

Eeeesh.

'But I can buy you a piece and watch you eat it.'

'Thanks,' I said.

We took a seat inside, next to the window. Rosie ordered for both of us. At the opposite side of the square, a decontam crew were clearing the shell of a store. A Unit cordon enclosed the front. Strips of bent metal pushed up out of the foundations like tortured vines.

'Dirty bomb,' said Rosie, nodding towards the mayhem. 'Took out a couple of civvies and the store manager in the small hours of the morning. Some kind of turf war, apparently.'

I rolled my eyes. 'Have they caught whoever did it?'

'Yeah. He's been given to Twenty One for biological experiments.'

My stomach flipped.

'Anyway, I didn't bring you here to talk about work,' said Rosie brightly. 'I brought you here because I wanted to ask you something.'

'What?'

A waitress slid a tray onto the table between us, with a cup of hot water for Rosie, and Earl Grey tea and a huge slice of chocolate cake for me.

'How do you fancy coming out one night?' Rosie took a sachet of crystals from her hand bag and sprinkled them into the water, which turned dark and began to thicken.

'I'm not sure what the rules are,' I said. 'I'm supposed to take Mo everywhere with me. We haven't got as far as discussing a social life.'

Rosie rolled her eyes. 'What a killjoy. He'll cramp your style.'

I shifted in my seat, and stared through the window, where our reflections were superimposed over the mess opposite in a bizarre pastiche of bomb-damage and floral tea-cups.

'I'm not saying no, Rosie. I just don't know the rules, that's all.'

Rosie sighed. 'I know somebody who's interested in you, Jess. I think you should meet him.'

I dead-panned my expression so my panic didn't show. Clients, I'd had to deal with, but relationships?

Rosie picked up her cup. A metallic straw like an insect proboscis shot out of her mouth and into the liquid. I looked away. A faint slurping noise followed by a soft burp told me she'd drained the cup. When I looked back, the tip of the proboscis had retracted behind her lips. She was staring at me over the cup rim, her cheeks dimpled winsomely and her blue eyes glinting.

'Interested in me?' I said, weakly.

Rosie nodded and put the empty cup down. 'Come on Jess, eat up. I don't buy cake for people to sit and stare at. You've got to enjoy it. Facing me, so I can watch.'

I picked up a fork and rotated the plate.

'His name is Daryl.'

I stabbed the fork into the cake. Chocolate sauce oozed out. 'You don't mean Daryl from Letters and Packages?'

Rosie nodded. 'He might be a little younger than you, but he's smart, and he has prospects.'

'He looks about twelve, and has terrible acne and bright orange hair, Rosie.'

'There's nothing wrong with red hair,' said Rosie defensively, reaching up a hand to touch her platinum curls.

'And he's into rubber gloves, for god's sake,' I said, laying the fork down and picking it up again when Rosie scowled at me. 'Daryl lists Celebrity Botch It, dressing up and role playing games among his favourite pastimes.'

'Wow, he's usually so quiet. He told you all that?'

'No, he just thinks too loud.'

Rosie sighed and rolled her eyes. 'Look, I'm sure if you two get together over a drink, you'll hit it off right away. Despite the rubber gloves. Eat the cake, Jess.'

I broke off a piece. My lips closed around the chunk on the fork and I forced myself to chew. Rosie leaned forwards and scrutinised me.

'I've forgotten what it's like to chew food,' she said, hypnotised.

I swallowed. It wasn't bad cake, I'd just lost the impetus for enjoying it.

'So are you up for it?' Rosie's eyes followed the fork. 'I know a great place. It's called the Memory Banks. It's Unit owned, so Jane Public don't get a look-in. I'll get a few others together, and we'll go in a group. That way you won't feel under any pressure.'

Chocolate sauce slid out the corner of my mouth. Rosie's pupils expanded.

'Daryl isn't my type.'

'Come out anyway.'

'I'd love to. Once I've checked it out with Mo.'

Rosie rolled her eyes. 'Mo's supposed to look after you, right?'

'Uhuh.'

'Well, he isn't the only one who can fulfil that role.'

Rosie glanced towards the till. The waitress had disappeared. Rosie wrapped one hand around the leg of the table behind us.

'These are Kevlar tables, right, because the square gets bomb threats all the time?'

'Uhuh.'

Rosie lifted the table with one hand, keeping the top level. The metal groaned. The little vase on the tablecloth trembled and chinked against the sugar bowl. Rosie stopped when the table was above her head, then squeezed her fingers together. The Kevlar squealed and collapsed, indenting like soft putty. She put the table down and grinned.

'Ta-dah!'

A perfect hand print sat in the leg, its centre only millimetres thick. Rosie giggled and twitched the table cloth over the damage.

I dropped my fork and jumped to my feet.

'Rosie, the table was bolted down.'

'Uh?'

'Look,' I hissed, gesturing at her feet. 'You ripped it right out of the floor.'

'Oh, crumbs.' Rosie toed broken bolts and chunks of metal underneath the table.

'Where the fuck did you learn to do that?'

She shrugged. 'Like I said. Mo isn't the only one who's enhanced, Jess. I can take care of you. So now you have no excuse, OK? Sit down and finish the cake.'

By the time I pushed the plate away, I felt sick.

Rosie checked her com. 'You have precisely two minutes to drink your tea.'

'But we've only been here half an hour.'

'We have to leave.'

I'd barely drained my cup when Rosie grabbed my arm and propelled me out of Harry's and back towards HQ. We ended up at the same rest area she'd found me in. Rosie disappeared in the direction of the secure pods without a backward glance. Seconds later, Mo walked out the lift directly opposite.

'Hey,' I said.

'Hey.'

'How was the meeting?'

Mo shrugged. 'Oxton isn't happy. Not surprisingly. And I got you this.' Mo held out a vendor package. 'You haven't eaten.'

I glanced through the wrapper at the dull, cloned fruit skins inside. 'It – it's very thoughtful of you. Thank you.'

'What's the matter?'

'Nothing.'

'You don't like cloned fruit?'

'Of course I do,' I lied, taking the package.

'You have half an hour before your appointment with Reginald.'

'Appointment?'

Chryst, not another session with Mr Undress You Eyes.

'Yes. With Reginald.'

'I didn't know I had one.'

'Oxton has just scheduled it.'

I ran my fingers along the surface of the package, listening to it rustle, feeling the unnaturally smooth skins of the fruit inside.

Mo frowned. 'What's the problem?'

I shrugged. 'No problem. No problem at all.'

Mo regarded me for a moment. I looked away, towards the vending machine, which sensed my presence and tried to spark up a conversation. I ignored it and turned my head the other way.

'Do you have issues with Reginald, Miss Green?'

I dropped the fruit into my pack and straightened up. 'Of course not.'

Mo cocked his head to one side. 'You aren't telling me the truth, are you?'

'Why shouldn't I be?'

Mo's mouth curled up at the corners. 'You've become too sure of yourself, Miss Green.'

I glared at him. 'What do you mean?'

'You're under the mistaken impression that only empaths can pick up things that don't get said out loud.'

A flash of heat burned my cheeks.

Mo suppressed a smile. 'So, are you going to tell me about it?'

'It's nothing.'

'Reginald is a bit of an odd-ball, but he's harmless. Whatever impression he's given you, just remember that.'

The lift door across the corridor shot open and Oxton appeared.

'Miss Green, Mr Okoli.'

'Oxton,' I said, relieved.

'Change of plan,' she snapped. 'We're going to Archives, right now. For once, I can't pull Mr Le Blanc away from the comfort blanket of his files, because we need them.'

Oxton set off towards the chute. Mo shrugged. We followed in silence. Inside, there was barely room for the three of us. My stomach lurched as we set off. I shut my eyes and hung onto the hand rail, but it didn't help the queasiness. When the door shot back, I reeled like a drunk.

Oxton went ahead of us, striding off into the gloom.

'Are you OK?' said Mo.

I nodded.

On the way to Reg's station, my 'night vision' let me down. I elbowed a robotic hoist and almost fell over a stepladder, which amused Mo, although he tried to cover it. Reg was waiting for us, his skin glowing faintly in the shadows. His desk was loaded with boxes, and pieces of Old World paperwork that fanned out over every available surface. Several holographs danced around the com, some rotating, some scrolling at speed.

'I'm almost there, Oxton.' The myriad froze mid-air and dissolved into tiny sparkles as Reg brandished a chip with triumph. 'Here it is!'

He slid the chip into the com. A single image appeared, of archaic script scrawling across a stained background. The tiny hairs at the nape of my neck stood to attention. A beat later, the sensation vanished. I guess I must've scratched my neck, or rubbed my arms or shivered, because Mo turned his head almost imperceptibly and watched me through the corner of his shades. I ignored him.

'Could you be precise about what we are looking at, Mr Le Blanc?' said Oxton.

'I don't have a full translation yet, but I'm working on it.' Reg's voice was high-pitched with excitement. 'It's all down to Miss Green, I'm afraid.'

He laughed a strangled little laugh, and plaited his fingers in front of his waistcoat.

Down to me?

Reg's eyes were hard as beads, taking all of us in and yet seemingly concentrating only on me.

Oh, crap.

Reg knew about me using his access, I could feel it. He was playing with me.

He cleared his throat. 'According to Miss Green, neither of the crime scenes showed life-lights from the perpetrators.'

'Correct,' I said.

'And yet, Miss Green, you clearly felt a large presence at the crime scenes. You identified men running.'

'I did.'

'Then we have limited options to explain why.' Reg's eyes darted between us. 'The most likely contender is androids. They wouldn't leave a life signature, they can move just as fast as mechanically enhanced humans, and in humanoid shape, they would afford an empath a view of running people.'

Oxton swivelled her head around to face me. She looked impossibly old, as though she'd just been unwrapped from a shroud. 'Miss Green?'

'No. I'm sure there were no androids involved.'

'Would you care to explain?' said Oxton.

I tried, but when you're talking to non-empaths, there are only so many words you can use to describe instinct. Their faces looked as blank when I'd finished as they had done before I started.

'How about mechanically enhanced humans?' Mo said.

He stood with his back against a file rack. His chair, swept of debris, sat empty between us. I explained that the introduction of bio-mechanics doesn't remove the essence of humanity completely. What I didn't say is that Rosie still confused me, because I couldn't figure which was the greater portion. Either her block was utterly flawless, or bit by bit, year by year, her biological parts had been slowly swallowed and overpowered by her cybernetics.

'There is only one more possible explanation,' said Reg, smug.

He gestured to the hologram with a flourish. It flipped over and jetted out a gauzy close-up. Text hung off the parchment, spidering over the desk.

'This is a Pre-Old World text. The original was lost over a thousand years ago, but some bright spark thought to copy it and store it in the memory vaults for the future.'

The words were barely legible.

'I don't know how you read this stuff,' I said.

Reg huffed. 'Perfectly well, thank you. I'm fluent in thirty six dead languages and I read nearly twice as many, for your information. Look here, see? It describes the activities of an Old World cult known as the necromancers. They were a clever lot who used the dead to do their bidding.'

'Nice,' I said.

'Exactly,' Reg paged down to an illustration. Inside a circle, a naked man with outstretched arms and legs hung in limbo. 'In certain parts of the Old World, there were entire cults dedicated to the undead. Our Brotherhood is a new take on an old theme. Add a dash of modern technology, and you've got neo-necromancy – re-animated human corpses used to do the bidding of whoever is in charge. In this instance, they're taking organs. En masse.'

Oxton's shoulders contracted inside the expensive jacket. The others noticed it, too, but none of us dared look right at her. God knows what grief they were giving her Upstairs. The heat seemed suddenly more oppressive, the racks pushing closer, bowing under the weight of their files. Or maybe Oxton's emotions were leaking. We sat in silence until she pushed back her chair and stood.

'I'm due Upstairs to discuss these findings,' she said. 'Mr Le Blanc and Mr Okoli, you will accompany me. Miss Green, you will remain in Archives and record a verbal account of the second crime scene for Reginald's file. No detail is too small. Do you understand?'

'Ah – Oxton?' Reg's voice was silky. He wrung his fingers and picked at his waistcoat buttons. 'Miss Green cannot stay in Archives without me.'

Oxton wheeled around.

'Miss Green will not burn down your archives. Neither will she deface your desk or sully your holo-photograph collections, Mr Le Blanc. I simply want her to speak into a com.'

Reg lowered his head but his fingers didn't stop working his buttons and his eyes didn't stop glittering underneath the knitted brows.

'It was just that I, er, thought it best that I should remain here too, just in case-'

'At the Unit,' snapped Oxton, 'we like to think that a way forward for our professional relationships is in the building of trust, Mr Le Blanc. You are needed Upstairs, and Miss Green is needed here. I trust that is a satisfactory explanation.'

Reg lowered his head meekly. Oxton headed for the lift without a backward glance. Mo peeled himself out of the shadows and followed, with Reg bringing up the rear. He shot me a black glance over his shoulder. I smiled and waved. Reg responded by whacking me with a surge of fury.

When their backs disappeared, I hit 'reveal' and suddenly every screen around the desk jumped to life, ticking with data. Gossamer-fine holograms shot over the table, some spinning through each other, making weird hybrids. I vanished them, and tried Reg's access.

It was blocked.

That proved it - he knew.

I tipped my head into my hands and slouched forwards onto the table, drained. As though it wasn't enough to be caught up in some weirdo Brotherhood's freezer-fest mutilation spree, now I couldn't even use Unit resources to get answers to questions that'd thrashed around in my head for too many years to count. The heat, the darkness, the oppressive atmosphere… drowsy, I pressed my forehead onto the cool wood, and closed my eyes.

*

I shot up in my seat, banging my knees on Reg's desk. I found myself staring into a hologram of Mo's face, which hung over the table in the gloom, sparkling faintly.

'Miss Green?'

I flexed my neck with a groan.

'Miss Green? Are you alright?'

'I fell asleep.'

'You didn't answer your com.'

I rubbed my eyes. 'Like I said, I fell asleep.'

The tension in Mo's face unravelled. 'Our meeting went on longer than expected. I'm sorry. Do you want me to take you home now?'

I checked the time on Reg's digi-display, and swore softly. Working for the Unit had screwed my body clock. I glanced around at the files, then remembered Oxton's last words.

'Give me a few minutes to finish up,' I said.

'Com me,' said Mo. 'I'll be in the square, at Raymonds. It's a birthday and I've been asked to show my face.' If I'd been able to see his eyes, I guessed he would've been rolling them. 'I can be back with you in minutes.'

'OK,' I said.

Mo disappeared. I ran a hand across my forehead. My hair was slicked to my skin with sweat. I peeled my shirt away from my body. This was pointless. Reg would be on his way down right now, and I was as good as live bait sitting at his table. The crime scene file could wait until morning.

I checked my pockets and my pack, but my com wasn't there.

Something moved in the shadows, a flicker that slipped across a shelf in a flash. I spun around, but whatever it was had already gone.

'Hello?'

The tiniest sound, like a finger sliding one sheet of paper over another, came from the rack opposite.

'Reg, is that you?'

My voice set off a volley of shuffling as though something very small was trying to get away very fast. A single chip fell from a shelf part way down the nearest aisle, and landed on a box underneath with a soft pat.

I scanned the racks. Nothing. Panicking, I checked the floor for my com, but it wasn't there. I fumbled through my pockets and pack again. As I straightened up, tiny invisible eyes burned little holes in my skin from hidden places all around me – I was being watched.

I grabbed my pack and my jacket, and ran for the chute without looking back.

VII

The temperature outside had plummeted below freezing. Frost sparked off the stones, and overhead, the moon sat in a rainbow corona. I pulled my jacket tight and headed across the square. The food vendors were closing up. Android enforcers stood in tight groups observing the flow of bodies. I dodged under a tree to avoid two old guys who lurched towards the cab rank.

'Don't talk rubbish Ralph. The Disaster wasn't caused by a comet. The Old Worlders would've blasted it out of the sky before it hit.'

'What with, David?'

'Nuclear power.'

'Ever heard of meltdown and fallout, Ralph?'

'Rubbish, David. Plague, plague, plague, every time.'

'How the fuck did the plague make an effing great hole?'

'How do you know there's a hole?'

'Everybody knows there's a hole, Ralph. It's in the centre of the Disaster zone, isn't it?'

'Have you ever seen it?'

'Well, no, but …'

'Don't believe everything they tell you, David. Propaganda. Keeps us frightened, keeps us small.'

An enforcer shot out a beam towards them and the men put their heads down and slunk towards the cab rank. I stepped out from underneath the shawl of fairy lights that hung from the branches. My reflection stretched over the plexi-panels of Raymonds, a grotesque watermark on the curves.

Inside, customers squeezed around tables, colourful as tropical birds, their gestures loosened by alcohol, but strangely silent now the doors were closed and the awnings gone. A flash of blonde caught my eye, and I recognised Rosie. She had on a skin-tight purple dress, with her hair piled up on top of her head and wispy bits pulled down over her naked shoulders. Next to her stood a group of off-duty guardians, some of them still in uniform. Mo was flanked by a man with a pale face and a suspicious expression, and a woman taller than any I'd ever seen, with slanted eyes and long hair in a cascade of little plaits. Mo stepped out of the group, his back to me. He'd taken his jacket off. He wore a pale fitted top that tautened over his shoulders. In one hand, he held a bottle of water. Rosie seemed to catch sight of me, but I must've been mistaken, because she turned away from the window. She stretched out one arm towards Mo, then traced a single finger down his spine, light as a feather.

Girls touched guys like that at Torches, but it was part of the job. Rosie looked like she meant it. I slid behind one of the trees. Rosie looped an arm around Mo's waist. It hung, casually, the tips of her fingers resting ever so lightly on his hip. Mo was deep in conversation with a guy wearing a silly hat and a 'happy birthday' badge. I moved towards the window, drawn like a desert moth to a glow-ball. Rosie's fingers trailed along Mo's waist, until just the tips of two were touching his belt. Before I knew it, I was so close my breath had steamed a little 'oh' on the plexi-panel. On a table only inches away was a tiny purple handbag the same colour as Rosie's dress. Sticking up out of the back pocket were two coms. One of them was mine.

I cupped my hands and squinted through the window.

Had Rosie picked it up earlier, at Harry's?

But if so, why hadn't she returned it to me right away?

I stepped back. Mo turned around, as though a sixth sense told him he was being watched. His face tautened with recognition that quickly turned to shock. He pulled away from Rosie, leaving her fingers outstretched after him, and shot towards the exit. Seconds later, he appeared around the side of the building.

'What the hell are you doing out here on your own?'

'You told me where you'd be. I came to get you. I – I didn't mean to spy.'

Mo manoeuvred me so that my back was pressed into the corner of the building. He checked both ways, as though expecting we were being watched, which seemed ridiculous.

'Anybody could be out here, Miss Green - and here you are, standing in the middle of a public walkway, staring in to a busy bar. You know you shouldn't leave HQ alone!'

'I want to go home,' I said. 'The streets are almost empty. Even the enforcers are heading back to their docks.'

'Why didn't you com me?' Mo hissed.

'Because my com went missing.'

'Missing? What do you mean, it went missing?'

'Rosie has it. It's in her bag. I've seen it through the window.'

Mo shook his head, his mouth hanging open as though lost for words. He cursed softly.

'Why didn't you use Reg's desk com, then?'

'He's blocked my access.'

Mo exhaled. Behind the shades, I sensed his eyes were closed.

'Then why didn't you send a call out from HQ reception?'

The truth was, it hadn't occurred to me.

A group of customers stepped out of Raymonds into the street. Mo shifted in close so that neither of us was visible. He watched their backs retreat in the opposite direction until they were out of sight.

Mo hooked his thumbs into his belt loops and stared into my face. 'I'll take you home immediately, Miss Green.'

'You've forgotten your jacket,' I said.

'What?'

'Your jacket. Your arms are bare, and it's cold.'

Mo shook his head in a confused way as though he hadn't got a clue what I was talking about. The tap-tap of spindly heels preceded Rosie peering around the corner, blonde tendrils of hair flaring prettily in the breeze, picked out by the up-lighters.

'Jess!' she squeaked.

'Can I have my com back, please?'

Mo turned around. 'Is this true? Do you have it?'

Rosie looked from one of us to the other, her eyes wide. 'I picked it up off the table this afternoon,' she said, drawing the com out of her bag. 'I only realised just now that I hadn't given it straight back to you.'

I snatched it. 'Thank you.'

Mo gestured to the walkway. 'We'll leave now.'

I dodged past him.

'Are you coming back?' said Rosie.

Mo glanced over his shoulder. 'No. I'd be grateful if you could make my apologies. I won't be coming back.'

'What about your jacket?' Rosie called, but Mo didn't answer.

Rosie watched us for several seconds before disappearing back the way she'd come, her heels tapping a diminuendo.

We made the journey to HQ in an electro. The cab took us the long way round town to avoid a mini-riot outside a Clone It store, which had escalated beyond the scope of the enforcers and now, after curfew, needed Unit intervention.

'What's happening?' I asked.

'Subversive element,' answered the electro. 'You will be able to observe the riot for yourself as we detour onto the only lower-stream road remaining open.'

Moments later, we pulled past a disorganised rabble surrounded by a handful of reluctant android enforcers who kept a safe distance. The crowd lit up briefly in a fire-flash. Half of them hit the ground and threw their hands over their heads, the others froze in the light like hunted animals. Our electro hung a left and they swung out of view, but the image remained imprinted on my retina in monochrome like an Old World photograph.

'I communicated directly with Unit HQ to request a pass for the upper travel stream,' said the electro excitedly, 'but I was denied. Therefore we have no choice but to travel the lower-stream and take the long way round.'

'Good job,' said Mo softly. 'This damn thing would fall straight out the sky if it rose more than four feet off the ground.'

The electro, nettled, pretended it hadn't heard. 'Allow me to take the opportunity to inform you about cause of the riot.'

'Go on,' said Mo tiredly.

'Cybernetic parts were illegally introduced into the Clone It catalogue last year,' said the electro. 'Customers have been building hybridised animals ever since.'

'But it's a children's birthday party outfit,' said Mo, incredulous.

'Yes,' replied the electro, 'Clone It is in the top three birthday destinations for the age group five to eleven. Parents are encouraging their offspring to select razor teeth and Kevlar spines. Once the birthday party is over, the children pit-fight the clones to the death. Large amounts of credits are believed to change hands between the parents. The Unit turned a blind eye until today.'

'Why today?'

'At oh-nine-thirty-a-m, a clone with laser claws took the face off a three month old baby in East Side. Customers are rioting for compensation.'

'The same customers who caused the problem in the first place?' I said.

'Your understanding is correct,' said the auto.

Mo grunted. 'Voice off.'

The com snapped off and I couldn't help but wonder if, somewhere inside its electronic casing, the cab's limited consciousness was wondering what it'd done wrong.

We continued in silence until we were safely inside Mo's hop above the building, watching the landing lights shrink below us.

'You've given me no option but to request a tag, Miss Green.'

'What?'

'You heard me. You have to be tagged. First thing tomorrow morning. It's the only way I can protect you.'

'Tagged like a criminal?'

'Uhuh.'

I began to laugh. It wasn't funny, but all the stress and misery came bubbling out of my throat as though it was the most hilarious thing I'd ever heard anybody say. I laughed until my throat ached, then slid down into my seat in exhausted silence.

Back at my apartment block, Mo didn't leave me at the security gate. He walked through the grounds right to my front door and waited outside until I shut him out and threw the laser lock. I called goodnight, but he didn't answer. He retreated down the stairs, slowly. I waited at the other side with my ear to the panel and listened, then I put him on hallway cam and watched him go.

That night, I dreamed that I looked down at my body, and that it was no longer there, as though I'd been rubbed out, and all that existed of me was a mess of cerebral connections that hung, formless, in the air.

I awoke with a start, to find it still dark. A splinter moon shone through the half-closed blackout, silvering the shape of Claws who slept, unmoving, at the foot of my air-hammock. I drifted back into uneasy sleep, in which images chased themselves behind my eyelids: an empty cot, its covers stripped, a single Old World button laying underneath; a Spider People wise-woman telling me the story of the schaduw, the evil force which channels the most abhorrent crimes through the hands of men; the glint of a nightbeetle's body as it rattled over the sand in the moonlight; and red eyes that glowed from the centre of something small buried in the sand, which burst into flames as I reached out my fingers to touch it.

When grey dawn broke, I slithered gratefully out of bed and into my water-blaster, my skin slick with sweat.

VIII

The following day, Oxton's face sprang into my lap the moment I opened my com. Her skin was sallow, her eyes bloodshot and rimmed by dark circles.

'I need you on the North Side immediately, Miss Green,' she said. 'I'm afraid one of our victim's organs have come to light. Rosie has organised your hop. You'll find it waiting out front.'

Oxton vanished in a shower of pixels. I shut down the com and scooped up my jacket. A victim's organs, on North Side? Surely Nineteen hadn't busted a shifter delicatessen because a human bleep-code had turned up in the pate?

I checked out at the main door. A two-man hop sat waiting in the square. The driver jumped out to open the passenger visor. He was blonde, and younger than me. I'd never seen him before.

'Where's Mo?'

'Sorry Miss, I don't know,' he shrugged. 'I don't ask questions, I just drive when I'm called.'

I jumped in, and fastened my harness.

We crossed the river in silence. Flinty sparks shot off the grey surface where the sunlight kissed the water. Clouds reflected in the driver's headset, steel-grey, billowing, ominous. Curiously, for a Unit employee, he didn't have the over-cautious block I'd become accustomed to. Instead, his thoughts rolled free-form, giving me colourful glimpses of another life so vivid and surprisingly uncomplicated that I began to wish they were my own.

Above the cobbled streets of the old district, the crime scene was impossible to miss. Nineteen were securing the area, subtle as a circus act in high-vis uniforms with megaphones and cones. Two officials were directing pedestrians away from a building. We dipped towards the roofs and skimmed the Old World chimneys, flying through ribbons of smoke that unwound from the wealthier stacks.

'It's safer if we land a street or two away. Attracts less attention,' said the driver. 'The word is, Nineteen are making quite a spectacle of things already.'

'I can imagine.' I craned my neck for a last glimpse before the hop dropped below the rooftops.

The pilot put down in an empty back-street. He slipped off his headset and smoothed out his hair. Patches of fine stubble sprouted below his sideboards. The skin of his hands was soft, with shiny nails that had pure white tips. I opened my side visor.

'Hey. Be careful.' He caught hold of my arm as I swung my legs over the side of the seat. 'I'm serious. On North Side they might have designer faces and private vehicles, but there are some nasty critters out there.'

'You aren't superstitious,' I said, looking at his fingers, feeling them loosen from my jacket and pull away. 'Most Unit won't even brush arms with me.'

'Sorry. I didn't mean to.'

'That's OK. You've made a nice change. What's your name?'

'Guthrie.'

His eyes were blue, very bright like a frozen winter morning, the kind they put down to global cooling until some bright spark discovered that the Sky Skin Corporation were fiddling the weather pattern analysis to sell self-contained environment bubbles in readiness for an Ice Age. Rumour has it the MD of Sky Skin ended up on a shifter banquet table with a real apple stuffed in his mouth, courtesy of the Unit.

I jumped out the hop and slid the visor closed. The bodywork immediately took on the colours and textures around it. By the time I reached the road, the hop was no more than a shimmering outline on the cobbles, the sort you'd look away from, thinking your eyes were playing tricks.

I headed towards the alley I'd seen from the air. It was narrow and dark and smelled of decay. Tall buildings stretched up on either side, with crinkle-crankle brickwork warped by the passage of time. When I emerged onto the main drag, I found myself at the edge of a crowd. Pedestrians, mainly shifters, drifted past in willowy groups, elegant and deceptively fragile, their feline gene giving them more grace and power than seemed decent. Nobody knew whether the Disaster was responsible for their mutation, or the Old World labs that operated before the Disaster, and shifter folklore wasn't to be trusted with all the answers. None of it mattered, so long as you remembered never to trust appearances on this side of the city. I pushed my way through and made for the cordon which formed a makeshift barrier around the scene. A man with a megaphone and a jacket saying Department Forty was patrolling the border with his chest puffed out.

'Move on, miss, no gawking,' he snapped.

I flashed my ID.

'Body's this way.'

'You don't have to speak through your megaphone,' I said. 'I'm right in front of you.'

Behind the tape, Forty were slotting a makeshift solid boundary into place. Blood spattered the cobbles, and streaked the glazing of a boutique with lopsided Old World windows. The shop sign said Mephisto. Underneath, the words Fine Clothing were inscribed in curly script. Above, a small balcony several stories up had collapsed.

'What happened?'

'We had a jumper,' said the chief, glancing at the mangled balcony. 'He nosedived from the sixth floor. Only human. Didn't stand a chance. Spent two days on a bender first, though. Went out in style.'

How the hell had a victim's organs turned up in a suicide?

'Where's the body?'

'Under there.' The chief pointed to a shapeless lump, which somebody had covered with evening gowns.

'You covered the vic in dresses?'

'From the boutique,' said the chief, gesturing at Mephisto. 'Forty aren't used to dealing with this kind of incident. He had to be covered up.'

'And you scanned the body?'

'Uhuh,' said the chief, pulling out his com. 'Sent some kind of alert to HQ. Then I get a call to say that you're on your way. Not exactly usual for HQ to be interested in a North Side suicide, Miss.' The chief's eyes narrowed speculatively.

'Not exactly,' I said. 'I'll need to take a look at your scan report. And the body.'

'Whatever,' the chief shrugged. 'This way.'

As I passed the boutique, a man dressed entirely in black rubber appeared at the doorway, crazily angry and not bothering to block, his eyes glowing yellow.

'Your shop?'

He nodded, setting his hair beads rattling. 'Thousands and thousands… that's what my stock is worth. And these yobs picked the evening gowns. I mean, why? If they'd gone for the rubber coats, at least I could've rinsed them off afterwards.' His voice juddered as he spoke.

'They're dresses,' I said. 'Surely they'll wash?'

'You don't understand,' said the shifter, his voice breaking with emotion. 'Some of these gowns are hand-sewn with rare plastics and obsolete glass-based crystals. Some are copies but most of my stuff is genuine Old World. You can't just shove them in a particle cleaner and hope for the best.

They'll come out looking like those frittatas they sell in Veggie No Death.'

I laid a hand on his arm. 'You will be compensated.'

The shifter looked at my hand, along my arm, and up into my eyes. His sulphurous pupils swam.

'What are you?'

I snatched my hand away.

'I'm with Thirteen,' I snapped. 'I'll see to your compensation personally.'

I left the shifter in his shop doorway and headed for the pile of dresses on the pavement, where the chief stood waiting. Blood seeped through the gaudy fabric. A wide purple pool sat on the stone. Beyond it, thread-like splatters made a paint-flick spider's web.

'Raphael been bothering you?' said the chief, sidling closer.

'He's upset, that's all.'

'A shifter? Upset by a human death?' the chief snapped. 'Pull the other one.'

People without empathic skills listen too much to speculation and rumour. That's what fuels the shifters' mythology – yes, they're crafty and strong and clever and beautiful, thanks to whatever Disaster mess-up gave them a feline gene, but no, they aren't capable of shape-shifting or doing half the things that most of South Side think they can. That's just plain superstition.

'I don't think it's the death that upset him so much as the dresses,' I said.

The chief scowled. 'I did what I had to.'

'I need to access your scan of the victim.' I turned my head away from the mess as I spoke.

The chief pulled his com from his pocket. 'This little beaut has a direct connection to the bleep-code database. It pulled something up instantly.'

I got out my com and leeched the information. 'Thank you.'

I scrolled down and skimmed the report. The victim's liver had, until the first big frozen crime scene, lived inside an office worker called Martinez. Martinez had his organs bar coded under the Rights and Privileges of Unit Employees scheme, as a birthday present several years previously. His signature had come up, unmistakeably, in the chief's scan, which had sent an emergency report to Oxton. I glanced back at the pile of gowns. Somewhere underneath them, an unidentified man was wearing Martinez's liver, or what was left of it. But at least I wasn't in a deli.

Next to me, the chief waited expectantly.

'I hear the suicide was implanted,' he said. 'Couldn't get an ID on the body m'self.'

I ignored him. He cursed softly and shook his head, wandering away to shout at the shifters through his megaphone. Raphael sidled up behind me while I was reading. I turned the screen off.

'You never introduced yourself,' he said silkily.

'My name is Jess Green.'

'You're not like the others.'

He leaned closer, giving me a whiff of expensive aftershave, and sniffed my hair, carefully, as though I was some kind of non-cloned exotic flower in an expensive display. I stepped backwards. Raphael's irises began to swirl with kaleidoscope patterns.

'It won't work on me,' I said, 'so you might as well forget it.'

Raphael grinned. 'Exciting.' He reached out one forefinger and ran it lightly over the front of my jacket. 'You don't know what it means to me, to come face to face with somebody who can stand up to me, who isn't another shifter.'

'Well don't get any ideas,' I snapped.

'Don't worry, you're not really my type,' said Raphael, dropping his hand and looking me up and down with a wink. 'You're the wrong side of the tower block, if you get my drift. But you could still be fun, though. Variety is the spice, so they say.'

'Excuse me,' I said, 'I've got a body to scan.'

I twitched a flare of purple fabric aside with one foot and held out my com.

'Ughhhh.' Raphael looked down dispassionately.

'Move away. You shouldn't be this side of the cordon.'

'I'm not abandoning my clothes to those bitches,' Raphael spat, glancing towards Forty, who were wandering up and down the boundary, leering at the shifters on the other side. 'Given half a chance, they'll start mopping the pavement with my lingerie.'

The scan results flashed up on my com. Martinez's donee wasn't on any database, even the classified Unit version.

'This one's well and truly slipped under the radar,' I said.

'Probably came from the Disaster Zone. Shit. I recognise that face. What's left of it…'

'You do?

'Hell, yes. It's Dante, the cage dancer. Used to work the Fork Tongue club.'

'How recently?'

'Within the last few days. Until he had a big row with his boyfriend. So loud everybody in the block heard. Then he vanished.'

I flicked my com shut and stowed it in my jacket pocket. 'Was the row big enough to make him want to fly face down into the cobbles?'

Raphael shrugged. 'I guess so. He was pretty cut up when they split. Oh sweet Mary Virgin, they put my pink chenille right over the damaged bits…' Raphael turned away and seethed, one fist blocking his mouth.

I toed the dress back over the remains. 'Do you know Dante's boyfriend?'

Raphael took a quivering breath. 'Yes, I know him. The guy has an act at a club over the way. We're on nodding terms, nothing more. He isn't my type.'

A fleet of Unit hops appeared above us. They descended in formation, sending the shifters scattering with squeals of excitement. The chief retreated from the boundary with the rest of Forty, his megaphone resting on one thigh.

'Thanks for your help, Raphael. And I'm sorry about your dresses.'

Raphael had his finger underneath my chin before I could step away. My skin fizzled along the line he traced down my throat. His irises began to whirl again.

'Come into the shop,' he whispered. 'Take a look around. You're so pretty yet so austere. You really don't make as much of yourself as you could, you know.'

'Thanks, Raphael, maybe another time. I'm on duty.'

Raphael's finger carried on down, tracing my collar bone and skipping onto the collar of my jacket. I snatched his hand away and dug my nails into his flesh. He winced.

'Black,' he said wistfully. 'You have a history with black, don't you, Jessica?'

I didn't respond.

Raphael stared at me from underneath lowered lids. 'I'm only making an observation. You need to throw the black. Get a little colour into your life.'

The jewels in Raphael's irises stopped whirling. Just for a split second, my block fell away. Had I lost concentration? Had I wanted to? Or had Raphael's crafty feline intuition worked its magic and pushed me over that invisible line so subtly that I hadn't seen it coming? I'll never know. Raphael's eyes widened with alarm, and something I couldn't read fleeted across his face. It only lasted a fraction of a second. Then we were back to the way we'd been before, standing behind a crime scene barrier, two strangers on a blood-spattered pavement staring at each other, the status quo resurrected. He wasn't touching my jacket any more.

'You've been invited to a function,' said Raphael. 'I can see it weighing heavy on your mind. You need a cocktail dress, don't you?'

'I don't think my boss would agree to fund real glass beads.'

Raphael laughed, his huge shoulders shaking, the muscles on his arms taut underneath their rubber casing. Behind us, the noise from the crowd died to a stunned silence as Twenty Three disembarked in formation. Uniform has that effect on shifters. They love a show.

'Bring me the compensation credits yourself,' said Raphael. 'I want to dress you. You're a challenge. And you're far more interesting than the average South Side customer.' He glanced towards the chief, who was ogling a slender shifter with a hypnotised smile pinned to his face. 'I could make your visit worthwhile.'

'How?'

He spoke in an undertone: 'Information.'

'Information on what?'

Raphael smiled. 'Information on everything. I deal in it. If you want something specific, something that might help... well, you'll just have to come back soon, won't you?'

'Goodbye, Raphael,' I said, turning away.

I passed Forty, who stood with their mouths open watching Twenty Three swarm the scene. I squeezed through a gap in the barrier and set off towards the alley. Nobody even so much as acknowledged me as I headed in the opposite direction. Sometimes, not standing out is a bonus.

'You'll be back,' Raphael called from the kerbside. 'Sooner than you think, Jessica!'

I headed into the shadows, the sound of the crowd washing away into the background. My footsteps rang hollow and metallic off the twisted walls. When I emerged into daylight, a small crowd of shifter children had gathered near the hop. On my side of the city, the kids were in school right now, but here, things ran differently. They were throwing bits of twig that'd fallen off a real tree, and laughing as the ends sparked on the cocoon. They scattered when they saw me coming. I slid the visor open. Guthrie was cringing in his seat. His knuckles were white and his eyes were wild, not blue any more, but grey, like the river on a bad day.

'Those shifter kids can see through the cloaking system.'

'I know,' I said, fastening myself in and shutting the visor.

'Then what the hell is the point in having a cloaking system at all?'

'There isn't. At least, not on North Side. How long did you say you'd been with the Unit?'

'I didn't,' Guthrie's voice was sullen.

He crammed his headset on and took the hop up, only relaxing when we pushed through layers of chimney smoke. Below, the shifter kids emerged from the alley, jeering and chucking bits of twig into the air after us.

'Criminal way to treat a real tree,' said Guthrie. 'They don't have values this side of the river.'

'They do, just different values.'

'Why aren't they in school?'

'They are,' I said. 'They just learn on the streets, here. Have you only ever worked for the Unit, Guthrie?'

'Followed my father and my grandmother before that,' he replied with a set in his jaw that could've been pride or duty, but not both.

'I'm afraid we aren't going back to base yet.'

Guthrie stiffened.

'I've got a stolen liver and a flattened cage dancer. I haven't got a clue what the connection is, but I need to be at least one step closer by the time I get back to HQ. Oxton is with the suits Upstairs, and if I don't take her something, my neck is on the line.'

'Where do you need to be?' Guthrie's voice became hoarse and professional.

'My dead dancer worked a club called Fork Tongue. Do you know it?'

'Yes.'

'Great. I think it's time to pay a visit.'

'Fork Tongue will be closed up now until dark. You won't get in.'

'All the better for taking a look round the outside without being disturbed,' I said.

Guthrie pulled the auto-map down over the steering column with a grimace. We veered left, and turned our backs to the river, where sunlight fractured the surface of the warming water. As we flew, the buildings beneath us got smaller, then the chimney stacks disappeared, until eventually, the only thing between us and the Cinderlands were the bone-yard headstones that chewed at the edge of the wilderness.

'Just look at that,' said Guthrie, motioning below. 'Every time I see it, it freaks me out.'

'The Cinderlands?'

'No, the bone-yard. Who'd believe that they gave so much space for burials in those days? And whole bodies, too? How gross is that. No wonder they all died of plague.'

'Nobody can be sure that the Disaster was a plague. It could've been a meteor hitting the earth.'

'You'll be telling me it was a nuclear accident next,' Guthrie smirked.

I didn't respond. The hop lowered as we approached a row of buildings that were part Old World, part modern. In one, the remains of an ancient church were engulfed by a newer, more angular design.

'Here it is,' said Guthrie. 'Fork Tongue.'

We set down in the vehicle park, which was empty except for two rhine-stoned retro-wagons with huge old-fashioned thrusters and tinted windows. A sign saying Fork Tongue winked from the club roof, feeble and flickery in daylight.

'I'll only be a few minutes,' I said, sliding out and shutting the visor before Guthrie could give me a lecture on personal safety.

A bitter breeze slid across the open lot, wrapping itself around my legs. I pulled my jacket tighter. The bone-yard and the wilderness beyond weren't visible, but I felt them, in a stillness and quiet that stretched further than sight, and soughed around the edges of my consciousness like wind through broken glass. I shut them out and hurried towards the facing wall. It had no windows, but I didn't doubt there were security cameras. I glanced back at the hop. Guthrie was watching me, unashamedly, his face tense.

I set off clockwise around the perimeter. The club was on several levels, some made of Old World brick. A steeple rose from the centre, an arcane statement from a destroyed past. Sister Rose used to say that Old World temples were built in the shape of male fertility symbols that no self-respecting worshipper of the Virgin would dream of reconstructing. Mad old hag.

The newest part of the club was enclosed in blacked-out plexi-screen and alloy framework, the kind they could dismantle in days and take somewhere else if the need arose. One murder too many, shifter turf-war, human parts being found in the fast food – it's all happened before, and when it does, they slink away to start again somewhere else. I glanced up. A security-eye passed over the hop.

Along the side of the club was a flight of stairs that went down. I peered over the edge. Below ground level, a barred window looked onto an enclosed yard. The gutters were blocked with detritus and sprouted flares of green and black mould. Down the steps, the smell of decay got stronger. I reached the window and crouched down. The room inside was small and dark. A pinprick of light shone through an open door from somewhere distant. Several tables were pulled back against the walls. An assortment of chairs that looked as though they'd seen better days were arranged in a loose circle. Scanning for residual memories wasn't worth the risk: the shifters would pick me up from all over the building. Being converged on by a bunch of over-excited heavies was the last thing on my wish-list. I'd heard what they did to South Side females, given the chance.

The floor was empty save for a couple of glasses, a dining plate smeared with dried gunk, and a crumpled leaflet. The leaflet had an illustration on it, drawn in old fashioned ink: a ram's head. I pulled back and leaned against the window bars. My head felt so tight I was dizzy.

A premonition.

A leaflet in a nightclub basement.

A dead cage dancer wearing a liver stolen by the Brotherhood.

I set off back up the stairs.

When I rounded the corner, Guthrie was in the same position, looking right at me. I turned away again, towards two doors set in the modern section of the club. Holo-leaflets crowded the plexi-panels. A band leapt out and started to play death metal, then a woman with black lips and a shaved head promised me a night I'd never forget. I ignored the sparkly finger that reached out and stroked me underneath the chin. An understated promo bearing the words The Eternity Fund promised a key to anti-ageing. Underneath it sat a small, white leaflet bearing the sigil of the ram's head. It was pasted over the top of two competing holo-promos which struggled to burst out as they sensed me pass. Beneath the ram sketch, a list of dates and the words Fork Tongue were printed in an arcane font. I took out my com and recorded the image. Only the last date hadn't passed: it was in ten days' time.

I turned to leave. A huge man in black stood in front of me, casting out foul temper. His pupils swam dark yellow.

I had nowhere to run, and Guthrie couldn't see me.

'What the hell are you doing wandering round my back yard?' he glowered, his arms out to each side as though they didn't fit comfortably next to his body.

I flashed my Unit ID.

He ambled towards me and snatched it.

'This had better not be no forgery,' he said, scrutinising the card and looking at my face.

The shifter felt far older than he looked. If he was an elder, I'd drawn a short straw. They get meaner with age. And they take more risks.

'I'm not a fake, but I came unannounced. I didn't want to make a scene.'

He prodded my ID into my chest and scowled.

'I don't like Unit sniffing around,' he said, rolling his eyes and stepping too close.

I moved back. The plexi-panel creaked behind my shoulders. Even if Guthrie could pick up a mental distress signal, mine would ring like a claxon. They'd be all over me in seconds.

'I especially don't like Unit sniffing around incognito. What is it this time? That bitch from The Hellhole tell you I'm distilling my own hooch again?'

'No,' I said, sliding my ID into my inside pocket and moving sideways. 'I'm investigating a death. A guy who used to dance here.'

'A death?' the shifter's eyes narrowed.

A lock of hair fell across his forehead. He brushed it away, without letting go of my eyes.

'Went by the name of Dante.'

The shifter rubbed his chin, sending sparks off his stubble like only an elder can do. The guy had power alright, and he was masking more than half of it. I swallowed, but my throat was so dry it had already seized up.

'Dante is lying underneath a boutique off Shifter's Alley, splattered across the pavement.'

'Huh? Dead, you say?'

'Yes. Did you know Dante?'

The guy searched my face as though weighing up his response. 'I might remember him.'

'That's a start. When did you last see him?'

The shifter pulled a drugstix holder out of his pocket. It was Old World pink enamel with diamante jewels and pictures of kittens on the front. He slid out a drugstic, snapped the holder closed, and struck a spark from his fingernails.

'Dante was a good dancer. Didn't turn up for work the night before last.'

'Do you know why?'

The shifter drew on the stick and shrugged. 'I suppose I figured he'd been poached by that bitch from The Hellhole. All I know is, I had to get Sabrine on stage early. She's a good girl. Obliging, for a South Sider, if you know what I mean,' he leered, searching my neckline for cleavage. His face fell when he came up against the throat-high shirt. 'Other than that, dancers come, and dancers go. I don't ask questions.'

'Dante wasn't poached by The Hellhole. He went to a private room above a boutique, downed a cellar full of liquor over two days, then took a solo flight out the window.'

'Look, Miss Unit,' the shifter said, pluming vapour from both nostrils, 'just because a guy dances for me, doesn't mean to say I control what he does or where he goes. And between you and me, any human who tries jumping is nuts. You people are so soft you're pate already. Dante didn't drink the liquor here, and he didn't go flying off my roof, so there's nothing I can help you with.'

The shifter threw his half-smoked drugstic down and crunched it into the dirt.

'If you spill to me, now, you won't have Unit crawling over the club later on, when the punters are around,' I said, with more confidence than I felt.

The shifter grunted.

'You let out your basement for group meetings?' I gestured towards the damp stairwell.

'Yeah. Helps pay the bills. You got a problem with that?'

'Did Dante attend any meetings?'

The shifter shrugged, sending his mane of wavy hair shimmering over his shoulders. Even ugly shifters have beautiful hair. It's a big cat thing. 'Maybe. Maybe not. I don't keep tabs on my staff.'

'Did you notice anything odd about Dante, or the way he was behaving recently?'

The shifter rubbed his chin again. He didn't spark, but the rasping went through me.

'Dante used to dance naked, but he stopped doing that a couple of weeks ago. The word was, he'd had an operation. Had a scar he didn't want to show.'

'Must've been a big scar.'

'I have no idea. Naked South Side men aren't my thing.' His expression changed, and his eyes roved my body greedily. 'South Side females I can tolerate, but only on my terms.'

'I'm not available,' I snapped.

The shifter's gaze flickered to the corner of the building, as though he'd remember the hop, and Guthrie. He grunted.

'Who is Dante's lover?'

The shifter shrugged. 'Some half-breed from the Well of Souls over the way,' he jerked his head in the direction of the bone-yard. 'Goes by the name of Leo. You'll have to ask Ava at the Well for the details. And when you see her, tell her she's a fat slag, and that Charles-William Fortescue sent you.'

The shifter turned away and sloped off towards a door that swung in the wind like a broken wing, creaking as it smacked repeatedly into a plexi-panel. He disappeared and pulled it shut behind him. The hinges and outline vanished. I turned towards the hop, and ran.

Guthrie's face hung ghostlike above the controls, pale with panic. The engine was already powered up. He brought the hop closer when he saw me, taxiing across the lot. We took off before I'd strapped myself in, rising up over a single window that opened at the apex of the club roof. It was small, and barred. Somebody stood behind it, watching us go – a girl in her late teens with a black eye and frazzled hair implants. Her bare arms were dappled with bruises. She stepped backwards and melted into the shadows.

*

Leo was completely naked. His eyes were bloodshot, with deep shadows smeared underneath.

'I'm sorry to disturb you,' I said. 'I'm here about Dante.'

Leo blinked. 'Who?'

'Your boyfriend.'

Leo smothered a yawn. 'I've only just got back from work. I fell asleep on the sofa. What the hell do you want at this time in a morning?'

'It isn't morning anymore. Can I come in?'

Leo turned away, leaving the door open, and giving me an unimpeded view of his tanned buttocks and broad back. A snake tattoo traced down his spine, ending in a fanged head just above his coccyx.

The flat was small and open-plan. Leo grabbed a pink dressing gown from a hook on the back of a door, and wrapped it around his body. He moved like a trained dancer.

'I smell Unit,' he said, looking me up and down.

I fumbled for my ID, but Leo waved a hand. 'Don't bother. It's the clothes. Nobody except a Unit rookie wears cheap, ill-fitting black with their hair scraped back. And no makeup. Tut tut.'

'I'm afraid I've got some very bad news. You might want to sit down.'

Leo pulled a beaker off a shelf and poured himself some just-like-juice. 'Nothing can shock me. Not anymore. Go on.'

'Dante – your boyfriend – he threw himself off a balcony above a dress shop on North Side. I'm afraid he's dead.'

Leo swigged, swishing his mouth before swallowing.

'Dante...' his voice was dreamy, his eyes far away. 'What makes you think he was my boyfriend?'

'That was the word on Shifter's Alley,' I said. 'I was led to believe you were his next of kin.'

Leo snorted and ditched the beaker. 'We had sex a few times. He bought me flowers. Real ones too, not the cloned sort. Must've cost him an arm and a leg. Probably stole the credits that paid for them.' Leo swung away and tightened the cord around his waist. 'Dante always did have expensive taste.'

'Dante died earlier this morning. He went on a two day drink binge before he flew.'

Leo kept his back to me. 'Shit. You don't say.'

He reached a hand up to scratch the back of his neck, where the tail of the snake disappeared underneath his hairline. His fingers were trembling.

'I'm trying to piece together Dante's final movements. I believe he had surgery recently. About two weeks ago?'

Leo began rifling through things stacked on the table, tossing them aside with agitated movements.

'Dante fucked his liver up with too many drugs. I warned him, but he wouldn't listen. And before you ask, just because I dance naked to pay my way doesn't mean I'm hooked on crap too.'

'I wasn't going to ask,' I said.

'Well, you'd be the first. Most people assume I'm just like the rest of the crowd, but I actually want to get out, you know? One day I want a window garden with real carrots growing in it, and a regular table at Hex's. I gave Dante the opportunity to change and to come with me.'

'How long had Dante been an addict?'

'Long enough,' snapped Leo. 'He got so ill that his dancing suffered. He couldn't keep muscle on, couldn't work a shift without adding steroids to his protein shakes – couldn't stay awake for the high-tipping punters, you know, the ones from Upstairs at your place?'

'Nobody ever sees the ones from Upstairs. Not unless you work above floor Eighty Nine.'

'Don't you believe it.' Leo stopped looking for whatever he'd lost. 'I told Dante he had to live clean, or he wouldn't work at all. Who do you think is going to pay for you to shoot up then, I said, because it won't be me, lover boy.'

He snatched something poking from underneath an empty Veggie No Death snack-box, and held it to his chest.

'So how did Dante get hold of the new liver?'

Leo took a deep, shaking breath. 'Dante's condition had gone too far to be treated. He couldn't afford to pay for a new liver to be grown, so he said the next best thing was to go recycled.'

'You mean use a donor.'

'I prefer to think of it as recycling. I mean, you don't have to ask the person who originally grew it why they don't need it any more, do you?'

'So Dante had a private op.'

'Yes. But I don't know how, on his wages.'

'I've traced the donor.'

Leo's head snapped to attention. His eyes widened with alarm, and his fingers loosened around whatever he was holding. It was a photograph, but not a holo photo: it was one of the old fashioned sorts that flick between a couple of static images. Retro, they call them.

'You've come to the wrong place if you're looking for a bankroller, sister,' he snapped. 'I certainly didn't pay for a transplant. Hell, how would I do that living in a dump like this?'

My eyes roved the ceiling, which was peeling, and the corners of the room, blackened with dirt. Leo opened a drawer. There was nothing inside. He put the photograph face down and closed it, then began to pull a pile of clothes off the settee. His movements were rapid and bird-like, his fingers pecking at the fabrics. He looped everything carelessly over one arm. I didn't say a word. I knew I didn't have to. He'd talk, when he was ready. Eventually, Leo stopped and stood, like one of those kid's toys with its solar panel covered, motionless, but weirdly so, as though he'd got stuck in the middle of a manoeuvre when the power cut out.

'Dante said he didn't need dropping off or collecting from the clinic. I don't even know where he had the op. All I know is, it was a good place, with anti-rejection therapy and sonic scar healing. Said he'd be dancing again within days. Said that's what you got if you were prepared to pay for the best.'

'Did Dante's operation take place in River City?'

Leo shrugged. 'I never found out. And I don't want to know either.' He picked a shiny body suit up, and shook it out. The material tintinnabulated delicately, as though it was made of myriad tiny parts. 'Real lizard scales,' he said, holding it up.

It glittered in the light.

'I thought all the real lizards were dead.'

Leo laughed bitterly. 'You can get anything providing you've got the money. But then again, you should know. You're Unit.'

'Tell me about the meetings at the Fork Tongue club, Leo.'

Leo waved a hand. 'There's always some group or other holding meetings downstairs. I didn't get involved. If you want to know more, just look at the flyers. One month there's a run on political lobbying, the next they're making cloned flower arrangements for the rich.'

'What about Dante's interests?'

Leo slung the clothes over the arm of the settee. 'Apart from the drugs, I have no idea what interested Dante. All that sex, and I never really got to know.'

'But you said you wanted to start a new life with him, away from here.'

Leo shrugged. 'It's the same speech I give everybody.'

'Did Dante ever mention a group who use the sigil of the ram's head?'

Leo picked up the feather boa and ran it through his fingers. 'Yes. Dante was into new groups. I used to joke he'd be doing yoga next.'

'Did you go along to the meetings?'

'Only once.'

'What happened?'

Leo tipped his head on one side, remembering. 'It was just like you'd expect. Some fat guy stood at the front whipping everyone into a frenzy, asking would you like to change your lives, would you like eternal happiness, how about if death and disease no longer existed... the usual trash.' A single feather detached itself from the boa and floated like a fluffy parachute, dipping and swaying towards the floor. 'Dante went a few times, but I never joined him again. Then he stopped talking about it.'

'Was this just before his transplant?'

Leo nodded. 'Yeah, I guess it was. Now if that's all, I really do have to catch up with my beauty sleep. I've a gig tonight and I have to look fresh.'

'Are you OK?'

'You win some, you lose some, honey,' he smirked. 'I'll never be short of somebody to take me out to dinner. Poor Dante. Be sure to kiss his corpse for me. Was he... was he pretty mashed up?'

'You can visit him in the Unit morgue... although I can't guarantee how much of him you'll be able to view.'

Leo looked thoughtful for a moment. 'Nah. The doormen give me the creeps.'

'Thank you for your time. And I'm sorry.'

I let myself out of the flat into a gust of cold air. As I took the steps down to street level, something fragile smashed against the back of the door, and Leo began to wail.

IX

Guthrie had barely cut the thrusters when Mo ran over and yanked the pilot-side visor down. Guthrie jumped out, leaving me fumbling with my harness. Mo said something I couldn't hear, then reached out and flipped the peak of Guthrie's cap. It flew off his head and somersaulted to the ground. Guthrie let it fall. He watched Mo stalk back to the rooftop door, fists clenched by his sides. As the harness sucked back into the seat, I scrambled out.

'What the hell was that about?'

Guthrie turned to face me but his eyes didn't leave Mo's back until he disappeared inside.

'Your handler needs to speak with you. About the trip we just took.'

Guthrie stooped to snatch up the cap. The peak was dented. I mumbled an apology, and headed for the entrance.

Past the security scanners, Mo was standing by a water cooler in the rest area, his back turned. He drained his cup, crushed it, and tossed it into a recycler.

'What's going on?'

Mo spun around.

'Jon Guthrie wasn't authorised to take the hop, or to take you.'

Mo spoke softly, but sparks of badly-contained anger danced around him.

'Guthrie was sent to pick me up.'

Mo inhaled deeply and glanced upwards, as though steeling himself for divine intervention.

'Since I was reassigned, Miss Green, I've had nothing but trouble with your interpretation of protocol. You aren't supposed to travel without me and yet, once again, this appears to be something you refuse to grasp. I have Twenty One on standby to fit your tag. The sooner, the better, as far as I'm concerned.'

Anger knotted my throat. 'Oxton sent me to North Side, and Guthrie was appointed to take me. If you have a problem with that, then talk to Oxton, but don't take it out on Guthrie. He was only following orders.'

'Nobody else flies you. Only me. They are Oxton's orders.'

A flash of frustration burned the air between us.

'Is this why you were reassigned, Mo? Because you can't control your temper?'

Mo's expression blanked.

'You wanted to punch Guthrie out there just now, didn't you?'

He clasped his hands front, and pressed his lips together.

'What's with the blank face? A coping technique you learned in therapy?'

Just for a moment, Mo's features crumpled, caving in around his shades with the unmetered emotion of a child.

'We have to build a relationship based on trust, Miss Green. In spite of your personal opinion, I only have your best interests at heart. How am I to convince you that you only leave HQ with me, and nobody else?'

I swore under my breath. 'You're getting me tagged. I don't think convincing me comes into it.'

Mo held up one hand. 'Hear me out. This isn't a game. Guthrie doesn't have the experience to take care of you properly. He's only a junior pilot. I understand you went to North Side?'

I nodded, remembering the whites of Guthrie's eyes, the blood on the pavement, and Fork Tongue. Guthrie had barely coped with waiting for me in the hop. What if something had happened out there?

'Please tell me that Guthrie didn't let you wander around on your own.'

'Of course not,' I lied.

Mo shook his head, and ran both hands over his close-cropped hair as though he'd just run for miles and was utterly exhausted.

'Something isn't right, Mo. I com you, you don't answer. I try to leave a message, your mail is switched off. You call me, but I don't hear because my alerts are disabled. And now I get sent out on a job with a driver who's waiting for me, and you nearly punch him because he shouldn't have been there in the first place.'

'I never switch my com off, or disable my messages,' Mo said slowly, as though speaking to a child.

'That's my point. This isn't about getting me tagged so you can track my every move – it's about finding out who or what is screwing up our communication.'

Mo's expression was blank, but behind it, I knew his mind was working fast. He gave one quick nod, then turned away and headed down the corridor. I jogged to catch up.

He ignored the lift door and slipped into the narrow gangway that opened into the fire escape. Above, a sign read 'For Emergency Use Only'. The entrance was dark.

'Don't you want to know what I found out, on North Side?'

'Of course I want to know, Green.'

I dodged through, behind him. In the stairwell, thin tubes of low-glare lighting lined the walls.

'Aren't you going to slow down?'

'No.'

He pulled away, disappearing around a bend.

'What about the tag? You said Twenty One were on stand-by.'

Mo ignored me. Breathless, I hung my head over the banister. The lower floors were an abyss.

'There are easier ways to deal with your aggression,' I shouted.

My voice chased itself around the shaft. Mo didn't stop.

'I don't like dark spaces,' I added, setting off again.

Mo's footsteps were faint now.

'What floor are we on?' I yelled.

'You're on ninety six.' His words disappeared in a boom of reverb.

'Shit.'

*

Ten minutes later, I was slumped in a rest area with my jacket slung over the arm of the settee, and my top shirt button undone, a canister of water in my hand. The vendor slid two coffees onto the table in front of us.

'You need to do some fitness training,' said Mo.

'I danced nearly every day until eight months ago.'

'That was then.'

The table top was littered with com parts, the panels prised to bits so Mo could fiddle with them.

'Why won't you tell me what's going on?' I said.

'I'll talk about it as soon as I know what my conclusion is,' said Mo softly, holding up a tiny chip and examining it at close range.

'They enhanced your eyesight, too?'

'Uhuh.'

'Must've done a pretty good job. Those parts are microscopic.'

The Eye on the ceiling twisted towards us and extended its viewer, fascinated by the chip in Mo's fingers.

'There's nothing wrong with either of these coms.'

I rolled my eyes, drained my cup, and grimaced. 'I'll take your word for it, Mo.'

He reassembled the parts.

'So,' I said.

Mo sank back into the settee and slid his com into his pocket, then pushed mine across the table towards me. 'I've amended the settings so that nothing can prevent you from contacting me, or vice versa.'

'What about Oxton?'

The Eye ticked as its auditory facility upped.

'What about her?'

'She gave the order for North Side. Guthrie told me he was scrambled.'

'Leave it with me. Don't mention this to anybody. And meanwhile,' Mo scrutinised my face, 'if you find somebody waiting to fly you who isn't me, don't get in the vehicle, and call me immediately. Is that clear?'

'Yes.'

'Good.' Mo pulled the fronts of his jacket together in a single brisk movement. 'Now. The field operation, tomorrow afternoon.'

'You mean the cocktail party for The Eternity Fund?'

'It isn't a party. It's an operation. You need to look the part. Did you find anything to wear?'

I slid back into the settee. The slouchy sides swallowed me. 'Not yet. What's the guest demographic?'

'The seriously rich. The Eternity Fund is researching halting the ageing process, without resorting to cybernetic enhancement. We know that the fund is connected to the Nemesis Corporation, but that isn't common knowledge.'

I nodded. 'I already saw the public blurb. The long and short is, people with more money than sense are going to splurge a few credits so that if Barber hits the jackpot, they're the first in the queue to get the jab.'

The corners of Mo's mouth twitched up. 'A harsh but accurate assessment, Miss Green. The Eternity Fund has already attracted several major backers. It's fast becoming the city's buzz-word.'

'Why can't they just pay for the same alterations you and Rosie had?'

Mo's eyebrows shot up. 'The Unit's cellular strengthening technology will never be released to the public. And The Eternity Fund are proud of their non-cybernetic ethics.'

I thought of Rosie, draining her cup through a metal proboscis, and shuddered. 'Maybe that's a good thing. Did you know that Rosie can crush Kevlar with her bare hands?'

Mo stood up. 'Come on.'

I picked up my back pack. 'Where are we going?'

'The boutiques in North Side. You need something formal to wear.'

*

Outside Mephisto, the Unit cordon had gone. A clean-up team had removed Dante's remains, the pile of dresses and the stains from the stone. Through sparkling glass, Raphael's re-stocked hangers glinted with a plethora of colours. A new balcony clung to the crumbling brick-work, as though none of it had really happened and perhaps Dante had never existed at all. Mo gestured to a bench outside.

'I'll wait here. But please choose something appropriate, Miss Green. Ask the staff for help.'

'What's that supposed to mean?'

'I'm not sure your past at Torches would make you the best equipped to make an appropriate clothing decision by yourself.'

Mo turned away. The ghost of a smile pulled at the corners of his mouth. I swore, softly.

Inside Mephisto, Raphael was fussing over a mannequin-like African girl. His hands smoothed imaginary wrinkles out of her snakeskin cat-suit while he muttered soothingly. She walked away to admire herself in a full-length. Raphael spoke without looking up.

'So. You came back.'

I turned to rifle through the 'sale' rack and grimaced at the prices. Raphael's yellow eyes flickered with amusement.

'I have just the thing,' he said, 'in a colour that'll set your eyes off a treat. You really don't make enough of yourself, Jessica, darling.'

He reached deep into a recess and pulled out a hanger. A tiny scrap of sea green fabric drizzled off its fastenings and landed in a pool on the counter.

'That's not a dress, Raphael. That's a dishcloth.'

'Not for three thousand two hundred and forty seven, it isn't. You have to pay for class, Jess. Anyway. On to business. I hope my compensation is huge.'

'It is. I saw to it myself.' I pulled a Unit bleep-code from my pocket and handed it to Raphael. 'You can load the credits into whatever account you want. All I need you to do is retina and print for me.'

I took out my com and held it towards him. Raphael eyed me warily and pushed the green dress back into its alcove. He took my com, then the bleep-code, and slid it into the till. He whistled.

'Jess, darling, I owe you one.' Raphael cocked his head to one side. 'You ever eaten at The Eye?'

'On my wages? Do me a favour. They serve real veg that's grown on a secret site, not the stuff from the Klone Zone. You must've heard the rumour about their protein – that at top table, it comes from real live animals, not meat racks.'

Raphael smothered a laugh. 'All the real animals are dead – except the ones the uber-rich have in their conversation-piece collections.'

The African woman turned away from the mirror and slunk back towards us.

'I'll keep the cat-suit on.'

There was no mistaking her voice as male, nor the fuzz of chest hair that poked out above the pert breasts.

'There's somebody at The Eye,' Raphael whispered, appraising his customer as she bent over a shelf of shoes. 'I think you should pay her a visit, Jess.'

'Who?'

'They call her the Sybil.'

Raphael opened an empty box and began to pack it carefully with tissues. He put on the lid, and slipped it into a 'Mephistos' bag.

'And who is this Sybil?'

'It's not so much a who, as a what, if you get my drift. She's a fortune teller. A good one, too.' Raphael's pupils glowed sulphurously.

'I'm not sure I get your drift.'

He rolled his eyes. 'I told you yesterday that I deal in information. That's why Oxton likes me so much. I take bribes, darling. But sometimes, the money isn't important. Sometimes, I don't have any control over who I give a message to – like now. You have to see the Sybil. She knows about your past, and she wants to tell you something about your future – something that might prove useful.'

My stomach knotted. Raphael, sensing it, smirked.

'You know you want it, Jess,' he whispered.

The African passed her bleep-code to Raphael with a flirtatious smile. Her nails were long and curly, like miniature animal horns. Raphael scanned, then handed the code back, holding the tortured fingertips slightly too long. She took the bag and turned to leave. Raphael's eyes ate her rump all the way out. When she disappeared, he opened the till drawer, and drew out a small round disk.

'What is it?'

'The token, of course,' he said, as though I was stupid, sliding it over the counter towards me.

I picked it up and flipped it over in my hand. It resembled an Old World coin, made from stone. Both sides were blank.

'The Sybil only reads for people who have the token. You hand it over, she does her thing.'

I tossed it into the air, watching it spin under the lights. The surface glittered, as though it was Old World granite, or the hardest kind of blackglass.

'Go to The Eye,' Raphael turned back to the sale rail and began to reorganise hangers. 'Back entrance. Kitchen. That's all I can tell you.'

A shadow cut the doorway. Mo leaned against the frame and stared inside. He locked eyes with Raphael briefly, then disappeared again.

'Oooh, who's lover boy?' Raphael craned his neck.

'That's my handler.'

'The body!' Raphael rolled his eyes. 'I bet he works out.'

'I imagine he does,' I said. 'I've never asked.'

'Treat him carefully,' Raphael whispered, leaning in close. 'He's got a past, that one. Dark rivers run deep.'

'What do you mean?'

'He needs delicate handling, hon.'

'I don't handle him at all. We work together,' I said, my face beginning to burn.

Raphael laughed. His teeth glinted and his hair beads rattled. 'Whatever, Jess. Whatever.'

I shoved the token into my pocket.

'And now, are you going to let me dress you? Your expensive dishcloth would be my first choice.'

Raphael pushed the hanger into my hands.

In the dressing room, I loosed my hair so that it fell in a dark cascade around my shoulders. I piled my clothes on a chair in the corner, and pulled the dress down over my head. The bodice clung in all the right places, the gauzy straps showing off my shoulders, still honed from years of dancing, but softer after eight months off. The neckline plunged to reveal more cleavage than I'd shown since I left Torches. When I moved, the fabric changed colour like holo-pix I'd seen of the sea, greeny-grey and foamy white. I stepped out of the dressing room and turned around slowly. Raphael whistled.

'I can fetch you more, but the first choice is always the right one, Jessica.'

'I'll take it,' I said.

'I haven't finished with you yet.' Raphael took a pair of strappy heels with sparkly bits out of a cubbyhole and put them on the counter. 'I sized you up as soon as you walked in. I never get it wrong.'

I whistled through my teeth and teased my fingers along the delicate ankle lashes. 'I'll never manage to walk in these.'

'You won't need to do anything more than balance, when you've got lover boy on your arm.'

'It's work, Raphael,' I snapped.

Raphael shrugged.

In the changing room, I scraped my hair into a ponytail band and slipped on the ankle-to-neck black that I'd arrived in. Uniform, that's all - just like the trashy stuff had been at Torches. Nothing more, nothing less. Guys just didn't seem to get that.

I stepped outside with a bag in each hand. Mo was waiting by the bench.

'Did the shifter help you choose?'

'Yes,' I said.

Mo reached for the bags. 'Good. The only thing that lot have going for them is dress sense. Let me take those.'

He slid the handles out from between my fingers. It was the first time in my life that anybody had ever carried my bags. Hell, it was the first time in my life I'd been to a boutique and come out with bags to carry.

Maybe, to anybody who didn't know any better, me and Mo looked like a regular couple enjoying a day out in North Side, sauntering along in the weak sunshine as though we had all the time in the world. It's good to pretend, sometimes. But when we got back to the hop, Oxton's hologram was waiting for us on the dash.

'Prepare to leave immediately,' she snapped. 'We have another crime scene.'

X

The sky was unbroken cobalt blue, too beautiful to be flying to another scene of multiple deaths, feeling sick to the pit of my stomach. On the distant horizon, gauzy green lights shot nebulous fingers through the stratosphere, beautiful but deadly, a legacy of the Disaster. Story was, ground zero was still unstable, and the aerosol particles that flooded the air from time to time refracted light into rainbow colours on clear days. Today was a green day, whatever that meant. Sometimes it's easier just to be afraid than to uncover the truth.

Mo, tiring of the holo-boards that shot oversize promotions at us as we navigated the traffic system above the blocks, took us half way between street and rooftop level, a perk of being Unit.

Below us, the crime scene stood out where a flea-fest of black suits pock-marked the plaza. The cordon team were still putting the bunting out when we touched down. Mo got out the hop and opened my door. My palms had begun to sweat.

In front of us, Block Seventeen was a patchwork of reflected sky. Mo led the way, but he stayed close to me, this time, averting his eyes from the rest of the Unit crowd the same way I did.

Inside, the doors shushed closed behind us. A rivulet of sweat traced down through my hair and slid onto my neck, yet I was cold. I wiped it away with the back of my hand. Mo watched me.

'OK?'

I nodded, and switched my awareness. Life lights sprang up from the floor, reception desk, and the walls.

'It's the same story as before,' I said, my voice echoing over the potted jungle and up into the mezzanine. 'Three hours. I don't see a single life light younger than that.'

Mo didn't respond.

I headed for the lift. This time, instinctively, I pressed 'up'.

We travelled in silence, and stepped out onto the top floor. The open-plan was empty, desks abandoned and chairs pulled back as though their occupants were due to return any time. At the end of the corridor, the security door was code locked. I swiped it with my Unit flash card. It flew open with a beep.

Half a mile above the city, the roof was eerily peaceful. The slightest trace of haze hung like a fine voile curtain around the evacuation hatches, blanching the surrounding buildings. I slumped down with my back against the nearest vent shaft. Mo headed past me and stood by the barrier, staring out over the city. I closed my eyes.

Thought-streams flared up around us, teeming through the surrounding buildings like a wave of North Side fairy lights. I sank down and moved between them. The closest were the clearest: some guy alone in an office watching porn on his com, hoping that the rest of his virtual conference wouldn't notice the flush on his face, or what his hand was doing underneath the table; a reception temp pissed off by her boss's failure to notice the tight-ass mini she'd poured herself into because he preferred the ditzy blonde with the big tits he'd taken on at the same time. I pushed them away and moved on. I learned a long time ago what can happen if you get caught in the undertow. I have Torches to thank for that.

It came from the East. My first impression was of black ants in formation. In my mind's eye, they resembled the Army Ants that you see in Old World books, the kind that give children nightmares, destroying homesteads and eating their way through anybody stupid enough to stay put. I sensed ranks, hyper-organised, formidable, in formation on the horizon like a seething black scar.

They vanished.

I scanned again.

Nothing.

Somebody, something within that rank, knew I was trying to listen in. They'd snapped closed like a fortified door, pulling the plug before I could get any further. I opened my eyes and cursed, softly. Whatever I was dealing with was intelligent, organised, and now, in hiding - my enemy knew that I existed, and that I was hunting them down.

In the washout, the faintest trace of something unsettlingly familiar conjured the long, dead convent nights, and the darkness that had suffocated the place when the disappearances began. It was unthinkable that anything I encountered here could dredge up my childhood, and yet it'd happened, subtly, creeping into my psyche and leaving me trembling and disturbed. I turned to face Mo.

His silhouette was motionless against the barrier, his fingers poking through the cage like a captive animal. I stood up, and walked over. I rested my hands on the grille, following his gaze out across the rooftops.

'Insects,' I said. 'That's what they remind me of. We're dealing with some kind of a hive mind.'

Mo turned his head fractionally. A sheen of sky reflected off his lenses.

'I picked them up, but they vanished. They know we're on to them, Mo.'

He turned away and walked towards the rooftop door. 'Let's go find the bodies.'

We took the lift to the basement.

The whiff of death trailed along the bottom corridor. The air temperature dropped. When Mo kicked open the screens that led into the vehicle park, I didn't have to see the bodies to know that they were close by.

They lay, bloodless and wan, stacked opposite the lift in a vehicle bay, bleep-codes and fingers and neatly-cut clothing hanging out of the pile. This time, the bodies touched the ceiling. My stomach heaved. I put one hand over my mouth and looked away.

'De ja vu.' Mo took out his com and began to scan. 'How long?'

'Nearly three hours.' My voice quavered. 'Modus operandi identical.'

I recorded the scene with my head averted. It was easier, somehow, to check the footage afterwards than it was to comb over the corpses with my eyes. A series of holo-reports ticked and fluttered around Mo's head. They riffled themselves into a virtual pile, and vanished.

'Chemical scans complete. Do you want me to call in Twenty One, Miss Green?'

'Give me five more minutes.'

The cold coming from the bodies pierced the thin fabric of my trousers. Goose-pimples ran in a wave up my legs, and my breath bloomed roses of vapour. I closed my eyes.

Impressions spun around me, faint as whispers: black wraiths flitting past, with wizened hands and shrivelled faces. Trails of dry ice that fell away like curtains around the cast-off bodies. The flash of a scalpel, a stack of packing boxes, then blackness.

Whatever happened here took place so fast, I could barely break it down into separate events. The Brotherhood peeled away in a swathe of darkness like a fog that sucked out through the windows. They moved, as one, out of the block and away from the business district to the edge of the city. At the perimeter, they vanished into the Cinderlands, drawn away like an outbound tide. The vision snapped off and my mind reeled. Instinctively, I stretched out one arm to steady myself on a wall, but I hit Mo's arm, and hung on. He didn't shuck me off.

'OK?'

I nodded, and let go.

I prodded Archives.

Reg answered too quickly, as though he'd been waiting. He was close to the camera, which had the effect of making his nose look huge and his eyes slide down the sides of his cheeks.

'Miss Green,' he said, breathless, 'we have to talk.'

'That's why I called. I have more bodies.'

Reg's eyes flickered left to right. 'Are you at the crime scene now?'

'Yes.'

Reg almost swallowed the camera. 'Show me.'

'Reginald, I have a situation. I wasn't briefed to give you a tour of the dead. I need your expertise.'

Reg stepped back and ran a hand over the hair that stood to attention above his ears, smoothing it down. 'As you wish. But we have to talk.'

'We're talking now. I've picked up something that could be vital in tracking the Brotherhood.'

'Go on.'

'A hive mind. They work as a team, with an extreme sense of order. I see them in ranks, communicating without words, almost as though they're governed by a single consciousness.'

Reg pondered for a moment, one forefinger tapping his chin. 'If we're dealing with a hive, then it stands to reason there must be a controller – somebody in charge, like the proverbial queen bee of the organic age. Do you sense anybody?'

'Not clearly. Somebody picked up on me, that's all I'm sure of. I lost them. I'm sorry.'

How could I tell Reg I'd felt something from my past, a whisper, faint as a ghost, that'd made my flesh crawl with half-remembered truths I didn't feel able to confront?

'What about the golden ram, Miss Green?'

Somewhere on the periphery of my consciousness, the ram's head glittered, half-hidden in the darkness.

'Yes. It's here.'

Reg's face moved so close to the camera that all I could see was his mouth and the tip of his nose. 'Do you want to tell Oxton?'

I ignored him. 'There's something else. The drones, the ones who actually commit these crimes – they have no life signatures because they're all dead.'

Reg's pupils flared in the shadows. 'Then this is indeed a form of neo-necromancy, as I suspected, Miss Green.'

Reg's gaze flickered over my shoulder. He craned his neck.

'Can I see the edge of the pile behind you?'

'What?'

'Feet, Green. I see feet. Dead feet. If you could turn a little to your left-'

I swung around in the opposite direction.

'Call me when you get back to HQ,' Reg scowled, 'because we really have to talk face to face, Miss Green.'

I flicked the com off and slid it into my pocket.

The lift doors pinged open. Oxton appeared, flanked by Twenty One, who disembarked with their black coats flapping. I swear one of their heels struck a spark as they stepped out the lift.

'This time they've taken out two hundred and twenty nine staff,' Oxton snapped, eyeing the bodies dispassionately. 'What have you got for me, Miss Green?'

'We're dealing with a hive mind. I've got Reginald onto it.'

Oxton swung away and began to bark orders at the men in black. When she turned back to face me and Mo, her skin was ashen, her eyes bloodshot.

'My rear end is under fire from the suits Upstairs.' Oxton spat each syllable as though she was trying to get rid of something unsavoury from her mouth. 'Particularly

Perseus. There's only so long Upstairs is prepared to wait for the definitive solution. Given time, heads will roll. Our heads.'

Mo stood with his back to the bodies. His face was devoid of emotion. What must he have seen, over the years, that a pile of corpses touching the ceiling got no response?

Oxton turned on one grinding heel. 'Follow me, please.'

The men in black had already decanted half the corpses, and were using a steri-box to collect stray items which had fallen out of the melee: an ID tag; an earring; a personal com; a single faux-leather shoe.

Oxton waited until the lift doors closed us in before speaking. 'I didn't want to say this in front of the others. We already have another crime scene.'

'What?' snapped Mo.

'I'm taking you there right now. No news has been released at present.'

Exhausted, I leaned against the lift wall and faced my reflection, my face pale, my eyes bloodshot and hollowed. I guess I looked like Oxton used to, forty years earlier.

At the next scene, something had gone badly wrong for the Brotherhood of the Golden Ram. Two office workers had been hacked to pieces haphazardly, the body parts left where they'd fallen. Blood ran down the plexi-panels in elongated smears, as though the victims were still conscious when they'd fallen. Only a handful of frozen corpses were stacked in the basement. The others were abandoned in and around lifts shafts, waxen white and drained of blood, propped against walls, or face down in the corridors. They showed no surgical marks. They were simply discarded, like over-size dolls tossed carelessly around after a nursery party.

Underneath a thin veneer of control, Oxton's flesh was grey. Her left eye muscle-ticked continually. When Upstairs bleeped her, she flinched. I turned away as she answered, and headed for the front of reception, where a glass screen opened out onto a view of the plaza. Mo followed. A hop waited out front, its rotating light the same scarlet as Oxton's nails. I plaited my fingers behind my back. My palms were damp. Mo stared outside in silence.

'They were interrupted, weren't they? Bodies abandoned in the corridor? Organs left un-harvested? This isn't the Brotherhood's usual MO.'

Movement on the plaza drew my eyes. Several rows of short, squat men wearing blue uniform disembarked from a Unit carrier, and headed towards the cordon in drill formation.

'Who are they?'

'Seventy Seven,' Mo said. 'Oxton brought them in.'

Seventy Seven didn't look particularly friendly. They didn't look particularly human, either. Their faces were identical.

'Clones?' I whispered.

'Worse,' said Mo. 'Droids.'

Seventy Seven marched towards the cordon in rows three deep, their black boots beating an even meter. The double door opened, letting in a waft of air loaded with the scent of hot metal and hop fuel. The men passed me and Mo without a glance, and headed for reception. Oxton emerged from behind the screen of greenery looking wan. She beckoned to us from the faux-leather desk. Seventy Seven stopped in neat rows in front of her.

'We need to ascertain what this scene can tell us,' she addressed us all. 'The Brotherhood is as unfathomable as it is deadly. The assailants access their target buildings unseen. They strike quickly. They leave, with the body parts, before an alarm is raised. But this time, something went wrong.'

Oxton flicked out a hologram of two clumsily dissected bodies. Seventy Seven shuffled into a circle around a spectral rope of entrails that hung over the back of a chair. I looked at my feet.

'One of our mutilations,' said Oxton. 'These victims were cut down in situ, at their desks. Instead of flash freezing them, instead of using clinical cuts to remove the desired organs, the Brotherhood botched it. We also have the bodies in the corridors.'

She replaced the image with one of a dark-haired young man lying face down by a lift door. The colour and texture of his skin resembled something I'd once refused to eat in a Veggie No Death – waxy, and pallid.

'These bodies are drained of blood, but no organs are removed. This is not the modus operandi we've come to expect of the Brotherhood. What I need to know is, why were things different this time, and how can this knowledge help us to stop them?'

Oxton signalled to the first rank of Seventy Seven, who led off in single file towards the stairwell, unravelling row by row until they'd disappeared. She waited until the door closed before turning to Mo and me.

'Right now, Miss Green, I need your insight like I've never needed it before. If not, at this rate, River City will be depleted within a year. The extrapolations are simply horrendous.'

'We need to predict the Brotherhood's next target,' said Mo.

Oxton's mouth set in a grim line. 'Exactly. But without fully understanding the Brotherhood, we clearly cannot.'

'The answer is in the Cinderlands,' I said.

Mo's eyebrows shot up. Oxton's nose wrinkled with distaste.

'Could you please explain yourself?'

'The hop driver on North Side, the one who disappeared into the Cinderlands - I know he's connected to this somehow, because-'

'Miss Green has a theory that may not hold water,' Mo cut in.

Oxton swung around to face him.

'We're collecting the facts to present to you as soon as we're able, Oxton.'

Mo spoke quickly, the words tumbling out of his mouth. Behind the shades, I sensed him flash me a warning glance.

'You will both remain on continuous call until you have the information you seek. And you will report back to me immediately you discover anything at all.'

Oxton turned to the exit, her heels snapping on the tiles. Outside, the speed hop powered up, its lights pulsing. The door whooshed closed, leaving Mo and me alone.

I faced him. 'Why did you do that? You didn't want me to be the one to tell Oxton I'd got a handle on it, did you?'

Mo tipped his head back, as though staring at the ceiling, but behind the shades, I knew his eyes were closed.

'There's a right way and a wrong way when dealing with Oxton. You have to learn that, Miss Green.' He focussed on my face. 'Perseus is a suit, and his personal symbol is turning up at frozen crime scenes. Oxton can't openly admit that somebody Upstairs could be involved. Add to the mix the fact that the Nemesis Corporation are big Unit buddies, and you've got an extremely unhealthy cocktail. Before we try to convince her of anything, we need hard evidence.'

'But-'

'Trust me.'

Mo began to pace along reception, staring blindly at the desk and the walls as though he hoped something, anything, would spring out at him.

'If Perseus is involved,' he said, 'this needs careful handling. Nobody can touch Perseus, but the Unit can't stop people deciding where to invest their credits. Once the public get wind of the situation, he could be bankrupted. And when Perseus gets pissed off, the bad feeling trickles down the chain and affects us all.'

Outside, Oxton's hop lights vanished into a cloud-bank. The plaza was empty. The cordon, and the silence, were the only signs that anything was wrong.

'Not only that, there's the possibility that Quimper could be involved.'

'Another suit from Ninety Nine?' I said, confused. 'Why Quimper?'

'Rosie must've warned you about the rivalry between certain Unit departments.' Mo phrased it as a fact, not as a question.

I shrugged. 'I guess she mentioned something. I didn't really take much notice.'

'Take it seriously,' he said. 'Quimper and Perseus are both Ninety Nine but they're far from on the same side. Quimper backs some causes, Perseus backs others. It's more than just petty differences - these guys hate each other.'

'How does that affect us?'

'It isn't impossible to believe that Quimper is framing Perseus to get one over on him.'

'And these people are entrusted with running the known world?' I said, incredulous.

Mo laughed mirthlessly. 'You're either for Perseus, or Quimper, but never both. I've known suits above Eighty get too much in the pocket of one, and get bumped off by the other.'

'Who are we for?' I asked, stunned.

'Perseus, of course,' said Mo as though I was stupid.

He joined me at the window, and stared out beyond the cordon, his thumbs hooked into his pockets. 'We collect the facts first. You have to understand that Oxton has personal reasons for wanting us to avoid the Cinderlands.'

'Am I allowed to ask?'

Mo looked uncomfortable. 'She lost somebody out there. A long time ago.'

'On an operation?'

'Yes.'

'And I shouldn't know about this, right?'

Mo shrugged. 'Those of us who've been around a long time know the story. It isn't spoken about openly. Not anymore.'

'So Oxton's even older than she looks?'

Mo's lips twitched. 'Much older, Green.'

'With the same enhancements you have?'

'More or less.' Mo grimaced. 'Cellular rejuvenation. End of conversation.' He pressed his lips together and stared outside, where a wind teased the leaves of the fake-trees in the plaza, pulling them in ragged circles as though it couldn't decide which way it wanted to go.

I ran one hand through the bank of ferns that stood next to main desk, listening to the susurrus created by the fronds against my fingertips. Random objects littered reception: a personal com; a neatly stacked pile of holo-zines; a scattering of virtual business cards. Each of them wore the life-lights of human contact, from people who were now dead.

I got out my com and leeched the Block's security report. The brotherhood had entered undetected, as always, and not through the main entrance. The slightest blip in a scanner told me exactly when they'd been disturbed. One of the bodies in the lift had set off an auto-alert when central computer had recognised a human form with no life signature.

'Mo, what time were we on the roof at the last crime scene?'

He shrugged. 'Two hours ago.'

Two hours ago, I'd cast my mind out towards the Brotherhood. I'd locked on and felt them retreat like an outbound tide, with no idea that, at the time, they were conducting another mass-harvesting elsewhere.

'I did it,' I whispered.

I wheeled around to face Mo, who was searching the ferns as though for a hidden clue.

'I locked onto the Brotherhood and scared them. That's why they ran. They weren't responding to a physical interruption. They were responding to a psychic interruption.'

The brotherhood had been frightened away by me.

XI

Back in HQ, Rosie was waiting at reception, her arms full of digi-pads. Her eyes flickered up and down Mo before she turned to me, and smiled too cheerfully.

'I have to take you to Twenty One,' she said.

'I'm supposed to be meeting Reg.'

Rosie's smile didn't waver. 'Not until after your appointment with Twenty One.' She moved in close and lowered her voice. 'You do know what this is for, don't you, Jess?'

The tag.

'There's no need to look as though you're enjoying yourself so much,' I snapped.

Rosie took a step back, her expression wounded. 'I'm not programmed to take pleasure from circumstances like this, Jess.'

Like hell, Rosie.

'But for what it's worth, in the spirit of friendship, I won't take it personally. I understand you've had a rough time out there, what with the bodies and everything.'

Sometimes, silence is the best policy.

I followed Rosie into the nearest lift. Mo had conveniently disappeared, just melted away into one of the corridors. Bloody coward.

We took the ride in silence. Outside Twenty One's glass frontage, Rosie gestured for me to palm print.

'You told me they'd stopped my access,' I said.

Rosie cocked her head to one side, her curls bobbing over her shoulder. 'I sorted it, Jess. Go ahead.'

Inside, the lab coats shot curious glances in my direction. Rosie and me were ushered into a small room with blinding white walls and high-tech medical equipment banked in the corners. A surgical couch sat in the middle.

'The doctor will be with you in just one moment,' computer said.

I turned to Rosie. 'Are you staying to hold my hand?'

'Wouldn't miss it for the world,' she beamed.

I glowered at her. Rosie cleared her throat.

'Actually, I can wait outside and pick you up later. You're in safe hands. If you'd rather.' She lowered her eyelids and looked up at me through a thick fringe of lashes.

'Rosie.'

'What?'

'I'm the wrong sex to fall for fluttery eyelashes.'

Rosie turned away. 'I'll wait outside.'

The door slammed.

'Please, lay on the couch,' said computer.

I eased myself into the seat and plaited my fingers in my lap. The walls were stark. I'd just got round to examining the ceiling tiles when a tiny woman with limbs like sticks and jet black hair came into the room, carrying a tray.

'Miss Green. You're here to have your tag fitted, right?'

She smiled, as though it was the most natural thing in the world, like booking a table at a restaurant or having a dental. I didn't respond. She pulled a small table up next to the couch, and laid the tray on it. In the centre was a box.

'Please tell me that isn't it,' I said. 'The bloody thing's huge.'

She laughed. 'The tag is inside the box. It's tiny. You won't feel a thing.'

The doctor pulled on a pair of surgical mitts that sucked down flat onto her skin, giving the surface a sparkly sheen. She flipped the lid off the box and took out the tag. It was tiny, and flesh-coloured.

'This is the latest technology. It's what we send field operatives out with. Amazing what can be done these days.'

I crossed my legs. 'Where exactly are you going to put it?'

She glanced at my locked knees and smirked. 'Externally. Behind your right ear. Lean forwards, please.'

The surgical mitt squeaked against my skin as she brushed my hair away. Her fingers pressed down, hard. A sharp click sent a burning pain down my neck. A second later, it fizzled out.

'That's it. All finished.' She stepped away.

I ran a finger over the tag. It lay flat to my skull behind my ear. I tapped it with a nail.

'It might be tender for a couple of hours, especially if you fiddle with it. Your hair will start to lay naturally around it before close of play today. Nobody will be able to see the tag. All I need you to do is palm print this file to say you understood the procedure.'

I sat up. The doctor shoved a digi pad under my nose and I reached for it instinctively.

'Thank you, Miss Green. The tag cannot be removed by yourself. Any attempt to do so could damage your nerve endings and your skull. It will also send an alert to Unit security, who will take immediate action. The small print is in the file you just signed.'

She smiled, too brightly, and picked up the tray. Hell, she could've been a waitress reading the specials menu, for all the emotion in her voice.

'I'll send the secretary back in.'

I didn't watch her go. I hooked a nail underneath the tag and pulled. Pain flashed down one side of my neck. I grimaced and checked my finger nail. The underside was smeared with blood. I pulled a wipe from my jacket pocket, and dabbed behind my ear. The door opened.

'You missed all the fun,' I said, checking the wipe.

A scarlet stain bloomed the surface like an Old World ink blot on paper, intense, velvety, a colour I would've like to paint my apartment walls.

The door clicked closed.

I looked up.

Mo stood in the corner, his hands in his pockets.

'What the hell are you doing here?'

He walked towards the couch, slowly, his eyes averted.

'I told Rosie she could go. I thought it better if I came to get you myself.'

I dabbed behind my ear.

'You got what you wanted,' I said.

'You're bleeding.' Mo stood next to the couch and peered at the wipe. 'Please tell me you haven't tried to pull it off already.'

'Thanks for your concern,' I said, but the sarcasm was lost on him.

'Where is it, right ear?'

'Uhuh.'

I rolled the wipe up into a tight ball, and closed my fingers around it.

'Can I look?'

I jerked my head to one side. Mo's fingers ran over my hair, brushing it back, so unexpected that I flinched even though the sensation wasn't unpleasant. Angry, I threw the wipe at the recycler. It missed and landed on the floor.

'Happy?' I said.

'No,' said Mo. 'It's not like that.' His hand fell to his side. 'That's why I came. I didn't explain properly, and I realise it's upset things between us.'

I swung my legs over the side of the couch.

'I have to be able to protect you, Miss Green. The tag is just in case you... forget yourself. Only for as long as it takes you to get used to living this way. Then it will be removed. I promise.'

'Thanks.'

'Seriously. You think you can take care of yourself, but the truth is, you can't.'

A mirthless little laugh bubbled out of my throat. Mo moved away from the couch, leaned against the wall and folded his arms. Against the white background, he stood out like Old World decoupage, sharp-cut.

'You don't realise just how vulnerable you are.'

'Do me a favour, Mo. Don't patronise me.'

'You think I don't understand how difficult this job transition is for you.'

I ignored him. Mo sighed.

'You remember when I told you I did some background checks?'

'I remember you bluffing,' I snapped.

Mo took his com out of his jacket pocket and tapped it. The Eye on the ceiling died, its lights fading to blackness.

'How did you do that?'

'It doesn't matter. I bought us a little privacy, but it won't give us any more than forty seconds before the alarm kicks in.'

Reflected in Mo's shades, the couch stood out like a gash, split by my figure, hunched and frail-looking.

'I know about the other tag, Green.'

Instinctively, I glanced at my left ankle.

'Before you ask, I haven't seen the scar. I know about it from Archives.'

Shocked, I stared up into his face.

'And don't tell me there isn't a file. If there wasn't, I wouldn't know you stripped your own tag, would I?'

I crossed my right ankle over my left, as though I could forget. The night of the fire, it had all happened so quickly: a sharp knife, a strip of torn fabric, a stolen quickskin wipe from a client who was careless with his personal belongings. A client who might've died in the fire, for all I knew. Then, freedom, whatever that had turned out to be, through the wet streets, hiding in back alleys...

Mo studied my face. 'The file came from an interview Fifty Three did with a guy who called in a fire at a sexclub. He gave his occupation as club manager and his name as Luca. I didn't make the connection until you mentioned Luca that day in the Cinderlands. That, and the name of the club. Put together, everything fell into place.'

What a fool I'd been.

I'd spoken about Torches the day we'd gone through the broken barrier, following Graham and his vanishing hop. The day Mo had caught me off balance and got under my guard.

'Luca,' I said.

My voice came out as a whisper.

Luca who'd looked after me. Or that's the way he'd sold it, back then, a lifetime ago. The memory of his face was already beginning to fade, blurring his features at the edges, as though he might've been made from modelling material and left on one side before he was properly finished. I hadn't realised I'd forget him so readily.

'The file contains a description of a young woman who could be you. She had longer hair and significantly less clothing, but...' Mo shrugged.

Behind my right ear, the flesh began to throb.

'Didn't you realise that the manager of Torches put out a seek-and-find on you?'

I should've known it wouldn't be easy. Luca always threatened he'd never give up on a girl who got away.

'They never knew my full name,' I said. 'Except Saskia.'

'And of course, your bleep-code was never connected to anything.'

'I'm not stupid.'

Mo shifted his weight from one foot to the other, as though he was warming up to saying something difficult.

'What?' I said.

'The tags they used at Torches were nowhere near as sophisticated as the tag you have now. That's why you managed to strip and ditch the old one. Please don't be fooled. If you try with this one, the consequences will be severe.'

Consequences? How could they be any more severe?

What a fool I'd been.

I was already hunted, even before I'd got a price on my head with Thirteen.

'By law, you were, and still are, the private property of the club, Miss Green. You had no right to leave without buying yourself out of your contract.'

I swung my feet. Mo stepped away so I didn't kick him.

'I wasn't paid a wage. How could I buy myself out of anything? I never even signed a contract.'

'You know as well as I do that the contract would've come into effect automatically when you accepted lodgings at the club.'

'What are you trying to say?'

Mo hesitated. 'I know it's wrong, Green. I don't like this any more than you do, but so long as the Unit has its hands full fighting shifters and terrorists and trying to monitor the Cinderlands, there will be no time for legal bills protecting sexclub hostesses. You know how it is.'

I stopped swinging my feet. 'Has Oxton made the connection?'

'No, and she never will because she's got better things to do than trawl random files. I'll never tell her.'

'What about Reg?'

Mo shook his head. 'You gave a false name for the club in your employee file. Reginald may have read it, but without mention of Luca or Torches, he won't make the connection either.'

I stared into my lap at my hands, the flesh bluey-white underneath the intense lights. 'And if Luca finds me?'

I looked up, into his shades, into the eyes I could never see.

'I didn't want to tell you this, but I'm going to. Luca didn't just put out a seek-and-find. He attached a large bounty to it, for your safe return.'

A rush of panic swept my skin. 'Safe' and 'return' weren't two words I'd put in the same sentence, where Luca was concerned.

'Now do you understand why I'm trying to keep you safe?'

I stared at my feet, focussing on the flash of white that reflected off the toe of my boots.

'What the hell happens if he finds me, Mo?'

Mo's face gave nothing away, but when he spoke, there was something akin to a smile in his voice.

'If Luca comes looking for you, then he's got to get through me first.'

Mo flicked his com and the Eye powered to life, spinning momentarily as though disorientated. Its lens did a close-up of both our faces before it settled.

He slipped the com into his jacket. 'Do you understand?'

I nodded.

He took my arm and helped me off the couch. 'I have to take you to Reginald, now.'

I felt sick to the pit of my stomach. As though sensing it, Mo said:

'I can't come with you, unfortunately. I have to be elsewhere. But I will come fetch you afterwards. Just com me.'

I nodded, miserably.

At ground floor, Reg was already waiting in the lift, his face hidden behind his ocular mask. I stepped inside. Mo stood in the corridor and watched the doors close us in, his face impassive. Reg dimmed the lights and pulled off his mask.

'I didn't ask to see you for another crime scene interview, Miss Green.'

His eyes glittered like black beads. I leaned back against the wall, exhausted.

'I'm quite happy for you to record your summary in the comfort of your own apartment, then send it to my com.' Reg's stare was intense, screwing holes in my face. 'You may have realised that I have an alternative motivation for our chat in Archives.'

I didn't respond.

'You used my access to search the memory vaults, didn't you?' Reg's voice held a note of triumph. 'I know this because my com was turned off. I never turn it off. It didn't take me long to work out that you'd deleted an action request, Miss Green. The computer, once prompted, confessed everything.'

Reg slid along the interior wall of the lift towards me. I stepped backwards into the corner.

'You can't deny it for much longer,' he whispered. 'I have something you want, Miss Green. I've invited you to make the most of my position. But you haven't given me an answer. Yet.'

Reg leaned so close that my reflection stared back at me from the centre of his expanded pupils.

'You owed me a favour, Reginald. Remember the steri-sack? The wriggling things? I put them in your briefcase just like you asked. When I shut the lid I noticed that your com was on. I figured it was only fair to call payback.'

'The idea was that we'd trade, not that you'd simply help yourself to what's mine.'

I started to speak but Reg cut me off.

'You didn't get very far, did you? Don't tell me you don't want more. Everybody wants answers, Miss Green. And I can provide them.'

The lift stopped and the door shot back on the hinterland of Archives.

'I'm a little concerned about your price,' I said.

Reg stood in the open doorway, grinning, dwarfed by a backdrop of storage towers.

'Why would you have a problem with my price? It's a fair proposition. Nobody need know. In fact, I'd prefer it if they didn't. It's illegal, for a start.'

We were alone, countless floors below reception, too deep in the bowels of HQ for security to respond to a distress call.

'I'm only asking for a little,' Reg wheedled, 'now and again. I don't expect something every time you come downstairs. In fact, if you prefer, I'm sure we could arrange to 'trade' on the higher floors. We'll just have to be careful that nobody catches us, that's all.'

The top of my back pack, which I'd raised like a body shield, hit me under the chin. 'Come come, Miss Green, surely you're not coy about business?'

Even at Torches I'd never had to put up with this.

'I can't trade information for sex,' I snapped. 'You just don't do it for me, OK?'

Reg jumped back like a mugger bitten by a taser. The file in his hand shot into the air, sending an explosion of ancient paperwork and several computer files and a bleep code in cartwheels around his head. The stuff rained down around us. Reg fell to his knees, scrabbling.

'I can't believe you just said that,' his voice quavered.

'What, that you don't do it for me?' I shrugged, lowering the backpack. 'I'm only being honest.'

Reg choked. I put my pack down and stooped to help him pick up the mess.

'Don't,' he said, snatching a file from my hand.

I stood up. Reg scooped the remaining bits and pieces together. When he'd finished, things were poking out of the file haphazardly. The ruff of hair above his ears stuck out at random angles.

'You don't understand,' he said, backing out into an aisle.

'There's no need to explain. You've been down here for years, you get lonely, and when you find yourself in the company of a young woman, your hormones take over, blah

blah blah. It's nothing I haven't heard before. Let's forget all about it, shall we? We'll probably laugh about it one day.'

Reg was sweating profusely. The snakeskin tattoos around his neck and wrists looked red and mottled, even in the half light. He backed away, catching things as they fell from his arms.

'No,' he said, 'you really don't understand, Miss Green. When I asked you for favours, I didn't mean... I wouldn't have... I mean I could never... you're the wrong species, for heaven's sake!'

We stared at each other in silence.

A bleep code fell from Reg's file to the floor. Neither of us made any move to pick it up. The storage racks seemed to close in around my head.

'I wasn't asking you for that kind of favour,' Reg said at last.

I fiddled with my backpack straps. 'Oh.'

Reg turned away and began to walk, quickly. I followed at a distance, feeling his embarrassment drift behind him like the wake of a boat in the water, smacking into me with every step. It was the first time I'd felt anything from Reg at all - it was the first time he'd forgotten to block.

'Reginald,' I said, but he didn't stop.

When we reached Reg's desk, he put the file down and sat at his com. He smoothed his hair. His fingers were shaking.

'I can see that I owe you an explanation,' he said, his eyes averted. 'I collect things. But it's not permitted. Not the things that I collect, anyway. I have a small secure pod here, in Archives. I use it for storage. I've picked up all sorts over the years. When I asked you to trade favours, I thought that perhaps you might be willing to add to my collection.' Reg breathed a great, trembling breath. He spun his chair round to face me. 'I don't get out of Archives very often, Green. I know it's my own fault, but I don't really fit in upstairs. So I collect. It keeps me in touch with the cut and thrust of life above basement.' Reg scratched at the tattoo on his neck, which stood out like a livid scar. 'I like to touch the things that people like you get to handle every day. Things that carry the scent of criminality, of death, of... well... crime scenes.' He shrugged.

I sagged against the table, my legs weak with relief and embarrassment.

'You should've explained,' I said. 'All this time, I thought you wanted something different.'

Reg tried to muster a laugh, but it came out as a pained squeak.

'Oxton thinks I've had too many years down here. Says I should get above ground more. Thinks my social skills have deteriorated. She's wrong, of course, but I can't afford to fan the flames.'

'Reginald,' I said, reaching out to give his hand a quick squeeze, then changing my mind, aware of the tremor in his lids as he watched and tried to pretend he hadn't noticed, 'forget about it.'

Reg snatched his hands off the table and folded them in his lap. 'It's illegal to take anything from Unit crime scenes, unless you're above Eighty Nine, and they aren't open to trading because they have total access to everything, and better collections of their own than I'll ever get. You were my big hope, Miss Green. I haven't had anything for years, and then you arrived. And now, I suppose that chance has gone up in smoke like the Disaster Zone…'

I dropped my backpack on the desk and sat on one corner. 'I've only been here a few months, Reginald. And like you said, it's illegal.'

Reg looked at me from underneath lowered lids. His expanded pupils took everything in, somehow seeing around me and through me at the same time. Freaky.

'Let me show you something. I'm going to give you a taster of what could be yours.'

Reg scooted his chair underneath the desk, and accessed the memory vaults.

'Now, let's see... you mentioned your mother.'

'I didn't,' I said. 'I never do.'

Reg's eyelids closed from side to side. 'I'll phrase it differently. When I checked the log you deleted, I found her. In a little more detail than you did.'

Reg spoke into the voice-reader in a tongue I'd never heard before, full of hisses and clicks. A holographic record spun onto the table between us. In one corner was a photograph of my mother in a formal ID pose. She rotated in front of me, close enough to touch, for the second time in days. My stomach somersaulted all over again.

'When I saw the holo-photo, I knew there couldn't be a mistake. You're her double. Even though the official records say this woman had no children.'

'What?'

Reg nodded. 'See for yourself. It's here, look. I can get further, but there are risks.' His eyes hardened to blackglass. 'All you need to do is tell me to go ahead.'

My mother's face, insipid as a watermark, was superimposed over Reg's head. Had I been born when this holograph was taken? Had my brother? Why had she given birth to us, just to leave?

'Would it really be so much to ask?' Reg said. 'I could find out why your mother was investigated, what happened to her all those years ago at Fort Burnout...'

Reg vanished the file. The com sucked it in, snuffing it out like a glow lamp. She was gone.

'I have something in my backpack that you might be interested in,' I whispered, my voice strangely flat.

I pulled it onto my lap and unzipped the front pocket. I slipped my hand inside, ignoring the tremor in my fingers, and felt for the steri-wipe I'd used on my head at the second Brotherhood crime scene. With my hands still concealed in the bag, I pushed the wipe into a sample sac and quickly sealed the tape. Reg hovered over my lap. I drew the sac out. His hands crawled towards it. I snatched it away and slid off the desk in one quick movement. Reg made a funny choking sound and half fell onto the desk, his palms outstretched.

'I'm breaking every promise I signed up to,' I said.

Reg nodded, his eyes fixed on the sac. 'If it's any consolation, you won't pay the price alone. But the label is blank…'

'I didn't get chance to fill it in.'

'I need to know, Green.' Reg's voice trembled.

I picked up my com, tapped the screen, and discharged a label. Reg snatched the sac and held it against the reader on his com. The screen flashed.

Steri-wipe. Crimescene 48692. Subject of investigation suffered minor venous rupture to head.

'Thank you, Jess,' Reg's voice was soft with awe. 'If you wouldn't mind, I'd like to put this in my secure storage. You can see yourself out. When you're down here next, I'll give you fair exchange. Right now, I need a little privacy…'

Reg slipped away down an aisle without a backward glance. I swear his eyes hadn't left the sac once. He pattered somewhere out of earshot singing softly, a strange little tune unlike anything I'd ever heard before.

I turned away, and headed for the lift.

*

By that evening, Oxton had closed down every business building in the district. Reel after reel of Unit tape festooned each block frontage like fete bunting. The last hop to leave was the one carrying me and Mo. We rose up through the darkness into a starless sky, the entire West side of the city spread out beneath us like a ghost town.

XII

Reg burst onto my coffee table as I opened my living room blackout, sending Claws off the settee in a flash of black and white fur. I was still wearing my pyjamas. My hand crawled up to the throat button.

'Reginald! Can't you organise some kind of advance warning?'

'I'm sorry, Green,' Reg's eyes rolled around my living room until he found me. 'I forget how much rest you people need. You're permitted to put me on voice-only if you don't want me to see you in a state of indecency.'

Great.

I sat on the settee, and shoved my mug of Earl Grey onto the coffee table. A cloud of steam billowed into the hologram.

'Have you just put hot tea underneath me, Green? And please, can you engage the blackouts? The sunlight is frying my retina.'

'Reginald, why is your face on my table so early?'

'Last time we spoke, I'm afraid that I was so uncharacteristically… overcome… that I neglected to ask you something.'

I hit the blackout control, plunging the room into darkness. 'You have that needy look I've begun to recognise, Reginald. Shall we cut straight to the chase?'

Reg wiped a tear from one cheek with the back of his hand. 'I need your report on the newest Brotherhood crime scene. Immediately.'

I picked up my tea and blew steam into the hologram. Reg flinched.

'Please don't look at me like that, Green.'

'I sent you the report last night,' I said.

Reg feigned surprise. 'Really?'

'You're a terrible liar That's not why you're here, is it?'

His eyelids fluttered. 'It's a favour. Just a very small thing. I'm putting together a file, on the Disaster Zone. So far, there isn't much in it. I was wondering if you could help.'

I leaned back and rested my feet on the coffee table, right under Reg's nose. He moved his chair back.

'Why should I be able to help you with a file on the Disaster Zone?'

'Because according to your personal record, you were brought up there.'

I pushed my mug onto the table. 'I was not brought up in the Disaster Zone. I spent a while on the edge of it, in a far part of the Cinderlands. There's a big difference.'

Reg fiddled with his waistcoat buttons. 'I'm sorry, Miss Green. It's just that I'm aware you spent two years in an orphanage-'

'Convent. Not orphanage.'

'My misinterpretation,' Reg inclined his head. 'Miss Green, is it true about the nightbeetles?'

An image sprang into my mind before I could stop it, the creature rising like a leviathan out of the sands, sinking onto its short legs and hurtling towards me, a grotesque pantomime animal, moonlight glancing off its shell, squeaking with excitement.

'I don't have time for this.'

Reg didn't notice my glance towards the tip of the nightbeetle pincer I kept on the mantle piece, the bit that I'd taken with me in my leg, to be fished out years later. I never knew what made me keep the damn thing – maybe the disbelief on Sister Enuncia's face when she realised I'd survived the attack.

'Do the Spider People really offer girl-children as sacrifices so the beetles will leave them alone?'

I shook my head. The Spider People were the only adults I remembered fondly from my time at the convent. At least they hadn't carried cat-o-nine-tails and dispensed punishment on a daily basis.

'What utter drivel. I have work to do,' I said, reaching for the control.

'Do you have any mementos? Skulls from real creatures? A bottle of sand, perhaps? A piece of nightbeetle pincer? I've heard tell they make amazingly good cutting knives...'

I held up the com and poised my thumb over it.

Reg spread his fingers in a gesture of surrender. 'I understand you're on work-from-home to prepare for the cocktail event, Miss Green.'

'Twenty Seven got us in. They convinced Barber's financial wing that me and Mo are a husband-and-wife team worth a fortune in cloned protein. Now all I have to do is learn the legend.'

'Good luck,' Reg smirked.

'Apparently, I have a hyper-warehouse full of meat-growing frames that I've grafted several hybrid species onto. My speciality is selecting the best genetics for high yield.'

Reg raised his eyebrows. 'Tasteful. Let's hope that Veggie No Death aren't on the guest list.'

'That isn't what's worrying me – it's the fact that Mo did a senior guardian job for the Nemesis Corporation a couple of years ago. They're connected to Barber, and to the Unit. What if somebody recognises him?'

Reg smiled, his hologram stretching at the corners. 'Relax, Miss Green. Senior level Unit employees aren't precluded from having their own business interests. Mr Okoli will simply be playing himself, with a dash of fiction. You are the one who needs to worry.'

'Why?'

I slid further into the cushions, clutching my tea. Reg's eyes followed the cup to my lips.

'Your sexclub. I don't know what class of establishment it was, and I don't wish to enquire, but what if one of Barber's super-rich guests was on your client list at one time?'

He had a point. At Torches, you never knew who you were entertaining. Some of the most perverse clients were so rich they thought money could buy anything... and at Torches, it generally could.

I stared at my reflection in the mirror on the opposite wall. Three quarters of my hair had been cut off. My clothes were now plain. My faketan had gone, leaving my skin naturally pale. The heavy stage makeup, the false eyelashes and bold colours which had completely transformed my face at Torches, seemed like a lifetime ago. I'd said goodbye to that look the night I'd run.

'Don't worry. Nobody will recognise me.'

'Well I hope you're right. Oh, and one other thing. Oxton requested that the movement sensors on the broken perimeter be taken down.'

I jerked upright. 'What? I'm tracking the hop driver who's been using the Cinderlands as cover.'

Reg shrugged. 'Oxton is more concerned about the Brotherhood, and since there's been no movement at the perimeter for several days, she's shelving the case.' Reg shifted uncomfortably in his seat. 'I'm sorry. Not my decision, I'm afraid. A repair team were dispatched this morning. The breach should be fixed by now.'

Reg disappeared before I had chance to reply.

Great.

Graham had vanished into the desert, taking his old hop and his lifeless cargo with him, and now Oxton had closed my best line of enquiry, by sealing off the Cinderlands with Kevlar panels. The vaguest sensation of unease wound itself around my shoulders. I shivered, involuntarily, watched by the cat who sat in the entrance to my bedroom, his pupils huge and his tail flicking.

I killed the blackout, flooding the room with daylight, and opened up my desk com.

At noon, I showered and dressed. The sea-green gown that Raphael had packed in tissues hung on the back of my water-blaster door, its long, gauzy layers frighteningly insubstantial. I'd never been a 'guest' at a cocktail party before. I wanted armour, not skimpy fabric. I pinned my hair up on top of my head, about as far from the Torches look as possible, and used a little mascara and some clear lip balm. The one thing I'd rescued from my previous life was a long black shawl that Aunt Connie had given me. The night I'd run, I'd taken it to cover my half-naked body, and the wound on my ankle. I shook it out and wrapped it around my shoulders. The dress was almost completely hidden. The shawl fringes hung over the last inch of pale hem, tickling the tops of the sparkly shoes Raphael had chosen.

Outside, the whir of a hop engine told me Mo had arrived. I stared out the window. The vehicle was a private one, not Unit. Smart. Now we looked super-rich.

I hated to admit it, but Mo looked stunning in a suit.

'Are you ready?' he asked as I fastened my harness.

I nodded, once, and we took off.

*

I'd heard rumours about our host's wealth, but nothing prepared me for the show. The entrance hall to Barbervil Towers had a chequered floor and a vaulted ceiling. Gloved waiters distributed cocktails, and housemaids wearing black discreetly relieved the guests of jackets and wraps. A cloud of excitable emotions assailed me, so I blocked them, consciously, in the same way that colleagues who know I'm an empath block me. The guests' cerebral shouts became whispers and then ceased to be, although I remained aware of them, simmering only just out of reach, waiting for me should I forget myself and relax. Overhead, a poster hung from the minstrel gallery, with the words 'The Eternity Fund: Together Forever' picked out in holographic fireworks.

Mo took two glasses of sparkling water from a passing waiter, and handed one to me. I took it, and sipped, watching him from the corner of my eye. The splash of starched white between the jacket lapels showed off his brown skin to perfection.

Around us, security were stationed at regular intervals. Several wore X-ray eye-lenses, and one had a portable hormone-scan unit.

'Get the kit,' I whispered.

'Don't draw attention to yourself, Jess.'

An aerial Eye dodged between the bodies, jerking itself above head height and skirting the perimeter of the crowd. A couple of guests ducked and laughed.

'You used my first name.'

Mo smirked. 'We're married, remember?'

Around us, the guests fluttered like birds. I switched my awareness, but they drowned me out: too many people, too much excitement, and too much alcohol. Reminded me of some of the longer nights at Torches.

'Try to look more natural,' Mo spoke close to my ear. 'For goodness sake, ditch the funeral cape. And loosen up. You're as stiff as a board.'

Piqued, I slid the cloak off my shoulders. A housemaid appeared at my arm and took it. He even called me Mrs Okoli. As he walked away, the hem caught on one of my strappy shoes. My foot jerked and I stumbled, slopping water onto the tiles. The glass flew out of my hand and landed on the floor with an expensive tinkle, which brought the bodies around us to that awkward kind of silence which is always much more fun if you're not the one who's caused it. As I hit the floor palms first, my clip snapped off and spilled my hair out, the broken halves scuttering away over the tiles.

The silence only lasted a second.

Several hands wrapped themselves under my elbows and around my arms, and hauled me up. Between the curtains of hair that fell over of my face, I spotted a man with a hooked nose and thin lips, taking in my dishevelled appearance with an intensity that suggested he was trying to work out where he recognised me from.

'She must've hit the drinks too fast,' somebody whispered. 'Look at the puddle on the floor. I'll bet that's neat Old World vodka…'

The housemaid who'd taken my wrap, which was still attached to my heel, sprang back to my side muttering profuse apologies. I struggled to balance, snatching his arm. Female hands smoothed my dress out, and fell away. The guy with the hooked nose turned away just as I remembered the last time I'd seen him, the night with the ripped fabric and the raw fish. Sheesh, he looked different with his clothes on.

My first cocktail party.

I shoved my hair back with one hand, teetering precariously on the heels. Mo stood in front of me, staring down into my face.

'Oh, Jess,' he said, I couldn't tell whether with amusement or disappointment.

Or maybe a bit of both.

Around us, the crowd had started to talk again, animatedly. A waiter appeared with a sonic mop and began to neutralise the spillage. Somebody pushed another glass into my hand, and a second housemaid appeared. He stooped down to pull the fringe off my heel, glaring at his colleague. The pair of them melted into the bodies.

Mo reached out and brushed a strand of hair behind my ear.

'Are you OK?'

'I'll live.'

His fingers lingered, trailing my jaw before he dropped his hand.

'You look much better with your hair down.'

The line he'd traced along my skin tingled.

Was he acting, or did he really mean it?

Chryst, it was simpler treating the whole thing as a business transaction - at least you knew where you stood.

'And you look... different... in a nice dress.'

I didn't know what to say, so I looked at my feet. The sequinned shoes glinted from underneath my hem.

Mo laughed. 'I don't know how a girl with your background manages to blush at such a small compliment, but you're definitely blushing, Green.'

That's when I saw her.

A woman with brown hair wound into a tight chignon appeared through the crowd in front of me. Her pale dress fell in long, gauzy folds to her feet, and twisted around her legs as she turned to face me. I grabbed Mo's wrist.

'That's her.'

Mo tensed. The aerial Eye dipped in close, its lens extended into my face. I did exactly what I'd been told in my basic training, and stared right at it. It scanned, retracted, and shot off across the room.

'Are you sure?' he whispered.

'Of course I'm sure.'

She dipped behind the bodies.

Mo shook his head. 'That's Shem Barber's daughter, Alicia. She runs his labs – and she's the face of The Eternity Fund. Unmarried, workaholic, fabulously intelligent and totally dedicated to her father. To my knowledge, she's never put a foot wrong.'

Mo didn't bother to mask his confusion.

'She may simply be a connection,' I whispered. 'I can't pick and choose the things I see, Mo. The vision could've been leading me to her father, or to somebody else close to her. At this moment, I have no idea.'

Alicia appeared again, working her way through the crowd towards us. My broken hair-clip sparkled between her fingers.

'Mrs Okoli? I believe this is yours.'

'Thank you. And I'm so sorry about the glass.'

Alicia waved a well-manicured hand. 'Don't worry about it. My father has too many to count. I keep joking I'll auction some off when he isn't looking.'

Her scent enveloped us, something heady and unusual distilled from priceless real flowers.

'It's lovely to see you again, Miss Barber,' said Mo.

'I thought I recognised you,' Alicia smiled. 'Of course, a senior guardian. You looked after a little meeting of ours a couple of years ago. Please, let's dispense with the formalities. We should all be on first name terms.'

Her dress, her hair, the eyes... Alicia Barber was the woman I'd seen in my visions, but right now, I was so hyped, my sixth sense was screwed. I wouldn't have known if she spent her evenings watching armoured grandmas laser-frying unarmed children on the Geriatrix show, or embroidering cushions for sick pauper babies - I couldn't see any further than the maquillage.

Alicia turned to face me. 'How's the new bio-flesh hybridisation policy suiting your production, Jess, isn't it?'

I took what I hoped was a casual sip of the drink in my hand, and almost gagged because it wasn't water. Some idiot had given me neat vodka. Mo tensed at my elbow.

'Very well, thank you,' I said, stifling a cough. 'Although our lab was already one step ahead when we created a hybrid that wasn't governed by existing policy.'

'I'm so pleased to hear that. Tell me, Jess, do you have hobbies and interests outside the business?'

'Vintage hops,' I said, pinning a smile to my face. 'I've just started collecting. I don't suppose you could point me in the direction of anybody who might be able to help?'

'Of course. The amount of old machines my father has stacked up in compounds all over the place, he really should be doing something about moving them on. Maybe you can tempt him with an offer.'

She laughed, a tinkling little laugh with just a hint of vulnerability, the kind men find terribly attractive. It'd certainly worked on Mo. Behind the shades, his eyes were eating her up.

'My father has stockpiled hundreds of vintage hops,' Alicia continued, laying one hand delicately on Mo's sleeve. 'Your wife really would be doing him a favour – me, too. One of my duties is to account for all the company hardware. It gets tiresome.'

Alicia peeled her hand off him slowly. Mo glowed unashamedly and without blocking.

'Where does your father keep his hops?' I said.

Alicia hesitated, her eyelids fluttering. 'The Cinderlands. My father is pushing for an agreement to spread his lab facilities out there. We're not allowed to say anything official yet, but Ninety Nine have been so helpful, I'm sure it'll all be under license soon.'

A security guard appeared and whispered something in Alicia's ear. She smiled and nodded, her pendulous earrings sweeping her shoulders.

'Please, excuse me.'

Mo watched her rear end disappear into the crowd.

On the minstrel gallery, a man in an expensive suit addressed us through a hover-mike that shadowed his lips.

'Shem Barber,' Mo whispered. 'Perhaps Alicia was connecting us to him? He is her father, after all.'

'I never make snap decisions,' I said softly. 'I'll give you all I can, I promise, but I can't pretend this is clear to me yet.'

Barber was impossibly well preserved, considering his age. His dark hair showed a controlled peppering of grey around the temples, designed to show wisdom, I guessed, rather than decay. Something told me he was already using whatever The Eternity Fund was trying to sell today. Beneath the minstrel gallery, Alicia stared up into her father's face, listening intently, turning once to seek me out and give me a quick wink.

'Looks like I've made a new friend,' I whispered, acknowledging Alicia with a nod.

'Milk it,' said Mo in an undertone. 'Use her.'

If Shem Barber was involved with the Brotherhood, what did he stand to gain from it?

Why would the city's richest philanthropist darken himself by getting involved in mass murder?

That's when my sixth sense started to kick in.

The buzz of the crowd, the thinly-restrained excitement and avarice and the huge egos, began to peel away in gauzy layers, revealing an essence that wound its way between the bodies in the hall, percolating upwards from below. Whatever it was, was subtle, and invisible, and had the feel of partially-masked life signatures that weren't entirely human.

Something was underneath us, in the basement of Barbervil Towers.

I upped my awareness.

Whatever it was, it was trapped.

The life signatures slid into a jumble and retreated, sucking away as a holo-presentation began above our heads. In it, the face and body of an old woman tightened and brightened until she'd turned back the clock by forty years. The crowd gasped and cooed, but I couldn't shake the unease that stroked the nape of my neck. Ignoring the voice-over narrative, I slipped away from Mo, and out of the crowd. He didn't notice me go.

At the back of the hall, one of Barber's famous collections was on display. I guess the rich get bored of spending on useful stuff. I pretended to read the information screens which sprang out in auto-grams. Beneath my feet, the life signs flickered and faded.

Somebody moved behind me, so close that a jacket button brushed the naked skin of my shoulder. I spun around, too fast, and swayed on the heels. A hand reached out to steady me. Shem Barber stared down into my face, his dark eyes amused.

'You're more interested in my collection than you are in learning about the Fund?'

'I-'

Barber laughed. 'It's all right. In fact, it's quite refreshing. Mrs Okoli, isn't it?'

'Please, call me Jess.'

Barber took my hand and squeezed it, whatever lemony scent he wore enveloping us both. Torches had taught me that powerful men always had plenty to hide, but most of them didn't have such a flawless mental block in place as Shem Barber.

'Tell me, Jess, what do you think to my archaic little curios?'

I hesitated.

'You don't like them, do you?'

'In my opinion, rarity doesn't always equate with beauty, Mr Barber.'

When he laughed, it sounded genuine. 'Please, call me Shem. It's not often I meet somebody prepared to speak their mind. The older I get, the less often it seems to happen.'

Barber turned away and beckoned to a waiter. Moments later, she re-appeared carrying a tray heavy with two crystal flute glasses and a genuine Old World bottle.

'Champagne.' Barber took the bottle and filled both glasses. 'Real Old World. An absolute luxury, but one I insist on, from time to time. Especially when I'm in good company.'

'In a real glass bottle?' I reached out and stroked the label, running tiny beads of condensation into streaks. 'I've never touched an Old World bottle before. Aren't they supposed to be fragile?'

Barber held the bottle aloft. 'If I dropped this, it'd end up the same way your glass did earlier, in a thousand little pieces on the floor.'

I flushed and took the drink. Barber was enjoying teasing me; I could see it in the set of his mouth, which turned up at the corners. Bubbles rose in inverted cascades up the sides of my glass. Barber's body angled towards me, just a little too close, the lapel of his jacket touching my arm. He turned away in one quick movement and snapped his fingers, twice, in the direction of the serving staff. Footsteps made away hastily. Moments later, a butler returned with a silver tray. Whatever sat on top in little pieces was so hot it was still sizzling.

'Have you ever tasted real meat, Jess?'

The butler lowered the tray between us. Maybe it was primeval instinct, or perhaps sheer greed, but the smell of those little glossy squares speared onto Kevlar skewers was enough to drive me to distraction.

'Go on,' said Barber, 'take one. I promise you won't be disappointed.'

I reached out, pulled a skewer off the pile, and sniffed. 'This is a first for me. I've never had fresh meat before.' Not even in the convent, I almost said, and then didn't. 'What is it?'

Barber helped himself, draining a little cooking juice onto a bed of wilted leaves that formed the base of the dish. 'An Old World animal called cat. This one was cloned especially for the table.'

I tossed the skewer back onto the pile. Claws might've been over-rated as a pet, but the idea of dicing him up and forcing scraps of him onto sharp metal spikes didn't do much for my appetite.

'Jess? What is it?'

I took a step backwards.

'You haven't even tried it.'

'They didn't eat cat in the Old World, Mr Barber.'

Barber laughed, incredulous. 'Don't talk nonsense. My researchers worked on Project Cat for four years before beginning the building process. Cat played a huge part in the lives of the Old Worlders. Limited references remain, but my people searched them all out carefully.'

I shook my head, a little dizzy. 'No, you're wrong. Cats were pets. Some of them survived the Disaster.'

I ran the hand that'd held the skewer up and down my dress as though cleaning off the intention to eat it.

'Pets?' Barber's voice was short and sharp. 'I'm unaware of this. What was a pet?'

'A kind of companion animal.'

Barber looked bemused. 'Myth and legend, surely? New Worlders attempting to turn small creatures into Old Worlder's familiars, just because they were ignorant enough to believe in witchcraft. They were far smarter in the old days than most people today give them credit for. Plus, the brain size of small mammals is incompatible with them being able to converse.'

'No, they don't – I mean didn't – talk back.'

'Then what was their function?'

I shrugged. 'Sleeping on your air-hammock. Something to groom. You have to feed them and give them water.'

'And pet gives what, exactly, in return?'

Bemused, I thought of Claws. Feisty cattitude and the odd turd on the water-blaster mat when he was seriously pissed off?

'I don't know,' I said, truthfully. 'Maybe the Old Worlders didn't like being alone.'

'Take it away,' Barber hissed to the butler. 'And next time I request real meat, bring racoon instead.'

The butler scuttled off leaking a huge sense of embarrassment. The tray in her hand oozed the fragrance of cooked cat all the way to the exit, thickening in my nostrils, cloyed with the sickly sweetness of death.

'I've never heard of racoon, but I'll give it a miss if you don't mind,' I said, queasy.

'Of course. I'm so sorry to have offended your sensibilities,' Barber inclined his head. 'It appears that your knowledge of certain facets of the Old World excels mine. I would be most interested to chat with you about your sources, at some point.'

I forced a smile. Perhaps it was best if I neglected to mention Claws. Just in case.

One shirt-sleeve had pulled free of Barber's wrist. It glinted with an old-fashioned cufflink in the shape of a ram's head.

'You like my cufflinks?' Barber pulled his jacket sleeve further up.

'Yes. Are they real gold?'

'They are.' He rotated one arm slowly, setting the faceted eyes glinting. 'The stones are rubies, some of the last in existence from the Old World. The cufflinks were a gift from Perseus. He's my daughter's godfather, and a family friend. And a big backer of The Eternity Fund, obviously.'

A shoal of bubbles shimmered up my glass, set off by my trembling hand.

Barber pulled his sleeve down. 'Alicia tells me that you collect vintage hops.'

'It's a new thing. I have very little experience.'

'I've an entire decommissioned fleet you could take a look at any time you like, Jess.'

'That's very kind. Are you so welcoming to all your guests?'

Barber tilted his glass and, just for a moment, his block slipped. A flash of white wall, a security grille, and a laser lock reeled through his thoughts. He'd visited the basement just before the party started. It felt like a laboratory of some kind. The scent of whatever was down there hung off him like a shroud: pain; distress; violation. The impressions spooled off into darkness and the sensations cut out.

'No, I'm not so welcoming to all my guests. Not everybody gets to share my champagne, either. But I like you, Jess. You're up front. It's a rare quality, these days.'

Barber's gaze roved my naked shoulders just as Alicia spun past the edge of the crowd. She and her father caught each other's eye, and a flash of anger lit up between them.

'Is the champagne not to your taste?'

I blinked.

'Jess?'

'I'm sorry...' I took a gulp, half-emptying the glass.

Barber reached for the bottle and topped us both up.

'Tell me about your science labs,' I said.

Barber smiled indulgently. 'I have labs all over the settled world. At the moment, genetics are my thing. That, and anti-ageing, of course.'

'Do you have a lab facility here, in your home?'

Barber's expression flickered. 'Yes, I do. It's in the basement, but it isn't in use at the moment.'

'Really? Do you have plans for it?'

He hesitated. 'Yes. Do you know anything about horse racing, Jess?'

'You mean race-droid-horses?'

'No. I mean real horses.'

'They don't exist.'

'Wrong. I have the DNA of several old bloodlines downstairs, safe in my lab. Thanks to the Old World, I'll soon have the only stable of real thoroughbreds in existence. I suppose you could call them... pets.'

I choked on my champagne. 'Here? In River City?'

Barber laughed. 'No. My private lab will take care of the genetics, but I have a facility elsewhere to build the animals. I'm shipping the components out at the end of the week.'

'But if you're making real horses, what will you use them for?'

'Racing, of course.'

I pushed my empty glass onto the tray. 'What a criminal waste of protein. Surely they should be harvested for meat grafting.'

Barber spluttered into his glass. Two security guards stared in our direction. An Eye zipped around the side of the room and surveyed us from a discreet distance.

'Spoken like a true businesswoman.' He pulled out a white handkerchief, and dabbed the corners of his mouth.

'Do you ever give lab tours?'

Barber poked the handkerchief into his top pocket. It slid down, leaving one perfect corner exposed.

'No.'

'And you never make exceptions?'

Barber's lips pursed and then stretched into a smile. 'Perhaps. But not today.'

'What a shame. I'd love to know what horse DNA actually looks like.'

The holo-presentation erupted into an orchestra, which appeared on the minstrel gallery and began to play.

'The River City Phil,' said Barber. 'They recorded a twenty minute slot especially for this party.'

The musicians were shrunk to fit on the balcony. Their bodies were vapid, the back wall visible through their instruments.

'Do you think it's true, that in the Old World, the musicians really used to play together, in the same hall, at the same time?'

Barber shook his head. 'There's a lot of rubbish spoken about the Old World. I bet they weren't as backward as everybody seems to think.'

The crowd began to loosen, small groups breaking away, chattering over the music.

'Please, make my apologies to your husband, Jess. I have something urgent to attend to before the Q and A session. It's been a pleasure.'

Barber pressed his hand into mine, and melted away. Mo appeared from the back of the crowd, and stared after him.

'Are you OK?'

I nodded.

Mo stared into my face, and down at the glass in my hand. 'What are you drinking?'

'Something called champagne. It survived the Disaster, in real glass bottles – god knows how.'

He snatched the glass, sniffed the contents, grimaced, and pushed it back into my hand.

'Are you drunk?'

'Of course not.' I slid my arm into his. 'Come on. Let's circulate.'

Afterwards, we headed outside to the hop park with an armfull of Eternity Fund holo-literature. I didn't have to turn around to know that Shem Barber was watching us leave from a first floor window. His eyes burned holes in my back, and sent a little frisson down my spine.

Inside the hop, I sagged back into my seat, and flicked the harness onto auto-fasten as Mo did a spy-bug sweep.

'We're clear. And well done, Green.'

I glanced at him.

'I'm serious. You handled it perfectly.'

'Apart from the falling face down and smashing a priceless Old World glass. But I don't think anybody noticed, do you?'

Mo laughed, a real deep laugh that bubbled up from somewhere inside. Barbervil Towers shrunk beneath us as we pulled up into the clouds and swung around.

'Now, tell me everything.'

'Shem Barber is conducting experiments in his private basement lab. I think Alicia knows, and I don't think she's happy about it.'

Mo swore softly.

'Whatever he's got down there, it's pretty mashed up, in more ways than one. Unfortunately I couldn't persuade Barber to offer me a tour.'

Below us, the river had a greenish tinge. The hop's shadow cut the wavelets.

'But no experiments are illegal providing you've got the right permit,' said Mo.

'Something's telling me that these aren't standard experiments, and that the Unit might not know anything about them.' My spine prickled as I remembered the anguish emanating from beneath my feet, and the ambiguous life signatures. 'I don't think Barber is simply using human detritus to cut and paste under license. I get the feeling he's doing something that crosses boundaries even the Unit doesn't have a handle on.'

'Did you get anything on the Brotherhood?'

I shook my head. 'Barber wears cufflinks in the shape of the same golden ram I saw at the crime scenes – Perseus's golden ram. Maybe Barber is moving out into the Cinderlands to keep his work very private?'

We continued in silence, descending through a cloud bank onto HQ roof. We landed, and Mo slid off his headset. The underside caught his shades and just for a second, I caught a glimpse of his lower lid, and his long, black lashes. He put the headset on the dash.

'What?'

'I'm sorry, I... I just wanted to see your eyes.'

'Why?'

I shrugged. 'It's normal, isn't it, to want to look into somebody's eyes?'

Mo ignored me and slid out of the hop. I followed, wobbling above the strappy heels.

Rosie was waiting outside the lift door when we arrived at ground floor.

'This is for you,' she said, pushing something small into my hand. 'Rescued files. From the guy who jumped in North Side.'

'Thanks.'

I leeched the contents of the chip onto my com, then flicked it into the laser recycler on the wall. Dante's surviving files were mostly music, stuff with a heavy beat and not much tune, just the sort of thing I could imagine him dancing to. He'd taken out a subscription to a dance com-zine, and sent a few sexually explicit messages to a variety of guys including Leo, but the jump had mashed most of his stuff beyond recognition. I checked 'recent activity' and found a post from The Wellbeing Clinic. Leo had received it two days before he'd died.

The file was blanched and incomplete, with only a few phrases clear: ...no way of knowing that the liver... treatments for diseases such as this... team care councillor... unfortunately cannot provide this service free of charge...

I cursed under my breath. I'd found Dante's clinic, all right, and the reason for his jump off the balcony as well. Dante's liver, the liver that had been illegally taken from Martinez, and was supposed to save him to start a new life, was a dud. I hit delete and kept walking. Poor bastards, both of them.

'Green!'

The voice was a hiss. It came from between two vending machines in the lobby. Ahead, further along the corridor, Mo and Rosie were talking, their heads close together. Reg stepped out of the shadows.

'I've been waiting to catch you. I don't trust personal coms. You never know who's listening in. It's about your mother's file.'

An Eye on the ceiling nearby rotated in our direction.

'I couldn't get any further, I'm afraid,' Reg whispered. 'Access is restricted. I thought it was a matter of just finding the right door, but it's not. There's a total blocker on your mother's information.'

'Why?'

'Because your mother's file is with Perseus.'

Perseus.

That name kept cropping up like a broken Clone It toy.

Reg fiddled with his face mask and pulled out a handkerchief to mop a tear from one cheek. The Eye on the ceiling began to glitter, a row of lights pulsing underneath the lens. I passed my bleep-code over the vending machine.

'All is not lost. I have something for you.' Reg selected a withered-looking fruit. 'It isn't what I hoped for, but it's something. What do you know about your biological father, Green?'

'Nothing. I can't ever remember him being mentioned.'

'Well, I have a lead.'

Frustrated, I jabbed the selection screen. What use was the identity of a man I'd never met? He and my mother must've been estranged since before I was born.

'I have two words for you: Paradise House. It's here, in River City. The place doesn't advertise, and there's nothing on public access that will tell you what it does. I suggest a visit. In person.'

Reg reached into the service recess and pulled out his fruit, a cross between a strawberry and an apple. One corner was bruised. He wrinkled his nose.

'And that's all you can tell me?'

'The name was at the top of an old document appertaining to your mother. The rest of the document had been severed and sent Upstairs. It's fortunate that somebody made a mistake. That's the best I could do.'

I reached inside the vendor, and pulled out a shake. 'Thank you.'

I jabbed a straw into the carton lid. Something pink and viscous erupted through the hole and slid down the sides.

'Let me know what you turn up.' Reg polished the fruit on the breast of his shirt, leaving a smear on the fabric, then hurried away to the lift.

The Eye turned to follow him. I sucked on the straw, hard. The shake was too sweet. On the way past reception, I chucked it into a disposal chute.

XIII

Paradise House sat on the wealthy side of town, on a tree-lined avenue heavy with the scent of real sap. Horsetail ferns splurged luxuriantly over the high walls. If they weren't real, they were expensive fakes.

'This is weird,' I whispered.

'This is Unit,' said Mo, flashing his ID card at the main gate scanner. 'What do you expect?'

'And you can just get me in?'

'A senior pass can get you in anywhere, but it can't keep you somewhere you shouldn't be. You probably have half an hour tops before they catch on they have an uninvited guest.'

'And then?'

The laser wire flicked off and the gates began to open.

'Let's worry about that later. Just make sure you get what you came for in under half an hour. And Green, you're safe in there. Unit property is probably the one place I can leave you.'

'Thanks, Mo. I mean it. You didn't have to do this.'

Mo retreated onto the pavement, where the breeze riffled a delicate shower of leaves into the air. I wanted to pick up a handful to keep (there wasn't an android enforcer around to stop me) but the set of Mo's face told me now wasn't a good time. I stepped inside, and turned towards the main entrance, feeling his eyes never leave my back.

Reception was plush. The interior was real hardwood with just a whiff of illegality about it, with velvet sofas that would've been more at home in a shifter penthouse. A receptionist with immaculate makeup flashed a smile that'd definitely seen work, and proffered me a seat. From a table in the centre of the room, a com-zine shot a story feature towards me.

'Switch off,' I said.

I wasn't in the mood.

'Everybody gets nervous on their first visit,' said the receptionist. 'It's perfectly natural. Oh, I'm sorry, I don't appear to have your name...'

'Green. Jess Green.'

'Miss Green. Your tour will begin in five minutes. We're only waiting for one other lady.'

I glanced around. Nothing in the room carried a holo-display or graphic literature that told me what Paradise House actually did.

A little woman in a grey suit with big, tearful eyes arrived at reception desk.

'I'm Alice,' she whispered.

Alice had the same high cheekbones and freckled skin as Saskia. The memory of her hurt like a punch in the ribs. I had to pick up the courage to com Saskia, soon, but I couldn't risk Luca finding out.

'Then we're ready to start,' said the receptionist. 'Please, ladies, follow me - my name is Marianne and I'm here to give you the best advice I can about the important choice you're about to make.'

Together, we took the lift. The door pinged open on a lobby filled with tables and chairs. Soft music played in the background. In a corner, two women huddled over Old World menus, whispering conspiratorially.

'The menus detail the current donors we have on offer,' Marianne said. They were set on every table. 'Some clients prefer to choose this way.'

'Is - is there another way?' I said, sneaking a glance inside the closest menu, which revealed a flash of naked flesh.

'Of course,' said Marianne. 'If you follow me, I'll take you to the viewing gallery.'

We passed through another set of double doors, and entered a light-filled room with a domed roof. Behind a glass partition, a line of muscled young men worked out on various fitness machines. Their blank pouts suggested their side was mirrored, but that nobody had bothered to tell them they had an audience.

'Some clients prefer to view in the flesh,' said Marianne, gesturing towards the men.

I loosened my collar. The room was unbearably warm.

'The menus are a bit of a gimmick, a bit Old World, but if viewing face-to-face isn't for you, then of course you can view by electronic profile. We have viewing booths featuring the donor's specifications.'

'Of course you can see the donors naked if you'd prefer. Would you like me to take you to the sauna?'

Panicking, I glanced at my wrist com. Alice fluttered her hands to her mouth, stifling a giggle.

'That's perfectly fine,' said Marianne. 'It is quite usual for a first time visitor to require a second or even a third visit before feeling more at home.' Marianne steered me and Alice towards another door. 'I understand it's all a bit emotional at first, but I can assure you that every one of our clients thinks that Paradise House is the perfect solution to add that magical something to your life.'

Magical something?

These women were either buying themselves toy boys, or looking for something more specific....

Donors.

Of course.

This place wasn't about relationships.

It was about fertilisation.

My mother had come here to conceive.

Aunt Connie's voice jumped out of my distant memory: If anybody asks about your parents, just tell them they're both dead. It will stop any embarrassing questions. OK?

We'd come full circle, back to reception, where the dark wood and horsetail ferns suddenly looked fake and overblown, and the red sofas might as well have come from a shifter clearance warehouse.

'...and of course, if you didn't want to plump for the IVF option,' Marianne whispered, 'there is the natural method ...the Pleasure Rooms are this way...'

Marianne indicating several doors leading off the lobby. All were marked 'Private'. Had I started life behind any of them?

An alarm sounded from reception. Marianne flinched. Almost immediately, a woman emerged from the lift opposite. She had small eyes and a pointed nose. Whoever had taught her to use a mental block had taught her very well. She scowled at Marianne and turned to me.

'Miss Green, I assume? Follow me, please.'

We travelled up one floor in silence. In the corridor, two uniformed guards stood either side of a door marked 'Dr Dana Dawkins'. Both were armed with enough kit to scan, sample and laser-cook a small army. They didn't move as we passed between them.

Inside, Dr Dawkins slid into a high backed chair, and directed me to sit in a smaller one facing her desk.

'Miss Green. You cannot seriously believe that our security wouldn't pick you up, coming in here unannounced?'

I didn't reply.

'What I fail to understand is why your bosses didn't go through the regular channels. Upstairs still audit me regularly, and expensively. They had no need to send an undercover.' She folded her hands on the desk and eyed me beadily.

'I'm not here on Unit business.'

'Please don't take me for a fool.'

'I'm looking for information.'

Dr Dawkins squinted. 'When I had my team check, they discovered that your personal records have been virtually erased, Miss Green. You are Unit, from an unspecified department with a high level of security. Therefore, by definition, I don't trust you.'

'I'm with Thirteen, but that's not why I'm here.'

'Thirteen?' Dr Dawkins sucked in her cheeks. It heightened the effect of making her look like a small rodent. 'There is no such department as Thirteen. Some foolish Old World superstition, so I was always told. Last time I was at HQ, the entire thirteenth floor was given over to storage.'

'Things have changed. Thirteen is new - we're Crime Solutions. But my enquiry is personal in nature. It has nothing to do with my employer.'

Dr Dawkins tipped her head to one side and regarded me shrewdly.

'Is donor sperm your main business?' I said.

'That and the stress toys.'

'Tell me how Paradise House works.'

Dr Dawkins pointed to a mission statement on her wall. 'We started more than twenty five years ago. In those days, the premises were privately owned. By me. I merged with the Unit under enforced license. We're fully vetted and approved, now. Paradise House provides a route for the discerning woman to attain pregnancy discreetly, using the male of her choice.'

'As for our advertising policy, I'm not in breach of guidelines,' Dr Dawkins said stiffly. 'We do not advertise. Everybody who comes to Paradise House is referred by word of mouth. We're below the radar. Except, apparently, when it comes to paying taxes.'

Dr Dawkins pulled something out of a drawer in her desk. She unfolded her hand. Sat in the palm was a small, pink, hairless creature, with a delicate face and two big, glassy eyes. It crooned with delight as she stroked its head. So this was the other half of the Paradise House business:

the genetically engineered stress toys Rosie had told me about. As though sensing my surprise, the creature turned its eyes on me. Its nose twitched, the small whiskers vibrating as it tested the air. It began to purr.

'SafeSperm is our trade name, but our hotels go by individual titles. Paradise House, Nirvanah Beach, Club Heaven; all located strategically, all empowering wealthy women with positive fertility choices.'

Professor Dawkins pointed to a holo-photo of a man in Old World spectacles, beside her desk. The words 'Matteus Finkler - Unit Business Award' were engraved in the frame.

'Matteus was my business partner until he retired. Without him, I wouldn't be sat behind this expensive desk. Then again, without me, he'd still be working on the difference between long ears and short ones.'

'What can you tell me about the early days, say, twenty five years ago?'

Dr Dawkins looked startled. 'Why?'

'Because the nature of my enquiry relates to your early practices.'

Dr Dawkins shifted uncomfortably. She tapped the stress toy with a manicured nail. It flinched.

'If you know about my license revoke, there's no need to play games. That was a long time ago. I went through investigation, I served my suspension, and here I am now. It was the Unit who started me off again.'

'With Mr Finkler as your sidekick?' I gestured to the photo on the wall.

'They weren't about to let me go it alone again, were they?' a flush of anger crawled up Dr Dawkins's neck. 'Still, I can't complain. Matteus has been good for business. In many ways, I'm better off now than I was in the old days.'

'Even with Bill and Ben stood outside with their huge laser arms?'

'My security arrangements are private,' Dr Dawkins snapped.

'I'm not interested in your license. I want to know about your records.'

'They took everything away.'

'Ok. Let's do it without the files. Tell me about the men.'

Dr Dawkins was speechless for a moment. 'The men? You mean the donors? What on earth would you be interested in them for?'

'I'm trying to... trying to trace somebody.'

Dr Dawkins began to laugh. It was high pitched, and a touch wild. 'Nobody tries to trace a donor, not then, not now. It simply isn't done.'

'But what if one of the fathers-'

'They are not fathers, Miss Green,' she snapped, 'they are donors. They lend their gametes to provide a service. There it ends.'

'So there's no way that-'

'No. The systems were encoded then as they are now. It's impossible to match an embryo with a donor once insemination has taken place. The files are scrambled.'

'Then what about afterwards, when the donors retire?'

Dr Dawkins dug her nails into the stress toy. It squealed. I flinched.

'We don't allow our donors a retirement in the traditional sense. It's the only way we can be sure that nobody will try to claim. What would become of SafeSperm if, half a dozen years down the line, a client of ours found herself in sticky financial circumstances, and decided to pursue her donor for maintenance?'

I shrugged.

'Exactly.'

She squashed the stress toy face down into the desk. Its naked skin squeaked on the varnish, and its legs thrashed. After a short struggle, it wrenched free and scuttled behind a plant pot where it cringed, sobbing softly.

'The donors are released when their contract expires.'

'And they just walk out the door?'

'They may leave the premises… just not in the same molecular order that they walked in here.'

'What?'

Dr Dawkins reached for the stress toy, which had squeezed itself between the plant pot and a file box. She hauled it out by the tail.

'Come now, Miss Green, there's no need to be squeamish.'

The toy swung like a pendulum from her fingers, wriggling. She flicked it, hard. It whimpered. She responded by whacking it down on the desk. Its body landed with a thunk, the skin reddened and blistered in patches, the delicate little mouth bloody. It lay still.

'You… you killed it?' I said, incredulous.

'They're genetically engineered,' Dr Dawkins replied. 'The important parts will be recycled. We prefer not to think of it as death.'

'But it whimpered… it was afraid of you. It had feelings.'

Dr Dawkins smirked. 'The addition of my empathic gene makes the stress toys more lifelike, and much more of a pleasure to play with. Ingenious, don't you think?'

Stunned, I sat back in my chair.

Dr Dawkins forgot the stress toy and ran her fingers delicately along the underside of an orchid. 'So, you want to know what happens to the donors. You see this plant? Retired donors can remain here, eternalised in our gardens, or they can leave the compound bagged up as a resource. We like to think of it as putting something back.'

Chryst, my father was probably pushing up roses in the private gardens.

Dr Dawkins picked up the motionless stress toy and hurled it into a bin underneath the photo of Matteus Finkler. It hit the side with a clang and slid down into the detritus, its eyes glazed, an expression of horror frozen on its little pink face.

'I'll tell you exactly why I came,' I said, 'just please... please don't get another one of those things out.'

Dr Dawkins folded her hands on top of the desk. Her nails gleamed like predator claws.

'I last saw my mother when I was ten years old. I have reason to believe she came here, to the original Paradise House, before the Unit took over.'

'I've had many clients. Why would I remember your mother?'

'You might not. Her name was Abigail Tempest Green. She would've been here twenty four years ago. She had a daughter.'

Dr Dawkins's cheeks blanched and her lips went slack. She stared at me without blinking as though time had stopped, and we were in a bubble, suspended, just the two of us.

Her fingers pulled at her top button.

'I – excuse me, Miss Green.'

Dr Dawkins reached inside her desk drawer and pulled out a bottle of calmers. She slipped three in her mouth and reached for a canister of compressed water that sat on the desk. The hiss of the stream went through me.

'I haven't heard from your mother in many years,' she said at last, her voice weak. 'I do remember her, unusually, because of the circumstances surrounding her visits.'

'Circumstances?'

Dr Dawkins's lips quivered. 'Women who come here are desperate for children. Some of them already have spouses, some don't. Your mother fell into the don't category. Just let's say it was very difficult for her to pay for the treatments.'

'She was a laundry assistant. She wouldn't ever have been able to pay for treatment at a place like this.'

'Which is why I remember her. Ladies in your mother's circumstances made special arrangements.'

'You provided the treatment free under a condition, didn't you?'

Dr Dawkins inclined her head. A plethora of tiny capillaries chased like crazy paving across the whites of her eyes. Something came down behind them like a Kevlar airlock, sealing whatever she was thinking behind it impenetrably. 'All I can confirm is that I treated your mother on several occasions but she miscarried every time except once. She had a daughter, nearly twenty three years ago...' her eyes searched my face. 'My work stopped when the Unit took my license. Believe me, Miss Green, if you are Abigail's daughter, then you are safer knowing no more than that.'

Shaken, I tried to focus on Dana Dawkins's block in the hope that it would crumble, and that she'd reveal something, anything to help me understand what she meant, but I couldn't: my sixth sense was drowned out by my own shock.

'Did you know I had a brother?'

Dr Dawkins leaned forwards in her seat, her eyes searching my face.

'He was born six years after me,' I said. 'It looks like nature had the final word. We were separated at the convent.'

'The convent?'

'Near Fort Burnout. He vanished one night.'

He vanished one night.

It all sounded so deceptively simple, abbreviated into four words that skipped the nightmares and the loneliness and the constant, exhausting futility of unbroken hope. I sat on my hands so I couldn't reach for the button around my neck.

The Doctor shook her head, slowly, and tipped it into her hands, muttering something – it could've been a curse, or a prayer, I couldn't tell.

'A few days ago, somebody dropped a faked memorial card off at my secure pod at HQ,' I said, taking the card from my pocket and pushing it across the desk. 'It has my mother's name on it. Do you know why anybody might do that?'

Dana Dawkins reached for the card, running her fingers across the front. Her hand trembled. She pushed it back over the table towards me.

'I'm sorry. I wish I could help you, truly. But I can't. It was a lifetime ago. Where have you been, all these years?'

'After the convent? I was brought up by my aunt. We moved around.'

Dr Dawkins reached into a drawer for an inhaler. The delicate lapels on her blouse collar trembled as she clamped her lips around it and sucked. As she withdrew it, something moved behind her eyes, like a tremor, something from long ago that she quickly quashed. She rubbed the bridge of her nose, and blinked as though trying to clear a memory.

'You didn't have an aunt.'

'Of course I had an aunt,' I snapped. 'Why else would she have taken me in?'

Dr Dawkins pushed the inhaler back into the drawer and closed it.

'Miss Green, just in case I... remember anything, would you kindly leave me your private contact details?'

Just for a second, the Doctor's block dropped, and she resounded with notes of deep sorrow, like a huge cathedral bell that continued to hum long after it'd last been struck.

I pulled my com out.

'Put that away. Let's be discreet. Give me a paper copy only, please.'

'Paper?'

'Yes. Nobody would think to look for paper. I have to be careful. I'm sure you understand.'

I turned the memorial card over and fished a laser pen out of my backpack. I wrote, and slid it across the table. Dr Dawkins picked it up and ran her fingers over the script.

'Give me a couple of days,' she said, sliding the card underneath the base of a potted palm that sat on one corner of her desk. 'I need a little time to access some archived material. I prefer to do it in secret. I'm sure you understand.'

'Thank you,' I said.

'Marianne will be waiting downstairs to show you out.'

I stepped into the corridor. Behind me, the office door closed with a soft displacement of air. The security guards hadn't moved. Their eyes burned holes in my back as I walked to the lift.

Back at reception, Marianne flashed me a look of fury.

'I'm sorry, Marianne. I didn't mean to get you into trouble.'

She struggled with a smile. 'Allow me to escort you to the door, Miss Green. Please, do listen to the endorsements before you leave. You'll find them in the foyer. And remember that at Paradise House, you'll be welcome to view again any time. That all-important decision isn't to be made lightly.'

I had to take my hat off to her for professionalism.

In the foyer, the plummy tones of an over-elocuted woman told me that without Paradise House, she would have been forced to Will her life savings to the Unit. Now, apparently, she had triplets to fight over them.

By the time I reached the drive, I was running.

I didn't get very far.

A tide of people in hats, scarves and clumpy boots were gathered around the main gate. Banners and placards bobbed up and down, and voices rose in agitation. I slid to a halt, scattering gravel.

'Take the side exit, Miss Green,' said computer from a speaker somewhere in the foliage. 'Follow the lights.'

A hidden runway of tiny beacons throbbed through the gravel in the direction of a small exit beyond the lawn. As I reached the gate, a man's voice yelled: 'Say no to genetically engineered stress toys!'

Female voices began to chant: 'Ban the toys! Ban the toys! Ban the toys!'

'Thank you for your visit,' said computer from the gate finial, springing it open whilst warning me I only had three seconds to get through if I didn't want crushing to death.

Across the other side of the street, Mo stood by an electro-cab, his laser drawn. I raised one hand in acknowledgement. He radiated relief. From the edge of the crowd, a plump girl clutching a bunch of leaflets hurried towards me and thrust one under my nose. A hologram of a dismembered stress toy leapt into my hands, blood dripping from a severed limb.

'It's cruel and inhumane,' the girl snarled.

Her name badge, stuck onto lumpy boobs, said Mel.

'We are here today to bring Dr Death to justice, and to re-home the thousands of stress toys we believe are inside Paradise House, suffering.'

Holographic blood dripped from the leaflet onto the pavement.

'It isn't too late to join us, sister,' Mel said. 'We're going inside. When the security staff concentrate on the assault at the front, our men will penetrate the rear.'

Behind her, Mo, who'd circumvented the crowd, shook his head and looked at the sky.

'Those toys are the prisoners of their own misfortune,' Mel snapped, her fabulous frontage undulating. 'Trapped in packaging, waiting to be opened and tortured by wealthy, pampered Unit employees who have nothing better to vent their spoiled spleens on.'

Mel's open face told me that, until recently, she'd been shagging one of those self-same wealthy, pampered Unit employees behind his wife's back. Still, it's not for me to moralize.

'I mean,' she spat, whacking the leaflets into one palm, sending a cascade of holographic sparks fizzling into the air, and Mo onto the balls of his feet, 'can you imagine putting something small and pink to death for your own amusement, and then opening another packet and pulling out its replacement?'

'I've never really thought about it,' I lied, remembering the thugs from Fifty Seven.

Rosie told me they recorded the screams of the stress toys they pulled to bits, then replayed them in their coffee breaks. They had a 'squirt chart', too, for whoever managed to get the blood furthest with each dismemberment.

A blacked-out Unit multi-carrier appeared overhead, one of the new kind that run further and faster on fewer compression canisters. The protesters scattered. Mo took my elbow and steered me towards the electro cab. The hop landed, and the crowd rushed it, jeering. As Fifty One dismounted and began to seize people, the protestors squawked and threw themselves on the ground. The occasional flash of a laser cosh glinted in the weak sunlight as Fifty One bundled anybody they could catch into the hop. Within a minute, the protest was reduced to a rear-guard of middle aged women in knitted hats who scampered past us, yelling half-heartedly and bundling leaflets into their bras. The hop doors slid closed, and the vehicle rose up into the air, turning in the direction of HQ.

Mo opened the side visor of the electro and pushed me in. 'You've only run a few paces and you're short of breath. You have to exercise, Green. Your life could depend on it one day.'

The cab engine buzzed to life and we rose up off the roadway and skimmed towards town. Overhead, the black hop vanished into a cloudbank.

'What will they do with the prisoners?' I said.

Mo smirked. 'You're not getting sentimental in your old age, are you?'

'Course not. Next stop the Wellbeing Clinic?'

'Not in this pile of junk. We're going back to HQ to get a proper ride.'

*

The Wellbeing Clinic had discreet signage at the rear of a Health Matters installation on the outskirts of town. At the main entrance, two porters were unloading a robo-cart piled with boxes.

'What's the betting there are organs in those?' I said.

'They aren't marked,' said Mo.

'With organ thieves around, that's probably a good thing.'

The receptionist, disconcerted by our Unit IDs, called a senior colleague. She took us into an empty office and pulled up the details of Dante's transplant.

'The organ was legitimately purchased from Body Bay,' said Mo, flicking a holo-file towards me.

'Only hours before Dante had his op,' I added.

'Have you the supplier details?' Mo asked the senior.

She tapped the screen. 'We only deal with a small number of companies. Give me a few moments…'

Mo peered into the com and whistled through his teeth.

'What is it?'

He flicked the file out towards me.

A letter N in curly script hung in front of my face.

The Nemesis Corporation.

How the hell could Nemesis have got hold of a stolen organ, unless they were bona fide connected with the Brotherhood?

'Is there a problem?' the senior searched our faces, the tang of her fear sharp in the air.

'Can you pull up the details for this supplier?' I said.

She flicked through a stack of files, her eyebrows knitting together. 'I don't understand. That's impossible. There are no further details logged on our database. I'm so sorry, I can't imagine…'

'No problem,' said Mo. 'Thank you for your time.'

She watched us, all the way out to the hop, as though expecting us to change our minds and turn around and come back with a closure warrant.

'What do we do now?' I said, as we climbed in.

Mo shook his head. 'This isn't looking good, Green. If the Nemesis Corporation is running the Brotherhood, then the poison is inside the Unit, and Oxton's worst fears are realised.'

I fastened my harness. On the dash, the token glimmered dully.

I reached for it. 'Did you take this out of my jacket?'

'What?' said Mo, slipping on his headset. 'Why would I go in your jacket, Green?'

I turned the token over in my fingers, remembering Raphael's words.

'How far are we from The Eye?'

The hop rose off the ground, pushing up into the low cloud.

'Minutes,' said Mo. 'Are you taking me for lunch?'

'No, but humour me. I think it's time to try and call in some information.'

Mo shrugged, and turned us around.

XIV

The back entrance to The Eye was a little yard stacked with recycle units and a compression skip. The windows were wide open, belching steam. A youth appeared on the back steps, his arms wrapped around a box of vegetable peelings.

'I'm here for Sybil,' I said.

He grinned and slumped against the wall, the box in his arms lilting dangerously. A digi-display on the front said Real Produce. Sheesh. The rumours were true – no Klone Zone for this joint.

'I have this.' I pulled the token from my pocket.

The youth stared into my palm. He nodded towards a corner of the yard, and pushed past me down the steps.

Tacked onto the back of the restaurant was a unit with a crooked sign saying 'steam room'.

I knocked, but nobody came.

I tried the door.

It opened.

Inside was gloomy. As I crossed the threshold, a cloud of hot vapour surged around my head. The door handle, wet with moisture, slipped through my fingers and the door shut itself behind me.

The steam cleared to reveal a metal bench stacked with trays of real vegetables. A woman in a white apron stood over a cauldron. Her hair was wrapped in a cloth.

'Sybil?'

She took a handful of chopped vegetables and strewed them onto a mesh over the cauldron.

'I have the token,' I said.

Sybil stopped what she was doing, and looked up. One of her eyes was stitched down at the lid. The other was pale blue, and bloodshot.

'Raphael told me that you have information for me.'

I slid the token onto the table next to a tray of baby potatoes. They weren't perfect enough to be Klone Zone. They were Old World. I wanted to reach out, just so that I could say, I touched a real potato, once in my life. But I didn't - I plaited my fingers and stood in front of the bench like a schoolchild waiting for detention.

Sybil picked up the potatoes and cast them over the steam. The cauldron responded with a hiss, and a veil of vapour burst up between us.

'I've been waiting for you, Jess Green.'

I felt queasy. Underneath my jacket, my shirt stuck to my body.

'Raphael was right, I have something for you, child, but I'm afraid it isn't what you were expecting.'

Sybil's one good eye rolled in its socket. The other looked as though it'd been gouged out by a blunt instrument. She was tiny, smaller even than me, almost as wide as she was tall, but something in her pale eye glowed like molten Kevlar. Instinctively, I began to back away. Sybil advanced, slowly.

'Why are you afraid of me, child?'

I stepped into something metal that skidded away over the tiles and clunked into a wall.

'Your past, it gives you nightmares, doesn't it? It started when she left you in that place in the desert.'

Against a backdrop of steam, my memory replayed my mother walking away towards an arch door with her shoulders hunched, her heels ringing on the stone. She didn't look back. My brother flapped and screamed in Sister

Enuncia's arms until his bunny with the button eyes fell onto the floor.

'You own very little from those days, child, but the thing around your neck is precious to you, isn't it?'

Sybil gestured with one outstretched finger and squinted. My hand crawled up my neck and felt for the pendant where it lay hidden, stuck to my skin in the heat.

'And your brother. You lost him, didn't you?'

The cot, his head a smudge in the shadows, his mouth wet and pink where he'd fallen asleep, exhausted after crying. I never knew that night would be the last time I'd see him, or that the only trace the following day would be a single button on the floor.

'You think of him all the time, don't you, child?'

The button gleamed from underneath the empty cot, and my fingers closed around it.

'And the others. They haunt you. You want to know what happened to them, don't you?'

I closed my eyes, squeezing a single tear onto one cheek, but the inside of my lids was imprinted with the dorm beds, emptied one by one, and it wasn't Sybil's voice but Lindiwi's that I heard whispering across the years: 'Sister Enuncia takes them at night and drains their blood in the cellar. Then she leaves the bodies in the sand for the nightbeetles to snip to pieces. It'll be us next...'

Flames, burning, orange and yellow tongues licking at the walls...

I opened my eyes.

Sybil had reached one hand towards me through the steam, a pale hand with elegant nails and skin much younger than it should've looked, as though she was about to wipe the tear off my cheek.

I couldn't do it.

I couldn't listen to this stranger tell me things I'd never realised I was too afraid to hear.

I jerked away.

My fingers hooked round the door handle and I fell out into the yard. The door closed itself behind me as I scrambled to my feet. Mo stood was the hop with his hands in his pockets, watching the steam room just as I'd left him. I set off towards him, fighting with the lump in my throat and the feeling of utter bewilderment, my hair slicked to my head and my shirt stuck to my body.

All my life I'd told myself I wanted answers, and yet here I was, running like a coward, too afraid to hear anything at all.

I glanced back, once, half expecting the door to be open, and Sybil to be walking towards me with her hand outstretched, just as I'd left her. But the sign saying 'steam room' had vanished and so had the door I'd gone through. All that remained of the annexe was a blank wall.

I stumbled across the yard, dimly aware that something was burning my flesh from inside my shirt pocket. I slipped my hand in and pulled out the token - the same token I'd left on the table.

Cursing, I wiped my cheek with the back of one hand and shoved the token into my jacket pocket. The kitchen lad smirked at me from the compression skip, an empty box lolling from one hand.

'Chryst, what's happened to you?' Mo took in my lank hair and wet shirt with one glance.

'Never again,' I snapped, masking my shock with feigned anger. 'You shouldn't have left me alone in there.'

'The Sybil has a reputation,' said Mo, 'but it isn't as a skin-stripping laser murderer. I was outside, watching the only door into the place. You were perfectly safe. The Eye is much more secure than you might suppose. Rumour is, it's owned by Perseus. Green, what's the matter?'

At the warehouse, with the bodies and their stripped muscle and raw flesh and the blood, Mo had told me I had to find a way to cope. He'd said I had to toughen up, yet I was choking back tears for people who'd disappeared more than half my lifetime ago.

'I'm fine,' I said, my eyes averted. 'Let's go.'

We made the journey in silence. When you feel something strongly, you leak the emotion. That's the kind of thing I pick up on, anything from a small trickle to a great cascade. Nothing prepares you for the times you feel so bad that it washes back over you, amplified. Right now, I was drowning.

When we reached HQ, I made my excuses and took the chute down to Archives, alone.

Reg was fussing about with a robotic hoist, running it from floor to ceiling and back again. He let go of the controls when I stumbled out of the chute. The hoist flew to the top of the racking and clanged to a halt.

'You knew,' I said.

'What?'

'You knew what Paradise House did. You let me go in there to find out for myself, instead of being honest with me.'

Reg smoothed his hair down with one hand, the fingers of his other picking at his waistcoat buttons. 'I'm sorry. I didn't realise it would upset you this badly. Please, sit down. You look like you need to.'

I lowered myself onto a storage chest that was pulled out in the middle of the gangway.

'What was I supposed to do? You asked me for information. I gave you what I had. I thought it might be fun for you to go find out something in the real world, instead of Archives. I'd kill to be in your shoes.'

'Fun? Reginald, please don't ever remind me again that you and I have distinctly different ideas of what's fun.'

Reg had the good grace to look sheepish. 'Look, Green, this might make it up to you. I have something on your aunt. Follow me.'

He set off, pattering past boxes and files that were pulled out into the aisles at random, the contents spilled onto the floor. I followed at a distance, angry that my legs were still trembling.

'Don't mind the mess. I'm working on something for Sixty Eight. Just mind the delicate bits, will you?'

We arrived at his station, where the main com riffled through a blur of files. Reg sat.

'You told me that you were raised by your aunt.'

'Yes.' I slid onto the edge of the desk.

'But I assume that being a niece was an honorary title, Miss Green?'

'No, of course not. She was my mother's sister.'

Reg enlarged a file and pointed. 'Your Aunt Connie didn't have a sister.'

Dr Dawkins's voice slid into my mind.

You don't have an aunt.

I'd ignored her, hardly surprised that my mother had secrets she'd kept from more than just me.

'But she had to be my aunt. Why else would she have taken me in?'

Reg snapped a series of commands at the computer while I sat back, too stunned to do any more than watch the words dance in front of my eyes. He skimmed a pile of holo-files, sending them off to left and right in fuzzy stacks.

'Could you identify your aunt from a photo, even if it was taken more than a decade before she died?'

'Of course. I'd know her anywhere.'

The photo he enlarged showed a woman past her prime, but not so far past that her hair didn't show red between the white. It lay in thick curls over her shoulders.

'Yes, that's her.'

Reg rubbed his eyes. 'I don't know how to tell you this.'

My stomach tightened. 'Just say it, please.'

'I think I've discovered why I couldn't find Constanza Eckhardt in the main vaults.'

'Why?'

'Because she's classified. This is a limited access vault, Green. I searched it on a hunch. It came up with this photo and one small historical file.'

The flame red streaks in Connie's hair stood out like pennants. She'd been caught mid-movement, as though the image was taken outside when a breeze was blowing.

'Please, Miss Green. Read the file, and tell me if anything stands out.'

I scanned the words. Facts and figures were listed dispassionately, an abridged version of a life I only thought I'd known. Aunt Connie had once been married, and she'd had a child. She'd never mentioned a husband or a child to me. Neither had she told me that her daughter had been killed in an unspecified 'incident', when she was only twelve years old - the same age I'd been when Aunt Connie had taken me in, years later...

The ghostly irises of the woman I thought I knew stared through me, unravelling my past with alarming speed.

'Your aunt appears to be classified because she was once a Unit employee.'

The towers of files around my head suddenly seemed to close in. I sank back into a chair. Scenes from my childhood replayed themselves in disjointed fragments in my head: me and Aunt Connie on the balcony of a little flat we'd rented in Cliff, looking at the stars together; Aunt Connie telling me that lost loved ones wait in the sky as shining lights until it's time to be reunited; Claws as a kitten, picked up from somewhere he should never have been, covered in muck and cowering under the settee; me tossing the photograph of my mother down the kitchen disposal, the day Connie went into hospital for the last time. The memories were out of sequence, but vivid – truths, not lies. How could she not be my aunt?

Reg plaited his fingers. 'If I dwell on a non-case-specific file for too long, Upstairs will know about it. I'm closing down now.'

The light in Reg's eyes went out as the link to the memory vaults icon disintegrated and the screen went dark. The files shot back into the com, leaving a faint sparkle of holographic dust over the table.

'You closed the file without letting me finish reading.'

Reg waved a hand, irritated. 'Two things I've developed by necessity are speed-reading and an excellent memory. I can talk you through the small-print.' He steepled his fingers. 'The file describes Connie as a Unit sleeper. That means she worked field assignments, and rested in between. To any casual observer, your aunt must've lived what appeared to be a normal life. Then, for periods of time, she'd simply disappear. Now for the tricky bit. How old were you, Green, when Connie took you in?'

'I was twelve.'

Reg rubbed his chin. 'Connie was too old to be a sister of your mother's. Much too old, I'd say. According to the file, your aunt did a vanishing act at the same time she picked you up. Constanza Eckhardt absconded from the Unit. Her file is classified because she ran away and was never seen again, Green. And that, within the Unit, is utterly unheard of.'

'What?'

Reg inclined his head. 'When I couldn't find your aunt under a mainstream search, I guessed that something was amiss.'

He began rearranging things on the top of his desk: virtual pens; files; his briefcase. Something shifted inside with a hiss. Reg stood the case up carefully and slid it out of sight with one foot.

'Now, stand back and look at what happened from a different angle,' he said. 'Your aunt goes missing from the Unit at the same time she finds you at the orphanage. I mean convent. Whatever. She takes you away and you live with her, and she moves you around. You live in so many places you can't name half of them.'

I shifted uncomfortably. Talking about my past was something Aunt Connie had conditioned me not to do.

'I worked out that your employment at the sexclub began when your aunt died, and ended just before you came here, to the Unit.' Reg stopped fiddling with things and stared at me, hard. 'I'm an archivist, Green – the devil's always in the detail. It's obvious to me that you were a minor when your aunt died. You should've been taken into care, but you weren't.'

'I can't be the first underage to choose making my own way against being put in care,' I snapped. 'It was only two years. After that, I would've been free to make my own choices anyway.'

Reg held out his hands, placating, his voice soothing. 'I'm not criticising your decision in the slightest. In fact, I think I'd rather take my chances in the wider world than find myself being fed, clothed and educated by an auto-matron in a hostel. That isn't my point.'

'What is your point?'

Reg leaned closer. 'You didn't find yourself in a home and then run away, did you, Green? You knew right from the outset that you weren't going there. It isn't difficult for me to imagine that a woman who raised you to live below the radar would make sure you knew how to carry on that way. '

I reached for my throat and picked at the collar of my shirt. Somehow, I doubted that a sexclub was the destination Aunt Connie had had in mind, but I'd needed to move fast before the Welfare Team got hold of me.

'Your aunt needed to know that you were capable of staying off the system,' said Reg. 'She must've had her reasons.'

Reg waited, giving me space to speak. The silence expanded between us until he gave up.

'So your aunt, courtesy of her many years' service at the Unit, manages to fake your ID to such an extent that the Jess Green we have today can never be linked with the Jess Green who was placed in that orphanage. I mean convent.'

Half-forgotten snippets of conversation flew around in my mind: never settle in one place for too long, Jess... don't worry about your ID, I'll make sure you're safe...

Reg reached out and patted my arm, stiffly.

'There, there, Green,' he said, his cuff pulling back to reveal a flash of marbled skin that shone faintly in the half-light. 'I don't want to upset you, but if you want answers, then I'm afraid you're going to have to face some difficult truths. Including the fact that there's something about you that makes you different, dangerous, desirable or just downright expendable to whoever Connie wanted to keep you hidden from.'

The shadows around his head took on a surreal quality, swimming with different shades of darkness, as though I was staring into an abyss.

Reg lay his palms flat on the table. 'The information I've pulled up suggests that children in convent orphanages were sold to the highest bidder whenever the chance arose. The form-filling was minimal. If you were there for two years, you could've been taken out by anybody during that time. Yet you weren't, because the adoption rates from the edge of the Disaster Zone were terrible. Whoever put you there knew that. I think you were left in the desert for your own safety. I don't think Connie Eckhardt was your aunt, but I do think she knew your story.'

Since the day my mother left, I'd been running on guesswork, nightmares, and whispers. It'd brought me nothing but misery. How could I believe that she'd dumped me and my brother in a convent for our own safety? Accept that the woman who took me in was a stranger?

Reg leaned in closer. 'Are you ready for answers?'
I nodded.
He took a deep breath. 'Give me your bleep code, Miss Green.'
'What?'
'You heard. Bleep code, please, now. I'll hand it right back when I've finished.'

I pulled the code out of my jacket. Reg snatched it and held it over his scanner, muttering. A file materialised. My Unit ID photo rotated in the top corner. I looked away.
'So, your birth was registered in Cliff City.'

'Yes. I mean… I don't know. I don't remember.'

Reg eyed me shrewdly. 'Where did you first go to school?'

'I… I can't remember.'

'How about your graduation?'

I shrugged.

Reg scanned my file. 'Here, I see that you stayed in school until your late teens and got a college diploma in digital archiving?'

'I… yes, of course…'

'Except you can't have, because you worked in a sexclub. And you've got no idea who Jack the Ripper is. He's a stalwart of every digital archiving syllabus in the developed world, Green.'

Reg vanished my ID file and slid my bleep-code onto the corner of the table. I snatched it. The skin beneath his collar had begun to glow with the same faint, sulphurous light as the exposed wrist.

'How long have you suspected that your aunt forged your ID? Lied about where you'd been, what you'd done? Or did she tell you outright?'

When the time comes, your ID will keep you safe. I've given you a safe history…

'Come now Green, don't be coy. You're the most exciting project I've had chance to work on in a long time. I'm hardly going to turn you in, now, am I? There are no Eyes in here in archives,' he gestured around. 'You've no need to be frightened. You see, I've been puzzled about you since the day we first met. Too many things don't add up.'

Reg buried his head in a swathe of holo-files, muttering, dictating instructions, some in his own tongue, some in mine, but too fast for me to follow. He spoke briefly to a white coat in Twenty One, then vanished the portal and sat back, wearing a smug expression.

'Your DNA doesn't bear any familial resemblance to Connie Eckhardt's.'

'How did you-'

'From your bleep-code. Just let's say Twenty One owed me a favour.'

I watched Reg, in silence: the creases underneath his eyes that tautened as though somebody had pulled a string in his skin; the side-to-side flicker of his eyelids that he forgot to hide when he felt passionate about something.

'If we get to the root of what made your Aunt Connie take you out of the orphanage, then we'll find all the answers you're looking for.'

Be careful what you ask for, Connie had always said. I pictured her, as she was before the end, her hand a wasted claw above the bed clothes, her eyes dulled. In my mind's eye, she wasn't smiling any more. A sick feeling flooded the spaces where the unanswered questions sat around my heart.

Reg laid his hands on the desk. 'Knowledge is a terrific thing. But don't fool yourself you can just turn around and walk away. The desire for the truth runs through humanity like a thrombosed vein. You will always come back - and I can hold your hand throughout the journey. All you have to do it trust me.'

Reg folded his arms. This time, he didn't bother pulling his cuffs down.

'I – I need to think.'

He inclined his head. 'Of course. You know where to find me.'

I pushed myself out of the chair and turned away, in the direction of the chute. The racks of files swallowed the sound of my footsteps, as though, to a casual listener, the place could've been empty, and I might not have been there at all.

My mother had a Unit file.

My aunt had a Unit file.

And now, my aunt was not my aunt, and although I was still Jess Green, I wasn't the Jess Green I thought I was.

The chute door sprang open at reception. I almost fell into the corridor. Rosie was talking to HQ computer, pacing around with one hand on her ear and a worried expression on her face. She spotted me and cut the connection.

'Hey.'

'Hey, Rosie.'

She brushed a stray curl behind one ear. 'You remember we talked about going out?'

'Rosie, I-'

'Well, I cleared it. Mo's coming too.' Rosie screwed her nose up and giggled, which made her look even younger. 'It's my birthday today. We're going out after work.'

'Rosie, do you mind if I dip out? Only I don't really-'

'What's the matter?' Rosie puckered her lips. 'I've chosen the best restaurant in North Side. And I'm paying.'

'The Eye?'

'No way - that's for old people. And washed-up actors.'

I sighed.

'I'll take that as a yes, then.' Rosie squinted and peered into my face at close range. 'Are you OK, Jess? You look a bit pale.'

'Long day,' I said quickly. 'Rosie, why are we going to a restaurant when you can't actually eat?'

She shot me a withering look. 'There's no need to be so insensitive, Jess. I have a table booked at Hex's. Girls only. Except for Daryl.' She winked. 'Mo can wait in the lounge. OK?'

I feigned a smile and watched her disappear down the corridor, then slumped on a settee in the rest area. I guess I didn't realise how tired I was; I was woken by a hand on my shoulder, rocking me gently.

I blinked and yawned.

Mo sank into the sofa opposite, two coffees on the table in front of him.

'One day you'll remember I hate that stuff,' I said.

He glanced down at the cups. 'The good news is, you don't have to drink it. Come on, it's time to go.'

'Where?'

'Rosie's birthday supper.'

Reception stopped me as I signed out.

'Foreign object in left pocket,' computer said, flicking the laser barrier down. 'Authorisation required.'

I pulled the token from my pocket. Its surface sparkled faintly under the lights. The guards peered into my hand, and took turns to tap it.

'What's this, Miss Green?'

'I found it.'

'Where?'

I shrugged. 'Can't remember. I went for a walk and picked it up.'

'A walk?' said the second guard. 'You people don't walk. You take cabs everywhere. Paid for by the Unit.'

They guffawed, until Mo stepped in close behind me.

'She found it in City Park under a bench. It's a stone.'

The guards squinted into the monitor and glanced at each other.

'You can keep it if you want,' I said.

'Not likely.'

Reluctantly, I slipped the token back into my pocket. The barrier disappeared. I walked through and headed outside, Mo at my shoulder.

A fine mizzle of rain shimmered in the square. Night lights flicked on in dribs and drabs. The decontam crew had finally gone, leaving a spanking new bar frontage to replace the blown-out wreck opposite Harry's. Underneath its awning was a pavement café, crowded by customers with full glasses and short memories. We crossed the street and took a cab from the main point.

'I don't know why you wouldn't let me bring a hop,' Mo grumbled.

'So that we fit in. I don't want to be the only guest who turns up in a Unit vehicle.'

The driver refused to take us any further than North Side archway. He pulled off the main drag in a slosh of rainwater, and flicked the interior light on.

'You're perfectly safe,' I assured him, 'it isn't dark yet.'

'No way, lassie, I'm not chancing it. It's dusk now, but what happens if I get lost on the way out?'

'If you follow the signs, you can't get lost,' Mo said. 'Head for the river bridge. You can't go wrong.'

'Them shifters swap the signs around after dark,' the driver glanced underneath the archway fearfully. 'They do it on purpose. That's what happened to one of our lot, last year. Took a punter to a cage-dancing club. Thought he'd get out before curfew but must've got caught up in those cobbled alleys. Nobody saw him again. Cab turned up six months later, covered in rhinestones in some shifter's private collection.' The driver scanned my bleep-code and handed it back. 'What's a regular couple like you two doing in North Side anyway?'

Mo smirked.

'Birthday party,' I replied, fastening my pack.

I flicked the token onto the back seat as we climbed out of the cab. From underneath the archway, partly shielded from the rain, we watched the driver reverse. The cab stopped suddenly, and drove towards us. The driver waved.

'What's the matter?' I said as he let the visor down.

'You forgot something on the back seat, miss,' he snapped, holding out one hand. 'I don't approve of these new legal highs. I don't know if you wear it, eat it, sniff it, or rub it in, but I don't want stuff like this in the back of my cab. I've got a license to keep and a family to look after.'

The driver dropped the token into my hand. His door snapped closed. The cab pulled away, sending a slick of oily water onto my legs.

'Isn't that the token?' said Mo.

I ignored him, and tossed it into the air, watching it spin. It looked dull in the rain. I headed for the bridge and stared out over the water. Surely it couldn't find its way back to me if I threw it over the edge…

'Jess!'

Startled, I spun around.

Daryl from Letters and Packages stood in the middle of the road, his hair slicked to his face, his coat soaking. He skipped the puddles and jogged towards us.

'Am I glad to see you,' he said, looking Mo up and down warily.

'Daryl,' I tried to smile.

'Apparently, I'm an honorary girl for tonight only,' Daryl said. Mo coughed. 'Thought I'd save the money on a cab and walk. I see you had the same idea. Bloody terrified when I realised it was getting dark. What's that in your hand?'

I stuffed the token into my pocket. 'Nothing,' I said. 'Come on, we're getting wetter.'

We headed under the arch and into North Side, Daryl and me side by side, Mo behind. The streets were deserted. As the buildings got closer and taller, the cobbled alleys narrowed, and the chains of fairy-lights wound increasingly chaotic patterns over the old brickwork. The rain turned to mist. Daryl jumped at every corner, especially when yellow eyes retreated into the dark as we passed.

'Are you sure you know where we're going, Jess?'

'We're nearly there. You mustn't show you're afraid. That's half the battle, here.'

The curfew claxon rang out as we arrived at Hex's. Daryl slid in front of me and ran inside. Rosie was huddled at the far end of the restaurant, in a private room with an open archway entrance surrounded by girls I didn't recognise who were giggling and drinking from oddly-shaped glasses. I peeled my jacket off. A waiter held out his hand. I let go of it gratefully. Daryl had already pulled up a seat, and was dripping onto a real wooden table. Mo scoped out the private room before giving me a nod and melting into an adjoining bar.

'Hey, Jess!' Rosie yelled. 'What do you think of the venue?'

'Nice.' I glanced around.

'Real fuel license,' said Rosie, nodding towards an Old World fire in a hole in the wall.

I took a seat at the end of the table.

'I've already chosen,' said Rosie, waving a menu. 'You're all having the protein banquet, with cocktails – of course – followed by the most exciting entertainment you could imagine.'

A red-head pushed a spiral glass of something colourful and viscous towards me. I sipped, and gagged.

'Entertainment?' I said.

'Last year we had two hermaphrodite strippers who offered personal services after the show, but it was a bit naff, really,' said Rosie, to affirmative mumblings from the others. 'This year we've arranged something totally different. Far more North Side, if you get my drift.'

The girls giggled.

'Awesome,' said Daryl. 'Did you book a role playing game?'

'We're girls, Daryl. We don't do spangled capes and rubber gloves.'

Daryl flushed.

'I've booked a fortune teller,' continued Rosie. 'But not just any fortune teller.' She took out a sachet of crystals and tipped them into a glass. 'This fortune teller is the best in the district. And on North Side, that's something.'

'She reads a steam cauldron,' said one of the other girls. 'She's so famous she travels all over the world reading for celebrities. And she's here, tonight, in a private room upstairs. There's just some catch about a token, or something.'

'A token?' I snapped.

'Uhuh,' said Rosie. 'It's in the rules. Apparently, we won't all get one. It's the luck of the draw. Only those who need to see the Sybil get a token.'

'I've been told,' said the red head, 'that there's only one token given out all evening. But we're feeling lucky, aren't we, girls?'

An inebriated cheer went up around the table.

'We reckon at least half of us will get a reading tonight,' said Rosie. 'The other half will sit here getting wasted on cocktails. Perfect!'

Three waiters brought in covered dishes that oozed fragrant steam, and placed them in the centre of the table. My stomach somersaulted. I ditched the cocktail in Daryl's empty glass. When the next wave of dishes arrived, I slipped out of my seat and made my way to the cloak room.

'Can I help you, miss?' a yellow-eyed waiter appeared from the shadows.

'I - I'm looking for my coat.'

Without releasing my eyes, the waiter went straight to my jacket and took it from a hook.

'Do you ever give out the wrong coat?'

He smirked. 'Scent never lies.'

I snatched the coat and turned away. The pocket I'd put the token in was empty. I tried the other. That was empty, too.

What was it Rosie had said?

That you never knew how many tokens were handed out, but you only got one if the Sybil had a message for you?

Well, maybe it was my lucky day. Perhaps she'd decided to reclaim my token and hand it on to somebody more willing. I couldn't face the truths she'd promised me.

I slung my jacket on the closest hook and went back to the party room. Rosie's guests were ladling various protein substitutes in sauce onto expensive-looking crockery. I slipped into my seat.

'Here,' said Daryl, tipping noodles onto my plate.

I pulled my com from my bag and held it under the table.

'...and some of this, it comes highly recommended...' sauce splashed onto the table.

I popped my top button. The real fuel license had suddenly lost its appeal.

'...and finally...' Daryl scooped something green and cloned-looking onto the top of the pile he'd made on my plate, and slopped more cocktail into my empty glass.

I hit speed-call for archives. Reg sprang out in miniature.

'Green?' he sounded startled.

'Call me in,' I said.

'What?' Reg squinted.

'Call me in,' I hissed. 'I have to get out of here. Invent an emergency. Anything. Just do it.'

Reg's eyes darted left and right. He looked above his head. 'Have you got me underneath a table?'

'Please - send a Unit hop for me and Mo. We're at Hex's in North Side.'

'Tuck in, Jess,' called Rosie. 'This is the best protein substitute you'll find anywhere in the city, and it's all on me. Enjoy!'

I pushed my com into one hand, and picked up a fork with the other. The plate Daryl had filled seemed obscenely large.

'Don't panic, Green. I'll get you out of there.'

'I owe you,' I whispered.

'I know,' said Reg greedily.

He vanished. I stowed the com in my hand bag, and lifted the fork to my mouth. Before my lips had closed around it, my bag jumped off the seat. Amber lights shot through the fabric. A siren throbbed inside. The conversation cut out, and everybody lowered their forks, staring.

'You're joking,' said Rosie, her face sullen.

I pulled the com out of my bag. It stopped flashing. Reg, looking serious and sounding loud, appeared in the middle of the table and snapped:

'Amber alert, Green - I'm bringing you in!'

I put my fork down. 'I'm so sorry, Rosie - I'll make it up to you, I promise. I'll take you out to Harry's for cake later this week...'

Daryl slid my plate next to his own. 'You don't mind, do you, Jess? Only I couldn't stand to see it go to waste…'

I didn't look back.

Mo was already waiting in the lobby, his face creased with concern.

'Don't ask,' I said, 'not here. I'll explain outside. A hop is on its way.'

The waiter's yellow eyes followed us as we slipped out the door. Outside, the chill was welcome. My wet jacket clung to my arms, but I didn't care.

'Are you going to tell me what's going on?' said Mo.

At the end of the street, the slender silhouettes of a group of shifters paused to stare, their eyes glowing in our direction. A hop appeared above them. Guthrie had the controls - I didn't need to see his face through the visor; I could feel him. He touched down in the courtyard, and the visors flicked down. I swear I felt him wince when he spotted Mo.

'You owe me an explanation,' Mo hissed as we headed for the vehicle.

Guthrie took us up, and we hovered over Hex's, the shifters watching us from the ground, their eyes gold sparks in the dark. They vanished into the shadows as we pulled away over the rooftops.

'Thank you for coming out at short notice, Guthrie,' I said.

Night-lights flared along the side of his headset and across his cheekbones.

'Just doing my job,' he said, mildly, but with a glance towards Mo, as though making a point.

Below us, the river was a black snake fringed by coloured lights. Mo stared at it in silence. I sat back in my seat and slipped my hands into my pockets. Something small and round and solid sat at the bottom of one. My fingers closed around it. I pulled it out and held it up. The token twinkled in the light from below.

On impulse, I slipped the side-visor down ever so slightly, and dropped it. We were too far up to hear the splash, and it was too dark to see. Moments later, we pulled over the bank, turned for the gated estate on the posh side of town, and skimmed past the roosting river birds, sinking down in front of my block.

Mo slid out first and got my visor.

'Thanks,' I said. 'Why not come in? We can talk.'

Guthrie winced when Mo gave him a nod. The hop rose up and pulled away.

'I think he likes you,' said Mo as the tail lights disappeared in the direction of HQ.

I smirked. 'Come on.'

Mo checked the laser lock and re-set my security as soon as my apartment door closed behind us.

'Just-like-juice? Or something stronger?'

'Water, thanks.'

Claws was asleep on the sofa, stretched out, his distended stomach a little hillock in its black and white jacket. Mo hesitated.

'He's old,' I said, pulling two beakers from a rack in the kitchen. 'He's almost blind and deaf. And he doesn't like people. He has no idea we just walked in. Don't make him jump.'

Mo turned away from the sofa. 'I'll take a chair.'

I took both beakers into the living room and put them on the coffee table. Mo sat across the other side of the room, his long legs folded underneath a too-small chair. I asked the broadcast system for easy-listening, and it selected some syth mambo at low volume, having sensed I wasn't alone; I almost expected the darn thing to ask me why I had company.

'So, Miss Green, are you going to tell me why, on your first night out, which was supposedly so important to your sense of personal freedom, you barely lasted fifteen minutes?'

I threw my wet jacket into the Instant Dry that sat on the back wall, and slipped off my boots.

'You see this?' I said, lifting the cat's paw.

Something small and black and shiny lay underneath, as though it'd been sat there since before the cat had curled up and fallen asleep. Mo peered at it. I slid it out, and held it up. The surface glittered faintly.

'That's the token you were supposed to hand to the fortune teller.'

'It somehow found its way back to me,' I said. 'Then it wasn't in my pocket when I wanted to give it away, at Hex's – and just now on the way home, I threw it out the hop window.'

Mo frowned. 'You're kidding.'

I slid it onto the coffee table. 'No, I'm not.'

He picked it up and turned it over, then reached for his com.

'What are you doing?'

'You'll see.' Mo ran a scan over the token. He shook his head, a smile playing with the corners of his mouth. 'You've been taken in, I'm afraid. It's not as mysterious as you might think.'

I snatched his com and read the file. 'What the hell's a quintemp?'

'Eighty One have done some work on zone-to-zone transportation. It's a way of sending small objects to different locations in a fraction of a second, via quintemps, a sub-molecular particle. The technology needs a marker, which it can easily get by tracking, say, a com that's in your jacket pocket. So long as the marker is with you, the object that's being transported will keep finding you.'

'You're saying that Sybil is teleporting this thing back to me whenever I try to get rid of it?'

Mo smirked. 'It's highly likely. You're supposed to think it's mystical. What did she tell you, at the Eye?'

'I left in a hurry. I don't want to talk about it.'

Mo's eyebrows shot up. 'I knew something wasn't right when you came out. I figured it was personal. I didn't want to ask.'

I reached for my beaker and cradled it in my lap. The cat stirred, his whiskers twitching.

'I hope you realise you're never going to get rid of the damn token until you meet her face to face,' said Mo. 'The Sybil has a reputation which most people fall for, hook, line and sinker. In your case, it worked.'

I shifted position. The hiss of the fabric of my trousers against the settee seemed amplified in the silence.

'So, if you won't tell me why you left the steam room in such a hurry, are you going to tell me about Paradise House?'

I straightened up, disturbing the cat, who opened his eyes and flinched when he spotted Mo.

'Green?'

He waited, and watched.

'I had a brother,' I said, eventually, swirling the liquid in my beaker. 'Our mother abandoned us as kids. I never saw or heard from her since. My brother vanished one night.' I twisted the beaker in my lap, my fingers blanching where they pressed the surface. 'He was there when the nuns rang curfew, then gone the following morning. I saw his cot. It was empty, the sheets stripped and the mattress leaned up. It's what they did when somebody wasn't coming back… and I found this.'

I pulled the chain from underneath my shirt collar, and held the button up. Mo leaned towards me.

'May I?'

I nodded. He knelt in front of me and reached out one hand, slowly, and touched the button very gently, as though he understood how precious it was.

'It's Old World.'

'Yes. It's from a toy. It belonged to Michael. I found the button under his cot the morning after his bed was stripped.'

Mo's fingers trailed away. He pushed himself off his hunkers and slid back into the chair in silence. From behind the shades, I felt him study my face.

'When Reg found a link to my father at Paradise House, it seemed like a lead,' I said. 'I took the chance, but it was a mistake – my father's too long gone to figure in any of this. Then, in the steam room with Sybil, I bottled out. Whoever she is, she knows something about my past, and I shocked myself by being too afraid to stick around and listen.'

Mo picked up his drink and spun the water in circles. 'So if your father was a dead-end enquiry, and you were abandoned by your mother, then it's your brother you're really looking for, right?'

I must've flinched.

'Allow me some credit, Miss Green. I can be quite observant when I set my mind to it. How old were you both when he disappeared?'

'I was ten and he was four. We hadn't been at the convent for long. I was there another two years.'

Mo whistled through his teeth. The cat slid off the settee and ran.

'And your mother?'

'What about her?'

'Why did she leave the two of you in a convent?'

'I have no idea.'

'But it still haunts you.'

Mo phrased it like a statement, not a question. I didn't respond.

'If there's anything I can do to help, just ask.'

'Thank you.'

Behind the open blackouts, the moon, what little of it there was, vanished behind a cloud, and the glow balls brightened in response. Mo stood up and stretched his legs. He checked his com and put it in his jacket pocket.

'You're going?'

'I have to be somewhere.'

I slid off the sofa. 'Oh.'

Mo hung his head, and just for a moment, I sensed he didn't want to go.

'Am I allowed to ask?'

He hesitated. 'I'm meeting a friend.'

I shrugged. 'Maybe come back another time.'

Mo nodded, once, and flicked the laser lock off.

'Re-set your security protocols when I'm gone.'

On hallway cam, his body cast long shadows, multiplied by the plethora of security lights and angled over each other in complex patterns. Moments later, Mo's silhouette cut the laser wire at the end of the compound, and he disappeared.

'Energetic rock,' I said to the broadcast system.

It responded by switching into an overdriven game-show soundtrack it knew I hated. Exasperated, I reached into the sideboard, and pulled out a carton of Forty Per Cent Proof. Through the open blackout, the face of the moon played peek-a-boo with the clouds. I reached for my water beaker and sloshed the liquor in.

XV

If Oxton had thought that closing the business district would stop the Brotherhood, she was wrong.

They simply went elsewhere.

We were scrambled mid-morning.

My stomach heaved as we crossed town towards the Education District.

Mo took the hop down outside a playground, where a section of Kevlar fence had been burned away. The gap was big enough to drive a hop through. Whoever had operated the cutter hadn't touched the fence; there were no life-lights anywhere.

'They used a hydraulic winch,' I said as we headed for the cordon. 'There aren't even any tell-tale footprints.'

Outside the school entrance, the faces were grim. Nobody looked at me and Mo directly, but feet began to shuffle and the bodies parted as we made our way towards Oxton through the back of the crowd.

'It's all yours,' she said, glancing from me to Mo and back again. 'You have fifteen minutes on your own, and then you will be joined by two more departments. Make the most of it, Miss Green. Things have taken a particularly nasty turn. I'd hate for you to be caught in the crossfire.'

Oxton lifted the cord, and I led the way. Behind us, the bodies surged in to fill the gap, their eyes clamped to our backs until we disappeared inside.

The smell of traditional polish hung in the air, unsettlingly familiar. In the first classroom, toys were strewn on the desks and floor, as though they'd been dropped mid-game. A pile of holo-books was fanned out haphazardly on the floor. Near my feet, a miniature cab beeped and flashed. I moved to one side, afraid to touch it.

'Where to, ma'am?' an automated voice said cheerily.

On a screen at the back of the classroom, a holographic tiger cub stood with its muzzle pushed up against a force-field. Tiny sparks hung around its whiskers. The cub's eyes were wide with alarm. Another second and it would've backed away, but it was stuck, suspended above the teacher's desk with its lips curled back, waiting to be released when somebody hit play.

An avalanche of mini digipads collapsed onto my feet. I kicked my boots free and backed away.

'Concentrate,' Mo said softly. 'If you compromise the crime scene, Twenty One will be all over us like rabid tamewulfs. Feelings are high about this one – they have expectations.'

He said us, not you.

I turned away, and headed out of the room.

'Where are you going?'

'I know where they are,' I said.

Mo's footsteps followed me into the corridor.

The children were stacked in the far corner.

They'd been wedged in a gap between the secretary's office and the auto-cleaner. The bodies had tumbled away at one end of the pile, leaving two of them lolling out into the walkway, their tiny hands palm-down on the tiles: little girls with pig tails, tied with pretty ribbons crisped by ice. Their legs were in the melee, trapped between the other bodies, the sheen of death on their exposed skin. Their fingernails were bruised violet, the colour of flower petals. Strips of green and white gingham check uniform were sliced open with laser accuracy. Mo's hand squeezed my shoulder.

'Life sign,' I said, my throat tight.

'What?'

'One of the children is alive, Mo.'

Mo glanced at the motionless bodies and back to me.

'No. Not there.'

Winding towards me like a gossamer thread, something pulled - life attracted to life, magnetic, insistent. The signature was weak.

'This way,' I pointed to the classroom.

'But we've just been in there,' said Mo, drawing his laser.

Ignoring him, I headed back along the corridor. Inside, the toy cab sensed us and crossed the floor, negotiating scattered toys and furniture.

'Need a ride, ma'am?'

I walked to the centre of the room.

'Tell me where you are,' I whispered.

The thread pulled free with a delicate twang, and vanished. Panicking, I scanned around. The room had no other doors aside from a fire exit at the opposite end. It was closed.

'What's the matter?'

'I've lost it. Please,' I whispered, 'tell me where you are...'

The toy cab changed direction and crossed underneath the teacher's desk. It whirred towards a bank of cupboards. The bumper hit a door labelled 'toys' with a clunk.

'Anybody need a ride?' the cab said, then reversed, and drove forwards, hitting the cupboard door again. 'Anybody need a ride?'

The faintest quiver of a life sign reached out and locked on to mine.

The cupboard door creaked open.

A little boy with dark hair fell face down onto the floor with a thud.

*

'That child is our only living link to the Brotherhood,' Oxton's bloodshot eyes narrowed.

A hospital orderly with a trolley walked past. She waited until he was out of earshot.

'I don't care what it takes or how you do it, Miss Green - I need something from that child and I need it as quickly as possible.'

'The boy – Scott – he's under sedation,' said Mo.

'Then use it to your advantage,' snapped Oxton, glowering at us.

'The parents are with him,' I said. 'They requested restricted access. Nobody in except medics.'

'Hospital security just confiscated a media hop on the roof,' Mo added.

Oxton rolled her eyes. 'Reporters? Already? And family? Don't these people realise we've got a job to do? Information from that child could save lives!'

'I'll get in there the moment the parents leave the room,' I said. 'They need to sleep some time.'

Oxton nodded. 'The child is the only person to survive a Brotherhood attack. I don't care how deep the memories are buried, or how much decoding his young mind needs to give me exactly what he saw yesterday… do you understand?'

'Yes, Oxton,' I said.

Oxton's com flashed. She glanced at the screen. 'Preliminary scans show the boy is suffering from shock. The hospital pulled up a genetic disorder that nobody knew about. Apart from that, he appears to be fine. If one of our sleepers administers a counter-sedative, you should have him alert within minutes, Miss Green. Just tell me when you need it.'

'No,' I said. 'Leave him under.'

Mo twitched.

'It's a hunch. He's a child. He'll be more receptive.'

Oxton's lips set. 'I await your report with enthusiasm.'

She disappeared into a lift as two medics in white came out, poring over their digipads.

'How am I going to get into the room unnoticed?'

'Let me worry about that,' said Mo. 'If we wait at the junction, we'll see everybody coming and going. You'll get your chance.'

We sat opposite each other on chairs that lined the corridor. Mo stuck his face into his com, but at every sound, like the scuff of a shoe, or the change in air pressure as a door somewhere opened or closed, he tensed. I stalked to the rest room. Inside, the air was cool, the decor startling white with spotless tiles and rows of basins and mirrors. I turned a tap on and leaned over to splash my face, but as soon as I closed my eyes, I saw the little girls, their glazed eyes and bruised fingernails, their frozen hair ribbons. I turned the tap off and stared at my reflection. My eyes were bloodshot, with dark half-moons underneath. I had to get into Scott's mind as soon as possible. I dried my face and headed back to the corridor, then slumped in my chair, and waited.

Three and a half hours later, Scott's parents left his room. The mother, stooped and fragile, was helped away by a nurse. The father, a red-faced little man with a bald head, pattered after them looking confused. Mo slid his Unit pass into the door as they disappeared. The laser lock shone green. I slipped underneath his outstretched arm. The door closed behind me with a clunk.

The room was white. It brought back Aunt Connie's final weeks. I half expected to see her, one wasted hand like a claw on the bed covers. Instead, I saw the boy. He was tiny, dwarfed by the surrounding medical paraphernalia, his hair a sooty smudge against the bed linen. His eyes were closed. A flashback burst into my mind, of my little brother Michael asleep in his cot, his dark head on a white pillow, his long lashes sweeping his cheeks, forever four years old. I shut my eyes, and the image vanished.

Above the medical auto-alert sat a security camera. I pulled my flash card from my backpack, and skirted the edge of the room. By the bed, I stood on tip toe and held it up. A tiny light flared inside the camera, stilling the 'room empty' image. I eased myself into the visitor's chair. It was still warm. I touched the boy's arm. Bruises bloomed underneath his skin, doubtless from knocks he'd taken when he'd struggled into the cupboard. The wires that fed from his body into the gear overhead trembled as I ran my fingers towards his wrist. I felt for a pulse, and closed my eyes.

Inside his mind the space was dark and cold, as though everything had been switched off.

'Scott, are you here?'

The darkness distilled into light and shadow.

'I'm here to help you.'

Something flickered at the periphery of my vision. I turned towards it, and followed.

'My name is Jess. I found you in the classroom. Do you remember? You'd shut yourself in a cupboard.'

A shadow flitted past, and footsteps pattered away.

'Scott, there's no need to be frightened. I'm the one who called a medi-cab.'

Ahead, a series of doorways opened up, each leading into the other, scoring shadows down the walls. I passed through the first.

'Scott? Where are you?'

A child began to cry somewhere.

'I'm staying right here. I want you to come to me.'

Light flared, and the walls destabilised and slipped to the ground in pools of shadow. A head appeared through the single remaining doorway. A small hand clung to the jamb. He slid to the floor and hugged his knees.

'Any chance of some light around here?'

The shadows receded from everywhere but the boy. He sat in an inkblot of darkness. I joined him on the floor, crossing my legs.

'I'm not coming out,' he said at last.

'Your parents are in the hospital waiting for you to wake up. But you've had medication to make you sleep. It'll wear off, I promise.'

'My parents aren't dead?'

I shook my head. 'They weren't at school, remember? They were somewhere else, safe.'

'But what about my friends and Miss Cressey?' Scott's voice rose in panic. 'We were going to watch a film about animals. Wednesdays are my favourite.'

'I need to know exactly what happened, Scott.'

Scott shot backwards as though he'd been sucked down a tunnel. The space around him whirled like a kaleidoscope. When he spoke, his voice was torn to bits through the void.

'Scott, I can't hear you. Come back.'

I set off towards him, and reached out. My fingers closed on warm flesh. Scott flinched as I grabbed him. The tunnel collapsed in on itself, and spat us out with an audible pop.

'Don't take me back there,' said Scott, struggling.

'I'm not taking you back anywhere,' I said, hanging on.

'I won't come out!'

'Scott, you can't hide inside yourself forever. The memory is in a room somewhere here. You've closed the door. I need to find it - to see exactly what you saw.'

Scott stopped crying. I let him go. He pixilated, breaking up like a flaky signal on an Old World com. The room darkened around us. He vanished. Suddenly, I was squinting against bright sunlight. A tiger cub with sparks around its whiskers hung overhead, behind a woman whose name badge read Miss Cressey.

Outside the windows, a plethora of black shapes appeared. Their shadows cut the tables and darkened the faces of the children. The windows physically melted away, as though the men that hung on webbing straps at the other side had used a plexi-melting compound designed specifically for the purpose. I remembered the tower blocks, with the residue inside the empty window frames; Twenty One never had got a hundred per cent match on the traces I found on the floor. That's something we'd never banked on, that the brotherhood gained entry without crossing the designated threshold. It all seemed so perfectly simple now, and so logical. Entry without trace. As the schoolchildren sat, motionless, the mens' webbing straps released and sucked into their backpacks, and they were inside, their wizened hands greedy on soft flesh. A cloud of ice crystals swept away, revealing a pile of bodies, their clothes shredded where organs had been excised at impossible speed. Dazed, Scott fell from his chair and crawled to the back of the classroom. Outside in the playground, a battered hop with broken trim sat waiting. An overweight man played with a retro digi-pad from the driver's seat. His face was almost obliterated by the peak of a baseball cap.

Graham.

Half paralysed with fear, Scott scrambled inside the cupboard and reached for the door. His hand pulled it closed, and my vision went black.

I placed my forearms flat on the bed to steady myself. Scott stirred. Mo appeared next to me and knelt, searching my face.

'OK?'

An alarm was bleeping above Scott's bed. His eyelids fluttered and he groaned.

'We have to go,' said Mo, snatching my arm and pulling me off the chair.

We slipped out the door and rounded the corner as two medics came running, followed by a holo nurse barking instructions. Scott's parents chased after them, their faces masks of confusion and hope. We dodged out of sight, flattening ourselves against a wall.

'Green, are you OK?'

'It's Graham,' I said, my voice shaking. 'My hunch was right. He's transporting the Brotherhood to crime scenes.'

Mo's face crumpled. 'So the Brotherhood are Graham's mysterious cargo?'

I nodded. 'No life signature.'

He swore.

'The speed the Brotherhood work at is phenomenal, Mo. They're nothing more than a blur. I saw the children alive, then they were dead, frozen solid, in a second.' I slid down the wall until I settled on my heels, exhausted. 'Before now, I thought the Brotherhood used some kind of block so I couldn't pick them up properly. But now...' I shook my head. 'It's all over so fast, the victims die without any idea what's happening.'

'And Scott?'

'Scott hid in the cupboard afterwards.'

Mo squatted beside me on the floor. 'This isn't magic, Jess – it's hard-and-fast science.'

I stared into his face. 'Then how do they do it?'

'The Brotherhood is doing something that should be impossible – they're operating outside our time frame.'

'What the hell does that mean?'

'Whoever controls them uses some kind of temporal distortion. The physics is complicated, but in theory, temporal distortion can speed up or slow down time in isolated pockets.'

The squeak of rubber soles and the shush of trolley wheels followed the sucking sound of the door to Scott's room opening and closing. Seconds later, an expectant silence settled in the corridor.

'You said theoretically.'

Mo nodded. 'The Unit experimented with temporal mechanics years ago, but they could never get it to work reliably. I know because I guarded a wind-down meeting. There were a series of horrific accidents – people materialising inside solid objects when the technology cut out, fusing them to form SCH's-'

'What an SCH?'

'A Spontaneously Created Hybrid. Imagine you're inside a temporal pocket, and you're moving at the speed of sound - everything around you seems static. So you walk in front of a moving hop, but your temporal facility fails and suddenly, you and the hop occupy the same space at the same time.'

'Wouldn't you just get squashed?'

Mo shook his head. 'It doesn't work like that — and they found out the hard way. In the end, the project was shelved.'

'How the hell do I link this to Shem Barber's private lab and the Nemesis Corporation? This is too much to be coincidence, Mo, but all I have are visions and suspicions.'

Mo scrutinised my face. 'Get me one more piece of information, Green, to back up your suspicions, just one more... then Oxton will grant us whatever resources we ask.'

'Including a visit to the Cinderlands?'

'If that's what you need, then yes.'

XVI

Alicia Barber had left a secure message on my com, inviting me for drinks and nibbles to look over a digi-logue of her father's disused hop fleet. She'd gone to enough trouble to know I only ate certain kinds of grafted meat and Klone Zone veg, and even promised to break into her father's drinks store for a bottle of real champagne. Mo, eavesdropping as I played the message back outside my secure pod, whistled.

'You've found yourself a friend. Take her up on it as soon as you can,' he said. 'Why don't you ask her to invite daddy along, as well? You never know what you'll pick up when you get him alone.'

'Alicia invited me when her father is out of town next week,' I replied, peering into my pod for the delivery. 'I've no chance of accessing the basement lab, and she's too loyal to spill anything daddy wouldn't want me to know. I put her off.'

A small, white card sat on the middle shelf. I snatched it up and turned it over.

Come to Paradise House today. DD

Dr Dawkins had something for me.

In the electro, Mo didn't ask.

Instead, he took a call from Sixty Nine about an incidence of severe head injuries that'd happened overnight in Cliff City. Some bright spark had decided to introduce a little more reality to the popular com game Brain Snatch.

There were already fifteen victims, all clumsily butchered. The word on the street was that a video crew were following the 'contestants' and screening the action live at an underground bunker somewhere in the ghetto district. The frustration dripped off Mo in huge great globs as he scowled into his com and snapped quick fire instructions at a colleague. Upstairs had noted that live Brain Snatch was complemented by a drop in other crimes in Cliff City. While folks were watching other folks having their heads scooped out live on com, they weren't beating their spouses, thieving, peddling or pimping. Upstairs, it seemed, were seriously considering turning a blind eye.

Mo cut the call with a silent curse. I didn't ask.

We didn't speak until we pulled over by the perimeter wall of Paradise House, where a handful of demonstrators milled around outside the main gate.

'Knitted hat brigade here again,' Mo rolled his eyes. 'I'll watch you inside.'

'Thanks.'

Dana Dawkins was expecting me, and she knew I wouldn't just walk in the main entrance. I kept to the horsetail ferns, moving underneath the fronds towards the small gate. On one pillar, disguised as a static Eye, sat a com pad. I pressed.

'Hello?' The voice was female, with a slight tremor.

'It's Jess Green.'

An exhalation of breath hissed through the speaker. 'I diverted the gate com to my access only. Take the path around the back of the house. My private guards will meet you at the rear. The disturbance out front distracted security. We can play to that.'

The com cut out and the laser locks faltered and failed. The gate creaked open. Mo nodded, and stood back. I slipped through and took the path that ran around the edge of the lawn. I didn't look back, but I felt him watching until I was out of sight.

At the back of the house, a raft of fairy lights illuminated a retro-stone path that rambled past tiered lawns, and beds brimming with priceless real plants. Several static Eyes lined a framework that ran the length of the house, but the lenses didn't wink as I passed. I guessed Dawkins had disabled them. I cleared the lawn just as two guards detached themselves from the shadows on the veranda. They seized one arm each.

'Hey!' I struggled, but they didn't lose a beat, propelling me inside with my feet dragging.

Inside Paradise House, three different alarms were sounding. An automated message repeated: 'Code Amber Procedure. Code Amber Procedure.' Staff hustled along the corridors and vanished through doorways without giving me or the guards a second glance.

'What the hell is going on?' I hissed.

'Security breach,' a guard replied. 'Stress toy liberation protestors. So it appears, one of them has breached security and entered Paradise House.' He stared down into my face with a smirk.

'The woolly hat brigade?' I hissed. 'They couldn't organise a drinks party in a shifter warehouse. And I do not share their dress sense.'

'That may be the case,' said the second guard softly, 'but this way, Dr Dawkins gets you in and out un-checked. We're only following orders.'

I ducked to one side as an android janitor rushed past hugging the wall, beeping with excitement. If Dawkins needed to resort to this, she was in deep. Why couldn't she simply step into the gardens, to take a quiet walk with me? Hell, she probably even lived here, on the premises, with Pinky and Perky stationed outside her bedroom door at night. What had she got herself tangled up in?

Ahead of us, armed security herded three women in fluffy white robes towards a lift. Their faces were pale, their feet bare. The half-dressed studs further down the corridor, all bronzed muscle, frightened eyes and loin cloths, had a separate escort. The floral scent of aromatherapy oils wafted around them.

'Take the donors to Safe Room four,' barked a woman out front. 'I'll escort the clients to Level Five. The Quiet Rooms are evacuated and sealed.'

Talk about coitus interruptus.

The guards hustled me into a lift, releasing my arms once the doors closed. I rubbed my bruises as we travelled up in silence. On the next level, the main corridor was empty. Dr Dawkins's office door was closed. One of the guards knocked.

'Dr Dawkins?'

The second guard tried the handle. We spilled through into the office.

The room was unnaturally quiet. The alarms below were reduced to a dull throb as the door shut behind us. A draft sifted through the slat blinds from an open window, teasing the leaves of the potted palm.

Dana Dawkins lay across her desk, flat on her back, her arms outstretched, her legs dangling, her toes almost touching the floor. Around the room, chairs were knocked aside, a lamp was smashed, and wall-mounted holographs were skewed. Slogans were daubed across the previously pristine walls in red paint: Death to Dr Death; Stress Toy Witch. The photograph of Matteus was on the floor in front of the bin, his teeth mashed into his nose. Somebody had painted 'Scum' across the mangled frame.

'She's dead.'

Dr Dawkins's eyes were half open, an expression of horror fixed on her face. Her mouth gaped wide, the cheeks blown outwards in bulbous lumps. Dismembered stress toys bulged from her parted lips, their fingers clasping the skin as though they'd died trying to prise themselves free. From the bruises on her throat, I guessed Dr Dawkins had a few shoved down her gullet for good measure. My hands crawled to my mouth.

'We can't do anything more until forensics arrive. We'll be more use out there. Come on.'

The guards left the room.

I couldn't bear to look at her.

Dana Dawkins had been murdered as I was on my way up to meet her. Somebody had engineered it to look like a demonstrator crime.

I gazed around the chaos in the room.

Maybe, just maybe, there was something she could tell me.

I closed my eyes.

In my mind's eye, the Doctor's hands moved quickly, as though in her last moments she'd been startled, sensing somebody else in the room with her. Her fingers fluttered as she placed something underneath the base of the palm tree pot. I felt her shock, sharp as a sting, as she wheeled around and saw a figure.

I slid my fingers towards the base of the plant pot.

Nobody uses paper any more. I have to be careful. I'm sure you understand…

My fingertips touched something.

Whatever it was, was thin, and flat. I pulled gently.

'Hi,' said a girl's voice.

I swung around.

She was young, Oriental, with straight dark hair. In one hand was a laser, which she polished with the cuff off her jacket.

'Dr Dawkins died of laser burns but it won't appear in the report. It's a new weapon – no traces. When Twenty One take the body in, Upstairs will block the facts and put a fictional account in its place.'

'You killed Dana Dawkins?'

She shrugged. 'Rent-a-mob downstairs is the cover, but doubtless you've already guessed that. That's why I had to let them in. They've infiltrated ground floor, but they won't get much further.'

'Why?'

'It's work. I don't get a say in who gets hit next. Today, her; tomorrow, it might be you.' She giggled, pushing the weapon into her belt and rearranging the cuffs of her jacket. Something sat along her collar bone, pulsating with waves of light – like a necklace, except more high-tech.

'Won't be long before the cavalry arrive,' said the girl, rolling her eyes. 'We must do sushi some time. Must dash. You know how it is.'

She touched the front of the necklace, and vanished. Behind me, somebody skidded into the other side of the door. I jumped over the broken picture of Matteus, knocking his nose onto the floor, where it disintegrated in a sparkle. I jerked the window up, and pushed myself out onto the ledge as the door burst open.

I ran down the fire escape. The slip of paper I'd found underneath the plant pot was still in my hand. I stuffed it in my pocket. Intermittent shouts and crashes came from inside Paradise House, audible through ventilation shafts and the occasional open window. I hit the lawn, and hared into the shrubs. Behind me, the static Eyes on the framework flicked to life. I cleared the side of the house and skidded to a halt at the top of the drive.

The security gates were wide open. A handful of protestors were gathered around a warehouse-vehicle that had stopped half way through. The driver's visor was open, and a uniformed driver was curled up in a foetal position on the stones, whimpering as two women took turns to hit him savagely, one with a hand bag, the other with a chunk of broken loud-mike. An unshaven guy with a torn coat stood in the centre of the lawn, flapping a broken, pot-bound arm like a bird's wing.

'Free the stress toys! Free the stress toys!' he whined.

The women abandoned the driver, who seemed not to notice, and continued convulsing as though fending off imaginary blows. Security guards ran from the main door and began to grapple with the protestors.

A pile of boxes fell out of the wagon onto the lawn, releasing a tumble of stress toys. Out of their stasis, they woke, some sitting up blinking wide, frightened eyes, staring at their liberators in terror. Others, confused and disorientated, ran for the safety of the horsetail ferns. Several formed a group, twittering and shivering, their little pink hands wringing, moving like a shoal to avoid capture.

'You're safe now, my little ones,' crooned a woman I recognised as Mel, stooping and reaching out a hand towards the toys.

They scattered. Mel screamed and shot upright. A single toy hung off her finger by its teeth.

'Fuck! Fuck!'

Behind Mel, two protestors dragged down a security guard. One sat on his chest while the other tossed his laser arm into the bushes and bound his hands, yelling:

'See how you feel when you're cut to bits, heartless bastard!'

The guard writhed as one of them drew an Old World hack-saw from inside his coat.

I skirted the front of the building, searching for a clear run. The small gate was invisible in the undergrowth, but it would be laser locked. Main entrance was awash with fighting guards, partially blocked by the vehicle and a fresh stack of boxes that the unshaven guy was lobbing out onto the drive with his one good arm. The squeals of newly-wakened toys rang shrill underneath the shouting. A flash of Mo's dark head appeared briefly behind the wagon, then disappeared.

A two-man hop sat behind the pile of boxes, one of the new kind, with small square thrusters. The driver's seat was empty, and the visor was half way down.

I set off, hugging the foliage along the interior wall. A stress toy darted between my feet. It curled its lips back and hissed at me, then scuttled into a discarded packaging box.

In the centre of the lawn, one protestor's efforts with the bound security guard and the hack-saw had toppled him over backwards. Three toys clung to his face with their teeth. Blood streamed down his cheeks.

'You fucking little bastards!' the protestor snarled, throwing the hack-saw onto the gravel.

He heaved himself to his feet, and snatched at the toys, tearing one away. He dashed it onto the stones, splitting it open in a splurge of gore. The bound guard flipped onto his front and wriggled away in the direction of the warehouse vehicle, his hands still tied. I ran, dodging the bodies, and jumped his legs just as he elbowed himself underneath.

I leapt into the hop and passed my Unit swipe-code over the ignition. The vehicle trembled and its control panel flared to life. I revved the thrusters. In the rear view, a confusion of faces and thrashing body parts ran like a film on fast-forwards. Mo wasn't among them. A thin veneer of sweat broke out on my skin.

Through the front visor, I spotted Mel carrying a box of panicking stress toys onto the lawn. They hurled themselves up at the open rim in a frantic bid to escape. I slid the side-visor closed and activated the auto-harness. A toy leapt out of the box and bit Mel's's face. Her lips curled back in agony and she threw the box up into the air. Toys shot out around her head and rained down around her in animated silence. Mo slammed himself into the visor at my side, his face and both palms flattened into the plexi-panel. I released the visor and scrambled out of my harness into the passenger seat.

Mo cursed and pulled himself in.

'Hell, Green, are you trying to get us both killed?'

I clung on as we rose and tilted dangerously. Below, the man with the hack-saw hared across the lawn in the direction of a guard who was pinned down by a screaming woman. The guy with the toys on his face dislodged the second of the three, leaving a livid hole in his cheek. As the toy hit the gravel he stamped on it, grinding his boot until all that remained was a lumpy red smear. The last toy clung on grimly, its little pink limbs dancing a frantic jig as he swung in circles, his features contorted with pain.

The hop levelled off and moments later we were up in the sky and pointing towards HQ, the tree-lined avenue shrinking beneath us.

'What the fuck happened in there?' Mo's voice was a squeal of fury.

Stormy sunlight shot across his lenses, and the hop cabin danced with flashes of uncontained rage. I'd never seen him so angry, not even with Guthrie.

'I don't know,' I said, truthfully.

'Those protestors were amateurs, Green – there's no way they were capable of penetrating that level of security.'

'It was a set-up.'

Speechless, Mo shook his head.

'Dawkins is dead. She'd been murdered by the time I got to her.'

For several seconds, neither of us spoke, all the unrestrained emotion drowning us inside the hop cabin as though it was a sealed bubble. We stopped above the river.

Mo turned the hop lengthways, tracing the course of the water. The waves lashed grey and white against the dirty banks.

'Mo, please, don't hover. I don't like deep water.'

Mo flicked the controls onto auto and folded his arms. 'This is where we stay, until you explain yourself, and tell me all the bits you're missing out.'

I closed my eyes. My legs tingled, that helpless rush you get when you're sure something dreadful is going to happen and there's nothing you can do about it.

'I met an assassin.' My voice shook. 'At a guess, she had the same technology the Brotherhood use to slow down time.'

'What?'

My palms were damp, and a sweat broke over my forehead.

'She got into Dawkins's private office and fried her with a laser. The window was open. When she left, she passed her hand over some kind of neck plate with flashing lights, and vanished. I never saw her leave, but when I went to get out by the fire escape, somebody had already shut the window. The only explanation is that the girl did it, the one who killed Dawkins. She sped up time, but not for me – just for herself.'

I closed my eyes and stared into the red haze behind my lids. A bead of sweat traced down one temple.

'Do you realise what you're saying?'

'Mo, take us away from the water. I'm going to be sick.'

The controls engaged.

Mo swung the hop around and took us towards the bank.

My mind spun. Below us, the buildings spread out in a grey splurge, dappled with weak sunlight. I pulled out the piece of paper I'd taken from underneath the plant pot.

'What's that?'

'She left me a message,' I said, turning the paper over.

It trembled in my hand. Both sides were blank.

I closed my eyes, and upped my awareness.

The paper held a memory, of Dana Dawkins fumbling to hide it underneath the plant pot, frightened. The images were fragmented, superimposed over each other like a collage. The memory was already fading, the colours leeched and pale, the emotions no more than a whisper.

I opened my eyes and turned the paper in my hands. The texture was thin as a butterfly wing, already deteriorating at the corners. An image solidified in my mind – a face: Matteus Finkler, in the holo photo I'd last seen crushed on the floor of Dawkins's office.

'Matteus Finkler,' I said.

'Who?' Mo snapped.

Dana Dawkins hadn't left me a written message, she'd imprinted the notepaper with a thought before sliding it underneath the plant pot on her desk.

The paper crumbled and fluttered through my fingers. By the time the bits hit floor of the hop, they'd disintegrated into powder.

'Don't take us back to HQ.'

'Where do you need to be?'

'Get on to Rosie, and ask for Matteus Finkler's retirement address.'

Mo swung the hop around, and flew into the sun.

*

Matteus Finkler's retirement strip sat on the outskirts of the South side of town, in rows of plexi-and-chrome, with gardens that had real plants. The absence of skeleton bikes beloved of the poorer, busier suburbs was complemented by the occasional lower-stream electro that ponderously crossed the tree-lined avenues at an intersection; even the transport moved geriatric-style. I slipped out the side visor, and hurried towards the entrance. Mo cloaked the hop and followed.

Finkler let us through the guest-scan without any questions, into an Old World-style hall with chequered tiles which reminded me of Barbervil Towers, except smaller, and less expensive. He looked much older than his photo. His hair was white and thin. He still wore Old World spectacles, the same ones as in the photo, and his trousers had grubby patches on the thighs where he'd wiped his hands. He ushered us into his apartment, where the scent of polish suggested the furniture that bulged from the walls was proper Old World and not retro. The settee, table, chairs and floor were alive with stress toys who sat up, alert, as we entered, fixing two dozen pairs of eyes on us.

'Good god,' I said.

Matteus shambled in behind us. 'Meet my babies.'

He reached out a hand to a high-backed armchair and a toy scrambled onto his arm with a croon. Matteus smacked his lips in encouragement. The toy scampered onto his shoulder, and nestled in the folds of his neck.

'This is Charlotte. Say hello to our guests, Charlotte. This lady is called Jess Green. She tells me she works for the Unit.'

Charlotte had faint grey markings. Her eyes were sapphire blue, and her nose was longer, and more mobile, than the escapees I'd seen at Paradise House. Charlotte blinked and chattered.

'I think she likes you,' Matteus's voice trembled slightly as he spoke. 'If you look around, you'll notice no two are alike. I was always against identi-cloning. Every one of my little children is unique.'

They were all different. Eye colour, body length, ears, skin – different variations of pink nakedness, some with tabby markings, or black patches. One had whiskers, others were missing ears. Some had fingers on their toes. Mo clicked his tongue and held out one hand towards the table. A tabby toy sniffed his extended fingers, and hopped onto his arm.

'Please, move one of the team and take a seat,' said Matteus, sinking into the well-worn dent in his chair.

Immediately, half a dozen toys leapt onto him, snuggling in his lap, running up his arms. Within seconds, they'd formed a jacket of eyes around him, all pointed in our direction.

'My original brief was to create low maintenance pets, Miss Green. You'll notice that they have no hair. They don't eat or drink, shed skin, or produce waste. These little creatures are perfect for busy people, young families, and allergy sufferers. There are no travel restrictions, as they can't harbour or pass on disease. The perfect pet.'

I stroked the closest toy. Its skin was warm and faintly fuzzy, like peach-clone-fruit.

'I didn't originally call them stress toys.' Matteus's voice darkened. 'That, unfortunately, came later.'

The toy licked my fingers. Its tongue was dry and soft, like Old World velvet.

'My original design was low maintenance and affordable. A handbag pet for ladies who lunch. A best friend for only children. A comfort blanket for lonely old bachelors, like me.'

I slid a resentful toy to one side and eased myself into the warm patch it'd left on the sofa. 'Where did the Unit and Dana Dawkins come into this?'

'Looking after Dana wasn't my idea. The Unit promised me unlimited facilities to develop my project. Their one condition was that I kept an eye on her. Of course, once I'd said yes, they changed the goal posts.'

'They employed you to spy,' I said.

Matteus shrugged. 'Police is a better word.'

'I'm afraid that Dana Dawkins is dead,' said Mo.

Matteus jerked his head off the back of the chair, his face a mask of shock. Something rippled through the stress toys like a wave. Several began to tremble, and one or two to cry.

'I don't get it,' Mo muttered. 'I didn't think the toys were sentient.'

Matteus reached for an old fashioned handkerchief and dabbed his eyes with trembling hands. 'They possess empathic qualities. It was something Dana is – was – excited about, way back at the beginning. The genetic modifications she made to my original design added a new dimension to my little pets. Then the Unit requisitioned the idea and made them into stress toys. My hands were tied. What happened to Dana?'

'She was found dead in her office,' said Mo.

Matteus's face blanched. 'Murdered?'

I nodded. 'Officially, the deed was done by a stress-toy-liberation group. The truth may be very different.'

Matteus pulled Charlotte gently from his neck and cradled her close to his chest. Her nose quivered, the whiskers beating the air.

'Do you know what Dr Dawkins was afraid of?' I said.

Matteus's eyes narrowed. Through the physical decay and increased vagueness of age, I saw the shrewdness for which he'd been recruited.

'What do you want from me, Miss Green?'

'The truth, Mr Finkler. Dana Dawkins called me this morning. I think she had something very important to tell me, only she never got the chance. She was dead by the time I reached her office.'

A single tear ran unchecked down the side of Matteus's face.

'Then what led you to me?'

'A psychic impression on a piece of paper. I never told Dana Dawkins I'm an empath, yet she knew.'

A thrill of shock ran through Matteus. The toys stopped moving. The silence amplified the slow tick of an Old World clock hidden somewhere in the ranks of furniture.

'I never thought I'd meet this moment.' Matteus's voice cracked with emotion.

He stood up, leaning into the high chair back. Toys clung to his trouser legs, sending the fabric quivering.

'Whatever Dana worked on before she came to me, it wasn't your average run of the mill genetic servitude. She might have gone under the public guise of granting professional women babies without a man attached, but that was only the cover story. Underneath, it was bigger... something else entirely. That's why the Unit closed her down and took her over. They'd planted a mole.'

Sensing my discomfort, a little lilac toy with a snub nose broke away from the group on the settee and nuzzled itself under my arm.

'I know that Doctor Dawkins engineered me before she was taken over by the Unit,' I said. 'My mother wasn't able to have children naturally, or so she thought. But she had no money to pay for the treatment, so she came to an agreement with Dr Dawkins. I never got to find out exactly what that agreement entailed.'

Matteus stared into the bloomed glass of an old mirror on the wall opposite. Looking back at him through the haze seemed to be a younger man, cheeks less withered, brow smoother.

'Then I can guess exactly who, and what, you are.'

Matteus sat again, stiffly, his face a mask of discomfort. 'I assume that Dana sent you here, to me, to find out. She wanted me to tell you as much as I could.'

'Please,' said Mo. 'Tell us everything.'

Matteus took off his glasses and rubbed the bridge of his nose. 'Do you know about Dana's expeditions to the Disaster Zone?'

'Impossible - it's illegal,' snapped Mo.

'Only when you do it without a Unit license,' said Matteus. 'Dana didn't have one. She collected DNA taken from subjects who'd lived in or near the Disaster Zone for more than four generations. Her expeditions were all privately-funded. Back at the lab, she isolated DNA strands from the subjects.'

The smell of furniture polish was beginning to make me queasy.

'Whatever happened to create the Disaster Zone, all those years ago, produced human and animal mutations,' Matteus continued. 'We already know that feline DNA somehow fused with human DNA, and that other cross-species genetics occurred with humans and reptiles. But that wasn't all. The human mutations Dana found possessed a high level of empathic ability unheard of in the mainstream populace. People who practiced psychometry, precognition and telepathy as a way of life. I suspect that she used a diluted form of the empathic gene to enhance my little pets, but I could never prove it.'

Mo's eyes rested on me. Underneath the careful control, the faintest trace of something he was trying not to show leaked out, stamped on before I had time to identify exactly what it was.

I pulled the lilac toy from underneath my arm and wrapped my hands around it, feeling the little thing tremble as it chattered at me.

'Dana must've used the DNA to implant into human gametes,' said Matteus. 'But the procedure was illegal, so she needed women who were desperate for children but who couldn't afford to pay.'

'And you knew this all along?' Mo spoke softly, but his voice was loaded with emotion.

Matteus sighed. 'I suspected. I built a theory, over the years, made up of the odd thing she'd drop into conversations at unguarded moments, and the occasional note I spied in her work journal.' Matteus moved in his chair with the discomfort of somebody in more pain than drugs could deal with. 'They took her research away. They wanted everything. I guess she knew too much for their liking.'

'Then somebody at the Unit is carrying on where Dawkins left off?' said Mo.

'No.' Matteus sank back in his seat, his fingers white where they gripped the side arms. 'Dana destroyed everything in a chemical leak. It was acid, a really violent bio-strain. I guess she wanted it to look like an accident.'

'It doesn't make sense,' I said. 'Why would she destroy her work?'

'You're not thinking in terms of the Unit, my dear,' said Matteus. 'What do you suppose would happen if Upstairs got their hands on people – or the ability to make people - with unique abilities? The resulting individuals would be enslaved. Take gambling – can you imagine knowing the shake of a dice, or the spin of a wheel before it actually happens? Or theft – where and when priceless objects are being transported, and the time at which they'll be most vulnerable? Then expand into politics and power games. If you can second-guess somebody's moves, you can outsmart them – the possibilities would be endless. Absolute power corrupts, absolutely. Dana realised that she'd opened a whole can of worms that should've stayed closed. She had to stop the Unit getting its hands on the thing it wanted most.'

Dizzy, I sank back into the cushions.

'Dana clearly decided it was time to pull the plug when she discovered she had a mole in her department. She thought the mole, whose identity she never discovered, stole information about her work. She was closed down as a result, which suggests the mole was a Unit informant.'

I thought of my mother, and felt sick. Dana Dawkins had created enhanced embryos using women who were desperate for children, like my mother, and I was one of the results. And now, the Unit had me after all, forcibly conscripted.

I leaned forwards and tipped my head into my hands.

'Dana staged the chemical leak so the Unit would believe her work had literally gone up in smoke,' said Matteus. 'She said the embryos had all been destroyed.'

'Even those that were already implanted in viable hosts?' snapped Mo.

Matteus shrugged. 'I'm not privy to the details, I'm afraid. How many of there are you, Miss Green?'

'I have no idea,' I said.

And what about my brother, conceived naturally? Or should I say, my half brother... Michael flashed through my mind, drawing in the sand with a stick, laughing, his mouth pink and wet, his teeth like little pearls... he vanished, the way he always did, leaving me remembering the cloying incense and the unforgiving heat, and the long, silent nights wracked by torment. I didn't realise I was squeezing the button until I caught Mo watching my fingers move.

'Dana's worst nightmare came true – they finally came for her, after all these years,' said Matteus, wiping his eyes. 'She lived in fear. Whoever did this could've killed her years ago. They tortured her by keeping her alive, knowing that, when the time was right, they'd snuff her out just as they threatened.' Matteus pushed his handkerchief back into his pocket. 'You survived against all the odds, Miss Green. Your existence would've been a secret to everybody except Dana Dawkins… and your mother.'

The tick of the old clock pounded my head. So my mother had been trying to protect me.

'Jess, you must be careful,' said Matteus. 'If you are who we think you are, then officially, you don't exist. Dana never knew who the mole was, but somebody wanted those embryos. If somebody wanted the embryos, then it stands to reason that same somebody will still want you.'

Just for a second his block slipped, and I saw the white coats, the labs, the machinations of Unit life and the prickly Dana Dawkins who over the years learned to trust and respect this man. I saw a good man, and a dying man.

'I'm old and tired,' said Matteus, his voice trembling. 'Your secret is safe with me.'

XVII

'When did it come through?' snapped Mo, snatching the com out of my hand.

'Moments ago,' I said.

He cursed under his breath and began to flick files out around our heads, hitting the control panel too hard, causing a few to collapse in on each other in glittery puffs.

'Hey, go steady with my com! What's the matter?'

'The message self-deleted,' he said. 'Whoever is trying to entice you to the Memory Banks left no trail. If I can't find the source, I can't find the messenger, and I can't trust the situation.'

I snatched my com back. 'Somebody wants to meet me about Dana Dawkins. They can hardly be open about it, considering the history. I don't have a choice – I have to go.'

Mo spun around, and then back again, as though he needed to pace off some energy but couldn't move from the spot. 'And this person didn't say anything about giving me the slip? The message didn't specify that you had to be alone?'

'Of course not,' I said, pocketing my com. 'It was just a few words from somebody who signed themselves as a friend, and said they had news. We can go together.'

Mo ran a hand through close-cropped hair, the air around him crackling with frustration.

'OK. But I don't like it.'

'One more thing. Rosie has organised to meet a few friends in the Memory Banks tonight. I know, I know, it's utterly bizarre considering we're waist deep in eviscerated corpses and we have Perseus breathing down our necks, but I've given up trying to understand Rosie. She invited me along too. I didn't feel I had any choice but to tell her we'd already be there.'

Mo leaned against the wall and looked at the Eye in the ceiling, shaking his head.

'She doesn't have to know why,' I said, laying a hand on his arm. 'I don't trust Rosie either. We just say we're getting out of HQ for a while. It can't possibly hurt.'

Mo pushed himself off the wall with his shoulders and shoved his hands deep into his pockets. 'You've never been to the Memory Banks before, have you?'

'No, but I know it's Unit owned. What can possibly go wrong?'

*

We took a skeleton cab into town and climbed out by an alleyway marked Carver Lane. The streets were busy, with enforcers ignoring shifters opening dealing, and adverts for the Deformathon spinning between the pedestrians - horrific images of children whose abnormalities were said to be the legacy of the Disaster and the mess the Old Worlders made of everything before it happened. A moon-faced girl being chased through woodland by a pack of slobbering tamewolfs; a little boy with stumps for legs desperately trying to negotiate a tightrope over a pool of liquid. Colourful fumes rose like spectres around him, and his face contorted as he struggled both to breathe and to stay upright. I yelled at them to leave us alone. The ads retracted and flew into the upper traffic stream, heading straight for a row of blacked-out hops who looked just the type to bet on crap like that. It was a relief to vanish into the shadows of Carver Lane, and to hear the bustle retreating behind us.

The further we went, the taller the buildings got, rising on either side as though they were trying to meet in the middle. Some had Old World style windows, but none of them were lit. The dusk turned to darkness, showing a smattering of stars that peeked between the rooftops. I pulled my wrap around my shoulders, and shivered.

Mo stopped abruptly, next to a double door set into a wall. A sliver of light shone through the crack. Inside, the corridor was bare.

'I can smell disinfectant,' I whispered.

He tutted.

The corridor led to a dead-end. Mo took a retina scan and the wall slid sideways, revealing a plush nightclub with a bar down one side.

'I'll be sitting here at the back,' Mo gestured to a table. 'I need to give you some space, but I won't go anywhere. Go to the bar and order a drink. Try to relax.'

I glanced around. The glasses were genuine breakables, the tables had napkins, and the décor was lush, but the place felt odd. Most of the customers were crammed together at the far end of the room. Their voices simmered in the background, an indistinguishable burr punctured by the occasional high-pitched laugh. Eyes turned in our direction and away again. I didn't see anybody I recognised.

How was I supposed to know who I was meeting? I didn't even know if it was a man or a woman. I glanced back at Mo. He was watching me, intently, and chewing a thumb nail. Near the bar, Daryl from Letters and Packages stood underneath a neon wall sign, alone, looking uncomfortable. Before I had chance to shout, the bodies ingested me again and I was bobbed further along. Daryl had gone when I looked back. I pushed my way free. Outside the crowd, the bodies looked fewer. I couldn't see Mo any more.

A waiter appeared at the bar. The up-lighters hollowed his eyes. I'd taken him for about twenty years old, but now, he looked freakily ancient. Behind him, the backlit optics glimmered like arcane jewels. He smiled, flashing white teeth.

I ordered a water and slipped him my bleep-code with trembling fingers.

At my feet, the words 'Door Two' were reflected backwards on the tiles. I slipped through the shadows, and carried on down.

The room was smaller than the main bar, with red velvet seating and a real wood floor. Two table waitresses stood chatting in a corner. Their skin-tight dresses might've come straight off a hanger at Mephisto. The tallest, a girl with an afro like a helmet of gorgons, looked up.

'You're bang on time. She's waiting in the booth in the back corner.'

I opened my mouth to speak, but she'd already turned away.

The booth sat in the kind of corner you'd walk past without a thought. A heavy drape on a pole hid it, as though spare chairs were stored there. The faintest prickle chased up my spine. I tugged the curtain aside.

A woman sat behind a desk, tapping into a table-top com. She wore white, something long that trailed, and a head scarf with wisps of hair poking free. She regarded me through one bloodshot eye. The other was scarred and stitched down at the lid.

'Sybil?'

Sybil snapped the table-top closed and folded her arms. 'I tried to reach you the conventional way, Miss Green, but you didn't seem to want to listen. I realise our last encounter shook you up, so I won't bring you news you don't want to hear, but we need to talk.'

Sybil gestured to a chair that faced her desk. I fell into it.

'What are you doing here?'

Sybil waved a hand. 'The small-print's irrelevant. Smoke and mirrors come in handy from time to time, but on the odd occasion that somebody fails to listen, I resort to less psychic approaches.'

Sybil pulled open a draw in the desk and pulled something out. She slid it towards me.

'You might recognise this.'

A collar necklace, inset with a display. The design was familiar... the assassin in Dana Dawkins's office, and the flashing lights around her throat – this was identical to the collar she'd worn.

'It's a time-collar. I won't bore you with the details of how or why it's been developed, except to say that if you want to do a little research, then a good starting place in Mr Le Blanc's Archives is The Bermuda Effect. The name may be Old World but the principle is universal. It deals with the folding of time. All you really need know is, it's yours. Take it. You'll need it.'

My hand hovered over the thing.

'It's perfectly safe,' said Sybil tiredly. 'When used correctly.'

My fingers closed around the collar. The panel flashed to life, setting off dim spirals of light across the front. The two end pieces snapped together.

'It's programmed to auto-close. When you need to use it, make sure your neck is between the ends so that you're sealed in. Only then will it work properly.'

'What the hell is it for?'

Sybil rolled her one good eye. 'Your protection, Miss Green. You must wear this collar whenever you find yourself alone. We have reason to believe that there will be an attack on your person, and we can't afford the consequences.'

I shook my head. 'We? Forgive me for not understanding.'

Sybil regarded me over the desk, her one good eye steely. 'For reasons I can't divulge, Perseus is unable to contact you directly. But he follows your work with interest, and he needs you to do something for him. This collar is currently in use by enemies of the Unit. Only by wearing one yourself will you be on equal terms. When you find these enemies, Perseus trusts that you will know what to do.'

'But I don't understand,' I said, my voice rising in panic, my mind spinning.

Sybil shook her head. 'Your instructions are simple, Miss Green. Wear the collar when you are alone, and don't mention this to your handler.'

My fingers closed around the webbing straps and I pulled the collar into my lap. 'Why not?'

Sybil smirked. 'Because it's come to Perseus's attention that Mr Okoli doesn't believe you're particularly able. Silence is sometimes the best policy. We believe that otherwise, Okoli will remove the collar from you, in the misguided belief that he is protecting you.'

I draped it across my upturned palms. 'But how-'

'I'm afraid that's all I have time for,' Sybil interrupted. 'I have several more people to see before I leave.'

Sybil stood. She gestured towards the drape behind me.
'But-'

'No more questions. You have all the information I can give you. Thank you for returning my token.'

'But I didn't, it's here, in my-'

My pocket was empty. I spun around. Sybil was holding the token in one hand. She pushed it into the mangled recess of her missing eye, and blinked. The stitched lid was mended. She stared at me with two pale blue eyes.

'That's better. Go, Miss Green.'

Stunned, I turned away, to find the drape still open, its rich reds and golds opening out into the empty bar like a portal to another world.

'One last thing,' called Sybil. 'If you succeed, Perseus will reward you – by giving you what you're looking for.'

Before I had time to digest her meaning, a hand touched my shoulder. I flinched. The waitress, the one with snake-curls and cruel heels, was smiling down into my face.

'This way,' she gestured.

I stepped through, the whoosh of the closing drape chasing my legs like a breath.

Back in the bar, with the curtain closed, and the waitress gone, nothing seemed real. The second waitress sat on a tall stool filing her nails and singing to herself. I folded the collar into my hand bag, and took the stairs two at a time. She didn't look up as I left.

The dance floor was empty, but the tables were buzzing. A hand brushed my elbow and I wheeled around to find Alicia Barber staring down into my face. Her hair was wound into the same tight chignon that only women with truly magnificent bone structure can get away with. Her lobes were heavy with pendulous jewels. Her greeting died on her lips with her smile.

'Are you OK?'

I nodded.

'I saw you and came right over,' Alicia continued. 'I was going to ask if you wanted a drink, but you're looking very pale… are you sure you're alright?'

'Guess I must've eaten something that didn't agree with me,' I lied, my eyes roving the bodies behind her.

I couldn't see the tables at the opposite side where I knew Mo was waiting, but what panicked me more was that I couldn't feel him, either.

'I've just spoken with your husband,' said Alicia, as though she'd read my thoughts. 'He's on his own at a table by the entrance. I dropped by to distribute some literature for The Eternity Fund - Mo was the first person I met through the door.' She gestured to the far end of the ballroom. 'Do you want me to fetch him?'

'No, thank you, I'm fine-'

'Nonsense. You're as white as a sheet.'

Alicia turned away and skirted the edge of the crowd in Mo's direction.

Nearby, Rosie stood at the bar, so close to Daryl that her breasts were almost pushing him over. A pitcher of sparkly pink liquid sat on the bar top between them, a number of shot glasses next to it, upturned.

'Jess!'

Rosie moved towards me, and squinted into my face.

'What's the matter?'

The whites of her eyes glowed pink.

I leaned on the bar, dizzy.

Sybil, Perseus, the collar – it was too much to take in. I fumbled for the calmers in the pocket of my wrap, but the tub was empty.

Daryl slid away between the tables. Rosie pushed a shot glass of the pink liquid at me.

'You look awful. What's the matter?'

I shook my head, and slid onto a bar stool.

'Drink. You look like you need it.'

I grimaced and pushed the glass away. Rosie shrugged and downed it.

'I've had enough of this place, Rosie. Do you want to share a cab with me and Mo?'

She rolled her eyes. 'The night's hardly begun. I told Mo you wouldn't last long. I think he's already gone to get a cab.'

Mo – I had to find him. Alicia had disappeared in his direction but there was no sign of her now. I left Rosie mouthing behind me, and headed for the vanishing wall at the far end of the room. The waiter who'd served me stepped out, snaking into the gap between the wall and me.

'You had a good time?' he whispered, his eyes glittering.

'I took a wrong turn,' I said, stepping backwards.

He closed the gap between us. 'Nobody takes a wrong turn in the Memory Banks. We all get to exactly where we're supposed to be.'

The wall shifted, the waiter stepped to one side, and I was back in the empty corridor, inhaling the faint smell of disinfectant.

'Mo?'

The silence and dim light made my head spin, as though I'd stepped out of a dream, into another reality. At the door, a dim square of light from the corridor fell into Carver Lane, frosting the cobbles. I poked my head outside.

'Mo?'

The lane was swathed in darkness.

Rosie said he'd gone to get a cab.

He must've set off along Carver Lane – and now he was too far away to hear.

I walked back to the wall and took a retina scan. Nothing happened. I knocked. Nobody came.

'Shit.'

Outside, a smudge of silver topped the cobbles, cast by a fat moon that hung over the chimneys. I set off at a brisk walk. Even if Mo had got all the way to the main street, I'd run into him on his way back.

Behind me, the light from the Memory Banks doors disappeared. I'd only gone a short distance when I heard a footstep. I stopped and spun around.

'Mo?'

Silence.

Oh, crap.

I began to walk faster. The high heels I'd borrowed from Rosie hit the cobbles like drumsticks, the sound bouncing off the walls. Somewhere behind me, the sole of a shoe hissed over stone.

I ducked towards the base of a building. Out of the moonlight, the darkness was impenetrable. Carefully, with one hand, I slipped off the shoes. Under my feet, the ground was cold and slicked with damp.

We have reason to believe that there will be an attack on your person, and we can't afford the consequences... wear this when you are alone...

My hand trembling, I pulled the collar out of my bag and held the ends to my throat. They whipped together and auto-fastened behind my neck as my handbag slid from my fingers. The front of the necklace lit up with spirals.

How could Sybil be so sure that this thing would protect me?

By my side, my handbag stopped before it reached the ground. Its handle had solidified mid-movement.

An indeterminable shape moved into the shadows. I took hold of the shoes as though they were weapons, with the heels pointing outwards. For several seconds, silence, then somebody grabbed me. I tried to spin around, but an arm hooked my throat. I lashed out, hitting the wall with both shoes, sending sparks off the brick. My basic training kicked in, and, choking, I scrabbled for pressure points in flesh. The shoes scuttered away. A leg swept my feet, and I fell. Something grabbed my calf - a large hand, strong, the hand of a man. I twisted around.

Moonlight fell sideways across his head.

His face was blank.

The bridge of a nose, and the faint rise of lips where a mouth should've been, were there, but unfinished, as though they'd never properly formed, or as though a sheet of flesh-tone rubber was pulled taut across his face to blank out the detail. He had no eyes, just faint indentations where the sockets should have been.

I tried to scream, but I couldn't. My attacker scrambled over my legs and pinned me down with a knee in my stomach. In his hand, a syringe glittered in the moonlight, the Old World sort, with a sharp silver stem and a phial of liquid at the base. His hands were shockingly normal, with short fingernails.

He flicked the syringe, and a single drop of liquid shot off the needle. As he grabbed the top of my arm, I jammed the palm of my free hand into his face. The heel smacked his flesh, making a sickening sound, like the thwack of a rolling pin slapping a ball of dough.

His head snapped back. The syringe flew into the air, landing on the cobbles with a metallic twang. Something around his neck glimmered faintly, sending out spirals of light. A collar!

I kicked up with one leg, and caught him in the back with my knee. The place where his mouth should've been contorted and stretched as though he was screaming, but there was no mouth-hole, and he made no sound. I snatched at his collar with one hand. The binding loosened and it came away, the lights on the front blistering and then dying. The faceless man froze, his outstretched hands anticipating hard ground, his blank face strangely contorted, but motionless, as though somebody had set him in clear glue. I rolled out from underneath him, the broken collar in my hand. By my side, the handbag still remained above the ground, its strap twisted.

So this was how they did it – the Brotherhood's deadly method, its invincibility, its speed – this little device, worn in a collar. No wonder the victims didn't get to know what had hit them before they were drained, harvested and stacked in a pile.

The distorted sound of a slowed-down cry rumbled out along the lane. I scrambled off the cobbles to my feet. My head ached, my knees hurt, and my fingernails were raw where I'd scrabbled for purchase. In the distance, a silhouette hung mid-stride next to a slab of light that fell through an open door. The low rumbling hadn't stopped, bouncing off the walls in innumerable echoes.

Mo.

The moonlight silvered his hair and glanced off his shades. The angle of his legs and his fists suggested a frieze of a runner, a proper one who'd clocked up competitions, muscles defined through the fabric of his clothes.

Mo was moving in 'normal' time, like the faceless guy behind me, who still hadn't impacted on the ground, but remained there, like a statue tipped over and suspended in a freeze-frame. I was moving so fast that Mo wouldn't be able to see me.

I stowed the broken collar in my suspended hand bag, and pulled my own collar away. A tiny sound, the kind of pop you get in your ears when you come down from altitude, went off in my head as the ends came apart. The faceless man hit the cobbles behind me with a dead-weight thwack, and the bass rumble suddenly became a human voice, Mo's, calling my name. He burst out of stasis and sprinted down the middle of Carver Lane towards me.

I guess coming out of fast-forwards with my attacker right behind me wasn't the smartest move.

Hands closed around my throat.

I began to choke, and my vision went dark.

Something hit us with the force of a freight hop, sending us both skidding over the cobbles, the faceless man underneath, me laying on top on my back, until we separated, and I hit the wall feet first. Stunned, I struggled up on one elbow. Somewhere hidden in the darkness, the sound of fists hitting flesh didn't stop. My collar was still in my hand. My hand bag lay on the ground, now, its contents spilled out. I slipped the collar inside.

Mo reappeared dragging a body. He dropped the arm not far from where I lay. It fell, slapping the cobbles with an outstretched palm. Hands, normal hands, with neat white nails. I scrambled away.

'Hold still - I'm going to scan you,' said Mo. 'You could have a head injury, a haemorrhage, anything.'

I sat, propping myself up on my outstretched arms. My throat was raw. My stomach was bruised. I turned away so that I didn't have to look at the faceless man. Mo knelt next to me, his com in one hand, eyebrows knitted together.

'Thank god you didn't manage to get rid of your tag,' he said. 'Having it fitted is the best bloody thing I've done.'

'The injection,' I whispered.

'What injection?'

'I knocked it out of his hand.'

Mo exhaled sharply and carried on scanning.

'Where were you?' I said, disorientated.

Mo's lips squished together. When he passed the com over my face, his hand was shaking.

'You haven't heard a word I've said, have you, Green?' He turned off the com. 'You have bruising but nothing worst. Twenty One will still want to give you the all-clear.

You don't know how lucky you are. Why, why did you give me the slip?'

Mo helped me to my feet. Carver Lane swam as I got up. He shook his jacket out and hung it round my shoulders. The arms dangled down to my knees.

'I didn't give you the slip. I was looking for you. I saw Sybil – I thought you knew. She was the one who sent the message.'

'What are you talking about? And why were you outside in the dark, on your own? And what is it about women on a night out?' Mo snapped. 'Can't you dress for the weather? Your feet are bare, for fuck's sake – and you're half naked!'

I'd lost my wrap in the struggle.

'Is he dead?'

'I caught this thing with its hands around your throat,' said Mo with uncharacteristic savageness. 'Of course the bastard's dead.'

He stooped and picked something up. The syringe glinted in his fingers.

'I need this serum analysed. It could contain anything. Until I know what's in the injection, I won't know what this – this thing was trying to do to you. We're going in.'

I stroked my throat gingerly.

It hurt to breathe. It hurt to stand, and it hurt to talk.

'I'm only bruised. You said so yourself. I can't spend all night wired up to some bleeping machine being wittered at by a holo-nurse just to tell me what I already know.'

'I can't take any chances.'

'What are we going to do with the body?'

I stared at the bulk on the cobbles. My attacker's face was smothered in shadow. Apart from the pallor, from this angle, he looked almost normal. He even had hair.

'I've called backup to take it in. Why did you leave the Memory Banks on your own?'

'Because Rosie thought you'd gone to get a cab. I tried to get back in, but I couldn't. Alicia Barber was there. She went to find you, then she disappeared.'

Mo cursed. 'I didn't see Alicia or Rosie. But that's irrelevant. You know the rules.'

A hop appeared overhead, its searchlights picking out the cobbles in moving circles. Illuminated, the place looked like a holo-recreation of an Old World Victorian slum I'd once seen. As the vehicle came down, its thrusters riffled the clothes on the body, and the faceless man became an oversize puppet, not quite real.

I suddenly remembered Rosie's shoes.

'I have to find something,' I said, squinting against the lights and crouching down.

I found one and picked it up. The heel was hanging off.

'You've been attacked, and all you care about is your shoes?'

'She only shops on North Side.'

Mo shook his head and turned away. Two men climbed out the hop, shifted the body onto a stretcher, and fed it into the vehicle. The whole operation took moments, like an expertly choreographed dance.

'Come on, Miss Green, let's get out of here.'

The crew climbed back into the hop. I didn't move.

'You just saved my life.'

The moon sat behind Mo's head like a halo. His lips weren't squished and his eyebrows weren't furious, but from behind the shades, he was scrutinising me, and I couldn't tell what he was thinking. Maybe still wondering how I'd appeared in the middle of Carver Lane like a special-effect.

'It's my job, Miss Green.'

I wedged my hands into the pockets of his jacket, and stared down at my bare feet. My toes looked like dead baby mice, bluey white, smeared with dirt. Rosie's shoes had indented an ellipse in the skin.

'Come on. Time to go.' Mo hesitated, then took my arm, and drew me towards the hop. 'You and I need to talk, but it's nothing that won't wait.'

On the short walk to the vehicle, I started to shake. By the time I climbed inside, I was racked with tremors from head to foot.

*

Twenty One took care of my bruises and pushed me into a water-blaster with hot jets that pummelled my aching muscles. Half an hour later, I stepped into the corridor with wet hair and a red face, wearing a borrowed all-weather lab suit. My own filthy clothes were bagged up and stuffed into my back pack. Rosie's shoes, scuffed and broken, sat at the bottom. Mo slumped on a chair opposite, his head in his hands, elbows on his knees. He didn't hear me in the soft-soled lab pumps. For a moment, I caught half-masked emotions whirling around him like an undertow: fear (for my safety?); regret (about what?).

'Mo?'

His head snapped back and he straightened up, whatever he'd been thinking blanching from the space around him as though I'd imagined it.

'Did they give you the all-clear and a shot of anti-inflam?'

I nodded. He stood up. His jacket was smeared with dirt.

'I'm sorry about your jacket.'

'It's only a jacket. There's something I want you to see, Jess. You aren't going to like it.'

He motioned towards the entrance to Twenty Two.

Mo took a retina scan, and said 'plus one' into the com. The double door swung open. The corridor was like any other at the Unit, except white instead of grey. Through plexi-panels to either side, prone forms on sheet-covered trolleys lay hooked up to monitoring equipment. In one, a team were in the middle of an operation. They wore white mouth masks and had smears of blood on their hands. In another, organs that didn't look human were enlarged on a holo screen over the top of a shapeless lump covered by a theatre gown. Somebody in a full body suit gestured at the screen, watched by two others with head masks. Mo ignored them and kept going. We rounded a corner. He stopped and tapped a digi-display in the wall.

'It's in here.'

I followed him through. The room was the same as the others, plain white walls and unfamiliar equipment. A screen on wheels hid something. Two guys in uniform emerged from behind it, charts in their hands. Mo gave a nod. One of the men pulled the screen aside.

The man with no face lay on his back on a trolley, naked except for a cloth over his midriff. His skin was grey, like over-worked dough, his hair mid-brown and wavy. The beak of a nose, the mouth with no cavity, the dents where the eye sockets should have been, everything I might've put down to a blend of my own fear and a trick of the moonlight was in front of me, underneath bright surgical lights, undeniably solid. His face was out-of-shape, contorted, the chin extended downwards, a large indentation in the centre, maybe where Mo had hit him. I recoiled. Mo's hand squeezed my shoulder.

'Twenty One ran tests on the serum in the injection. It was knock-out juice, Jess. The contents would've put you out cold for about three hours, but it wasn't intended to kill you.'

I turned my head away and stared at the machine they'd hooked him up to. Wires and tubes fed from it into the dead man's arms and torso. A holo-screen fluttered through a series of graphs and charts.

'The facts tell me that this thing was sent to capture, rather than exterminate,' said Mo. 'It was supposed to put you out cold for a reason. Somebody wanted you abducted.'

If Sybil hadn't given me

the time-warp collar, the whole thing would've been over before I'd known about it.

'Perhaps he's a new kind of perv,' I said, my voice shaking. 'Maybe he's got a whole load of women stashed in a basement somewhere.'

Mo released my shoulder and lowered his arm. 'Don't try to be funny, Jess. This guy wasn't doing it for his own personal thrill. You saw the face.'

'Yeah,' I said miserably. 'What little there is of it.'

'We think this is a 'tracker'. It doesn't have any identifiable features for a reason. If its mission fails and it's caught or killed, it is impossible to trace. Which effectively means, so are the people who sent it.'

I jerked my head away. 'No voice, no face, no identity?'

Mo nodded. 'Something like that. You see this here?' he gestured towards the flickering screen. 'All these are readings. This thing not only has no face, it has no finger prints, no blood type, and engineered DNA.'

'But he has no eyes or ears,' I said. 'How did he see me? How did he even know he got the right person?'

'An array of sensors. The guys here are trying to find out how they work. This is sophisticated technology. These things are programmed not to stop. They're sentient, intelligent, and deadly. Even the Unit's bio-projects haven't got this far.'

Why had Sybil given me the collar, but so little information? She'd mentioned Perseus, but nothing more. And my handler, who I'd grown to trust, who'd lay his life down for me if he thought he had to, couldn't be part of the loop, in case he took the collar away. The whole thing was a mess.

Mo shot a glance at the men with the digipads, who turned away and left the room. He waited until the laser lock clicked before speaking.

'Miss Green, this is not good. You go looking for information about your birth parents, and the Doctor who treated your mother ends up dead. Now somebody sends a tracker to knock you out and steal you away. Matteus Finkler warned us that this could happen. Somebody out there has a positive ID on you – and whoever it is, they want you alive.'

I stared at my hands, where bruises were beginning to form on the skin. The nails were broken.

'Can't we roll the clock back a bit, Mo?'

'What?'

'You'd started calling me Jess. Now you've gone back to calling me Miss Green.'

Mo turned away and looked at the thing on the trolley. 'OK. Jess.'

I stared at the monitors, the blur of information a holographic fuzz. The faceless man's soles were completely smooth. The toes pointed outwards slightly, as though his legs had relaxed after a hard day's work. It seemed impossible that only an hour before, this thing had fought with me in a dark alley. Mo grabbed a sheet from the end of the trolley and jerked it over the body.

'I'd like to know the identity of Dawkins's lab mole,' he said. 'That would give us something more to go on.'

'Somebody who worked in her lab more than twenty years ago? That's no lead at all.'

'The mole, or somebody connected with the mole, is behind your abduction attempt. Whoever it is will send another tracker,' Mo said softly. 'And another after that. If I can't find out who it is, I can't stop them.'

I felt sick.

I guess I must've reached up behind my ear to touch the tag; pain shot down my neck and I flinched. Mo snatched my hand away and tilted my head to one side.

'You've been trying to prise this out, haven't you?'

'No.'

Mo tutted. 'I picked up something on the scan I did on Carver Lane. It seemed stupid to mention it at the time, when worst could've happened. You've caused an infection.'

He took his hand away from my head.

'Please, can we get out of here?'

'OK. Come on.'

We left the body on the trolley and walked out into the corridor. The place was silent.

'Does the tag really make you so unhappy?'

I stroked my hair back into place and shrugged. 'You said it yourself. If you hadn't used it tonight, I might be slung over the shoulder of that faceless hero on my way to a cellar somewhere in North Side.'

Mo stared down into my face. 'Rosie should never have told you I went for a cab. I was looking for you, Jess. You'd disappeared from the ballroom.'

I looked down at the lab slippers, which were soft and shapeless, like puppet feet. The outline of my toes stood out through the fabric.

'I'll take you home.'

'I don't want to be alone.'

Mo nodded. 'I understand. I'll come in for a drink. And to look at your music collection.' The faintest ghost of a smile pulled the corners of his mouth.

We headed for the lift in silence, my eyelids gritty with exhaustion.

*

Back at my apartment, I cracked two glow balls, and we sat in the living room watching tongues of light and shadow roll up the walls. Claws settled on Mo's lap, while Mo ran through the listings of my music collection in silence. In the background, the broadcast threw out a Mozart piano sonata, an interpretation by a state-of-the-art musicom programmed to re-create the timbre of the original instrument. I find fast runs of notes oddly soothing. The anti-inflam was beginning to settle and the first sensations of stiffness cramped my arms and legs. Mo scooped the cat off his lap and placed him on the chair. He knelt by the side of the settee.

'I'm taking the tag off.'

'What?'

'You heard me right.'

Mo reached one hand behind my ear. He swept my hair back and pressed. Something clicked, followed by a release of pressure. When his hand fell away, the tiny flesh-coloured chip sat on the tip of his forefinger. The surface was smeared with blood.

'I thought only Twenty One could do that.'

'Well, you thought wrong.'

Mo flicked the chip into the laser-recycler. The machine beeped as it fried it. He pulled a steri-wipe out of my wall dispenser and ran it over my skin. My skin went hot and my neck began to tingle as the cell-repair kicked in.

'I don't understand.'

'Some things are best handled... differently.' He stroked my hair down.

'Give me your hand.'

'What?'

'Your hand. It doesn't matter which one.'

I held out my left hand. The skin was pale, my fingers almost skeletal in the shadows.

'Turn it over, palm up.'

Mo took hold and poised his other hand over it, a forefinger outstretched. I might've laughed, or snatched my hand away, or asked him what on earth he was doing, but something stopped me. He traced a line down the centre of my palm with his outstretched finger. My skin began to tingle where he'd touched it. He When he'd reached my wrist, and my fingers snapped closed of their own accord, gripping his. I tried to snatch my hand away, but his other hand grabbed mine from underneath.

'It's OK.'

A moment later, my fingers loosed off. Mo took both his hands away, slowly. A faint light traced the line he'd stroked along my skin, hanging over the surface like a silvery thread. It sparkled faintly, and faded and returned, as though it ran with an invisible pulse.

'What have you done?'

Mo shifted back over the floor and leaned against the chair. The cat slipped over his shoulder and settled on his lap again.

'What have you put on my hand?'

The light seemed strongest when I looked away to one side, the same way faint starlight does. The skin burned.

'It's a mark,' said Mo. 'Something I learned from the Spider People.'

I remembered Rosie's words - Mo's fiancee, the fiancee he'd never told me about, the one who I was supposed to remind him of, was from the Spider People. Mo didn't know that I knew the Spider People from my time at the convent. I remembered their dances, by torchlight, and the clicking of the nightbeetle pincers as they wove their ritual patterns in the sand.

'What does it do?' I said.

'It's a link. Between you and me.'

'So it's another kind of tag?'

'The Unit isn't involved with this one – no security department, no enforcers. This is personal.'

My palm glowed. 'So you still get to know where I am.'

Mo shook his head. 'No, I get to tell if you're in danger, when I'm not around. Then I can use the mark to locate you.'

'Mo.'

'What.'

'I have to ask you something.'

Mo didn't respond, but watched me, intently, or perhaps warily, I couldn't tell. Light from the glow balls gilded one dark cheekbone, giving it the kind of shine that made me want to reach out and run the back of my fingers over his skin.

'You put a mark on my hand and yet I know nothing about you.'

Mo shrugged, but not a nonchalant movement, a tense one, his shoulders taut.

'How old are you?'

Mo exhaled sharply, a stifled laugh, as though he was both amused and relieved.

'Two hundred and two.'

'So how did they do it? And what age do you stand still at?'

'It doesn't work like that. I age the same way you do, then my cells regenerate from the inside.'

'And you have cybernetics?'

Mo nodded, once. 'My skeletal system is fortified with metallic elements. My tendons are enmeshed with Kevlar fibres.'

'So how did you end up working for the Unit?'

Mo straightened up, and began to stroke Claws, who responded by stretching languidly and purring as though he'd had a personality transplant.

'I left the desert to work in the city. I was recruited while I was chauffeuring for a law firm.'

'How old were you?'

Mo shrugged. 'Nineteen, twenty. I wasn't promoted to guardian for more than ten years, though.'

'And your parents?'

'Dead some years now.'

'Do you still have any family out there, in the desert?'

'Yes. But I don't go back any more.'

'You're not… you're not like Rosie, are you?'

Mo's head jerked to attention. The cat twitched.

'In what way?'

'In a metal-face-bits kind of way.'

Mo laughed. 'No.'

'Do you eat real food?'

'Love it. Enough questions.'

We sat in silence, but not the awkward kind; the companionable kind, soothed by a backdrop of the old cat's unbroken purr, and the piano sonatas of Mozart, played end to end at a speed surely no human hand could've managed.

I stared into my palm until my eyes began to close, and my head hung heavy on one arm of the settee.

I awoke in the small hours to find myself alone. The cat was curled up on the chair opposite, and a blanket from my bedroom was pulled up over my shoulders. The laser locks were activated and flashing. Two empty beakers on the coffee table were the only signs that I hadn't been alone.

*

The following morning, as I stir-fried noodles with protein blocks in my kitchen, the com flicked on with a newsflash. A holographic reporter bounced onto the coffee table. Behind him, I recognised the frontage to Matteus's flat.

'Department Seventy One are seeking witnesses for information in a murder enquiry,' said the reporter.

The wok paddle slid out of my hand and lay frying with the noodles.

'Matteus Finkler, retired business adviser to Department Twenty Four, was found dead in his flat yesterday evening. He'd been asphyxiated. Finkler was connected with a stress toy project which recently caused controversy with anti-genetic-engineering activists. Interviews with neighbours are ongoing. A number of defunct stress toys were found at the scene.'

I shoved the wok off the heat, and killed the holograph.

My last established link to Dana Dawkins and her secrets had just gone up in smoke.

I prayed that whoever killed Matteus hadn't forced him to watch his babies being dismembered first.

XVIII

Oxton granted me two days recovery leave, with the caveat that if anything dramatic happened, I was to take an adreno-steroid shot from Twenty One and get straight back into work.

Nothing happened.

No alerts, no newsflashes, no communications.

There comes a point when my stress levels build until they avalanche off the walls and smother me. I guess it comes from being stuck in a little apartment with a cantankerous cat and a Mozart collection for company. I listened to music until I couldn't bear it any more, and yelled 'Off!' at the entertainment unit. I set the Dust Bugs to 'full clean'. They scurried along the floor and up the walls and furniture, sucking in loose cat hair and neutralising cooking stains. I waited for them to stop so at least I could empty them out, but they didn't because the new sort fry the crap they collect on auto-cleanse and then return to their wall docks without human intervention.

By late afternoon on the second day, I had cabin-fever. I found myself in a hop heading for HQ. At my feet was a pack containing Rosie's broken heels and the lab clothes Twenty One had provided the previous morning. I left Mo in reception, and took the chute down to Archives.

It lurched to a halt and I shot out into the shadows with my pack clutched tight in my hand. Reginald was waiting for me on the next aisle.

'I knew you'd come, Miss Green.'

'I have it.'

Reg's eyes widened. 'Follow me.'

We headed to his station in silence. I tipped the contents of the pack onto one corner of the table. Reg's hands darted towards the broken shoe. He picked it up, holding it close to his face and studying the scuffed sparkles, hissing and clicking to himself under his breath. Eventually, he spoke.

'What happened?'

I pulled out a chair and eased myself into it, slowly.

'Green, are you all right?'

'I was attacked by a man with no face.'

Reg gasped. 'This broken shoe...' he held it up, and the top glimmered faintly, 'you were wearing it?'

'Yes. It came from North Side. It's Rosie's. I have to replace them before she realises anything's happened.'

Reg placed the shoe on the table, reverently. 'I don't know if I can accept this as part of our arrangement.'

'Why not?'

Reg plaited his fingers and fidgeted. 'Because – because you're not a stranger. I work with you. It seems... indecent, somehow.'

'You aren't serious.'

Reg's eyelids fluttered. 'I found out about the steri-wipe, the one you gave me back at the beginning. It was your blood, wasn't it, Miss Green? Your head injury...'

I rolled my eyes. 'Please don't tell me you did a DNA check.'

Reg shook his head and looked at his hands. His fingers tapped together delicately. 'I just... I felt it.'

'Oh, so you're an empath now, are you?'

Reg looked uncomfortable.

'Don't you want to know what happened?'

Reg pursed his lips and shook his head. 'That's not how I make use of this kind of material, Miss Green.'

'Oh.'

'I realise you think I'm… odd… but I do have a code of conduct.' Reg's eyelids fluttered. 'I'd prefer it if the tit-bits you bring me are anonymous.'

'So you don't want the shoes.'

Reg's eyes flickered towards them and he reached out. His fingers rested on the sparkly tops. He closed his eyes.

'I'll make an exception. On this occasion. But please don't mention it to Rosie.'

Reg snatched the shoes off the table so fast I hardly saw them move. He stowed them in an empty drawer in his desk and laser locked it.

'Lets talk about what you'd like in return.'

I straightened my back, and winced. 'I want you to tell me about somebody.'

'So who are we looking for this time?' Reg fired up his com and pulled his seat underneath the desk. 'Your aunt? Your mother? Brother? Got a new lead for me?'

'No. I want to know about Mo.'

Reg hesitated.

'About Mo Okoli?'

'Yes.'

'Well of course I can help, Miss Green. It's just that… this is a shift in focus, that's all.' Reg inclined his head and plaited his fingers. 'Where do you want to start?'

I slid down into the chair and folded my arms. 'At the beginning.'

*

Oxton reached into her jacket pocket and pulled out a pillbox. She tipped it into her palm, leaned her head back, and funnelled pills into her mouth. She crunched, her eyes middle distance, as though she'd forgotten we were there.

'Do you realise what you're asking?'

'Yes,' Mo and me spoke together.

Oxton slid out of her swivel and stalked to the window. She twitched the slats aside and stared down into the square. An Eye darted past. She released the blind with a snap.

'The Brotherhood started off taking out two kids in an empty warehouse,' I said. 'That was an easy target. But they grew so fast that within days they'd moved on to entire office blocks. Now, there's a school.'

'The Unit have blocked all reportage on the crimes.'

'Word of mouth and underground networks will never keep this behind closed doors, Oxton,' said Mo, the set of his jaw grim.

'I do not need anybody to remind me of this,' Oxton snapped.

'Then let's handle it a different way,' I said. 'The Brotherhood's slipstream took me away into the Cinderlands on more than one occasion. That's why I propose we go out there to look for them. You might not think we have much of a chance, Oxton, but it's the best one we've got right now.'

'If we can find wherever they hide out, we can assess the best course of action,' said Mo. 'It might be destruction of the lair, disabling the Brotherhood, taking out the controller, or removing the technology they use to reanimate the workforce... but we can't do any of it unless we locate them first.'

'And if senior Unit personnel are involved?' Oxton's voice was low.

'Then somebody has deliberately pre-meditated the attacks to look like terrorism. We mount a clean-up operation to show them they can't expect to play these kind of games unchallenged. The wider public need never know.'

Oxton walked slowly to her desk and slid into the swivel, the seat creaking as she leaned back. Her eyes flickered between us.

'Maybe Perseus's sigil is being used without his authorisation,' I said. 'We can't assume that he's involved. That could be part of the game — somebody is taunting him, from inside or outside HQ.'

'Either way, Jess is convinced that the answer is in the Cinderlands,' said Mo.

Oxton sighed and ran one hand through the gelled spikes on her head, which sprung back into place like defensive quills.

'An expedition into the Cinderlands hasn't been mounted for more than seventy years,' she said.

Mo looked down into his lap, where his hands lay, motionless.

'People – valuable people – were lost.'

'Seventy years is a long time, Oxton,' Mo said softly.

'The Unit has a long memory, Mr Okoli.'

Their faces told me they both carried old scars in common. Oxton sighed a great, rattling sigh.

'This operation will, by necessity, be covert. It will also be conducted by a minimum of operatives. Your findings will be reported to me and me alone. Even the Unit secretary will remain outside the loop.'

'But she talks to HQ computer through her head,' I said. 'I think computer actually covers for Rosie sometimes. They seem to have an understanding.'

Oxton smirked. 'I have my methods, Miss Green. Rosie won't know anything about this. Mr Okoli, you shall pick the team.'

'Senior guardians,' said Mo immediately.

Oxton inclined her head. 'I can only allow you two.'

'And me, of course,' I said.

Oxton and Mo stared at me, silent.

'What?'

Mo sighed. 'You can't run more than a couple of flights of stairs without almost collapsing. Plus you're a magnet for trouble – you admitted it yourself.'

'That's crazy. You need me. I'm an empath. I can save you days by homing in on the target as soon as I pick up life signs.'

I sensed Mo's eyes roll behind his shades. 'We have technology to pick up life signs.'

'It's too slow and it can be blocked,' I said, my voice rising.

'The time we'd save in using your skills, we'd lose in travelling at your slower pace and protecting you.'

The set in Oxton's jaw told me this wasn't the first time she and Mo had discussed me.

Unbelievable.

If I wasn't permitted to go out in the field, what use was I to Department Thirteen?

Oxton began to shuffle files. Mo looked away, towards the blind, whose slats sat in tightly closed ranks, reflecting the ceiling lights.

My voice rose. 'You can't cut me out. If I hadn't given you the information that led to this, you wouldn't be planning this expedition now.'

Neither of them responded.

'Begin your preparations immediately,' Oxton studied Mo from underneath heavy lids.

She slid her chair back. 'Dismissed.'

Stunned, I followed Mo to the door. It wasn't just the set of his shoulders that conveyed utter stubbornness that wouldn't be challenged. He wasn't bothering to block, just so that I couldn't miss his point. Mo's mind was made up, and he was letting me read it loud and clear.

I had only one option: stow myself in the hop before the team kitted up, before anybody noticed I'd gone. The service staff would park it in Mo's personal roof bay, soon. I was small enough to fit into a cargo roll. Once we reached the Cinderlands, I'd crawl out. They wouldn't risk holding the mission up to take me back. I glanced at my wrist com. How long would it take them to get ready? I guessed I had a couple of hours tops.

We headed for the lift in silence.

'Jess-'

'Save it,' I snapped, tapping the icon for ground floor. 'You know as well as I do, I'm useless to Oxton if I can't bring her results. I trusted you, Mo.'

The lift doors opened on reception and I walked away, fast. Mo stood in the corridor and watched me go.

The smallest rest area on ground floor was tucked away from the scanners, the lifts and the vending machines. I glanced each way down the corridor. I was alone. Even the Eye on the ceiling seemed to be in sleep mode. I slid into a chair in the corner, and pulled my com out, my hands trembling. I tapped in a contact.

She picked up.

'Saskia!' I hissed.

The pause at the other end, heavy with shock, was broken by a sharp intake of breath.

'Jess?'

I hadn't heard Saskia's voice for months. The distance between us pulsed with unspoken words.

'Wait on, Jess - I'm taking you somewhere more private.' Footsteps clattered over a hard floor. 'Put yourself on visual.'

Saskia sprung onto the table in front of me, her face swathed in shadow, her eyes dark and circled. The thick makeup and long eyelashes looked odd, after all this time. Over one shoulder, the single strap of a glittery top cut into her skin. She looked years older.

'How are you?' I whispered.

'What the hell have you done to yourself? Where's your hair gone? And why are you crying?'

I wiped my face and we laughed together, a soft wheezy snigger, just like we used to when Luca was out of the way and we swapped notes about what was going on in the other rooms.

'Shit, Jess, you look as rough as a tamewulf.'

'You don't look so hot yourself. Is that a black eye?'

Saskia's hand reached for her cheekbone, but she stopped before she touched her skin. Her lids fluttered and she looked away.

'Luca's started taking customers who want to do damage.'

'You're kidding me.'

Saskia shook her head. 'Apparently, they pay more.'

Shocked, I rocked back in my seat. 'Bastard. He used to have standards.'

Saskia's hologram fluttered as she turned and glanced over her shoulder. 'He also used to own a club. Torches doesn't exist anymore. Not since the fire.'

'What do you mean?'

She shrugged. 'He wasn't insured. He's working for somebody else now. A place called Torque. They built it on the wreck of the old club. The rules are different.'

'How different?'

'Management say I'm expendable now I'm nearly thirty. Luca just got a fresh crop of younger girls. Slave-trade, Disaster Zone. Some of them are younger than I was when I first joined up. So I get the guys who like to hit, know what I mean?'

I shook my head. 'You're one of the best girls he ever had, Saskia.'

She pushed her hair back with one hand, a nervous gesture I remembered from Torches, something she used to do when she had a customer she didn't like – or a disagreement with Luca. Her hair was thin, as though she hadn't been looking after herself properly.

'Look, Jess, I've got about five minutes, OK? What do you know about the damage here?'

My stomach twisted at the memory. It wasn't a blur, it was a clear sequence of events that returned in vivid snapshots, complete with sound and smell. The sparks, the alarm, the sprinklers that Luca hadn't bothered maintaining, the sour smell of smoke... then the shouts and screams, and the darkness. Back then, I was fit. I ran, until I couldn't run any more. Before I was picked up by the Unit.

'Just tell me that everybody is OK,' I said, my voice shaking.

Saskia exhaled sharply, in a hiss. 'No thanks to you. Luca's the only one who never recovered.'

She glanced over her shoulder again. Her hologram wavered and slipped onto the table in broken threads. A second later, it picked itself back up.

'I'm losing you,' I said.

'Bad reception.' Her face freeze-framed but her voice carried on. 'I'm in the basement. Look, Jess, I have to warn you. There's a-'

'Seek-and-find out on me? Yes,' I interrupted. 'I know. That isn't why I called.'

Saskia's face became hostile, her eyes hard as blackglass. 'Then why did you call?'

'Because… because I miss you.'

'Sentimental. I always said that'd be your downfall.'

'I just wanted to hear your voice. Things haven't worked out for me since I left. I'm lonely. And I wanted you to know that if you need to get out, I can help you.'

The hologram jumped and began to move again. Saskia's face was almost entirely obliterated by shadow, as though she'd slid down into a corner somewhere. She started to laugh, but it wasn't a happy sound.

'And what the hell would I do with myself outside these walls? I'm not registered. Who would feed me? Who would stop them finding me? I couldn't work, even if I was able to do something more than screw guys. I'd be first in the queue for the next street compressor run.'

My eyes began to burn with tears. 'You could come stay with me. It's the least I can do.'

Saskia pulled a weed-pipe out of the little bag she still kept slung across her shoulder, and dropped a pipette of liquid in the top with one hand. She kept hold of the com with the other; her image scuttered over the table when she nearly dropped it. She lit, and inhaled. Her eyelids drooped.

'If you show your face anywhere near Luca, he'll kill you. If he finds out I'm in touch with you, he'll kill me, too.'

'Shit.'

Saskia lolled back against the wall and pulled her knees up to her chest. The folds of her dress fell back, exposing her skin. The bruises stood out, even in the shadows, and her collar bones were set in hollows. She took another draw on the pipe, then started at a noise somewhere. The com image slipped away from her face, showing me a blur of storage racks before it blacked out. Saskia's voice said:

'Gotta go…'

She cut out.

I put my com on the table, and tipped my head into my hands. I wanted to cry, badly, but I couldn't – this was too big, too deep, for tears.

What had I done?

The only person who'd shown me true kindness after my aunt's death, and I'd left her in a whore-house without so much as a goodbye.

Footsteps from further down the corridor broke the silence. I recognised them: Rosie. I ran a wipe around the rims of my eyes and pulled out my digi-pad. When she rounded the corner I pretended to be engrossed in a building schematics file of Business Block Two.

'How's things? No, don't tell me, Jess, because you probably aren't even speaking to me. I have an apology to make.'

Rosie put down the pile of mobile scanners she was carrying, and slid onto the seat opposite me. She laced her fingers. The nails were painted exactly the same scarlet as Oxton's.

'The Memory Banks. Mo's given me a hard time about it.'

I pushed my digi-pad away across the table. The Memory Banks seemed like a lifetime ago.

'I shouldn't have turned my back and let you slip out of the Banks,' she rolled her eyes. 'I should've returned your com straight away, I should've called Mo myself to make sure he got you home safe that night. If Mo hadn't suspected that something was wrong and used the tag to locate you, you might not be alive now. So if you absolutely hate me, I can completely understand, but I'm here to apologise and to try and put things right.'

'Wow. You really learned the script on that one.' I folded my arms. 'It's happened, it's over. There's nothing you can do.'

Rosie jerked her head to attention, sending a spray of hair over her shoulder. 'You mean you forgive me?'

I didn't respond.

'There's something you can do for me,' I said.

'In the name of conciliatory behaviour, I'd be delighted to consider… so long as it doesn't involve breaching any protocol.' Rosie smiled prettily.

I leaned forwards and stared into her face. 'You lied to me.'

'Me?' she squeaked, throwing one hand across her chest, her fingers outstretched.

'Uhuh.'

'Jess, I cannot lie to you. It's impossible.'

'I took you at face value and I was wrong, Rosie. I think you like to have a little fun with new recruits. I must've made it easy when I believed everything you said.'

'That's a very serious allegation.' Rosie pulled the fronts of her blouse together primly.

'That slimy thing in the pod? That was you, wasn't it?'

She recoiled in horror. 'No way. Ughhh.'

'The remote block on my com alerts from Mo. You did that too, didn't you?'

She blinked at me, aghast. She wasn't a bad actress.

'Not to mention the hop requisitioning. You engineered it so that I couldn't get my handler when I needed him, didn't you?'

'Jess! How could you!" Rosie's voice rose an octave.

'Then, when I asked you about Mo's fiancé, you told me you weren't authorised to tell me what had happened. That's bullshit, Rosie. I just spoke to Reg. He told me everything. It's not a restricted file at all.'

Rosie fluttered and twitched. Her brows pulled together into an angry 'v'.

'Why would you want to sneak around behind your handler's back, finding out things about him from Archives?'

'That's between me and Mo. I just want you to know you've had your fun, and it won't happen again.'

Rosie scooped up the scanners and sprang to her feet, her mouth pulled into a smirk.

'Well, Jess, if we've dispensed with the niceties and you expect me to tell you the absolute truth with no consideration for your feelings, there's something you should know.'

The Eye on the ceiling suddenly fired to life, juddering as it spun towards us.

'Your handler has gone. He's heading for the Cinderlands right now, with a hand-picked team comprising two more senior guardians. Oxton is fully appraised, but you aren't part of the loop.'

I pushed myself up off the seat, burning with rage.

'They don't want you, Jess. You're a liability. I should imagine they're almost in North Side already, about to head through the perimeter.'

I gasped. 'They can't find the Brotherhood's lair without me. None of them are empaths.'

'The word on the corridors is, Thirteen won't be around this time next month.' Rosie laughed, a tinkling little sound. 'The whole floor is going to be given back over to storage.'

I grabbed my com and hit speed-call for Mo.

'There's no point. He won't answer.'

The alert rang and rang. She watched me, giggling, her curls trembling around her face. I cut the call and scooped my digi-pad into my pack.

'I'm getting a hop,' I snapped, pushing past.

'You won't get out,' Rosie called after me. 'You're under house arrest.'

The Eye extended and tracked me as I headed for reception, setting off every other eye in close proximity, each one taking over where the previous one left off. Rosie's footsteps disappeared in the opposite direction.

At reception, I asked HQ computer for a hop.

'Request denied,' she said.

'Why?'

'You are to remain in HQ as a guest of Department Two.'

The bloody hotel wing?

'How long for?' I snapped.

'As long as Oxton deems necessary.'

'What?'

Security, embarrassed, glanced at me from underneath lowered lids.

'You'll find the accommodation in Two much more favourable than the prison wing,' said HQ computer helpfully.

I walked away.

At the end of the corridor, Rosie appeared at a junction. I wanted to scratch the pretty dimples off her face. She grinned and waved, then disappeared around a corner.

So. Mo had conned me. He'd removed the tag as a symbol of trust, he'd marked my hand using some arcane ritual he'd learned from the Spider People, then he'd disappeared, into the Cinderlands, with his hand-picked team.

Now, I was trapped, in HQ, unable to leave.

I wheeled around, scanning reception. Security had doubled and from the glances they were shooting me, they'd known the score before I did.

'What about my cat?' I snapped.

'We allocated a virtual veterinary specialist to your apartment on River Bank,' said computer. 'Your things have been removed from home and brought here to Department Two. You will find your temporary accommodation spacious and pleasant.'

Stunned, I turned in a circle, staring down the grey corridors that enmeshed, each one the same as another.

Every guard, every Eye, every little snitch in the building would be on alert...

I walked, fast, around ground floor and to the secure pods then up and along every corridor I could find, willing myself exhausted.

Mo had gone, Saskia was trapped, Luca had a price on my head, and if the away team failed, I was as good as bio-fuel.

Eventually, I found myself back in the little corner where I'd started out. The Eye had gone back to sleep. One of Rosie's mobile scanners lay alone on the floor underneath the table where she'd dropped it from the pile.

I ground it into the carpet tiles underneath my boot heel.

*

Two hours later, under escort, I checked into level Two.

The hotel wing had spacious lobbies but the locks on the outsides of the doors gave it away, along with the laser coshes that hung from the receptionists' belts. Nobody raised their heads as we passed, but I didn't see a single other 'guest' around the place.

My guards took me to a suite. They left me inside the door. The lock buzzed as it shut them out. The place was huge. Under different circumstances, I might've enjoyed it.

I slung my pack on the bed. An Eye stared down from the middle of the living room ceiling. I freeze-screened it the same way I'd done the camera by Scott's hospital bed. Some prat would be in trouble for not removing my field kit, but that wasn't my problem.

I packed half a dozen water canisters I'd raided from stores, my sand glasses, an all-weather jumpsuit, some protein biscuits, and my com. I emptied out my handbag. The broken collar I'd wrenched off the faceless mugger spilled onto the bed, enmeshed with the collar Sybil had given me – the one that'd saved my life. Right now, it was my only chance of getting out of HQ, and following Mo and the others into the Cinderlands.

I held the threads either side of my neck. They snapped together, and the collar began to glow.

The time difference meant it took forever for my flash card to chew the door code, but eventually, the gap was big enough for me to slide out into the corridor. In the fire escape, the glow tubes and the sterile scent of untrodden stairs brought back a memory: me following Mo headlong into the abyss, yelling at him over the banister. It seemed like a lifetime ago. He'd saved my life; he'd started calling me Jess, he'd put his mark on my hand, then he'd disappeared on a mission without me - it felt like a betrayal.

Reception corridor was a still-life. Juniors carrying digipads were suspended mid-step over the carpet tiles, half-formed words hanging from open mouths. The guards around the scanner had been caught mid-movement. Half a holo-file shimmered in the air. In the rest area, a lab tech grabbed at his shake carton, which had spilled a solid gloop of pink across a table. The half-formed thoughts were the weirdest, though - not flashes, or colours and pictures like I'm used to, but clumsy slowed-down sensations tangled around the staff in rubberised coils.

Exhausted from the stairs, I walked between the bodies towards reception. Rosie stood by a scanner, mid-conversation with a guard. His eyes were on her face, his mouth part-open, but Rosie wasn't listening. She stared off to one side, her eyebrows in a furrow, as though something had walked over her grave and she'd stopped, for a moment, and shuddered.

Did she know?

Could she feel somebody move past her at hyper-speed, perhaps even sense that it was me?

I dodged under the laser bar and passed security. Computer started to speak, a long, low howl of a sound. I ran for the double door, which had stopped half way, and slipped outside.

All over the square, people stood like monoliths, casting long shadows onto the flagstones. Tree branches caught mid-swirl sat in odd knots and twists above my head. The search beam of an android enforcer extended half a metre into the air, sparkling with refracted light. I moved between them, fascinated and repulsed at the same time.

The Brotherhood were dead - they didn't get to feel what I was feeling now, but whoever controlled them was very much alive. Did he feel the same bizarre combination of horror and power as I did, now, when he wore a time-tag and walked among the living?

At the cab point, I reached behind my neck and snapped the collar off. Across the other side of the square, HQ alarm began to siren, and the double doors auto-locked.

'North Side,' I said to the electro.

'Only permitted to take you as far as the boundary bridge,' said the computer.

'That's fine, just step on it.'

I checked my com. One hour until curfew. The city slid past in a slick of grey until eventually, the cab pulled over in North Side. If I paid my fair, Rosie would track me here through central computer. On the opposite door, the auto-lock was broken. I slipped out of the cab and sprinted away. The auto-imager flashed a photograph as I disappeared underneath the archway. Rosie would find out, but by then, it would be too late.

I ran until I couldn't run any more. Mo was right, I had to do some fitness. The memory of him stung. The image of his face in my apartment, the dim light of the glow-balls glancing off his dark skin, the mark on my hand, the way I'd woken to find a blanket laid across me as I'd slept... I'd begun to think I could trust him, then this. The only chance I had to prove that I was useful, that Thirteen was going somewhere, snatched away.

The streets were quiet. Shifters watched from behind the grimy windows, and from the little jetties between the buildings, their eyes embers.

In the nightclub district, I kept my head down as I headed for the boneyard. A cold wind sifted blacksand in an ankle-high mist around the stones. Ahead, two gleaming pieces of Kevlar were set into the old boundary. I cursed under my breath.

The faintest essence of Mo hung like sparkling dust in the air, no more than a glimmer - I could bloody well feel him. He'd come this way a couple of hours before, with two others I didn't recognise. An invisible connection stretched between us, pulling me out into the dunes: the mark, his mark. I closed my eyes. All of them had sand-vehicles, the open-topped kind.

I cursed softly.

My fingers traced the panel rim.

Clever bluff.

Mo had clipped a small section so the three of them could pass through. He'd fixed a temporary repair to make it look solid, and to keep it open until they returned.

Two minutes later, I stood on the other side as the wind whined and died, the boundary tacked back into place. From the vehicle park behind Fork Tongue, gold sparks glowed from the shadows.

I pulled out my sand glasses, switched them to dusk vision, and slipped them on. In the distance, a flash of sheet lightening whitened out the sky.

Ahead of me, the dying sun sat on the horizon, veiled by sandstorm clouds. I slipped on the collar, and set off towards it.

*

The sand came at me in slow motion, in great gritty slaps that tore at my face. At every strut of metal, or boulder that a travelling group might choose to rest by, I scanned the surface for lights, but each time I drew the same answer: nothing.

When darkness fell, I switched my awareness. Ahead, faint as a glow-ball in the distance, Mo's life signature ebbed and faded at the furthest edges of my consciousness, pulling taut and then releasing like an invisible thread, fine as a spider's web. He'd gone to ground with the others to wait out the storm: I could feel it. My left palm burned underneath the glove.

Eventually, my legs grew heavy, and my vision began to swim. I sank to my knees and pulled the respirator out of my field kit. A savage blast took me sideways into something solid. I fell, and began to crawl. Great sweeps of sand hit my glasses and ripped at my clothes, layering blankets of darkness over my body. My palm began to throb.

The last thing I remember is pulling the collar off.

Mo told me later that I was two metres deep inside a drift by the time he found me. After he dragged me out, we stumbled into a metal shell that might've once been a building.

Inside, the walls echoed with the sibilance of moving sand.

Mo's com sent out multiple points of light that roved the walls and floor like miniature search beams. He pushed it onto a strut in the wall, and helped me pull off my respirator. The collar was clutched tight in my hand. I shoved it underneath my kit, out of sight.

'Don't ever tell me I outrank you again,' I said, breathless. 'That com's way higher spec than the one Oxton issued me with.'

Mo sank to his knees, pulling off his visor. The com lights followed his movement intuitively, sending fine silver stripes across his shades, glistening over his skin.

'Why did you follow us?'

I shucked off the top half of my suit. It lay on the sand like a flayed skin.

'You virtually signed my death warrant, Mo. I trusted you, and you betrayed me.'

'What?'

'By stopping me taking part in this mission, you've made me virtually useless to Oxton. How long do you think they'll let me live before they give me to Twenty One for bio-experiments?'

'You don't understand-'

'You let that happen, then you come flying through the sand like a bloody superhero, pretending you've got my best interests at heart. Well let's get something straight - I'm here to save my own skin.'

'My prime directive is to protect you. That's why I requested you were grounded. You can't cope with field work. You aren't strong enough, or experienced enough. It was for your own safety. I wouldn't be here now if your wellbeing didn't matter to me. Think about it.'

I ignored him, and began to strip the legs of my suit.

Casting exasperation around us both, Mo continued to undress, the roving beams silvering his torso.

'The mark drew you to me, didn't it?' I said at last.

'Of course it did. But how did you get this far, so fast?'

'I stole a vehicle,' I lied. 'I ditched it when the storm hit.'

'How did you know which direction we set out in?'

I held up my left hand. 'Whatever this mark is, it seems to work two ways.'

Mo reached for my hand. I snatched it away.

'You're looking in the wrong place,' I said.

'For what?'

'For the lair. You came from the North East, but the life signs are that way, in the opposite direction.'

I pointed, towards the back of the shell, towards where I felt people, out in the dunes, subtle as eels in a dark pool, no more than an occasional twitch beneath a still surface.

'That,' I said, 'is why you need me.'

'No,' said Mo, rummaging in his pack. He pulled out a scanner. 'I have this. You could barely walk when I found you. How the hell can I rely on somebody so fragile to lead three guardians? Who, incidentally, I left in a bunker over an hour's trek away to come find you.'

I slumped back on the sand. Mo flicked the scanner, and the screen lit up.

'You're too far away to pick anything up with that thing,' I said.

He walked to the back of the shell. His com tracked him with narrow beams, sliding over the naked skin exposed by his running vest and shorts.

I tipped a handful of glow balls out of my pack, cracked them, and rolled them over the sand. Soft golden light flared up the walls.

Mo cursed. 'The scanner's broken.'

'Then we have no choice. We do it my way.'

'No. Tell me where the life-signs are. Me and the other guardians will deal with it.'

Mo tossed the scanner onto the floor, and tipped his pack out on the sand. He picked out two water canisters, and rolled one over the floor towards me.

'You've never really trusted me, have you?' I said, as I cracked the top.

Mo didn't respond.

I pointed the nozzle into my mouth, and drank until the container was empty. 'Yet you trusted Rosie.'

Mo choked. He lowered the canister and wiped his mouth with the back of his hand.

'Who do you think messed with our coms and made sure my transport requests never got to you, Mo?'

His face deadpanned. He pulled the scanner into his lap, and tried to recalibrate the settings.

'It's OK. There's no need to give me the blank face. I know about you two. I worked it out for myself.'

The scanner slipped through his fingers and landed in the sand.

I shrugged. 'I just... I just find it difficult to imagine you kissing somebody with a proboscis, that's all.'

Mo's expression froze somewhere between incredulity and horror.

'Kissing had nothing to do with it. And for your information, most of Rosie functions quite normally.' Mo picked the scanner up and rotated it slowly on the tips of his fingers. 'If we're talking about trust, Jess, then you're not exactly in the clear yourself.'

'What do you mean?'

'You went to Reginald, didn't you? You asked to see my file.'

I hesitated. 'I asked him about you. It was Reg's choice to show me your file.'

Mo crushed the scanner and dropped it. 'You didn't have to do that. You could've asked me anything you wanted to know, face to face.'

I stared at the mangled metalwork that lay between us. 'I honestly didn't think you'd...'

'I'd what?'

'...open up as easy as that.'

Mo shook his head. 'So, you found out behind my back why I was reassigned.'

I nodded. 'Reg told me... not everything, but enough.'

Frustration shimmered around him. 'Then he will have misrepresented Zaphira.'

Zaphira. The girl Rosie said looked like me; the girl who'd died. An image of Reg's face swathed in shadow crept into my mind. He'd whispered when he'd told me about the bomb, and the casualties, about how Mo had only brought Zaphira from the desert weeks before the tragedy, shortly before they were to be married.

'Lights off,' said Mo, and his com responded, leaving us bathed in the softer glow of the balls. 'I suppose Reginald told you that I never forgave myself for bringing Zaphira to River City?'

I didn't answer.

'Most people, including Rosie, think that I never met anybody else because I never got over her.'

Outside, a squall of wind hit the side of the building, rattling the shell.

'Is that true?'

Mo stared down at the bits of broken metal. 'I was about to call the whole thing off. Only we never got that far.'

I began to stack the rations that'd fallen out of Mo's pack, not because they needed stacking, but because I knew the kind of silence that would follow, and that I had to let him talk.

'She was unfaithful. I found out. The afternoon of the... the afternoon she died, I was set to confront her. She was seeing another guardian, good service record, a guy I trusted.' He laughed, a small, sad sound, like a sigh. 'He got promoted afterwards. They moved him out of my reach. I swore when I saw him again, I'd punch him.'

The glow-ball in the corner flickered and began to die. The remaining lights ebbed and flared, sending veils of shadow across our faces.

'Turned out he'd been screwing my fiancee behind my back for months.' Mo's voice held no bitterness, only sadness. 'Apparently, they were going to get married. While she was still wearing my mark on her hand.'

I opened my left hand and stared into the palm. The mark had gone. The skin didn't burn any more. I snapped my fingers closed.

'What was his name?'

'Saul. Saul Gunner.' Mo's lips twisted. 'He was warming somebody else's bed before Zaphira's ashes were cold.'

I swore under my breath.

'I didn't see him again for years, not until just before you were recruited.'

'You lost your temper, didn't you?'

Mo stopped messing about with the broken scanner and stared at me. 'Yes.'

I looked away, at the things scattered around us, the detritus of a demolished landscape. The silence expanded between us.

'I punched him,' Mo said at last, 'so they demoted me. But you already know.'

'I'm sorry.'

'About what?'

I shrugged. 'Everything.'

Mo tossed the scanner bits into a corner. They clanged into the wall.

'It isn't your problem, Jess.'

'It is so long as you're my handler.'

Mo gathered some ration packs and divided them, passing half to me. 'At least we won't starve.'

He tore the top off a pouch and poured the contents into his mouth. I fiddled with mine, watching him from underneath lowered lids, the shadows that moved across his face as he ate, the way he sat, back rod straight, as though he'd sat like this often, waiting.

'Do I look like her?' I said.

Mo stopped eating. 'Like Zaphira? No. She was tall and fair. You're completely the opposite.'

I put the pouch down. 'Rosie said-'

'Rosie wasn't telling you the truth. It's not the first time she's played that trick on a new recruit. Eat. You'll need your strength for the return journey.'

Mo ditched the empty ration pack and picked up his water.

'You said Zaphira was still wearing your mark when she was unfaithful. As though the mark is some kind of a... symbol.'

Mo lowered the canister. A smile played with the corners of his mouth. 'And you want to know why I put the mark on you.'

I shrugged.

Mo laughed. 'There's a naivety about you I find puzzling, Green.'

'What's that supposed to mean?'

He shrugged. 'As though underneath the front, there's a lot you just don't get.'

I bridled. 'Like what?'

'There's never been anybody special for you, has there?'

The nearest glow ball flickered inside its shell, morphing into delicate strains of gold and yellow. He watched me with an intentness that made me want to look away, as though trying so see something inside, something private that he'd never looked for before.

'Those years in the club… didn't you meet anybody?'

'That's a stupid question. The club was a job. I met customers, and other girls.'

Mo shrugged. 'The customers, then. Didn't anybody offer to buy you out? Take you away?'

'You have a very romantic idea of what club clients are like. I had plenty of offers to buy me, but it wasn't to give me a better life.'

'So you refused?'

'No, Luca refused. Said I was too good for business.'

'So what about the other girls?'

'The other girls?'

Mo shrugged. 'How about you and Saskia? Were you two ever-'

'No. She was a friend, that's all. Although plenty of customers asked for us together.'

Mo's eyebrows shot up. 'I just meant if you'd been put off guys for good, I could understand.'

My palm began tingle. I stretched my hand out, slowly, between us. A faint blue line hung over the skin, so faint that it shintled when I moved, sparkling and vanishing like a faulty hologram. Mo took hold of my hand and tilted it. His eyebrows knitted together. The mark flared and disappeared, leaving the skin hot.

'What's the matter?'

'It's still there.' He drew his hand away.

'You sound surprised.'

Mo moved away, rocking back on his heels, then stood, his top half disappearing into the shadows.

'Where are you going?'

'I need to stretch my legs.'

He snatched his com and disappeared into a little annexe at the far end of the shell.

'The wind,' I said. 'It's dropped. Listen.'

Sand hit the walls in lazy hisses, punctuated by periods of silence.

I emptied the rest of the ration pack into my mouth. Mo reappeared and sat opposite me, further away this time, his expression clouded.

'If you want to call the others, you're safe to use a flare,' I said.

'How do you know?'

'Because the installation we're looking for is underground.' I ditched the empty pack and reached for a fibre biscuit. 'I can feel the life-signs, but they're hidden. At first I thought it was the effects of the storm, but it isn't.'

Mo didn't respond.

'How can you say you don't need me?' I took a bite of the biscuit and grimaced.

'Jess.'

'What?'

A squall blew sand into the far side of the shell, followed by silence, which seemed to stretch over the dunes around us. I stopped eating. Mo leapt to his feet, and grabbed his sand-suit.

'I'm setting a flair.'

He disappeared towards the hole we'd got in through, suit, mask and glasses in one hand.

XIX

The others arrived at dawn.

Three shadows broke the lilac light that sent long fingers onto the floor around the entrance. I scrambled to my feet.

Outside, the dunes were eerily silent. The black, shifting skies of the previous day were cloudless blue, scored by three silhouettes of identical height. One was slender, with long, beaded hair. She was tall and muscular, her plaits tied back untidily, her eyes two green slants above high cheekbones. The other, a man with pale skin and a suspicious expression, had an empty laser hand that twitched uneasily. The muscles of his arms and shoulders stood out like moulded Kevlar through his skinsuit. I remembered the night at Raymonds, when I'd stared in through the window and spotted my com poking out of Rosie's bag. They'd both been with Mo that night, celebrating somebody's birthday.

'Meet Jody and Max,' said Mo. 'We go back a long way. And this is Jess Green.'

'So,' I said. 'When do we leave?'

'We reconnaissance immediately,' said Jody, her eyes roving my body with disapproval.

Mo motioned towards the shell. By daylight, it sat at an angle, embedded in a dune, as though a terrific force had tossed it there with ease. Jody and Max loped past me, peeled-off storm gear flapping around their mid-riffs. They ducked through the entrance. Mo hung back.

'After you've guided us to the target, you must return here for your own safety, Jess.'

'And what am I supposed to do? Play solitaire with lumps of blackglass until you turn up to collect me?'

'You can do whatever you want,' said Mo, disappearing inside, 'so long as you stay put.'

At the rear of the shell, Jody and Max set their coms as lights. Mo gave me the nod. I closed my eyes.

Somewhere over the dunes, life signs twitched and wriggled like grubs in a honeycomb, responding to my probing, then falling still as I pulled away. Around them, a darkness unfurled itself and began to spread. My eyes snapped open. The guardians were watching me intently.

'There are more than ten people,' I said. 'A dozen, maybe. Dead cargo too. But I'm picking something else up – messed up life-signatures, the same as Barber's basement lab. And a kind of gathering momentum. Something's happening inside the installation.'

'What?' Mo radiated tension.

'Can't explain it. Maybe the Brotherhood are powering up, ready for another attack.'

The guardians began to strip their storm gear in silence. There's nothing weirder than standing in a dark hangar with three near-naked titans who can communicate without words. I looked away, but my eyes were drawn back to their muscled bodies, the long limbs, the perfect skin. A fine gauze of dawn light from the entrance fell across Mo's back as he pulled some clothes from his kit and began to slide them on. I shut my eyes. The image sat behind my lids like a photograph. Seconds later, they stood by the entrance, checking their laser weapons, and sliding kit into their leg pockets with the ease of people who'd done the same thing hundreds of times.

'Jess, to the front, with me,' said Mo.

For once, I didn't argue.

We travelled in silence.

The horizon undulated, one dune melting into another. Jody and Max scanned each flank with long-sights. All the while, the life signs ebbed and faded, pulling me towards them inexorably.

Beneath our feet, the sand was no longer black – whorls of golden brown wove through it in random patterns. Over the top of the next dune, we found a hollow whose centre was green with real plants. An oasis – a bloody oasis, on the edge of the Disaster Zone. Something circled the sky above our heads. The keen of its voice carried on the wind. A bird – a real wild bird, riding the thermals.

'There aren't supposed to be any free birds out here,' I said. 'They're all supposed to be owned and licensed, or dead.'

Nobody responded.

Behind a screen of plants, several hops sat in a row. Most of them were old, but one was unmarked, black, and new: a speed hop, the most expensive kind.

Beyond, an unguarded bunker door was set into a mound.

Somebody opened a man-hatch in the door. Two men appeared. The largest turned to glance at the ridge, briefly. He radiated nervous energy, the sort you get when you're about to do something dangerous. His baseball cap fell off.

Graham.

He turned away and both men disappeared back inside, closing the hatch behind them.

Beyond the door, a string of vents stood out along the sand like the spine of a huge buried lizard. Jody and Max slipped off the top of the ridge and headed towards them.

I turned to Mo. 'How did they-'

'I gave the order.'

'But you didn't speak or move.'

Mo's lips twisted up at the corners. 'I have to return you to the shell.'

We traced our footsteps back over the dunes. A sensation of spreading darkness wrapped around me. Something was powering up inside the installation, something powerful and remorseless, something that leaked out through the ground.

'What will Jody and Max do?' I said.

'They'll find an entry point and wait for my return.'

'There's really no need to take me right to the entrance. I'll be fine from here.'

'I'll watch you inside,' said Mo.

The sun had risen, sending up faint heat ripples. Half way back to the shell, I turned around. A golden sheen across Mo's shades was broken by the single speck of a bird's silhouette from somewhere up above.

'I'll be back for you as soon as I'm able.'

I headed back to the shell, pushed through the entrance, into the shadows, and took the collar out of my pack.

*

Mo was frozen mid-stride, half way down a slope, one leg outstretched, when I caught up with him. Sand sprayed up around his back foot in a solid swathe. I didn't stop to study his expression, just in case I found the same suspicion I'd seen in Rosie's face as I'd passed her, immobilised at HQ reception. I ran on, my feet skimming the sand.

Jody and Max were statues, each of them crouched over air vents with the tops popped off, ready to descend. Max had a length of rope in one hand, solidified into a lasso. Jody's beaded plaits flayed out at odd angles.

I chose the furthest vent. The fixings were solid, but nothing Kevlar cutters couldn't handle. The top was too heavy to lift. I pulled the micro-hydraulics from my pack, attached them, and gave the lid a flick, then took out my torch and shone it inside.

The vent chute ran in one direction. That made it easier: I didn't have a choice.

I lowered myself in, and wriggled onto my stomach.

The darkness was punctuated by slats of light at regular intervals. I elbowed myself along. Behind the first grille was an accommodation chamber, small and disorganised. Next came an empty room, shiny white like a half-finished medical bay. Somebody was talking. The retarded voices echoed through the shaft, taking on a manic tinge. At the far end of the room stood two pairs of feet in heavy desert boots, the kind that looked decommissioned. I kept moving.

The vent shaft changed direction at a corner. A sigh of cool air came from the next grille. I pushed my face up to it. A low-level strip light ran around the room at floor level. Rows of identical pods lined the far wall, visible only as outlines in the shadows. Each was sealed by a plexi door. The pods stretched as far as I could see in both directions.

My hands trembled so violently that the laser clipper slipped through my fingers. It hit the bottom of the shaft with a boom. Carefully, I picked it up and began to remove the fixings. The cut-out was small – so small that if Mo and the others were here, they would never have got through it. I slid the grille to one side, tossed my pack to the floor, and slithered head-first onto it.

Every pod contained a body that sat like a dark stain behind the panel. The eye sockets were empty hollows, the mouths pulled taut over yellowed teeth. The dome of each skull was shrivelled and covered with tufts of hair. The figures leaned forwards, as though they'd been frozen while trying to claw out of the restrains that clamped their shrivelled wrists. The tops of the pods glowed softly in the dark, as though each dead man was joined at the skull to a power source. Sickened, I turned away.

If I could find the controller, I could guide Mo and the others right to him; and if I could find whatever power source prepared the Brotherhood for action, I could deactivate it.

I switched my awareness.

At the centre of the installation sat a core that resonated with strong emotion. A single life signature emanated from within: dark, obsessively driven, acquisitive.

Somewhere above, on the dunes, Mo and the others were moving in slow motion towards the vent shafts. I had to pull them in the right direction – I wasn't a match for the Brotherhood's controller on my own. My palm flared, a flash of blue searing across the skin. The mark pulled taut like a spectral thread.

Out in the corridor, the lights were failing. I began to run. Ahead of me was a double door, which opened into a lab. Medical equipment and operating tables were organised in rows, lit by cold, bluey-white lights that hung in racks from the ceiling.

In a bay enclosed by clear panels lay a man a little older than me, his face frozen in an expression beyond agony. His upper body was bruised and burned, his lower body gone – at the waist, he disappeared into the seat of a sand vehicle as though man and machine had fused together. Bloodied skin sat in patches over the metal, stretched like living fabric. Leg bones jutted from the vehicle's underside as though they'd been deliberately modelled to form part of the frame. He wasn't wired up to a monitor or a painkilling unit – he'd simply been dumped in the pen and left to die.

Further along, on a slab, two entwined bodies lay facing each other. Their nakedness was barely covered by a surgical gown thrown carelessly across their middles. The man had his back to me. An arm pushed out through his spine. He faced a girl whose eyes were glazed with the sightlessness of the newly dead. The skin was unbroken between her elbow and his vertebrae, healed as though she'd punched through him and they'd fused together. I staggered backwards, my hand reaching for support, and toppled into an equipment trolley.

Something shifted on the surface. I spun around to face a child's head inside a tank, wires and probes coming off the shaven scalp. It could've been boy or girl, I couldn't tell, no older than seven or eight; the eyes were open but sightless, the skin sloughed off in patches where tree bark pushed through from underneath.

Dizzy, I stumbled out into the walkway. Something popped inside my head: the space around me became heavy with the weight of physical pain and utter helplessness, split by a crash and a slop of lukewarm fluid that drenched my legs.

The collar lay on the floor.

Next to it, in the wreckage of the broken tank, the child's head mouthed silently, its lips smacking, a pool of viscous liquid spreading fast around it. The bark-fused skin glistened underneath the harsh lights.

I snatched the collar up, my hands shaking.

Shem Barber wasn't messing about with the DNA of race-droid-horses – these were the messed-up life-signatures I'd picked up in the basement of Barbervil Towers, the afternoon of the Eternity Fund launch. No wonder he needed to move out into the Cinderlands fast. But what was he doing it for? Kicks? Had an unlimited supply of credits and the futility of his endless collections finally pushed him over the edge, to commit atrocities for his own entertainment?

I turned around, slowly, my cheeks wet with tears, the stifling stench of death and pain thick in the air. Every person in here had been fused with something, cut and spliced, stuck together and kept alive… but why?

'Jess…'

The voice, no more than a whisper, came from somewhere close.

'Jess…'

I spun around. In the far corner of the room, the lights were out and the shadows deepened.

I ran.

A trolley stood at an angle, as though somebody had abandoned it in a hurry. On top lay the bulk of a prone body.

'Jess…'

An Old World style baseball cap hung off the corner of the headrest.

Graham.

'Jess,' he whispered, his eyes glazed and unfocussed, his jowls trembling with effort.

'Graham,' I said, taking his hand.

His skin was cold, as though the life was leaking out of him.

I squeezed his hand.

How the hell had he known my name? The man was hardly conscious and yet he'd called out to me as though he'd known I was here!

I closed my eyes.

The space inside Graham's head was dark, and light, and fractured like smashed bits of Old World stained glass. Snapshots of thoughts and memories lay around my feet like broken objects, mangled beyond recognition. Half-formed images flashed through my head and spun off into the ether, colliding. His mind was mashed. Somewhere deep within himself, Graham responded to my presence, drawing me further in, to where a tiny kernel of him remained, untouched.

'Graham, tell me.'

It came in impressions that tumbled over each other in shades of grey.

'You're an empath,' I whispered, 'a bloody empath…'

Graham was my living link to the Brotherhood. It was him who'd sensed me when I locked on to them, on the rooftop at the second crime scene; Graham who'd snapped the doors closed and retreated, who'd drawn me towards them from day one.

Graham disappeared like an outbound tide, rushing away into total blackness. I opened my eyes and gripped the side of the trolley to steady myself.

As a mark of respect, I closed his eyes.

If Graham had known that I was tracking the Brotherhood, if he'd lay on his deathbed whispering my name, if he'd drawn me here intentionally, then he'd told somebody else that I was coming…

The door swung open.

I turned around.

Harsh light fell onto the crown of a neat chignon.

Her pale blue eyes sparkled with malice.

'I've been expecting you.' Alicia Barber stood inside the doorway, the hem of a white lab coat swishing around her calves. 'You got inside without me knowing. I'd be interested to know how you foxed my technology, because it's better than the Unit's. But we've time for that later.'

Alicia gazed down at the entwined bodies dispassionately. The man moaned, the low guttural sound of somebody beyond speech. Alicia's face flashed irritation. She pulled the cloth off their midriff and twitched it over their faces, then pushed back her lab coat to reveal an impressive laser arm on one hip.

'Just to be on the safe side. I know you'll understand, Jess. This little laser is the newest technology. I don't have to hold it in my hand for it to vaporise you.'

I stepped away from Graham's body. The collar dangled from my fingers, hidden behind me.

'Bring your hands out where I can see them,' snapped Alicia.

Her laser arm bleeped and flashed.

Slowly, carefully, I slipped one throat lash into the back pocket of my trousers, leaving the rest of the collar dangling down my leg. I kept my palms face-out and moved them to the front of my body. The laser powered down.

'Don't think about running. I've an armed guard outside instructed to blow your head off if you try. That's if I don't get there first.'

'What do you want, Alicia?'

'Come out into the light, where I can see you.'

I took two steps forwards. Alicia looked down at the puddle of liquid, the smashed tank and the child's head. She tutted, scooting a chip of plexi-glass back into the mess with a pointed toe. It lodged in the child's open mouth, the soft lips mumbling silently around it.

'What do you want?' I repeated.

Alicia slid onto the corner of an empty slab with a bloodstain in the middle, one foot on the floor. 'I've always known you were out there somewhere, Jess Green. My problem was finding you.'

The laser sight on Alicia's hip was aimed right at me. If I pulled out the collar, I took the chance that the laser would be faster than I was, and it wasn't a risk worth taking. But with the collar off, Mo and the others were moving again, already on their way inside with no idea that I was already here, and no way I could reach them in time to warn them.

'Your mother took you away and put you somewhere I couldn't reach you, Jess.'

'Why?'

Alicia's eyebrows shot up. 'You mean you honestly don't know?'

Alicia shifted slightly and the laser compensated, altering its position. Either side of her face, her long jewelled earrings swayed like Old World nooses.

'Disaster Zone DNA. I helped splice it in a fertility lab. I worked with a woman called Dawkins. You met her, I believe. Little rat-like thing. Smart, though. She isolated a strand that we knew could create a more able race.'

Dizzy, I shook my head.

'Dawkins was clever, but she didn't have the stomach for seeing the project through,' Alicia began to swing her foot, eyes distant. 'When she realised what I had planned, she ruined the work for the good of humanity. We could've done anything, had anything, but she wouldn't do it. Stupid woman had scruples.' Alicia's pale eyes snapped back to my face. 'Anyway. The embryos were supposedly all destroyed but I discovered a file, the day before the chemical leak. The file told me that a small number of children were already born. Their DNA was taken from Dawkins's earliest collections, and the results were mixed, but viable. You are one of those children.'

Words ran through my mind in broken threads.

I think she was trying to protect you.

Something about you makes you more desirable, or downright dangerous...

You're at risk.

With a jolt, I was standing in the convent chapel at prayer, choked by the smell of incense. By my side stood a little boy with sooty hair and big tearful eyes, a toy bunny dangling from one hand, its button eyes gleaming dimly in the candlelight.

When is mummy coming back?

'And my brother?'

Alicia waved a hand dismissively. 'I'd no interest in him because he didn't have your DNA. I considered taking him as a trade-in but by then I'd already caught your mother.' She smiled. 'You didn't know that, did you? I put her somewhere a little inhospitable so she may not have made it, Jess. But we're straying off story. I never found the others, but I did find you... and so, here we are.'

I stepped backwards, into the shadows, and slumped against the wall.

'Move away from the wall,' snapped Alicia.

I obeyed.

'You were Dawkins's lab mole, weren't you, Alicia?'

She laughed. 'It only took you forever to work it out.'

'How? You must be twice the age you look, to have worked with Dana Dawkins before I was born.'

Alicia smirked. 'I work in regeneration and anti-ageing, darling. The Eternity Fund is my baby, not my father's. What do you expect?'

The corridor beyond the lab rang with footsteps. Alicia's eyes flickered, but neither she nor the laser at her hip moved.

296

'I sent the grave card,' she continued. 'I knew I had to find out whether you were the Jess Green I was looking for, or merely a mistake. I waited at the cemetery, knowing that if my suspicion was right, you'd come. I sent the janitor as a spy. It called me when your identity was confirmed. I flew straight in. My intention was to pick you up immediately.'

I remembered the cemetery, the fine rain spinning webs of mist along the paths, and the private hop, its lights slicing the darkness as they passed overhead. I'd run, first into the chapel, and then out of the perimeter into a cab.

'When I didn't manage to pick you up at the cemetery, I wasn't unduly worried. I had the advantage. What I didn't realise was how damn tenacious your handler is. Really looks after you, doesn't he?'

'Mo,' I whispered, casting out my mind, searching for him.

The mark on my palm tightened. He was inside the building - I could feel him.

The Mo I'd doubted, the Mo I'd questioned. This was what he'd tried to protect me from.

Alicia slid off the table. 'I wanted to lift you quickly. I tapped into HQ computer and tampered with your com messages, but your handler fixed it. I planted a fake driver to pick you up, but there was no chance he was going to let that happen. I went to the Memory Banks the same evening you did, and sent out a tracker loaded with sedative and a time-collar, but Mo Okoli must've got to my man before it activated. I've not seen the man or the collar since. Mr Okoli's performance has been impressive.'

Alicia's expression tautened, and suddenly, she looked much older, her eyes hollowed with fatigue, the cheekbones sunken. A finger of fear wound itself around my throat. If I couldn't put the collar on, then I couldn't help Mo and the others.

'He'll be here soon, I expect.' Alicia glanced towards the door. 'I have plans for your handler, too. But I won't bore you with those. Not yet.'

'I don't understand. Why here, like this?'

'This was my last chance,' Alicia shrugged. 'Graham was useless aside from one thing: his empathic abilities. He's nothing like you, of course, but I had to make do. You were foolish, Jess. Graham reeled you in like a fish on an Old World bobbin. Unfortunately, he developed a conscience towards the end.'

I glanced at the bulk on the trolley, and the baseball cap tilted over the head board. 'What did you do to him?'

'Used an experimental piece of kit I've developed. It fried his brains from the insides,' Alicia smirked. 'But let's not talk about me. Let's talk about you. I want your DNA, Jess.'

'Then why didn't you just ask me for a cell sample?'

Alicia laughed, a tinkling, flirtatious little sound.

'I need you, Jess. All of you, for extraction purposes. I won't go into the chemistry, because it's highly technical and more than a little messy, but I'm sure you get the drift. I don't expect you'll survive the process.'

'But if you wanted me, then why the Brotherhood? Why did you do all this?'

Alicia folded her arms. The laser extended towards me. 'Haven't we the huge ego? Not everything's about you, Miss Green. The Brotherhood belong to a friend of mine. I love the name, by the way. Very imaginative. I suppose it was Mr Le Blanc who thought of that one. Horrible, tedious little man. Needs to keep more abreast of his personal hygiene, from what I remember.' Alicia strolled across the lab, the laser moving intuitively on her hip as it remained trained on me. 'The truth is, Jess, my story is a long and complicated one. You can't imagine what it's like to have a father like mine. He wanted a son. Nothing I did was ever good enough.'

I turned on the balls of my feet, following her progress, feeling the collar lash brush against my leg. If only there were something between the laser and me, even for a beat, I could reach for it.

'My father stumbled on a few of my little experiments the morning of the Eternity Fund launch.' Alicia gestured to the trolleys and bays where the deformed bodies lay swathed in silent agony. 'He's under the mistaken assumption that all my work is linked to The Eternity Fund. He's wrong, of course, although the organs have come in more than useful. I'd been experimenting with time distortion and reanimation, with the help of the friend I mentioned earlier. My father didn't know. The time-collar wasn't my design but the perk of working in partnership is that I got to borrow it and have a little fun. Until it became tedious. Once you've stolen a few priceless antiques, attended free concerts and seen celebrities naked in their own bathrooms, it all gets a little staid. What really fascinates me are the wonderful things that can happen when a time-collar is deactivated at an inappropriate moment. Look around you, Jess. People conjoined, fused with mechanical devices, even melded with organic material… the possibilities are endless. My father was most perturbed. He insisted I stop. I refused, so he threw me out.'

'So having failed to win his approval, you're trying to get a response by making him hate you?'

Alicia's mouth stiffened, and the muscles along her jaw flickered. 'Thank you for your analysis, but it's quite unnecessary. My business partnership isn't just to get back at my father; I'm actually enjoying myself. I'm too driven to be fulfilled by anti-ageing alone.'

Sensing Alicia's mood, the laser flashed and extended towards me.

'Where does Perseus come into this?' I said.

Alicia eyes were unfathomable, icy blue. She pressed her lips together.

'Reg didn't call them the Brotherhood of the Golden Ram for nothing, Alicia. We know Perseus's symbol is in there somewhere, we just don't know how or why.'

She blinked, her face suddenly youthful again. 'All in due course. Be patient.'

'Come on Alicia, you don't need secrets. If I'm not going to leave this lab alive, then at least put me out of my misery. I don't just want to know why – I want to know how you did all this.'

A smile stretched across Alicia's face. A flush of pure arrogance bathed my skin, the sort that comes with absolute power and no conscience whatsoever. Somewhere, from an unguarded recess of Alicia's mind, came an image of whoever she was working with, the one she'd referred to as a friend and a business partner, a silhouette of a man whose face I couldn't see, but who resonated with a dreadful familiarity. In a beat, he was gone.

'I hacked your file, Jess. I know you don't do hand to hand combat, but I don't like the look of the pack you've got on your shoulders. Slip it off, slowly.'

I obeyed, careful not to dislodge the collar from my back pocket.

'Now put it on the floor and kick it away.'

She watched me do it, then slipped off her lab coat and tossed it over the bodies on the slab. The man convulsed, setting the dead woman's fingertips trembling behind his back. Alicia ignored them, and walked past me towards a door at the rear of the room.

'Come.'

I followed, into an air-lock, the firearm at her hip swivelling to retain a clear view of me. I moved one hand, slowly, towards the collar. The weapon beeped.

'Keep your hands front or my laser will fry you,' Alicia said without turning around. 'You've had two chances. You won't get a third. I'd prefer you alive, but I can still extract everything I need from a fresh corpse.'

A door whooshed closed behind, sealing us in. A frisson of electricity tickled my spine. Weeks before, the morning I'd sat on the office block rooftop and the Brotherhood had appeared to me as a seething mass on the horizon, I'd felt something similar; the vaguest whisper of horror and familiarity, too distant to process, but too powerful to ignore.

Whatever caused that sensation, it was in here, in front of us, behind the final air-lock door.

And whatever it was knew me just as I knew it.

The door whooshed open, releasing the grim smell of death. A surge of darkness powerful as a tidal wave knocked me, reeling, against the wall. Alicia seemed oblivious as she stepped into the room. I pushed myself upright and followed, gagging.

The room was small, and brightly lit. Stooped over an operating table, working underneath a stem light, stood a wizened man with blood-stained hands and a face mask. He raised his head and looked right through me, the whites of his eyes yellowed, the irises shrunken and cold.

Half his face was marbled by terrible scarring that decimated one cheek and ran down his neck in thick tracks of tissue. The injury ran underneath his robe and continued down, hidden from view.

Fire, tongues of flame, smoke, crawling up the arched windows and cracking the stained glass...

The eyes, dark as blackglass, regarded me unblinking as a wave of shock doused my body.

He reached one hand to his face, and pulled down the mask to reveal a half-destroyed mouth curled above crooked teeth.

'Meet my surgeon,' said Alicia.

We regarded each other in silence.

Layers of human misery had built up around the man, like an inexorable cancerous growth. They hung, tattered as funeral fabrics, ashy and blackened, about his body, each telling its own horrific story – the souls who'd suffered and died by his hand, snuffed out like candle flames. The air was so thick with them I could barely breathe. Alicia seemed oblivious.

'The surgeon is an expert in time-distortion techniques,' said Alicia fondly. 'He has a nasty little habit of leaving a trail of atrocities behind him. He's been known by several names throughout history. But none of that need concern you.' She smiled, her eyes sparkling with malice. 'And of course, the surgeon is a huge backer of The Eternity Fund. It seems that my work in anti-ageing has much in common with his own objectives.'

The surgeon pulled the mask back over his face, lowered his head and continued. His hand movements were deft, the fingers slender as an artist's. He lifted two dark organs from whoever or whatever was on the table, and lay them on a trolley. I turned away, trembling.

'So this is the genius who sees to the harvesting,' I said, fighting to keep my voice level.

Alicia smirked. 'Just let's say the surgeon makes an excellent teacher. Under his direction, the organs are removed. Nothing goes to waste. Between us, we've made the most of absolutely everything that's been harvested.'

My legs began to buckle. I collapsed against the wall but Alicia shook her head and tutted.

'Come now, Jess. Surely you have a stronger stomach than this?' she folded her arms and regarded me smugly.

'The organs,' I said. 'Only the faulty ones make it as far as Body Bay, unless they're rejected before extraction like Scott's were. Why wasn't the little boy good enough, Alicia? Was it because of his illness? The genetic disorder even his own family didn't know about, the one the hospital picked up?'

Alicia smirked.

'Did your surgeon teach the brotherhood not to bother with the ones who had genetic faults?'

She examined her nails.

'At least tell me what the hell you both do with the rest of the organs.'

My eyes flickered to the surgeon, who'd picked up a bloody rag and was delicately wiping his fingers.

Alicia shrugged. 'The surgeon has his own private lab, here. He likes to experiment. He wanted my empathic gene and I wanted a little fun, so we traded. We're virtually symbiotic,' she sniggered, glancing at the surgeon, who met her eyes briefly. 'My cell regression techniques are amazingly similar to the science behind the time collar. I can retard, I can accelerate, or I can send a cell back into its past to become young again. The thing is, I needed lab-rats to practice on. Well, lab-people. And that meant more blood, and more organs... the death is just a consequence of the science, I'm afraid.'

I remembered the convent, the disappearing children, the bloodstains on the cellar wall, and the empty beds with their mattresses tipped on one side; I remembered the schaduw, the thing that stalked the corridors bringing with it the evil of many lifetimes to infect whoever responded to its unholy touch. To the surgeon, death wasn't a consequence - it was a motivation.

Alicia's fingers wandered over the surface of a trolley which carried an array of steel tools. The surgeon picked up one with a fine metal probe, and held it into the light, its tip flashing.

'The empathic gene that's enhanced inside you is my birth-right, Jess. Dana had no right to destroy our work. I still haven't rediscovered every thread of it, which is why I need you. And of course, you're of great interest to the surgeon.'

'What use is an empathic gene to a man who deals in death?'

Alicia's mouth twisted into a smile. 'To use in his little dried army, of course. My gene will never make them 'live' again in the truest sense of the word, but its derivatives make the Brotherhood capable of so much more.'

'What about the organs from the children at the school?' I said, queasy with the memory. 'What has your surgeon done with those?'

She shrugged. 'I never asked.'

'The Brotherhood killed fifteen classes of children and took out all the staff in a single attack and you've never asked what he did with the organs?'

'Please, don't raise your voice, Jess.'

'What about the blood? Gallons and gallons of it, drained from little children… how can you not ask, Alicia?'

The surgical drapes moved, and an agonised moan came from the table. Whoever the surgeon was operating on, was still conscious. The surgeon's face illuminated with pleasure as he stooped closer to the bloody mess, his hands reaching inside the body cavity greedily.

'This is barbaric,' I hissed, my legs beginning to buckle.

'Then we'll move on,' Alicia said, turning back to the air lock. 'You first.'

I steadied myself on the wall and pulled the collar out of my back pocket. I scrunched the lashes up in my hand, and moved it in front of me as Alicia gestured me through. The laser ticked to itself, confused. Behind us, the life force of whatever was on the operating table ebbed and mercifully vanished. The surgeon threw his scalpel down, casting disgust around us.

'I'm going to show you my inspiration. Keep walking.'

We passed through the lab, and out into the corridor. Footsteps and voices funnelled from somewhere distant, distorted. Underneath the sounds, the darkness ran like water, swirling around us in eddies. My sixth sense was beginning to return. The palm of my left hand was hot, and it hurt. Mo was close, but I was too hyped to know exactly where.

'Take the door to your left.'

The door was inconspicuous, the kind you'd walk past without noticing, but something inside resonated with the same darkness that percolated through the Kevlar screen of the air-lock, and saturated the corridor.

Alicia motioned for me to open it.

The room was tiny, and dimly lit. The walls were bare. In the centre, stood a pod topped by a clear dome. Inside, a hologram glowed softly. Alicia gestured me closer. In my hand, the crumpled lashes of the collar cut into my palm. If I could get to the other side of the pod, I stood a chance of getting it around my neck before her laser took me out.

Inside the dome, the vapid strap of a holographic time collar was draped over a stand. The collar was worn and frayed. From its centre rose the emblem of an animal's head in tarnished metal. Its eyes were dark and crystalline, and slightly raised. De ja vu crawled along my skin like an army of insects.

'The first ever time-distortion device,' said Alicia, proudly. 'The surgeon keeps the original, of course, but the hologram fascinates me. Rare and beautiful as Old World gold. There are men who would pay a ransom in credits to possess it.'

She activated a control pad that illuminated the pod and spun the collar round on its stand. Under the lights, the ram's head glinted and its eyes began to glow softly, like embers.

'The original collar belonged to Perseus's family, but they lost it to the surgeon,' Alicia sounded amused.

Memories came back to me in snapshots: Lindiwi and me in the forbidden part of the convent, the candles guttering; the collar spilling out of the sand, its red eyes glittering; Sister Enuncia snatching it from us and holding it in her hand, entranced. The shadows that began to haunt the convent corridors; the eyes in the mirrors, watching; and the children vanishing one by one until finally, I'd found him, the schaduw, in the cellar, and I'd used the candle flame to light the soused rags and put an end to the terror once and for all... I pulled my eyes away from the ram's head, and back to Alicia.

A darkness sat around the hologram, welling inside the pod like poisoned gas.

'I recognise it,' I said.

'Impossible.'

I began to skirt the pod slowly, gazing into it. 'I touched the original.'

'Why would you want to lie to me, Jess? Ideas about saving your precious skin? Or is it your handler you're worried about?'

'I'm not lying, Alicia.'

The air around us quivered slightly, as though the collar had somehow woken up. The ram's eyes were brighter, glowing a deep blood red.

'How did you do that when I've got the control?' Alicia hissed.

'I didn't do anything.'

'Impossible. It's a hologram. It obeys commands.'

Frantic, she scanned the panel, a strand of hair working loose of the chignon. Something in the pod began to move, a blackness that unravelled and wound parasitic tendrils in front of my eyes. I stepped away.

'What?' Alicia whipped round.

'Look, Alicia – look at it.'

Agitated, she took hold of the top of the dome in both hands and stared down into it. Her laser remained trained on me through the plexi-panel.

'I see nothing,' she hissed.

The air inside the pod whirled with tendrils that sucked themselves slowly off the collar and hung above it. I guess that's what pure evil does when it's concentrated into one small space. The surgeon had used his precious time-distorting device during so many death-runs that it was tainted indelibly, even as a hologram. The ram's head began to glow with the sheen of recently polished metal. The eyes grew brighter, almost scarlet.

'What do you see?' Alicia leaned towards me, the uplighter throwing skull-like hollows under her eyes, which had darkened from blue to black. 'Tell me.'

'You don't know what you're dealing with, Alicia. This collar destroys lives because it belongs to your surgeon, and destroying lives is his stock-and-trade. You might have found yourself a business partner and cooked up a little plan that suits you both, but the surgeon will eat you up and spit you out in the process. You can't ever form a partnership with a man through which the schaduw flows.'

Alicia laughed, a hollow sound that bounced off the empty walls. 'Schaduw?'

'The essence of evil. The schaduw is the darkness that runs through humanity, the thing that makes some men torture and kill... When it finds a host as strong as your surgeon, the force becomes unstoppable.'

'I think you'll find that I don't believe in witchery and superstition, Miss Green. I deal in science and hard fact.'

'Then swallow this. I touched the original time collar because it was buried out in the desert by the first New World settlers. It was buried for a reason. They didn't bank on the fact that somebody would build a convent over the top and it would work its way out of the sand and call your surgeon back to it.'

'Your convent?' Her eyes narrowed. 'The convent I failed to find in all those years?'

I took another step away from the dome, nodding.

'Don't move any further.'

My palms were faced away from her, one concealing my collar, the other searing with pain. Mo was inside, but he was in trouble.

'Tell me what happened at the convent.'

'Me and another girl found the original collar. Sister Enuncia took it off us. Your surgeon did to Enuncia what he's doing to you. Enuncia started to kill in his name, then she went mad. By the time the convent burned down, there was hardly anybody left, and the remaining nuns were rabid with fear. You can't control the surgeon. And you can't control them.'

'Who?'

'The Brotherhood.'

'Don't be stupid. Between us, the surgeon and I created them.'

'You used stolen bodies and brought them back to half-life with some high-tech lab work. That was your mistake, Alicia, because it helped the surgeon con you into thinking you were his equal. He killed Sister Enuncia, and he'll kill you just the same once you've outlived your usefulness.'

'You know nothing!' Alicia's face darkened.

Her com bleeped and the light in the ram's eyes snapped off. She glanced at the screen. The laser still had a clear shot of me. A smile spread across her face.

'I've just had excellent news. I have a little surprise for you.'

A sting of adrenaline shot through my body.

Alicia took my arm and propelled me towards the door. She was surprisingly strong. The laser at her hip ticked and crackled to itself in irritation, only stopping when it extended far enough to get a clear view of me.

She hustled me back to the lab.

The pods and trolleys had been swept aside. In the centre of the room, three tall figures dressed in grey fatigues stood strapped together, arms by their sides.

Mo was in the middle. To his left, Max's face was torn by a bloody gash that ran across one cheek. Jody had a split lip and a black eye. Their bodies were bound with Kevlar straps at the ankles, mid-riffs and upper arms.

Mo's face, set with defiance, melted into despair as he saw me. Behind the shades, his eyes didn't leave my face.

Alicia gestured to the restraints. 'They're nu-Kevlar, much tougher than the old stuff, so don't think about trying anything heroic.'

She pushed me forwards, hard. I stumbled, clenching the collar. The flare on my left palm shone so bright that light bled out in needles through my closed fingers. They pulled towards Mo as though drawn by a magnet.

'I can use you two,' Alicia gestured either side of Mo. 'Well, bits of you, at least. But you, Mr Okoli - you're something special.'

Mo's jacket was torn from the throat to the waist, revealing bare skin. I backed towards the guardians as Alicia advanced, her eyes roving slowly down his body. Her lips parted and she licked them, delicately, just enough to make them shine.

'I understand that you've been... enhanced.' Alicia's pupils expanded as her eyes fell below Mo's waistline.

'Vicious rumour, I'm afraid,' said Mo softly.

'Maybe I'll be the judge of that.'

She traced the back of one finger along his jaw, delicately. Mo flinched.

Alicia pouted. 'I certainly think you'd make an interesting splice, Mr Okoli, perhaps with a vintage hop. Or with Graham over there. I've never fused the dead with the living before – they only ever seem to die on me afterwards. Could be fun.'

Behind the shades, I felt Mo's eyes close. Alicia dropped her hand, her expression tautening.

'I think you'll be surprised what you're prepared to do to save your comrades.'

Max's face was bleeding heavily, his skin deathly white and his eyes dulled with pain. Jody's split lip had swelled to twice its size. She was injured in the midriff. Although I saw no blood, her pain leaked out. Alicia's eyes flickered from Mo to me.

'Perhaps you'll do even more to save your girlfriend.'

I glanced at the laser. It had clear view of me. In my hand, the collar was slicked with sweat.

'Do you know that little Miss Green used to be a whore?'

Mo didn't respond. Alicia peered into his face.

'Yes, I see you do. Did you know she burned a sexclub down, absconded illegally, and has a price on her head?'

Mo didn't react. Max leaned into him as his knees gave way. The nu-Kevlar bands pulled taut. Alicia laughed.

'So. No secrets between you two. Nice.'

Alicia pressed her body into Mo's, pushing her breasts into his ribs. He didn't move. She rose onto the tips of her toes, sliding up him, and reached for his shades.

'I have a thing about eyes,' she said, taking hold of the sides.

Alicia began to draw them off, slowly. The laser on her hip was obscured by Mo's torn jacket. It beeped in alarm. I swung the collar towards my neck.

The sides pulled together and connected.

The laser had already extended round Mo's jacket.

The weapon discharged.

The laser beam burned a solid orange slash in my direction. It stopped inches from my body. I fell forwards instinctively, hit the ground, and rolled. Alicia's hands were motionless either side of Mo's face, his shades low on the bridge of his nose. I couldn't see his eyes. Max was collapsed against him, held up by the binding straps. Jody's glare locked onto Alicia, her eyes flashing fury.

I scrambled off the floor, and ran into the corridor.

In the main hangar, the pods were wide open. The blackened bodies of the Brotherhood stood in two rows in the centre of the room, as though they'd been taken out and placed there like oversized chess pieces. At either end, two janitors were frozen in motion, each holding an armful of time collars. Trolleys piled with syringes stood next to them. Was this Alicia's contribution, in the form of some kind of limited-liquid-sentience that enabled the Brotherhood to commit their next organ harvest?

An oppressive stillness smothered the bodies, the kind you get when kinetic energy suddenly freeze-frames with no chance to dissipate. I wove between them, repulsed yet drawn. These were the men who committed the crimes - dead, desiccated men who'd once lived and loved and suffered like the victims they now harvested. The Brotherhood were brought 'alive' only for the moments it took them to take down their prey at the speed of light, before returning to the nothingness of stasis.

Close up, they were fragile. Their skin was withered and dry, the epidermis separating from the muscle, hair falling out in clumps, their clothes no more than rags.

How would you feel if there was no more death or disease or suffering? whispered the dancer Leo's voice in my mind, the day he'd repeated the recruitment speech he and Dante had heard; the day I'd arrived to tell him his boyfriend was dead.

Something shifted behind me, the subtlest movement of air, the kiss of a sole over tiles. I turned around.

Standing in the doorway, his eyes glittering with malice, stood a wizened figure in a blood-stained theatre gown. A streak of overhead lighting glanced off his naked head, scoring his scarred tissue with deep shadow.

The surgeon.

Around his neck, a collar pulsed with spiral patterns – the original collar, grey and slightly frayed, the ram's head shining at his throat.

I stepped away from the ranks.

'You have something that belongs to me.' His voice was mild, with traces of an accent I didn't recognise.

He nodded towards my collar.

'This was a gift,' I said.

A smile twisted the surgeon's face. 'The collars all belong to me. There are no gifts, not even to my business partner.' His voice was mocking. 'The Barber woman thinks she is instrumental in my success, but her science is faulty. My interest in her empathy gene was a smoke screen to get me to where I need to be, into your HQ. As for time-travel, it's a hobby-horse of mine. Just like flash freezing. The freezing started with a study of cryonics, but it's led me to all sorts of exciting possibilities. But I digress. The collar is mine. Give it back to me now.'

I stepped away. The surgeon advanced, chin down, his eyes unblinking.

'Why the time-collars anyway?' I said. 'So that you can squeeze more victims into your little outings?'

The skin of his face fractured into wrinkles as he grinned. 'I rarely find anybody like-minded to work with, Miss Green. The Barber woman is interesting, but ultimately, dispensable. She'll do, while I'm here, but that won't be for much longer. And yes, historically, I've always preferred victims in large numbers. Over the years, I've tried everything from religious wars, ethnic cleansing and impaling to bathing in fresh blood and tinkering with gas chambers, but I have to say, now I'm getting into the swing of things, the novelties of flash freezing can't be ignored.'

My pack was in the lab with the rest of the weapons. I couldn't chance hand-to-hand. Underneath the withered muscle and yellow skin, I'd bet there was strength. Behind me was a door that led out into the corridor, the door the Brotherhood were about to leave through when I'd put the collar on. I took one step backwards, towards it. The surgeon didn't move.

'How do you do it?' I said.

'What, in particular, Miss Green? You've presumably already worked out how I pick
the men up? Sad, lonely no-hopers desperate to find a light to follow; that's the easy bit...'

'How do you turn them into un-deads?'

The surgeon's face crumpled as he laughed, but his eyes, their shrivelled irises hard as blackglass under paper-thin lids, showed no emotion.

'Over the years, I've immersed myself in cultures from different times and places. I've encountered things you wouldn't believe, Miss Green. From Zombie cults, brain transplants and limb grafting, to bio-necromancy and cybernetic enhancement. Just let's say that I take the best bits and then mix them all together.'

The surgeon drew something from the pocket of his gown with one fluid movement. The blade of an Old World scalpel glinted underneath the lights. He held it away from his body, poised like a poison dart. I stepped back.

'I have designs on those beautiful organs of yours. You owe me, after all. I haven't forgotten our previous encounter, at the convent.' He spat the words as though they tasted bad. 'Fire does extraordinary things to mortal tissue.'

The surgeon ran his free hand over his face and down his neck, pulling the robe below his collar bone. The scarring rutted and grooved his skin beyond recognition. I gasped.

'But why dead men?'

'Just another experiment. And the freezing adds a nice twist. I'm a big fan of cryonics, although of course, you can hardly bring the victims back once their internal resources have been removed. My challenge was thus: could I teach dead men surgical skills? Of course I could. They operate under my instruction and we have all the time in the world, with the collars. The only problem is their frailty. My desiccation chambers tend to make my little apprentices brittle and prone to falling apart. Which is why I only ever use them for one job before disposing of the bodies. But with so many social mis-fits and delusional weirdoes in our society, replacing them has never been a problem. That's why I leave the harvestees stacked up in their places of work, or play. I simply don't need them all. A nice touch, don't you think? A kind of signature, almost.'

I reached out one hand and touched the closest dead man, running my fingers along the threadbare jacket, feeling the desiccated muscle underneath. The surgeon radiated surprise. His scalpel hand lowered fractionally.

The only problem is their frailty…

I pushed the dried man, hard. He toppled like a skittle into the next in the row, where he stopped and froze, his shoulder impacted and half his head pushed off. Gauzy bits of fabric and flakes of blackened skin came to rest mid-air.

'You learn something new every day,' I said.

'Leave my workforce alone,' snapped the surgeon, his voice rising.

'If I let go of them, they revert to their own time frame,' I continued, 'but if I retain contact with them, they work in mine…'

I plunged between the rows and swung my arms and kicked out in a manic, ungainly dance. The men began to hit the floor, and damaged torsos, fingers, ears, and skull pieces shot out of torn clothing and flew around the room like litter in a wind.

'No!'

The surgeon darted into the melee, unsure whether to slash at me or to grab me with his free hand.

I dodged and ran through the rest of the queue, knocking the remaining bodies over, trampling them into the ground. At the door, I turned to look back. The hangar could've been a looted burial ground, with bodies of Old World mummies strewn over the floor, some resting mid-air like a weird Old World art installation. A fine film of dust hung around the trampled parts. The surgeon, who'd collapsed to his knees, was running his fingers through the detritus, scalpel still in hand.

'You fool,' he hissed, his eyes meeting mine.

For a moment his guard dropped and I understood his intention: the surgeon planned to take the Brotherhood to Unit HQ.

'She gave you her access codes, didn't she?' I said, backing towards the door.

He stood, slowly.

'Who do you want at HQ?' I pressed.

'There's somebody at the top I very much want to see.'

I slipped out into the corridor, and ran.

Behind me, the surgeon's footsteps followed with the unhurried metre of a funeral drum.

I pushed my way into the lab, the doors hanging open in my wake. The orange slash of laser beam hung static in front of the guardians. Alicia was motionless on her toe tips, her body obscenely close to Mo's. In the shadows at the back of the room, near Graham, lay my pack, too far away to reach.

Instinctively, I spun around behind Mo, slipping my hand through his ripped jacket down into the body holster he always wore. His skin was warm and smooth, but unyielding as I pulled out his laser arm. I ducked down next to Max's buckled body.

The surgeon stopped before he reached Alicia. He raised both hands slowly, his scalpel flashing.

'Drop the scalpel.'

His face split into a cruel smile.

'Come now, Miss Green, we needn't resort to-'

'Drop it,' I snapped, arming the laser.

The scalpel fell with a ting, bouncing back up in slow motion, suspending itself an inch above the floor.

The surgeon launched himself towards me, his hands outstretched.

I fired.

The laser jammed.

He slammed into Max's shoulder as I ducked back. Strapped to the other guardians, Max half-toppled, dragging them with him. They lilted and stopped. The surgeon scrambled round the side of them and lunged at me again. I stumbled on my pack, and feinted as he grabbed out, careering backwards into Graham's trolley, sending it into the wall with a crash.

I fired the laser again, but it still didn't work.

The surgeon stepped to the opposite side of the trolley and faced me over Graham's body.

'Before I leave for HQ, I'll have you on my operating table without anaesthetic. And it will take forever, because I'm very adept at what I do. Payback, for these…'

The surgeon ripped the theatre gown from his shoulder. The fabric rent in two to reveal the horrific extent of his scarring. His torso, yellowed and shrivelled, had the appearance of child's modelling clay that'd been spread inexpertly and then gouged as an afterthought. He pushed the trolley into my stomach, pinning me against the wall. I doubled forwards in agony. The laser flew out of my hand. A yellow beam shot out, narrowly missing the surgeon's shoulder. The beam hit a storage tower against the wall at the same time as the surgeon lost his balance. In a flash, I reached across Graham and yanked the collar from around his neck. It slipped through my fingers and landed at my feet.

The tower jerked away from the wall and rained equipment. As the collar pulled free and the surgeon froze, the contents of the shelves passed over him and through him before stopping, suspended. At the moment of fusion, a shelf embedded itself through the surgeon's skull like a cleaver, shearing his nose. Mo's laser arced through the air and hit the wall then rebounded, embedding itself in the surgeon's shoulder, flesh fused into its sights as though man and weapon had grown together from a single twisted seed.

The lab fell silent.

I pushed the trolley back and stepped away from the wall, breathless, my foot crunching the ram's head on its fabric strap.

The guardians' restraints had locks. I flicked them off, one by one, freeing first Mo, then Jody, last of all Max, who I knew would hit the floor the moment I took off the collar. I pulled the strapping away from their static bodies, and took it to Alicia.

Her ankles were easy to bind. I pulled the winching tight, cutting into her expensive boots, then secured her wrists. The laser was still in its hip-cradle. The beam remained a solid projection as I removed the weapon and slid it along the floor, facing the wall ready to discharge. Mo's shades were still in Alicia's hands, half way off. I prized her fingers apart and slid the glasses back up the bridge of his nose until they rested firmly against his face.

Next door, the holograph room was dark, the kind of darkness that sucks light out of anything it can drain. The hologram had disintegrated into a series of faint marks, but the eyes of the ram still glowed red.

I knocked the top off the pod and smashed the projector.

The collar vanished in a dim flare.

Back in the lab, I surveyed the wreckage.

The child's head in its viscous puddle, the bodies, the surgeon, fused with a shelf and a laser, and the guardians, beaten, injured, blackened by desert sand.

A price on my head, Mo had said.

A seek and find.

You aren't strong enough or experienced enough to go out in the field.

Exhausted, I reached my hand to my throat, where the collar pulsed, and tore it off.

XX

Jody lay Max's body on a sled outside the lab, and covered it. Neither she nor Mo spoke, but the expressions on their faces were set with grief as they hung their heads in silence. Mo had already shackled the surviving personnel together at the end of the main corridor, where a sliding hatch opened into a sand tunnel that led to the dunes. The survivors slumped, exhausted and dispirited. Around their ankles, the crumbled remnants of the desiccated Brotherhood shifted in the wind that funnelled through the hatch. Another storm was rising.

Jody stood and put one hand against the wall, wincing and holding her ribs. An electro-syringe and a snap-box of liquid were in her free hand.

'What is it?' I asked.

'Instant death. It's something we carry as a last resort. Painless, and fast. It'll put the survivors out of their misery.'

She turned away and disappeared into the lab.

'What about the surgeon?'

'He comes with us, back to HQ,' said Mo.

'Mo, you're hurt.'

A dark stain spread underneath his top. He pulled away from my hand.

'It'll wait. Where are the time collars?'

I gestured to a box by my feet. 'I collected them up.'

'All of them?'

'All except the surgeon's original. I stepped on it, in the lab, and crushed it. It's still on the floor.'

'You owe me an explanation,' said Mo, more softly. 'But for now, it can wait.'

Jody reappeared minutes later, her face pale, listing to one side. She dropped the syringe and snap-box on her pack. Without speaking, she began to strip. Within seconds both she and Mo were down to their underwear. They scanned and dressed each other's wounds in silence, pausing only to grimace or pull medication from their packs. I sat on my heels with my back pressed into the wall, watching them from a distance, an outsider.

'Please will you speak?' I said at last, after they'd pulled on fresh clothes from their packs.

Jody groaned as she tried to lift her hands to tie back her plaits.

'Here, let me,' I said, pushing myself up off the floor.

'We have to get back to HQ within twenty four hours,' said Mo. 'Jody and I have injuries that need treatment. They booby-trapped our way in. Let's just say the technology was more sophisticated than we'd anticipated.'

'We can still make it in Alicia's speed hop,' I said.

'Then we leave immediately,' said Jodie, her voice weak. 'Our brief was to disable the Brotherhood and return to HQ with any survivors. Oxton will decide what happens next.'

Mo turned away and headed towards the sand tunnel, limping. 'I'll load the prisoners. Get the surgeon on a sled and find the broken collar.'

Jody's face was strained, her skin ashen. She nodded, once, then disappeared back into the lab. The black cloth covering Max's sled fluttered in the tunnel wind as Mo dragged his body away.

When Jody reappeared, I couldn't look. The surgeon's remains slid past me on a sled, casting out a helplessness I refused to pity, hung with the wreathes of suffering he'd caused so many souls. Maybe he wore them as a badge of honour; I'd never know.

'I didn't find the final collar,' said Jody.

'I can go back in-'

'The collar will still be here when the clean-up team arrive,' she interrupted. 'We need to load the hop and move out, fast. Mo's lost more blood than you'd think. So have I.'

Together, we dragged the sled of mangled remains towards the square of light in the distance, darkness seeping from the surgeon like a tide around our legs.

'Where will we stow what's left of him?' I asked.

'Somewhere with absolutely no comfort,' Jodie replied. 'There's a cocoon on the top of the hop. It's big enough. I've injected him with endocrine stabiliser to keep him alive, but it doesn't dim the pain.' Her face twisted into a smile.

'Is the cocoon secure?'

'Triple laser-locked. Don't worry, Jess, this thing doesn't stand a chance of escaping, even if it could walk.'

Jody stopped short of the hop, out of Mo's earshot. She picked up my left hand. The palm flashed blue.

'You kept hold of the mark?'

I snatched my hand away. 'I don't know what you mean.'

'Mo put the mark on you to know that you were safe. When it activated, and he came to you in the storm, it should have disappeared.'

I remembered the wind, hurling sand against the shell walls, beginning to soften, and the gradual stillness that fell around us as we waited. I remembered Mo's confusion when he saw the mark was still on my palm, and the way he'd moved away from me, sitting at a distance.

'Well it didn't disappear, Jody.'

'Because you kept hold of it,' Jody repeated, as though I was stupid. 'That was your choice. Does he know?'

'Yes.'

'Then he knows that you have feelings for him.'

'No,' I said, shaking my head, stepping away. 'No. Absolutely not. No feelings at all. We work together. That's all.'

She narrowed her eyes. 'Mo's about to give you a hard time, Jess, but don't give up on him.'

'What?'

Jody shrugged. 'You're good for him. Don't let him push you away.'

She took the pull-cord from me, straightened up with a grimace, and dragged the sled to the loading platform without looking back.

*

The prisoners, dishevelled and bruised, sat together on the floor in the back of the speed hop. They were linked by a single Kevlar chain that passed through wrist and ankle cuffs, secured at one end. The blanket of exhaustion that hung thick as chemical fog above their heads told me nobody was about to try anything, but Mo insisted I have a laser.

Jody had trussed Alicia into a rear seat. The binding straps were too tight and the sled carrying Max's body was close enough to touch her feet. Alicia's expensive boots, made of real leather, hadn't a mark on them, as though the horrors of the day had simply glanced off her, leaving no effect.

The surgeon, or what was left of him, was triple-laser-locked into a roof cocoon large enough to accommodate the shelf fused through his face and the laser that sprouted from his shoulder. Mo had activated the locks himself, checking everything twice while me and Jody watched.

I fastened myself into the flip-seat against the back door, and leaned the laser Mo had pushed at me against my thigh. The muted greys and sharp reds of subdued pain and injury flushed through the hop. The vehicle hummed to life, rising off of the ground. Alicia glared at me above the seal-strip over her mouth. Her expression was one of utter derision, as though I was less than human. Strands of hair had unwound themselves from her chignon, and one of her earrings was missing, but she still looked the model of elegance, the evil bitch.

How had I been so easily conned?

The digi-screen in the cockpit lit up like a North Side twilight, fizzling and beeping in alarm.

'Sandstorm ahead,' said Mo.

The hop buffeted as a crosswind caught it side-on. The thrusters compensated, slowing then upping propulsion. Jody began to modify the stabilisers as the hop started to rock dramatically.

'Please, can you take off the blackouts?' I said, queasy.

The screens flicked off and we were assailed by clouds of blacksand that hurled themselves at the visors in waves. Alicia radiated a flash of fear.

'Take us lower,' said Jody. 'If we maintain this height we'll be ripped to bits by the updraft.'

Mo dropped the hop and cursed sharply as we veered. The prisoners rolled into one another, their chains rattling across the floor.

'What was that?' Jody snapped, leaning forwards.

We'd narrowly missed the tallest of the meltdown structures that stuck out the sand. Mo cut the speed.

'We don't have time on our side,' I called. 'Are you sure you don't want me up front to co-pilot?'

Mo paused, then nodded. 'Jody, you take guard duty at the back.'

'Jess doesn't know how to trim the controls.'

'You're losing focus,' he said, gently.

Jody nodded, dully, as though the effort was too much, and struggled out of her seat. I squeezed past Max's sled and into the front. The view through the visor was awe-inspiring. In the distance, the clouds had melted into a black horizon, through which needles of lightening erupted randomly, bursting in white-hot flashes. The wind scooped swathes of sand from the ground and hurled it with ferocity into the hop. Mo struggled to hold us level.

A blast of wind hit us at an angle and knocked the hop off course. Mo cursed. The chained bodies slid, accompanied by a feeble squeal from Alicia.

A strut appeared out of the sand and caught one of the stabiliser arms. The hop careered down at an angle. We hit the dune with a sickening thud. My auto-flex harness strained as I shot forwards. The accident protocols engaged with a deafening whoosh, and we were flung back in our seats, embedded in crash-foam. The soundproofing failed and the horror of the storm hit us in full volume, shrieking and howling around the crashed vehicle.

I released my harness. Mo swung around to look in the back while I struggled out of the crash-foam and flexed my neck. Jody was still cocooned, her face grey underneath a blinking roof light. She gave a feeble nod. The soundproofing came back on, leaving my ears ringing with the first stirrings and low moans of Alicia's surviving staff. Alicia's eyes were wild with terror. Only half her crash-foam had activated, leaving one side of her body twisted, thrust back at an awkward angle.

'She'll live,' snapped Mo dispassionately. 'She deserves to hurt just a little.'

Max's sled had tipped, throwing the black shroud off his face, which was waxy and grey-white in the flickering light. His eyes were closed, the gash on his cheek dark purple. Mo moved awkwardly across the sloping floor and pulled the shroud back in place.

'Mo, what the fuck are we going to do?' I said, my voice rising with panic.

Overheads had opened and strewed supplies, and kit bags had vomited their contents into the blood and debris.

'We get the vehicle out of the sand and we move as fast as we can,' he said. 'We don't have much fuel and we don't have much time.'

'It wasn't your fault,' I said.

Mo scrubbed his face with his palms, agitated.

'The strut we hit - it came out of nowhere.'

'The sensors weren't working,' he said, almost to himself.

He swung around to face Alicia, who turned her head slowly with a wince of pain.

'What the hell did you do to the sensors?'

Alicia's face twisted into a smile, just visible at the edges of the seal-strip over her mouth. Mo grabbed it and pulled it off with one quick movement. Alicia gasped and coughed.

When she spoke, her voice was weak. 'Surely you didn't expect that I would leave my personal speed hop all rigged up and ready to go, without leaving at least a couple of little alterations, just in case events took an unexpected turn?'

'Pity you didn't realise that you were putting your own precious skin in danger too,' I snapped.

Alicia tried to laugh but it came out as a choke. A finger of blood bubbled from the corner of her mouth, and slid down her chin.

'My father will find me. Our labs have the technology to rebuild and reanimate me, should my heart stop.'

'Except you'll have the mentality of a Klone Zone potato if you're brain dead for long enough,' Mo hissed, slapping the tape back over Alicia's mouth.

Jody pulled herself up, her eyes blood-shot and circled. She gestured at the bodies on the floor.

'Survivors.' Her voice was no more than a sibilant hiss, punctuated by laboured breathing. 'My kit.'

She clawed her belongings from the floor and began to fumble through for medical supplies. She searched out the snap-box I recognised from earlier: instant death. I looked away.

'The roof cocoon,' I said, instinctively.

'I'll check it. We have to get the surgeon back to HQ alive,' Mo said as he fumbled with the roof airlock.

'He's better off dead. You don't understand what you're dealing with, Mo. That thing has travelled the centuries killing countless numbers in terrible atrocities. No matter who tries to beat it, it comes back.'

Mo cursed as the airlock refused to budge. 'Oxton will extract information from the surgeon however she needs to, but she can't if I abandon him here.'

'How the hell do you extract information from a man who's fused with a storage tower and a laser arm?' I yelled.

'That isn't your problem,' Mo continued rattling at the hatch. 'Oxton will not rest until she's found out the how and why of the time collars and the extent of the surgeon's activities.'

The roof hatch gave fractionally. In one final jerk he released a shower of blacksand and a shush of wind. Above us, a circle of sky showed through the hatch, the clouds so low I could've touched them.

'You said it was integral.' My voice trailed away in a gust of wind.

From her seat, Alicia began to laugh, the sound smothered by the tape over her mouth, and tinged with pain as her body jerked in spasm. Mo slid the hatch shut, casting anger around us.

Jody struggled into the cockpit. 'It appears that Alicia made some alterations to the hop. The computer wasn't supposed to tell us, but I've been able to bypass security and restore the original settings.'

Alicia's shoulders stopped shaking but the top half of her face didn't un-crease itself. She listed slightly, as though, if the bands hadn't been there, she would've toppled off her seat.

'I should've checked before we took off,' whispered Mo, clambering into the co-pilot seat. 'Chryst, I'm sorry Jody... are you OK?'

'I gave myself another shot,' said Jody as the ignition lights flared on the display. 'It's the last I can take. We have to move.'

'The cocoon must've detached itself when we crashed,' I said, uneasy.

'There's no saying where it is or how long it would take us to find it,' Jodie replied. 'The wind's so powerful it could've taken the damn thing anywhere. We can't risk looking for it. We have to go back, now.'

She and Mo glanced at each other, as though exchanging a silent conversation, then the hop rose and lurched as the crash rectifier sent out sand paddles to right us.

'Come strap yourself in, Jess,' said Jody. 'A man fused with metal won't survive for long out here. We can come back and retrieve the body. Oxton will have to do what she can with that.'

Jody set a course for North Side. The thrusters powered up, and the battered hop limped into the air listing to its damaged side.

The sky cleared to a fiery red, threaded with green and lavender streaks, as we reached the perimeter. A Unit team had removed four pieces of boundary fence to allow the speed hop through. We limped past the boneyard, whose uneven stones glowed eerily in the disappearing light, towards the crowd inside the perimeter. Beyond, the tiny lights of North Side had begun to flick on, encasing the walls and chimneys in ghostly mesh.

Mo landed the hop next to a medical vehicle. Through the visor, my eyes found Oxton. I'd swear I caught relief ghosting across her face, and the corners of her mouth pull up fractionally into something resembling a smile.

As our visors opened, bio-suits swarmed the hop. Hands pulled us free, draped us with recovery blankets, and began scans. Silhouetted against the ruddy sky, Alicia's few surviving staff were hauled out. Alicia and Jodie were strapped into medi-chairs by droids, their eyes closed.

We reached Oxton and stopped, our entourage falling back. Oxton's eyes were ghostly pale, the circles underneath perhaps diminished, although it could've been a trick of the light.

'Miss Green, Mr Okoli.' She took in our bruised and filthy appearances with one deft glance.

'Permission to take twenty four hours to prepare a formal report, Oxton,' said Mo, his chin unnaturally high, his thumbs tracing the crease of his sandtrousers.

'Permission granted.'

The three of us continued slowly towards the medi-hop. The shifters behind the barrier drew back, their eyes flashing sparks in the encroaching twilight, as though afraid we carried some mysterious taint from the Cinderlands.

Oxton's face flickered with unspoken thoughts, her lips anus-tight. 'You will both require a full debrief as soon as you're medically approved fit,' she said.

That's the point I stopped listening.

Through the open hatch, I saw Jody. She lay on a trolley like those inside Alicia's abandoned lab, strapped to a mobile unit with a whole fleet of medi-droids moving fast to stabilise her. Somebody slipped a shot-box onto the side of my neck and pumped me full of something that made my vision recede at the corners. The last thing I remember is arms guiding me into a seat. As my eyes began to close, I thought I saw the shifter from Forked Tongue, his long hair shimmering, a drugstic in his fingers, watching. The travel bands tightened around my shoulders, and I slipped into drug-induced oblivion.

XXI

I drew the envelope out of my pocket, and held it up, between us, by its knife-edge.

'You haven't opened it,' said Mo.

'The last time I got one of these, it was a trap laid by Alicia Barber.'

'Which it can't possibly be, this time.'

'You haven't heard the news, then. Rosie told me Alicia has been released from custody.'

Mo's lips twisted into a smile. 'Not entirely true. Her father may appear to have bought her freedom, but it's not so simple.'

'What do you mean?'

Mo smirked. 'Alicia is in a luxury villa somewhere out of town, under twenty-four-by-seven armed guard.'

I whistled. 'I take it her father's influence saved her from being given over to Twenty One.'

'It saved her life, but she'll never walk the streets a free woman. Her lab equipment has been confiscated. Barber's trying to hush it up. He's in a meeting with Perseus, right now.'

We passed through security and stepped outside, into the square, where the first signs of frost shintled on the flagstones.

'Am I safe, Mo? Or am I going to spend the rest of my life looking over my shoulder?'

'You work for the Unit, Jess. You will always have to look over your shoulder. Now, open the envelope.'

We stopped underneath the fake-trees, whose leaves were bloomed with frost. I ran a fingernail underneath the seal, and pulled it open. A micro file fell into the palm of my hand, with a hand-written note and two faded tags. The number fifteen was printed on one of them, sixteen on the other.

'My convent tag,' I whispered. 'The other belonged to my brother.'

'You had numbers?'

I nodded. 'The nuns said it made things easier.'

Mo shook his head, incredulous. 'What does the note say?'

'It's from Sybil. She says the micro-file contains the information she promised me. She's giving me my mother's last known whereabouts, and details of my brother's… adoption…'

I sank down onto a bench, my legs weak and my mind spinning.

In all these years, plagued by dreams and flashbacks, haunted by the memory of my little brother, I'd never once considered that Michael might've been successfully adopted.

Why hadn't the nuns told me?

My hand crawled to my neck and snatched at the button at my throat, gripping it so tight my knuckles ached.

'This isn't bad news,' said Mo, taking the envelope and sliding the note and the tags back inside. 'This is good news. This is what you wanted. Answers, at last.'

'She said the information was a gift from Perseus.'

Mo's lips twitched up at the corners. He sat, so close our legs touched, and handed me the envelope back.

'There's something else you should know, Jess. Oxton has shown an interest in the convent where your mother left you.'

Behind the shades, I knew his eyes were fixed on mine.

'There's nothing left of it. The convent burned down, I told you.'

A smile flickered across his face. 'Please don't ever burn HQ down, will you, Jess.'

I ignored him, and slid the envelope into my pocket.

'Oxton's interest is connected with the fact that the surgeon, or schaduw, as you refer to him, was drawn to the convent by your discovery of the original time-distortion collar. If there's any information she can pick up from the site, what's left of it, then she wants in.'

'For Perseus?'

Mo shrugged. 'That's none of my business. All I know is, after we've cleaned up at Alicia's underground lab and recovered the cocoon and the remains, Oxton wants to send a team into the desert to map the area and find the site. I'm to head it up.'

'While I get to sit at HQ under house arrest for my own protection?'

Mo smirked. 'That isn't the way it's going to work from now on.'

'What do you mean?'

'You're coming too.'

Around us, the sun had begun to melt the frost, leaving smears of damp on the stones. The leaves above our heads dripped tiny jewels of melt-water. Inside my pocket, my left palm began to burn.

'Don't even think about it,' said Mo, pushing himself up off the bench.

'Think about what?'

'You're hanging on to my mark. Your decision, but I can't give you what you want, Jess.'

'I don't even know what I want,' I said, standing up.

Mo loped ahead of me across the square, the ghost of a smile evaporating in his wake.

EPILOGUE

Two weeks later, Mo and me sat outside Torque in the dark, watching rain run tears down the hop visors. We'd travelled to Cliff City in a borrowed high-speed, and cloaked it just outside the club. Torque's lights flashed baby pink and blue neon, their reflections smeared across the wet plexi-panels and the pavements. Along the street, a handful of rain-coat silhouettes hurried to their destinations. Tonight, even the enforcers seemed scarce.

'This has to be laid to rest one way or the other,' said Mo. 'I wouldn't advise you to try a second arson attempt, so I suggest we do it my way.'

'If he recognises me, he'll kill me.'

Mo glanced at me through the side of his shades. 'There's no way he'll recognise you. And like I said, he'd have to get through me first. But you need to be here, to see this for yourself.'

I felt sick.

'He'll kill Saskia.'

'I didn't want to tell you this until now, Jess. Saskia is no longer at the club.'

My hand flew to my mouth. Mo squeezed my wrist and pulled it back down into my lap.

'There's nothing you could have done. She left of her own accord.'

'Girls don't just leave of their own accord,' I said, my voice shaking.

'I think she was bought by a customer.'

'You know where she went?'

He shook his head. 'I have a lead I'm following up. I'll let you know as soon as I find anything.'

I nodded. A tear spilled out the corner of my eye. I turned my head so Mo wouldn't see but he reached out and brushed it off my face.

'Come on. It's time.'

We slid out of the hop, and crossed the street.

Torque was modelled on Torches, only more garish and with harsher lighting. I followed Mo, my hat pulled down over my unmade-up face, my hair tied back at the nape of my neck. As we walked to the bar, I scanned the faces, and the podiums. Less than a year, and everyone had changed. Sickened, I wondered what had happened to them all.

Luca was slumped on a stool at the end of the bar. He was thinner and greyer than I remembered, what was left of his hair shaved so close that the remnants looked like pale smears on his skin. He glanced at Mo, running his eyes over the broad shoulders and jacket, looking for a laser arm. Not spotting it, Luca's eyes roved to me. My throat tightened. He skimmed me, disinterested, and looked away.

'Luca?'

'Who's asking?'

Luca slid off the stool, glancing at two heavies playing holo-cards behind him. They motioned to stand but he held a hand out to stop them.

'I've come about a girl,' said Mo.

Luca laughed. 'Then you've come to the right place. We've got something to cater for every taste. Even those who like to share.' He flashed me a lewd glance.

'A girl who has a price on her head,' said Mo.

Luca's face straightened. 'What are you talking about?'

'A girl who worked here until nearly a year ago. Until the old place burned down.'

Luca's eyes rounded and then narrowed.

'You found the bitch? You come to claim your bounty?' he snapped, sending spittle flying. 'Where is she? I need her handed in so I can deal with her myself.'

'I have a bounty here,' said Mo, calmly, pulling a bleep-code from his pocket. 'This is for you, in exchange for her freedom. Remove the seek-and-find, take down the reward.'

The tag in his hand glinted underneath the spotlights.

Luca's face twisted into a sneer. He walked towards Mo and reached for the bleep-code. 'You're kidding, right?'

Mo raised his hand, too high above Luca's head for him to get. Luca glanced at the men behind him. They'd forgotten their card game. They watched, waiting.

'You heard my condition,' said Mo.

Luca gave a mirthless laugh. 'What is this?'

'Do we have an agreement?'

'I don't make deals with men I've never met before.'

Mo slipped the bleep-code back into his jacket pocket.

Luca threw the first punch.

Mo feinted. It landed wide.

Mo used his momentum against him and, in one fluid movement, took Luca down to the floor. I backed away. The two men abandoned their card table and headed towards us. The shuffle of footsteps and the sting of adrenaline told me that girls were coming out of the doors and walkways to watch from the shadows around the edges of the room.

One of the men pulled a laser. Mo floored him and his partner using an arm on each, then stamped on the hand of the man holding the weapon. Something crunched underneath Mo's foot, maybe the man's bones, or his laser, or both. He howled. Luca pulled a knife. The blade glinted, a slash of neon sliding from the hilt to the tip. Mo disarmed him and Luca fell. The knife flew backwards, towards me, its hilt spinning and hitting the brim of my hat.

The hat fell off.

Luca scrambled onto his knees and stared up into my face, his recognition painfully slow but gathering momentum. He purpled with fury.

'You fucking bitch,' he screamed, launching himself at me, 'you fucking whore!'

Mo caught him with one arm and tossed him on his back. The uninjured heavy skirted them, waiting for his chance. Luca scrambled to his feet and set at me again, his features distorted with fury. Behind him, the injured man scrambled away over the floor, nursing his crushed hand. His companion pulled out a laser arm. Mo drew and shot it out of his hand, leaving a seared stump. The smell of burnt flesh was sickening.

Luca threw himself at me, demented. His eyes stood out, and his mouth hung open, slack, drooling – he looked more animal than human. A table toppled behind me. I skirted it and kept going, towards the door. Mo flipped Luca on his back again and put one foot on his chest.

'You have my best offer,' he said, grinding down into Luca's ribs. 'You take your bounty, and you remove the price on her head. If you don't, I will kill you. The choice is yours.'

Luca thrashed and coughed and cursed until he was so exhausted he lay still, twitching. Behind him, the two men had crawled to the card table where they hunched on the floor, nursing their injuries and whimpering. Mo removed his foot and threw the bleep-code down onto Luca's chest. Luca, panting, sat up and snatched it. Mo crouched down next to him.

'I would kill you anyway but today you got lucky,' he hissed. 'I understand you work as a Unit informant. My boss wouldn't thank me for pulling you out of the food chain. But if you renege on our agreement, I'll take your head off, cut your heart out, and stick your dick in your mouth. Do you understand?'

Luca wiped blood and saliva from his face. He crawled backwards, until he found a bar stool to haul himself up. His eyes flickered between Mo and me as he slipped behind the bar, both hands in the air. He motioned to the till. Mo nodded. Luca slipped the tag in, and yelped.

'You're crazy,' he said, his voice trembling. 'This better not be a hoax.'

'It isn't,' said Mo.

Luca whistled. 'Keep the bitch. She's past her best anyway.' He snatched the bleep-code from the till and stuffed it in his pocket. 'You know why she started the fire and ran?'

Mo watched him, unmoving. I stopped when my back hit the door.

'She ran because I told her that her days as a table virgin were up. She'd done more than enough watching. It was time for her to cross the line to the other side, if you get my meaning,' Luca leered, his mouth lax. 'I told the bitch after that night she was going to be a regular working girl. I was going to break her in myself.'

Mo jumped over the bar and rammed Luca's head into the till. He slithered to the floor, limp. Mo stepped over his body and let himself out the barman's exit. Around the edges of the room, the girls drew back, melting into the shadows.

His expression deadpan, Mo curled his fingers around my elbow. Together, we walked out into the rain, where sheets hit our faces in cold slaps, and flashes of pink and blue neon jumped off the wet flagstones.

THE END

Cover reproduced with kind permission of Suna Cristall.

Printed in Great Britain
by Amazon